The Testament of Mariam

MORE BY THIS AUTHOR

The Anniversary
The Travellers
A Running Tide
Flood
The Secret World of Christoval Alvarez

Praise for Ann Swinfen's Novels

'an absorbing and intricate tapestry of family history and private memories ... warm, generous, healing and hopeful'
VICTORIA GLENDINNING

'I very much admired the pace of the story. The changes of place and time and the echoes and repetitions – things lost and found, and meetings and partings'
PENELOPE FITZGERALD

'I enjoyed this serious, scrupulous novel ... a novel of character ... [and] a suspense story in which present and past mysteries are gradually explained'
JESSICA MANN, *Sunday Telegraph*

'The author ... has written a powerful new tale of passion and heartbreak ... What a marvellous storyteller Ann Swinfen is – she has a wonderful ear for dialogue and she brings her characters vividly to life.'
Publishing News

'Her writing ...[paints] an amazingly detailed and vibrant picture of flesh and blood human beings, not only the symbols many of them have become...but real and believable and understandable.'
HELEN BROWN, *Courier and Advertiser*

'She writes with passion and the book, her fourth, is shot through with brilliant description and scholarship...[it] is a timely reminder of the harsh realities, and the daily humiliations, of the Roman occupation of First Century Israel. You can almost smell the dust and blood.'
PETER RHODES, *Express and Star*

The Testament of Mariam

Ann Swinfen

Shakenoak Press

Cover design by JD Smith www.jdsmith-design.co.uk

For

Katrina

Chapter One

Today I had word that my brother Ya'aqôb is dead. I have not seen him for more than thirty years, and now he has been gone three without my knowing. Our last meeting was brief and bitter, in the village house where we both were born. We shouted at each other over our father's bowed head before I left, putting that land behind me forever and the whole of the Middle Sea between us. And now he is the last of my brothers to die.

I watch a woman—the coppersmith's wife—on the other side of the square, as she catches hold of her son's hand and drags him away. He had taken a step or two towards me, where I stand with my jar beside the village well, but she keeps him at a distance. Turning away, she makes the sign of the horns behind her back. What is the coppersmith's wife to me, that I should care what she thinks? I tip the bucket to fill my jar, and lift it on to my head, a movement as familiar as breathing.

I remember how I used to lean over the well at home, when I was sent by my mother to fetch water, hoping to see my face reflected, but the shaft was deep and the sun behind my head so dazzling that all I could see were dancing stars of light in the dark unknown. And as I walked home with the cool clay jar balanced on my head, the stars still spun before my eyes, making my head dizzy and my steps faltering, so that the water slopped and splashed over my supporting arm and soaked the shoulders of my tunic.

My mother chided me for wasting the precious water, chided me for day-dreaming when there was so much work to be done. They all chided me as lazy and useless, all the family, except for my father, quiet and withdrawn in his workshop, and my eldest brother, Yeshûa.

When I was very small—it must be my earliest memory, I think—I was curled up once in the straw of the goat shed, sobbing with fear and horror. I had done something stupid, I suppose. Broken a cup or torn my clothes. The kind of accident I was always having, for I was a clumsy child. Ya'aqôb had turned

1

on me, lashing out with the flat of his hand and sending me sprawling.

'Spawn of the devil!' he shouted. Perhaps it was his cup I had broken. 'You care nothing for others. You will suffer for it, all the days of your life!'

I fled in terror for the goat shed, my usual place of refuge. Ya'aqôb was always so sure of himself, like those ancient prophets, whose words were read to us by the elders in the village synagogue, the *kenîshtâ*, on the Sabbath. Even burrowed deep into the hot summer scent of the straw, pricked by sharp stems and bitten by fleas, I could not escape my fate. By the time Yeshûa found me, I was gasping uncontrollably for breath, my whole body shaking and drenched with sweat.

He was twelve years older than I and must have been fifteen or sixteen at the time, already tall, but slender, lanky. This was deceptive, for although he never grew broad in the shoulders, with a thick neck and muscular arms like my other brothers, he had a quiet strength, a calm endurance. He picked me up as though I weighed no more than a kitten and cradled me in his arms, wiping my hot, wet face with the edge of his sleeve.

'Hush, *talithâ*,' he said, rocking me like an infant. 'What terrible matter is this, to bring on such a storm?'

I could barely speak, hiccupping and shaking still in my distress, but I managed to blurt out something about the accident and Ya'aqôb's words. His face darkened for a moment and his eyes grew hard with anger. Then he kicked open the door of the shed and carried me outside. Night had come on while I was hidden in the straw, and the breeze that often rose at nightfall cooled my cheeks. It carried down from the hills behind the village the scents of rosemary and juniper, set free on the air by the remorseless sun of the day. Yeshûa hoisted me up till I was sitting on his shoulders, my sticky fingers clutching his black curls for support.

'Nothing will hurt you if you are truly sorry for the accident, Mariam,' he said.

Now that I was growing calmer, my stubbornness was returning.

'Ya'aqôb should not have said that to me.' I was petulant. 'It *was* an accident. I hate him.'

'Now, Mariam, you do not mean that. He is your brother and you love him.'

I grunted. I did not feel very loving, but as always when I was with Yeshûa, I felt ashamed of my bad nature and wanted to please him.

'What must I do then?' I was ungracious, but Yeshûa didn't seem to mind.

'Tell him you are sorry, and kiss his cheek.'

'He should be sorry too.'

'If you show that you love him, he will be.'

I wasn't sure about this, but Yeshûa drew my attention away.

'Look at all the stars, Mariam. Aren't they wonderful tonight?'

It was a clear summer's night, the sky was cloudless and the moon not yet risen. The whole dome of the heavens glittered with the jewelled stars, as I always imagined the palaces of the ancient kings, Solomon and David, must have shone with rubies and sapphires and pearls. I was a fanciful child.

'Everyone has their own star, Mariam,' Yeshûa said. 'Each one of us, a single star of our own.'

'Which one is mine?' I asked, tilting my head and leaning back until he had to hitch me higher on his shoulders as I began to slip.

'That one,' he said at once, taking his right hand from my ankle and pointing westwards. 'There. That blue, pulsing star. See how it beats to the rhythm of your heart, and shines with the blue of your eyes.'

I was distracted for a moment from the glories overhead and wriggled on his shoulders so that he grabbed my ankle again to stop me from falling. I leaned forward and whispered in his ear, my lips brushing against his skin.

'Do I really have blue eyes?'

I had not known this about myself. Almost everyone I knew had brown eyes.

'Your eyes are blue,' he assured me, 'like Father's, only darker. It's a special gift. From time to time, someone in our family has blue eyes. It's rare and wonderful. Perhaps you will be a rare and wonderful person. And it will help you remember which is your star.'

I looked again at the star he had pointed out and as I did so it seemed to grow, outshining all the others in that glorious host. I would always remember it. And I tried to imagine what it would be like, to be a person who was rare and wonderful. Then Ya'aqôb would have to respect me, and would not dare to call me spawn of the devil.

'Come,' said my brother, lifting me off his shoulders and setting my bare feet gently on the stony ground of the yard. 'You must come and apologise to Ya'aqôb and finish your supper and go to bed.'

I apologised with as much grace as I could muster and when I was lying awake on my bedroll I seemed to feel my brother's soft curls between my fingers and his strong brown hands gripping my ankles. When at last I slept, I dreamt that I flew amongst a brilliance of stars.

ॐ

I still fetch water from a communal well, but I no longer try to find my face in its depths. Now I simply hoist the water jar onto my head and pace slowly back to my house on the outskirts of the village. After so many years, I no longer need to brace the jar with my hand. A straight back, a steady pace and a sense of balance are all that is needed. The women here have never learned the art. They carry their water in wooden buckets, sometimes strung in pairs from a yoke over their shoulders, so that they are bent and humbled as beasts of burden, but to them water is less precious than it was to us. Although the summers are hot and dry here in Gallia Narbonensis, the winter always brings rain enough to feed the rivers and lakes and to replenish the wells. The marshlands a little to the south and west of here are filled with the susurration of restless water all year round, soft murmurs and rustling, like the breathing of some hidden animal.

As I cross the village square, I see the woman and the boy eyeing me askance, but I ignore them and walk on, along the narrow alleyway between the bakehouse and the blacksmith. It is a steep climb up to our small farm and I could spare myself the walk, for we have a well of our own, but late in the summer the water is scanty and sometimes polluted with mud, while the village well always draws clear. It is the habit of a lifetime to labour, to endure, if at the end of it there will be a small spark of pleasure. I will cool the water in the shade of the orchard before I allow myself the reward of a sweet drink. But I am tired, for I rose before dawn to load the donkeys and set off for the market in Massilia. It is a walk of five Roman miles there and five miles back, and when I reach home now with the water I will permit myself to rest for a time under the vine arbour. My mother was right. I am lazy.

Yeshûa was forever comforting me when I was small, defending me, trying to make me understand that my bad behaviour always brought greater grief to me than to anyone else. My love for him was unquestioning, vast and implacable, like the great ocean that lies beyond the Pillars of Hercules, an ineffable part of my being, though its surface was occasionally troubled by waves of emotion—my emotion, for he was always constant in his love for me. When we were older, and he seemed to grow away from me, wrapped up in his own affairs, I was sometimes jealous. I did not want to share him with others, with strangers, some of them dirty, sickly and disreputable.

My love for his friend Yehûdâ, on the other hand, was passionate, restless, and hungry. Even fearful.

Why does the memory play such tricks? If I close my eyes, I cannot picture my brother's face, though every curve and hollow of it was known and dear to me from infancy. All I can summon up is a glow, like the embers of a welcome fire on a bitter night. There *were* bitter nights, some winters, high in the hills where our village lay. But his friend Yehûdâ's face is as clear as if he stood before me, though not with warmth in his eyes nor the joyous laughter of the brief, glad times. It comes to me always as I saw it last, in a shifting pattern of deceitful moonlight and the black shadows of trees, his eyes haunted, in an agony of pain, his voice hoarse with grief.

'Shall I bring you a drink, Mother Mariam?'

It is my daughter-in-law, Fulvia. She is a dutiful girl. Not clever, but kind and tolerant. It cannot be easy for her, living always under the shadow of an outspoken, opinionated old woman.

'Thank you,' I say. 'There's fresh water from the village well, there, in the shade.'

'I'll bring you a glass of the unfermented grape juice. You've had a tiring day.'

'Thank you,' I say again. My smile, I know, is tired and a little strained. My back is hurting and I regret my walk to the well.

From where I sit under the vine arbour, the whole bay of Massilia is laid out before me, and beyond it the wider sea. Sometimes I wonder whether I married my husband because his farm stood so high and looked so far. A merchant ship with red sails is making its way slowly into the harbour. She will hail from Sidon or Tyre, probably, for the merchants in Phoenicia favour red sails as bringing good fortune. Hardly a child's breath of wind fills her sails, they belly a little and then collapse, fill and sink. I almost think I can hear the gang-master shouting to the slave-rowers to run out the oars. Yes, there—the blades begin to flash and dip in the sun, and the ship slides a little faster towards the land. They must put their backs into it, the slaves, under the sting of the whip, or the ship will not reach the quayside before dark and must anchor out in the bay.

I spend many hours watching the sea and the life upon it, a curious pastime for one reared so far inland. I had never even seen the Lake of Gennesaret until I was nearly eighteen years old. It seemed a vast wonder to me at the time, though they say it is but thirteen miles long and no more than eight miles wide. A bucketful, a basin, compared with the Middle Sea stretched out below me here. No more than a teardrop, compared with the endless ocean away to the west of Iberia.

Here in Gallia Narbonensis, I go to the market in Massilia twice a week, but not always with the same produce. Today I took peas and honey and cheeses and a basket of eggs, but sometimes it is other vegetables in season, or summer melons. In the autumn, apples and pears, for we have a fine orchard. In the

6

winter there are always the fruits I have dried during the heat of summer, or preserves. This is a mixed farm and I take a delight in the variety, though my elder son, who now does most of the heavy work, has been spending more and more time with his vines for the last ten years. We have several warm, south-facing slopes which nourish the grapes and give a good yield. If it were not for my stubbornness, I know he would turn the whole farm over to viticulture.

When I reached the market down by the harbour at Massilia about an hour or so after dawn this morning, I set up my stall as usual not far from the quays. This is a prime location, for the foreign sailors, some of whom have been weeks at sea, are always glad to buy fresh produce after their poor diet of twice-baked bread, dried meat and salted fish. Business was brisk, and before midday I had sold everything but a few pots of honey. I had also bought sardines, fresh caught from a fisherman I know, which I had wrapped in damp vine leaves and stored under my stall in the shade until it was time to leave. We will grill them over charcoal tonight and eat them with olives and the new bread baked by my daughter-in-law while I was at market, and we will drink some of Manilius's wine.

I had begun to pack the donkeys' panniers when two sailors from a ship just docked strolled towards me across the square. At first I paid them no attention, until I realised they were speaking Aramaic.

'*Shalôm* to you,' I said, turning round and addressing them in their own language.

They looked startled and pleased, for I suppose they expected nothing but Latin or Gaulish here, or more likely Greek, for Massilia is an ancient Greek foundation, and most of its inhabitants are still Greek by descent. They began to chatter away like a pair of sparrows—Was I truly an Israelite? What was I doing here in Massilia? When was I last in the Land of Judah? I answered them courteously but evasively: I had left Judah long ago, when I was scarcely more than a girl, and had married a Gaulish farmer here in Gallia Narbonensis.

'Our ship sailed from Caesarea Maritima, two months ago,' said the older man. 'And we've been making our way all round the coast of southern Italy, then over to Sicily. We'll stay here a few days to unload the last of our cargo of olives and oil, before we reload and sail home.'

'What do you buy here?' I asked.

'Wine, mostly,' his companion said. 'And anything else that takes the captain's fancy.'

'My son Manilius would be glad to sell him wine. He can call on your captain tomorrow.'

The older man nodded.

'Good. He's anxious to return quickly. It's a worrying time at home. A dangerous time.'

There had been several risings, they said, new rebel leaders springing up everywhere. There had been skirmishes with the Roman forces. Soon it would be full-scale war. There had been villages razed to their foundations. There had been executions.

Their words wriggled into my brain like worms, but I would not let them lodge there. Long ago I had turned my back on Judah. Had cut off my past as cleanly as a newly sharpened butcher's cleaver will slice through a carcass: blood, flesh and bone. What was Judah—or her people—or her tragedies—to me? I had chosen this exile, this severance from my past and all that it had once meant. I was Mariam, widow of Petradix, Roman veteran and farmer of Gallia. The Mariam who once was, that Mariam was dead.

Perhaps an hour later, as I was making my way out of the city, able to ride one of the donkeys, now that I had sold my goods, the younger man appeared suddenly at my side, laying his hand on the donkey's neck to stop me. I realised that he must have been watching for me, but I was not alarmed, for his smile was warm and genuine.

'Lady,' he said, 'I think we distressed you with our news of home.'

'My name is Mariam,' I said. 'Yes. I was distressed. It is five years at least since I heard anything from those parts.'

From time to time word has reached me, through travellers and merchants, of my former family's lives and deaths, but I did not call it home. What is my home?

He glanced down at his hand, resting on the donkey's neck, then he traced, in the dust on its coat, a simple shape, an elongated loop, the symbol of a fish. A moment later he had brushed it away. I might have imagined it.

'Oh,' I said.

He looked at me enquiringly, and I traced the same shape on the donkey's neck. He nodded in satisfaction.

'I thought so. You are one of the followers of the Christ?'

'Well . . .' I would not commit myself to a stranger.

'I understand,' he said.

How little, I thought, *you can possibly understand.*

'I thought you would want to know more,' he went on. 'The rebels have risen against the Roman rule, and against the defilement of holy places. But the seed was partly sown amongst certain of us three years ago when the Christian bishop of Jerusalem was murdered.'

'Murdered?'

'Murdered. The Roman procurator died, and before his successor could reach Judah, a new high priest of the Temple was appointed at Jerusalem, Ananus.'

'Ananus?' I said. 'Surely not, after all these years.'

'Not the same Ananus. Not Ananus "the Great".' His mouth twisted bitterly. 'This one also is an arrogant man, greedy for power and eager to exercise it. He was the brother-in-law of Caiaphas and the fifth son of the "great" Ananus to become high priest amongst us. A man of violent temper and overweening pride in his aristocratic heritage. He arrested the bishop and several of his followers, and condemned them to death for transgressing the Law.'

'But under Roman occupation the high priest is not permitted—'

'Exactly. So good men, honest men—some of them followers of the Christ and some not—were outraged at what he had done and laid a complaint before the Syrian legate and King Agrippa. The high priest was removed from office, but there is still unrest.'

'And who was this bishop of Jerusalem?'

'A most holy man, who spent most of his life on his knees. He fasted regularly, and when he took food, ate no animal. He mortified his flesh, never cut his hair or shaved his face or washed his body. He drank no wine or other intoxicating liquor. It is said that he knelt praying so much that his knees grew as hardened as a camel's.'

'A most holy man,' I said, hoping that he could not hear the irony in my voice. 'And what was his name, the bishop of Jerusalem?'

'Ya'aqôb the Just,' he said. 'Ya'aqôb ben Yosef. Ya'aqôb brother of Yeshûa.'

And then he told me how the last of my brothers died.

⁓

The Temple guards bundled my brother Ya'aqôb to the highest point on the roof of the Temple, but their progress was slow, for the old man stumbled from the arthritis in his aged joints and the weakness brought on by the torture he had suffered.

'You'll soon be flying like a bird,' the captain of the guards cried, his small red mouth grinning within the frame of a thick curling beard. He poked the prisoner in the back with the tip of his spear and the old man fell to his knees. He began to mumble something, some kind of a prayer by the sound of it, but they hauled him to his feet and dragged and prodded him to the top of the stairs.

It was a dizzying height, the whole of Jerusalem with its hills and towers, its mighty walls and narrow dirty slums, laid out below them. Ya'aqôb was confused. Was this vision of the Holy City supposed to *mean* something? He was not ready for this. He had not performed the proper rituals. He tried to speak to the captain, but two of the strongest guards seized him by shoulders and ankles, and swung him up into the air. His emaciated body was as light as a boy's.

For a few minutes they amused themselves by swinging the body out over the terrible drop, then back inside the parapet, then out again. The old man was gibbering now, and the guards laughed. There had been little enough to entertain them since Ananus had become high priest, with his new rules, his diktats, his novel interpretations of the Law. Then, at a nod from the captain, on an outward swing, they let the body go.

My brother was wearing nothing but a dirty loincloth, and the rush of wind ripped it away, so that he flew through the air naked as a newborn infant, and crashed on to the unforgiving pavement below.

Making his leisurely way down the stairway to the ground, the captain was relieved the matter was dealt with. He would order the guards to clear away the body and hand it over to the man's friends if they wanted it. Then he could go home to his wife, his meal and his bed. The body lay sprawled at the foot of the tower, one leg stuck out at an unnatural angle. There was surprisingly little blood. The captain poked the body with his foot and it groaned. Then, unbelievably, it gathered itself together and crawled on to its hands and knees.

The captain jumped back, his heart throbbing violently, a rush of heat bringing out the sweat on his body and turning his stomach. The man was still alive! No one could have survived that fall. No one. He yelled at the guards, yelled at the gawping bystanders, yelled at some men mending the road.

'Stone him!' he shrieked. 'He must be stoned to death!'

They hurried to obey, everyone shocked and terrified by this man who had not died. For an hour they stoned him, till his hair was matted with gore, and every inch of his naked body was battered and bloodied.

And still he would not die.

The captain was almost out of his wits, his eyes stretched wide. He looked around desperately. What could he do? Then he caught sight of a passer-by who had stopped to stare at the gruesome execution. His clothes were stained with fuller's earth and he carried the club which he used to beat the cloth and soften it.

'Here, you!' the captain shouted.

The fuller came reluctantly, cursing himself for having stopped. The captain looked crazy enough to do anything.

'That club of yours, is it heavy?'

'Heavy enough.'

'Then finish him off. Club him. Smash his skull in.'

The fuller backed away. 'It will make me unclean.'

'Do as you're told,' the captain yelled, 'or I'll have them stone you to death in his place.'

The fuller did as he was told.

And so, finally, Ya'aqôb died.

✥

I sit here under the vine arbour and watch the Phoenician ship reach harbour and furl her sails. The air is sticky with the sound of my bees and dry with the rasping of the cicadas. My daughter-in-law is cooking the sardines. The smell of them floats out to me here. Let her cook by herself for once. I have done enough for one day. I can hear my grandchildren arguing in the orchard.

The sailor from the Land of Judah told me something else. Now that the Christ sect is spreading to many lands, there is talk of writing down the teachings and the whole story, before all those who were there either forget or die. Paulus, who was a posthumous convert, has been writing letters of guidance and instruction to some of the far-flung churches which have been set up amongst the Gentiles. The letters will be brought together into a book to be copied and circulated. Others are preparing testaments and books of the life, which they call 'gospels'.

I shut my eyes. My head is aching. From too much sun, perhaps. Or from the story of Ya'aqôb's death, which I have not allowed myself to think about until now. A testament. A testimony. Perhaps I should get out my writing quills, buy parchment and ink next time I am in Massilia. I have not lost the art, for Yeshûa taught me well. The Testament of Mariam?

Chapter Two

When my younger son Sergius was about fourteen, he asked me, 'Why do you and Father always speak Latin to us? It isn't his mother tongue, or yours.'

He was a thoughtful boy and deserved a careful answer.

'Your father believes the future lies with Rome. It is better this way. You are Roman citizens and should look to the future, not the past.'

'But Father's family is an ancient one here in Gaul. They held power in the land around Massilia, he's told me. And he has a Gaulish name.'

And one that must sound uncouth to Roman ears, I thought.

'All that has changed now,' I said.

Generations earlier the people of southern Gaul had been conquered by Rome and then, by that subtle process which has proved so effective throughout most of the Empire, they had become Romanised themselves. It was never a success in the country the Romans call Palestine. We were too stubborn, too separate, too arrogant and unshakeable in our belief in our righteousness, our Law, our special status in the world as the Chosen People of the One God, Yahweh. Petradix's ancestors, on the other hand, had taken gladly to Roman ways, Roman clothes, Roman baths, Roman hypocausts, and Roman cities. His grandfather had gained citizenship.

Petradix, however, was the youngest of five boys, with little chance of inheriting land, so he had joined the Roman army, risen to first centurion, and retired after his twenty years with several battle scars, but otherwise intact. His legion had been serving in Egypt at the time, so he was given his land grant there. A commendable Roman practice—to steal other people's land, then hand it out to army veterans as a pension. There were whole towns of these veterans on the far side of Gennesaret. With a little persuasion from powerful friends of his father's, Petradix was able to exchange his grant for land at home in Gallia Narbonensis—this farm, which had been seized owing to the non-payment of land taxes. He then looked around for a wife. He was ever a practical man, Petradix.

I had arrived in Gaul a few months earlier—an outcast, a refugee—amongst a group fleeing from the Land of Judah, and had found work serving food in a *caupona* in Massilia. Petradix came there to eat when he brought produce to market, and I suppose he thought I would suit as well as any. I was clean, well-spoken, something different from the other women who worked there, and who augmented their earnings on the street at night. I had not yet been driven to that, though things were very bad. I came to him a virgin. I shared a small, filthy room with three other women, all prostitutes. I possessed nothing but the clothes I wore, a bedroll and a small box. And if the owner of the *caupona* did not give us the leftovers to eat at the end of the day, then I did not eat. Petradix's proposal of marriage seemed like a miracle.

That is not a word I should use so lightly. And I am allowing my own cynicism to cloud the memory of a good man. Petradix loved me, fell in love with me, as unlikely as it may seem. And I was fond of him. He was . . . a dear friend. And I miss him surprisingly much.

I never told him who I was. To him I was a homeless orphan who had fled from the threat of persecution in Palestine. He had served in the lands around the eastern end of the Middle Sea, and he knew all about persecution. He never questioned me, for which I remain forever grateful.

We gave our two boys Roman names, Manilius and Sergius, and brought them up as good Roman citizens. Manilius has been happy to remain here on the farm, and like his father he is a good farmer, with a feel for the land, though he does not have my passion and my eccentric interests. Sergius is more restless and has moved to Massilia, where he works as a ship broker. He has not yet taken a wife. Both boys—both men, rather—are entirely their father's sons. I see nothing of myself in them, and that is good. Except, perhaps, that small itch of restlessness in Sergius. If we had had a daughter, she might have taken after me, but I do not really regret this. I regret nothing. Almost nothing.

୨

When I was seven years old, I was set, like other village children of my age, to watching our flock of goats when they were driven out to pasture on the higher slopes of the hills, the *midbar*. It was easy work, so long as you kept your wits about you and did not allow the goats to stray too far. And so long as the flock was not attacked. Mostly, my family owned a herd dog, but at that time our old dog had died and had not been replaced, so the responsibility for the flock was greater than usual. I was happy in the hills. It was cooler there, where the breezes blew freely amongst the pasture grass. There were small scrubby olive trees, self-planted from the olive orchards below, which provided shade.

Yeshûa's friend Yehûdâ had made me a reed pipe, and I was teaching myself to play it, though I am not sure the goats enjoyed my first attempts. I hoped they would gather around me, or even dance to my playing, as in some ancient myth, but they were inclined to distance themselves. There were other children on the hills, mostly boys, but the youngest of my brothers, Shim'ôn, was nearly eleven now and starting to learn the carpenter's trade with our father, so the herding of the goats fell to me. To give the goats the best pasture, we kept our flocks at a distance from each other, though sometimes when we stopped at midday to eat the food our mothers had provided, some of us would meet near a pool where the goats drank. A small stream cascaded into it over a smooth grey rock, worn down by centuries of water. At its lower end, the stream left the pool to run down the hill and join the river below the village.

One day I was walking back to my grazing ground after the midday meal, urging on three of my goats who had followed me down to the pool. I had lingered longer than I should have done, showing off my prowess on the reed pipe to three of the boys.

'No girl can play a pipe,' one had jeered.

'Mariam is so conceited, she thinks she can do anything a boy can,' crowed another, and they rolled on the ground laughing until they clutched their stomachs.

I was furious.

'Listen, stupid!' I said.

And fuelled by my anger, I played a simple folk tune right through without a mistake, a feat I had never achieved before. Now I was feeling pleased with myself, and sauntered along, swishing my thin hazel branch behind the goats whenever they showed signs of stopping to graze. I needed to get back to the rest of the flock and make sure none of them had strayed.

I climbed up a rock which projected out of the turf and began to count: one, two, three . . . There were only twenty-one. There should be twenty-two. It was not long since the nannies had dropped their kids and some were still very small. One was missing, but it might simply be hidden in a hollow or behind a boulder. I began to run from one end of the little meadow to the other, giving the chirruping cry I used to call the flock together. Nowhere could I find the kid. Could a wolf have taken it? There *were* wolves, lurking in the caves high in the hills. They did not hesitate to attack the flocks if there was no wild prey nearby. If I had had a dog, it would have alerted me, but I had seen nothing, heard nothing. I was searching aimlessly now, my sight blurred with tears, partly at the thought of the beating I would receive, partly at the image in my mind of the innocent kid, bloody on the ground, before it had even had a taste of life.

Suddenly there was a shape before me, there without sound or movement, a shape. I rubbed my eyes with the back of a dirty hand. At first all I could see was a radiance, like a cloud at night passing before the moon, then it seemed to gather together into the form of my brother Yeshûa. The sun was behind him, so that he floated gold-rimmed against the green of the grass, insubstantial as a painting.

Then the light was gone. I had noticed no change in the sky as I searched for the kid, but from nowhere, it seemed, a dark cloud wiped out the sun. And the grass of the *midbar* was leached of all colour and streamed flat along the ground like silver hair, moaning in a sudden wind. The short curls on the back of my neck stirred, and if I could have moved my feet, which were frozen to the ground, I would have fled to the high caves and hidden there even amongst the wild wolves of the hills.

Out of the darkness, I heard a voice. 'Was this what you were seeking, Mariam?' It sounded far away.

I was shaking so much, I could not speak, but covered my face with my hands.

Then as swiftly as it had come, the darkness was gone, and I peered fearfully between my fingers. The terrifying, intangible shape had become my brother Yeshûa, ordinary, substantial and real, and I saw that he had the kid draped round his shoulders like a cloak, its four feet held together with one hand against his chest, the way you will see a shepherd carry a sick or injured sheep.

'Is it dead?' I whispered, trembling. The kid lay passive, inert. Surely it was dead.

He grinned. 'Not at all. Just needing its mother.'

And he lifted it down from his shoulders and set it on the turf, where it skipped off, crying for its dam.

'Oh, Yeshûa,' I cried, 'I was so afraid!'

I could not have said what I had feared most. The loss of the kid. The attack of a wolf. Or the sudden manifestation of my brother—out of the sun?—out of the shadow of the cloud?—where, a moment before, there had been nothing. I flung myself at him, still shaking, desperate to feel the warm solidity of him, my brother, not some apparition. And he swung me up and held me, so that I buried my face in the hollow at the base of his neck.

And I remember as clearly as if it were here and now, his skin did not smell of the kid. His skin smelled sweet, of honey and cinnamon.

As a child what I knew was not the rich expanse of the Middle Sea, nor the bright glitter of sweet Gennesaret, but that narrow valley where our village lay, high in these Galilean hills. It was fertile—far more fertile than Judah to the south, with its desert and its barren rocky cliffs, its lifeless inland Sea of Sodom. The people of our village ate simply but well. I never remember going truly hungry to bed (except when I had misbehaved) and there were no village beggars. We were not rich, but neither were we paupers. My father possessed no cattle, though he owned the land of our own smallholding and a few fields. The only family with enough wealth and pasture for cattle was the family of the merchant Shim'ôn, father of Yehûdâ, who owned the largest farm and was landlord to many of the villagers. Shim'ôn of Keriyoth had bought land in our village before I was born, although he spent much of his time about his business in Sepphoris and Jerusalem. Later, he owned a great house in the tetrarch's new city of Tiberias. My brother would never go there, although Yehûdâ, who was his closest friend, often invited him.

'It is unclean,' Yeshûa said at last, one afternoon when they were perched on the low wall of the courtyard, and I was crouched at their feet. 'The whole city is being built on a cemetery and wherever you go, you walk over the bones of the dead.'

I was surprised when he said this. Ya'aqôb was rigorous in his observance of the Law and took every opportunity to rail at the rest of us for any minor infringement, but Yeshûa was much more easy-going.

I glanced up at him, questioning, but he was looking far away, over my head, and twisting the hem of his tunic between his hands until I heard a thread split and the fabric tear.

Yehûdâ laughed at him for his squeamishness, but my brother shook his head, and his face was serious.

'It's an evil thing Herod Antipas is doing, building a city there. Unclean.'

'He chose a site on the lake which would be profitable for trade and more central in Galilee than Sepphoris is,' said Yehûdâ reasonably. 'It's much better placed for his capital. My father thinks it promises to be a fine city, with magnificent buildings, a credit to Galilee and the whole Land of Judah.'

'I am not talking about what is good or bad for trade. It has nothing to do with fine buildings or convenience!' my brother cried out, then drew a deep breath, and I heard the cloth tear a little more, as if his very clothes cried out in sympathy. 'I'm talking about matters of the spirit. Myself, I care nothing for the petty religious rituals of the Pharisees, which are all form and no substance. But there are other things that are deeper, which touch the spirit of man, the soul . . .'

He broke off, and turned towards Yehûdâ, almost, it seemed, in exasperation with himself.

'I cannot find the words! But to walk upon the bones of the dead . . . To desecrate their graves and scatter their remains, just in order to dig the foundations of a new customs office or warehouse, or even a brothel . . . Their souls have fled, I know, but these are the mortal remains of men and women like ourselves.'

'They are ancient unmarked graves,' Yehûdâ said hesitantly, apologetically. 'The poor, buried in simple ground, not in ancestral burial caves.'

'Does that not make it worse? The poor—unregarded in life, to be defiled even in death?'

'I don't know. Who are we to judge?'

'It is a sacrilege,' my brother said abruptly, and closed the subject, as he so often did, by turning his friend's attention aside. 'Come, I thought we were to go fishing in the river today. Do you want to come, Mariam?'

I wanted to go with them, for I would rather be with my brother Yeshûa than anywhere else in the world. And his friend Yehûdâ was handsome and kind. He never mocked me, or scorned me, or treated me like a clod of earth on his shoe, like Ya'aqôb and my other brothers. At that age I did not altogether understand their discussions, but I was tantalised by a sense that there was something there, something my mind reached out to, but could not quite grasp. I would have liked nothing better than to tag along after them to the river, like a hopeful puppy.

But I shook my head mournfully. I had not the freedom of my brothers and their friends. It seemed that the women and the girls of the village worked from the moment they rose before dawn until they laid their aching bones down when the blessed darkness gave them leave to sleep. Somehow the men always had shorter hours to labour, and when the heat of the sun was at its most fierce, or the early evening brought an end to their working day, they would sit under the fig trees or in the shade of the awnings on the roofs, and sleep or gossip or play complicated games on wooden boards with bone or pebble counters, games to which we, the lesser sex, were never admitted.

'I have to grind corn in the quern today,' I said fretfully. 'And there are more figs to be picked and laid out on the roof to dry.'

The boys headed down the valley to the river, where they might fish for a while, but would certainly spend most of their time enjoying the delights of swimming naked in the cool water and gaining some relief from the merciless sun. I went away, dragging my feet through the dust so that it spurted up between my bare toes like water and flooded over my insteps, leaving them dyed a reddish brown. It reminded me of the Bedouin tribesmen who passed sometimes through the village with their camels and goods. They wore vivid colours, even when their clothes were a patchwork of rags, and they marked their faces and hands with dyed patterns, sometimes colouring their black hair an ugly orange-red with henna. As part of a woven garment or a rug, henna is a joyous colour, but matted in the tribesmen's hair, it turned my stomach.

The houses in our village were not laid out like a Roman town, in straight, unforgiving lines. They were clustered two, three, even as many as six together, round a shared courtyard, with narrow lanes zigzagging between these clusters. Our house was one of four built around two sides of a courtyard that was roughly square, with the other two sides enclosed by low stone walls to stop the small children and animals straying. The houses were cubes built of stone held together by a mortar made of mud mixed with dung and straw, then plastered all over in brilliant white to shield the inside from the sun. We had few windows, but the doors, front and back, were left open most of the time to benefit from any breeze. Ours was one of the few houses to have an upper storey, for my father was a carpenter and builder and the house was a way of displaying his skill. Like all the others, though, we had a stairway leading up against one outside wall to the roof, which we used almost as much as the inside of the house.

I made my way reluctantly to the corn mill shared by all four households, which stood in one corner of the courtyard, not far from the bread oven. Now that I was a big, strong girl of eight, I had to do my share of grinding corn for bread, an endless, thankless task that made my arms ache and my head pound from the heat. Hours every day were spent by the women and girls of the village grinding corn, and however hard we worked, the flour was gobbled up by the bread ovens, and the bread by the men and children, who seemed to have little care for our weariness and labour. Ya'aqôb often spoke of the perpetual torments after death which would be endured by those who failed to keep the Law or were imperfect in their observances towards Yahweh, but it sometimes seemed to me—as it seemed to me that day, with the sun setting fire to my hair and the boys away in the blessed cool of the water—that the torment was already here and now. I said a quick, apologetic prayer inside my head for my impious thoughts, as I tipped more corn from the sack into the hole at the top of the grindstone and with the end of my little finger cleared the groove where the ground flour trickled out.

'Why are you standing there, staring into the hills, Mariam?'

It was my mother. She must have been watching me from the doorway of our house, where she had been sitting at the loom, and had come up silently behind me on bare feet. She tapped me now sharply on the shoulder, as though she thought I was lost too far away in my dream world to hear her. I had jumped at the sound of her voice, but did not turn round.

'I have ground all this,' I said defensively, pointing to the bowl of flour and shrugging her fingers from my shoulder. The flour looked less than it had a minute ago. 'My arms are hurting and I was resting them.'

'There is no time for resting,' she said grimly, 'when there is such a large family to feed.' She was great with another child, which I think she did not want. 'If your father worked more quickly, instead of lingering over every spin of the lathe and stroke of the plane, we might have means enough to employ a servant girl.'

'But why can the boys go swimming and fishing when I have to labour in the sun?' I whined. I did not like her criticism of my father, whose work was beautiful, but I had complaints of my own today.

'Because they are boys, and the Lord made a different world for men and for women,' she said sharply. 'You must learn to accept it, Mariam. I want that bowl full before you stop, and then there are the figs to pick.'

'I know,' I snapped. 'And then the best must be chosen and laid out on mats to dry, and the rest put by to eat now. Surely there must be *more* work for me to do afterwards?'

For that, I got a sharp clip on the ear, and ground the rest of the grain through hot, bitter tears.

My mother continued to watch me, her most troublesome daughter, from the shadow of the doorway, where she had set up her loom to gain the benefit of the daylight but also some protection from the heat. Her hands moved automatically, throwing the shuttle, tamping down the weft threads with the heddle rod, tying in new colours as the pattern demanded. She could perform these tasks, practised since girlhood, while her mind was filled with other things. I knew that the unborn child, the unwanted child, stirred and kicked against the cramped position forced on it, as she sat cross-legged. This would be the tenth child she had borne, and eight still living. Only one lost, soon after birth, another son two years younger than I. Yeshûa, Ya'aqôb, Yehûdes, Yoses, Melkha, Shim'ôn, Mariam, Eskha. She was only thirty-five. She could be fruitful for another fifteen years. Perpetual mother. She laid her forehead against the tight fabric on the loom and closed her eyes. I heard her whisper, *Please, Lord, no more after this.*

The sound of sawing came from my father's workshop, mingled with the sound of voices. Some of the boys were there. *She should not have hit me,* I thought resentfully, but I suppose she was weary and hot, her back must have ached and the baby gave her no rest at night. I knew she thought I was old enough to be of more help, for Melkha would be gone to her husband's house in a few months' time. Today she was visiting her friend Martha on the other side of the village, where the two girls were working together on their dowry garments, embroidering and chattering. Probably more chattering than work. I saw a few tears squeeze between my mother's eyelids before she dashed them away angrily.

'Mariam!' she called sharply across the courtyard. 'Have you not finished that grinding? I need the flour for this evening's bread dough. It's time to begin preparing the meal, and I've not finished half the weaving I planned to do.'

I stooped and picked up the bowl of flour and the nearly empty sack of grain. *You cannot blame that on me*, I thought, full of self-pity. I began to trudge across the courtyard toward the house, dragging the sack through the dust behind me.

'You may leave the figs until tomorrow,' my mother said. 'Go and fetch Yeshûa home, and don't linger.'

Glad of the brief respite, I galloped down through the olive orchard in the direction of the river, but when I caught sight of the two friends, I slithered to a halt and squatted down behind an ancient trunk. I could not go on, for they lay naked on the lush grass of the river bank as the sun dried them. If I climbed back up the hill, they might see me. I was too embarrassed to move. They had put aside their fishing rods, for the fish were hiding amongst the rushes, away from the glare of the sunlight, and they had caught nothing. I knew they had not really expected to, for fishing was merely an excuse to escape for a few hours and enjoy the cool of the water, away from any work their fathers might set them.

Yehûdâ rolled over and sat up, leaning back on his elbows and squinting against the reflection of the sun on the water. There was the shadow of a fish half emerging from the clump of reeds opposite, but I could see he was too sluggish with water and sun to throw out his line.

'Yeshûa?' He turned and looked down at my brother's back, which shone like polished bronze, with a scattering of drops amongst the fine hairs.

Yeshûa lay with his head on his folded arms, his face turned away, and did not answer. He had fallen asleep.

'Hey!' Yehûdâ poked him in the ribs and Yeshûa grunted.

'Wake up. I want to talk to you.'

Yeshûa groaned and rolled over, shading his eyes with his arm.

'What?'

'My father wants me to marry.'

23

'Ah.' Serious indeed. Yeshûa sat up and wrapped his arms around his knees. 'Why so soon?'

They were twenty now, and it was the custom to wait longer, until a man had some goods put by, had established himself amongst the men of the community, then he would take a much younger wife. They were both boys still, living in their fathers' houses, subject to the government of their parents.

'I wouldn't have minded marrying your sister Melkha,' said Yehûdâ thoughtfully, 'if she were not already betrothed. She's beautiful and biddable.'

Hearing this, I stuck out my lower lip. I was tired of hearing Melkha praised for her beauty.

'She would have been married by now,' said my brother, 'for she's nearly fourteen, but the merchant Adamas has been away in Egypt. As soon as he returns, they will be wed.'

'My father has someone in mind, the daughter of a merchant from Tiberias.' Yehûdâ's voice was glum.

Yeshûa made a face at the name of the city.

'He's in haste, then?'

'Ever since he was ill last winter, he's worried about securing an heir. It's the penalty of being an only child. How fortunate you are, there are so many of you!'

Yeshûa laughed. 'Not so fortunate when food is short or the latest baby cries all night! You don't want this marriage, then?'

'No! I want my freedom! At least for a while longer. I have seen so little of the world. This village. A few visits to Sepphoris and Scythopolis and Tiberias. That one time we went with our fathers to Jerusalem to our make our *bâr mitzvâh* oath. I want . . .' he hesitated, 'I want to see something of the world before I am trapped.'

'Yes. I understand. Sometimes I want to . . .' My brother broke off.

'What?'

'I want to see the world too, outside this little village. But I promised my parents.'

'You mean, after what happened that time in Jerusalem?'

'Yes. But I can't get it out of my head. What I was saying earlier, about the poor.'

24

'The poor? I don't understand.' Yehûdâ turned towards him.

'Their unmarked graves. Their lives of terrible labour and hardship. Their cold. Their hunger. Their despair. Ending in nothingness. Somehow it has to change.'

'And how do you think that can happen? Do you think *you* can do anything about it? Change the world? A village lad from the Galilee?'

Yeshûa had been sitting forward, his arms clasped desperately about his knees. Now I saw his shoulders sag, his whole body go limp. Then he shook himself and leaned back on his arms.

'Probably not. As for your father,' my brother said, 'I think the solution is simple.'

Yehûdâ brightened. 'You think so?'

'Tell your father you want to learn his business better before you marry and settle down. Suggest that you accompany some of his caravans to Arabia and Egypt. Isn't he sending one into Macedonia this autumn? There's your chance.'

'Yes . . . yes! You're right. I can be the dutiful, conscientious son, and put off marriage yet awhile. As long as he hasn't made a commitment to this betrothal. Perhaps I could be betrothed to your little sister Mariam. She'll not be marriageable for years yet.'

I put my hands over my mouth to stifle my gasp of astonishment.

My brother laughed. 'I fear you would not find her biddable!'

'Or beautiful.'

'Oh, she may surprise us yet. But I'm sure my family is not well-born or rich enough to satisfy Shim'ôn of Keriyoth! You must look elsewhere.'

'How much easier life was when we were boys, studying in the *beth ha-sefer* with the *hazzan*—in those days it seemed our childhood would never end. You were always the cleverest, our golden boy,' Yehûdâ teased, poking my brother in the ribs again. 'Forever poring over ancient scrolls, still reading when the rest of us were released to play.'

Yeshûa shrugged and swatted away the flies that were beginning to be drawn to the warm scent of their skin.

'It was never a burden, I loved my studies. Even now, I study when I can be spared from my father's work. Hebrew, Greek, Latin.'

'Not I! I've put away such boyish things.'

'Boyish? I think not.' Yeshûa smiled, 'It's a kind of escape . . . from making window frames and kneading troughs, or mending table legs.' There was a note of desolate yearning in his voice. I had not realised he disliked his work as a carpenter.

'By the way,' he went on, 'Mariam is a promising young scholar. She can read and write in four languages now.'

I was both pleased and angry to hear him tell Yehûdâ this, for my lessons were a secret between the two of us.

'Mariam? A girl may be taught to read the Book. But anything else? Surely that is not permitted.'

'Ya'aqôb would probably agree, so I'd be glad if you did not tell him. With every passing year, he becomes more obsessed with the ancient Law, but I think . . . Could there not be another way? A kinder way than the Law? A better way to live in harmony? It's what I was trying to say before, about the way we live our lives. There is something awry in the world. There are so many *forbidden* things, but little about love and kindness. The Law says we should not kill, but should we not go further? Should we not refrain from anger? Without anger, men would live in peace, there would be no wars, no killing.'

Yehûdâ patted him on the shoulder and laughed, but kindly.

'You're too much the dreamer, Yeshûa. Look about you at the world, with a man's eyes. That's a child's belief. You'll never change men's nature. If others injure us, we will react with anger. Strike me, and I will strike back. Come along, it's nearly time for the evening meal.'

They knotted on their loincloths and pulled their tunics over their heads. The sun was slipping down in the west, the grass cool and damp under their feet with evening dew. They gathered up their useless rods and, with their arms thrown carelessly around each other's shoulders, climbed the hill back to the village. Keeping my distance, I followed them. I had not understood everything Yeshûa had said, but I had seen how passionate he was. He wanted somehow to change things, to make life better for the poor. Or to stop wars. I thought that was what he meant. But, like Yehûdâ, I did not see how it could be done.

Even then, I wanted to be part of their company, to share that easy companionship. I was not close to my sisters. Melkha, six years older and betrothed, already thought of herself as a grown woman. She was all that a daughter should be, in our mother's eyes: beautiful, skilled, hard-working. Only I knew that she could be spiteful when she was sure our parents and older brothers were not looking. Sometimes she would spoil my work, for the pleasure of seeing me scolded. I had learned long before that her word would always be believed before mine. Eskha, at three years old, was too young to be a companion. There were other girls of my age in the village. I met them at the well or when we beat the clothes clean on the banks of the river, but my secret studies with my brother somehow divided me from them. I thought their chatter stupid. I was arrogant and wilful. And I was lonely.

Yeshûa had little time to spend with me, and besides he was near enough a man grown now. How could he find pleasure in the company of a child? I had no illusions on that score and treasured every moment he gave me. I was fearful too that he might leave the village. There was a restlessness about him lately. Sometimes his temper was short, as it never used to be, and I watched him furtively for any sign that he might be planning to go off, as other young men in the village had done, to Sepphoris or Jerusalem, to seek his fortune. I feared he would not want to spend the rest of his life working with our father. When the new baby was born, then he might think the house had grown too crowded at last, and make that his excuse to leave.

Melkha's wedding took place in the autumn of that year when I was eight and Yeshûa was twenty. My mother was near her time and there was a sense in the family that the pattern was changing. One member was leaving, a new one was coming. There were other changes in the village. Yehûdâ had left home and gone with one of his father's caravans to Greece and Macedonia. He would be away for months, perhaps not returning until the following summer or even later. I knew my brother missed him, would have liked to go with him on this adventure beyond the village, beyond the Galilee, beyond even Judah itself, but there was no reason for him to go. He would never be a merchant. He was our father's eldest son and must follow his trade. All that autumn and the following winter and spring, he worked with a kind of desperate intensity, as if he were trying to find something in the work of his hands that would satisfy the restlessness of his mind. He seemed also to be containing with difficulty a kind of suppressed anger, though I could not understand why he was angry. Sometimes it would burst out, in a sudden sharp word; sometimes he would throw down his tools and make off into the hills, where he would roam alone until nightfall. In spite of this, or perhaps because of it, he found more time to teach me, whenever we could both escape from the seemingly unending work. It was easier for him. Our father had five sons to help him. With Melkha preparing for her marriage, our mother had only me.

When we could, Yeshûa and I would meet in the olive orchard which lay just below the village, on the slope leading down to the river. It is the practice in our dry lands to plant each olive tree in its own earth basin hollowed out of the ground, to encourage the rain, when it comes, to gather there and feed the tree. Olive trees grow as twisted and lumpen as old men, and their roots, writhing between these earthen basins, are like huge snakes turned into wood. Our trees were hundreds of years old, so the olive orchard was a place of mounds and hollows and bending trunks, where half a legion could have hidden unseen. Here we would sit, while my brother taught me.

I could read now in Aramaic, which he taught me first, and the Hebrew of the scriptures, and Latin. Recently he had begun to teach me Greek. Yet another alphabet, but I enjoyed learning new alphabets, it was like unlocking a door to a secret room, or being given a magic incantation which summoned up a whole new world of stories and people and ideas. My knowledge was still small, but I had an ear for languages, and each time we read together I was a little more confident. He taught me to write— first with my finger in the loose earth at the base of the trees, then with a charred stick on broad shavings from my father's workshop. That autumn he taught me how to split and shape a fine reed into a quill, and how to make a simple ink from lamp black and gum.

Sometimes we met for these lessons no more than once a week. On a few wondrous occasions we met three times. But as the day of Melkha's wedding drew near, my mother wanted me constantly at her side, sewing, cooking, packing up the store of goods that Melkha would take with her as her dowry. My mother's pregnancy tired her more than usual this time, and she was short-tempered, complaining that everything I did was wrong, then bursting into tears and apologising. Melkha had grown nervous and jumpy since the merchant Adamas had returned from his travels and she realised that she could no longer revel in the privileged status of betrothed girl. Soon she would have to leave her home and move to Sepphoris. She would have to share the bed of a man almost as old as her father, who had already buried two wives and had a grown-up son. And while he was in Egypt Adamas had grown fat and greasy. He touched me sometimes, with fingers like chunks of meat roasted on a skewer, so that I recoiled and he laughed. Melkha, in dread I suppose at what lay ahead of her, wept suddenly and without warning. Suddenly and without warning, too, she would turn on me. I seemed to be weeping a good deal as well, what with my mother and Melkha and Ya'aqôb's pious platitudes and Yeshûa's restlessness and a feeling in the house that made my head ache, as though a thunderstorm was brewing.

When my brother and I met for my lesson about a week before Melkha's wedding, it was to prove the last of these meetings for nearly two months, though I did not know it at the time. We found a comfortable seat on an old gnarled root under the shade of one of the oldest of the olive trees. There was a pleasant breeze blowing, with the heat of summer declining softly into autumn. Over our heads the wind lifted the leaves, setting their silver undersides glinting, like the jingling harness ornaments of a king in majesty, and from time to time a shower of ripe olives would patter on to the hard ground around us with the sound of some small animal scampering past.

Together we recited a *berâkâ*, a blessing on our lesson, and then he asked me to repeat in Hebrew the verses from the Pentateuch which I had been learning. It was a passage I loved, about Yahweh's creation of the world, and I repeated it without a mistake.

'Now, Mariam,' he said, 'we will write the name of each of the animals you know in Hebrew, as you have learned it, then in Aramaic, as you would speak it every day. Then we will see how many you can name in Latin and in Greek.'

His lessons were like a game, and soon I was reciting and writing the names of the animals in all four languages.

'Are there other languages I could learn?' I asked, for I was hungry for knowledge. 'How many languages are there in the world?'

He laughed. 'That I do not know, little sister. These are all the languages that I know myself. But there is Persian, and Egyptian, and Syrian, as many languages as there are peoples.'

'How I would like to see them all,' I sighed. 'All those strange people in the world. Where they live and how they speak and what they eat and wear.'

I saw that look come over him, that I had seen so often recently, as though he was looking beyond me to some distant place.

'But I don't suppose we ever will,' I finished.

'No,' he said firmly. 'I don't suppose we ever will.'

Years later, we were sitting on a stone terrace in front of a house in Capernaum after dining with friends. Behind us, the sun was sinking beyond the hills of Galilee and its last rays capered and sparked on the small waves of the Lake of Gennesaret. On the shore a few feet below us, some fishermen were unloading their evening catch, and my brother raised a hand to them in greeting. It had been a long and tiring day, but it was peaceful now, the palms casting their long-fingered shadows across our feet, the small town quiet after the bustle of the day. It was unusual for us to be alone, for most of our waking hours he was surrounded by his companions and followers, with more and more strangers clamouring for his attention, while I was busy about my duties with Susanna and Salome and Yoanna and the other women. Perhaps they had all retired early that day. I do not now remember.

'I have always wondered,' I said, 'why you taught me as a child. Taught me to read and write. Gave me the gift of languages. The gift of learning. No one else would have done it. Why me, out of all our brothers and sisters?'

He turned and gave me a slow radiant smile, and took my hand.

'Because you were filled with *ru'ah*, the gift of the Spirit. I knew it the first time I saw you as a baby, gazing up at me with those strange blue eyes of yours.'

I looked down at our joined hands, and felt my eyes fill with inexplicable tears.

Chapter Three

To this day I insist that we say a *berâkâ* over our meal, though I know my children and grandchildren think it is a sign of my foreignness, my not-quite-Roman outlook on life. The sardines are excellent and I congratulate my daughter-in-law Fulvia on not cooking them to a charred and broken mess (which she has been known to do). She blushes and stammers, and I am ashamed that I praise her so little. Perhaps I am turning into my mother? I must take more trouble with her, treat her more kindly. We can only afford two household slaves, and three to labour on the farm with Manilius, so all of us have to work hard at manual tasks. From time to time Manilius hints that if he could be allowed to build up his wine business, the farm would earn a much greater income and the whole family would benefit. However, he is an obedient son and will not go against my wishes while I live. I expect he will not have long to wait.

'I heard something at the market today,' I say, turning the glass of wine in my hand, then taking a sip for courage.

They look at me expectantly—Manilius, Fulvia, and the children: Marcus, the eldest, and the twins, Julia and Petronius. I see at once that they think it is news of Sergius. Perhaps he has decided to marry? Or he wants to come home to the farm? Could it support another adult—or perhaps another man's work would make us more profitable? I read these thoughts behind the eyes of Fulvia and Manilius. The children are momentarily interested, then somehow sense that it is nothing that impinges on their world.

'Two men from Judah—from Palestine,' I say. 'They bring news of trouble in the country. There is rebellion stirring. More Roman troops sent out there. Terrible reprisals. Villages burned, their inhabitants slaughtered.'

They look politely shocked. It is as if I told them a child's folktale of wickedness. It has no reality for them. I feel a sudden sharp ache. I have felt it more often of late. There is no one who remembers, who knows. Even amongst my family I am a

32

stranger. Incautiously, I let something slip, which I should not. The words fall from my lips before I can stop them and at once I wish I could call them back.

'Your uncle,' I say, turning to my son, 'your uncle Ya'aqôb, bishop of Jerusalem, has been murdered by the high priest.'

Later, I hear my son and his wife whispering together.

'Of course,' says Fulvia, 'she is growing very old.'

'I often hear her talking to herself,' Manilius admits it reluctantly. 'She seems to be holding conversations with someone called Yeshûa. There was no uncle. I suppose it happens to all old people, they begin to wander in their minds and memories. But I never thought my mother . . .'

They move away, out of earshot.

⤜

Melkha's wedding was a great occasion in the village, everything that my father could afford. There had not been a wedding for some time and, as was the custom, everyone was invited. Because she was the first of his children to marry, my father wanted to do all that was best for her. It would smooth the path to matrimony for the rest of us as well. The bridegroom's parents were long dead, but this did not seem to trouble Adamas, and—to speak of him in fairness, which is difficult for me—he did his part in providing for the feast, as well as paying my father the bride-price for Melkha.

My sister looked enchanting in her wedding attire. She *was* a beautiful girl and her eyes shone with delight. She seemed to have put aside her doubts of recent weeks and to be eager to take up her new role as a wedded woman. She had been marriageable for two years, since she was a little past twelve, and perhaps she was growing impatient at her lack of status. There had always been the worry that Adamas might die during his long journey into Egypt, in which case she would have been regarded as a widow. No woman, I suppose, wants to be a widow without first having been a wife.

After they made their vows before all the village under the linked crowns of fresh flowers (gentians and the little rock roses, which my mother and I had arisen before dawn to plait), Melkha threw back her veil to reveal her face to all the company. Her veil was of the most delicate silk, almost transparent, a gift from Adamas. With the help of her friend Martha she had been stitching it all over with flowers and leaves in the finest of threads. They had even worked long after sundown, with no light but the simple oil lamp which burned day and night in our main room, and their eyes had grown red and their fingers pricked and sore. But Melkha had bathed her eyes with cold spring water in which herbs had been soaked, and the redness had passed. I thought my parents were more red of eye than she, to see her leaving home, though it was a good marriage.

The bridal pair walked arm in arm from the *kenîshtâ* to the other side of the main square, where trestle tables had been set up for the wedding feast. Our own courtyard was too small to accommodate so many and the party had taken over the whole village. The table were heaped with honey cakes, dishes of lentils flavoured with precious saffron, roasted aubergines, artichokes, black and green olives, great loaves of wheaten and rye and poppy bread with fresh butter (unfamiliar to us) provided by Shim'ôn of Keriyoth from his cows, as well as the usual small bowls of olive oil for dipping, small rounds of goat's cheese wrapped in vine leaves, smoked fish from Gennesaret, slivers of dried beef also from Shim'ôn, great flagons of wine and small jugs of the potent date liquor that some of the men would drink as evening drew in. Downwind of the tables, a fat sheep was turning on a spit over an open hearth. Melkha and Adamas sat at the head of the table under a canopy, with my parents and the village elders, while my brothers were dispersed about the tables amongst the guests. I was relegated to a lower table with the children, having been given strict instructions to watch over Eskha, who had been over-excited all day and was ripe for mischief. I was resentful that my brother Shim'ôn, who had not yet become *bâr mitzvâh*, Son of the Law, was allowed to sit amongst the adults, but after a while, when I had stuffed myself with food and drink, I was glad that we were allowed to leave the tables and run about the village streets. It was two years and more since I had been allowed to play with a child's freedom.

Away from the adults, we ran shrieking through the alleys and courtyards of the village, scaring the street cats into streaking up fig trees for refuge and setting the house dogs barking on their chains. I slithered once on wet autumn leaves and sat down suddenly on the hard-packed earth, but one of the girls hauled me to my feet again and we ran on, eager to find a hiding place, for one of the boys had shouted that it was a game of seek-and-find-me.

The other girl, whose name was Judith, pointed to the chicken house belonging to one of her neighbours and we pushed our way inside. An indignant hen squawked and fluttered out, but the rest were scratching in the dirt outside, so we hoped we would not be discovered. It was smelly in there, and we sneezed once or twice from the dust and the feathers, but we covered each other's mouths with our hands to suppress the giggles and crouched there as quietly as we could. Judith's hand was warm and sticky and smelled of figs. Gradually the shouts of the other children died away in the distance and we relaxed.

'Your sister has got a rich man for her husband,' said Judith.

I shrugged. 'I don't like him. He's always touching me and he's fat and he smells.'

Judith put on a wise look.

'He's much older than she is, so he'll do everything to please her. That's what my mother says. Otherwise, another man might covet her. She's very beautiful.'

I was shocked. 'To covet her—that is against the Law.'

'It may be against the Law, but it happens. That's what my mother says.'

This was making me uncomfortable and I crawled forward towards the door. I had remembered that I was supposed to be minding Eskha, and I didn't know where she was.

'Wait,' said Judith. 'They may still be out there, watching for us. My eldest sister will be betrothed soon. She wants to get your brother Yeshûa, even though he isn't rich like Adamas.'

I felt suddenly sick and pushed past her out of the chicken house. There was no sign of the other children. I ran off, calling to Eskha.

It was nearly sundown before the bridal couple left for Sepphoris. My parents were worried because most of the journey would be made in the dark, even though it was no more than two hours away, but Adamas was rich and had provided for this. He had brought finely caparisoned camels to ride, and slaves bearing flaming torches to light the way. It seemed he was in a hurry to carry my sister off to his bed before there was any more delay. His son led off on one camel, Adamas following on another, pure white and immensely valuable, with Melkha sitting before him in the crook of his fat arm. She looked pale now, with heavy shadows under her eyes. I thought she was frightened.

We said a *berâkâ* for their safe journey, scattered seeds for fertility in their path, and crushed a pomegranate. Eskha began to cry, so I took her hand and led her home. My parents and their guests would continue with the feast until the tables were cleared, but I was glad of an excuse to leave. After I had put Eskha to bed, I carried my own bedroll and rug up to the roof. Before many weeks were out, it would be too cold to sleep up here, but I wanted to escape from the enclosing walls of the house.

I had fallen asleep at last, despite the discomfort of having eaten too much, and the stars had wheeled round to midnight or later, when I woke to the sound of someone coming up the stairway to the roof, then stepping softly over the straw mats. I raised my head. I recognised him from the silhouette cutting out his shape from the stars.

'Yeshûa?'

'I'm sorry, Mariam. Did I wake you?'

He laid out his bedroll a few feet from mine and sat down on it cross-legged.

'It doesn't matter.' I sat up and faced him, pulling my thin rug around my shoulders. 'Is it over?'

'Yes, everyone has gone home. Time to sleep now. Say the prayer with me.'

I did as I was bid and lay down again. I heard him take off his sandals and settle himself.

'Why did you come up here?' I asked.

'I thought you might want the company. Would you like me to go away?'

'No, please stay.'

There was silence for a while, but I could tell by his breathing that he was not asleep.

'Yeshûa?'

'Mmm?'

'Do you think Melkha will be happy?'

He did not answer at once. I heard him turn over, then he propped himself up on his elbow.

'I think she has what she wants at the moment. I think she has every chance of living a contented life.'

I did not think this was quite a straightforward answer.

'Yeshûa?'

'Yes, Mariam?'

'Will you ever marry?'

He was much longer answering this time, so that I turned my head to see if he had fallen asleep, but he was still leaning on his elbow and looking, not at me, but up at the sky.

'I do not think I shall marry, Mariam. I don't know yet what my life holds, but I think it will be something else, something that will demand everything of me, so that it would not be right of me to marry. Do you understand?'

'Yes,' I said, though I did not.

I lay back, searching the heavens until I found my blue star, and fell asleep smiling.

Although I knew that, being a mere girl, I would never leave the village, except perhaps to marry, I had even then something of my brother's restlessness. I tried to imagine the places Yehûdâ knew, like Sepphoris and the wicked city of Tiberias. I pictured myself walking through their streets, which I thought of as being like our twisting village lanes, only wider, lined with bigger buildings, but I sensed that I did not really understand what a city would be like. Above all, I wondered about the Holy City, Jerusalem. It was spoken about so frequently in the scriptures, with such awe, that it hardly seemed like a real place, yet my parents had been there, and all my brothers except Shim'ôn, the youngest, had made their *bâr mitzvâh* oaths there.

Once, I asked Yeshûa to tell me about it. It was after Yehûdâ had gone away and Yeshûa was down by the river, fishing by himself. I'm not sure how I had managed to escape from my tasks, but I was lying on my stomach, watching the water ripple over the stones, sometimes forming odd whorls and patterns before flowing onwards.

'My journey to Jerusalem?' said Yeshûa, lazily trailing the bait for the indifferent fish. 'I'll tell you some of it, anyway.'

He looked down at me with a rueful smile.

'It was a journey that changed me. Perhaps it would have been better if it hadn't.'

He paused, searching inside himself for the memories.

'I could hardly contain myself, you know, watching out for the caravan we were to join, but it came at last, and we set off, leaving the other boys and Melkha in the care of neighbours. My parents shared a camel; I was put to ride with a stranger, a taciturn man who'd travelled from faraway Sidon. I rode before him on the double saddle. I was glad of that, for if I'd been seated behind him I would have had my face pressed against the back of his *chalouk* and wouldn't have seen anything of the country we passed through.

'I'd never ridden a camel before, and I can tell you, Mariam, that it wasn't pleasant! A camel seems to roll from side to side, and sway back and forth, and all the while its head nods in front of your eyes, so that the whole world dips and gyrates around you. At the end of the first half hour, I vomited over the side of the camel the whole of my morning meal of bread and *shechar* (now I was to be a man, I'd been allowed beer). I think my fellow passenger had been expecting this, for he heaved me sideways and dangled me over the void by my belt, to spare his clothes. When I was back in the saddle again, he passed me a cool pottery jar of water and I drank thirstily, for the sun was growing hot on my unprotected head. I thanked him, wiped my mouth on my sleeve, and draped a cloth over my head.'

'Poor Yeshûa!' I said with a laugh.

'You may laugh,' he said, 'but we'll see if you laugh when you first ride a camel! By now our village had long vanished into a fold of the hills. Everything before me was new and strange, and riding so high on the camel's back, I could see the land of the Galilee stretching away for miles in all directions. I'd never understood before that the world was so large. We were descending southeast into the Jizreel Valley before turning south and following the ridge road along the edge of the Jordan Valley. After our small village fields, the rolling riches of Jizreel were staggering. I understood now why men called it the garden of Judah. The *hazzan* had taught us that it was the fertility of this valley that made possible the growth of the great cities. In ancient times, each family farmed its own land and grew its own food— as we do still. But once the land could be made to produce abundant crops, men could live idly in cities, feeding off the food taxes they took from the farmers.'

He drew his fishing line out of the water and laid the rod down beside him on the bank. He was quiet for a long time, looking thoughtfully down at his clasped hands.

I thought he had forgotten about me, and rolled over, shading my eyes with my arm. The leaves of the olive trees gave off a pungent scent in the heat, tickling my nose, so I thought I might sneeze. It was very quiet there at the end of the olive grove, beside the river, for the birds were roosting silently in the heat of the day. Only the cicadas kept up their endless, monotonous rasping, which seemed to blend with the cool music of the river in a strange counterpoint.

'That was the beginning of my unease,' he went on at last. 'I'd never before thought about the injustice to farmers, for the tithes and land taxes were my father's concern and not mine. Now I saw donkeys and camels loaded with baskets and bundles of foodstuffs, crates of chickens and ducks, great jars of wine and beer and oil, all heading towards the cities of the south. Eventually we met the wide road—beaten clay laid in some parts with stones—which runs north and south the whole length of the country. Along this even ox carts could travel, piled high with food.

' "Is that tribute for the Temple at Jerusalem?" I asked my travelling companion hesitantly.

'He grunted. "*Tribute* for the high priest, and for the Sanhedrin and all the other tribes of priests and Levites and scribes to live off.' He snorted scornfully. 'What you see going north is taxes for the Roman prefect and his troops at Caesarea."

'He leaned to one side and spat, as though the very words had polluted his mouth, then he lapsed into silence again.'

My brother paused, and began to arrange the fallen olives into patterns on the ground.

'You mean,' I said, not sure if I had understood, 'that the priests and the Romans hadn't grown the food for themselves. They hadn't *earned* it?'

'Something like that, Mariam. And in the villages we passed through, although the land was fertile, there were poor people, people going hungry, and I thought, *Shouldn't the food be given to the starving children, not to the Roman occupiers and the wealthy in Jerusalem?* It troubled me.'

'Did you stay at inns on the way?' I asked. The thought of an inn seemed very sophisticated to me at the time.

'Oh no! That would have been far too costly! Each time we halted for the night, we set up a *caravanserai*, with the camels and their Bedouin drivers forming an outer ring and the pilgrims in the centre. The Bedouins kept to themselves, preparing their own food, speaking their own language, and only addressing us in broken Aramaic to give us instructions: *You wake now; Make food; Rain coming.* They didn't use tents, but rolled themselves up in their blankets and lay down beside their camels. We had tents woven from coarse goat hair, which we draped each night over a rough framework of branches. We boys were sent to find stones to weigh down the edges of the tents and keep them in place. Yehûdâ and I always went together, for he was travelling to celebrate his *bâr mitzvâh* as well, though he's nearly a year older than I. He rode one of his father's own camels, but I didn't envy him. Terrible beasts! Our two families put up their tents together and our mothers prepared a communal evening meal, with the help of the two servants that Shim'ôn of Keriyoth had brought with him.'

'It must have been a wonderful adventure.' I sighed enviously. Oh, to be a boy, and have the chance to travel the world and see Jerusalem!

'Yes, most of the time it was,' he said. 'We suffered one storm, at the north gate of Jericho, a heavy spring thunderstorm, that soaked through our tents and flooded the ground. The next day everyone was drenched and bad-tempered from loss of sleep. Jericho was the first city I had ever seen, and I can tell you, I stood in awe of the wide streets and great stone walls. There were colonnaded public buildings, and a vast open marketplace where the camel drivers advised us to buy supplies, as everything would be scarce and expensive in Jerusalem. The city, however, was eerily quiet, with very few people in the streets. Yehûdâ's father, who often goes to Jerusalem for *Pesah*, explained this was because most of the population would already have travelled the short distance to Jerusalem for the purification rituals. We would only just reach there in time.'

Jerusalem! I sat up and wrapped my arms around my knees, waiting for him to tell me the rest of the story.

We started early the next day, *he went on*, but even so it was late, past sundown by the time we set up the *caravanserai* just outside the gate of Jerusalem, for it was a longer day's journey than usual. All the way the road was crowded with travellers, everyone heading in the same direction, and sometimes we couldn't move forward at all. As we approached the Holy City, the lights were coming on one by one, and it seemed to grow before our very eyes, spread out over its many hillsides. I was too excited to sleep, and only dozed off far into the night.

The next day was the seventh of Nisan, and the whole company, with the exception of the Bedouin, was to enter the city to begin the ritual of purification. For a few hours, while our fathers and the other men made the arrangements, Yehûdâ and I were allowed to explore the city. The women had remained behind in the encampment, otherwise I don't think we would have been indulged. Or trusted not to lose ourselves! We were to meet the men at the gate nearest the *caravanserai*, the Lion's Gate, no later than midday.

We were thrilled but a little awed by our freedom, Yehûdâ and I, and we stayed close together. The streets were so thick with people, even the main thoroughfares, that we were shoved this way and that, and could scarcely keep on our feet. Although it was springtime, the heat was intense. Yehûdâ plunged his head in a horse trough to cool it down, and flung back his hair so that I was spattered with the drops. The water was so welcome that I did the same, and we walked through the streets, with our hair streaming over our necks and shoulders, and our mouths agape, true country boys overwhelmed by all we saw. Eventually, after wandering with no particular goal in mind, we found our way into a square at the junction of several streets.

'Look, Yeshûa!' Yehûdâ cried, pointing.

The whole square was packed with market stalls, so close that the crowds could barely squeeze between them. Directly in front of us was a fruit stall such as we had never seen before. There were pyramids of pomegranates, cascades of figs and apricots, bowls of walnuts and almonds, bunches of fresh dates hung up on hooks, heaps of citrons and some fruit that looked like a citron but was orange in colour. There were melons of every shape and size. As we lingered before the fruit stall, the vendor, a small, weasely man who looked like an Arab, seized a cleaver and, with a single blow, chopped a huge melon with smooth green skin in half. The flesh was a crystalline red, and he carved us a thin shaving each to try. This was how manna in the desert must have tasted!

'I will take half a melon,' said Yehûdâ grandly, pulling his purse out from the breast of his tunic. He gulped a little when the price was mentioned, but was too nervous to try to haggle the price down. The man cut it in half again for us, and we found a seat on some stone steps to eat it. It was crisp and cold and wonderful after our poor food on the journey. We made it last as long as we could, spitting the seeds into the street. And received a torrent of complaints whenever we hit a passer-by. When we'd finished, we did as everyone else did, and threw the melon skins into the gutter.

Beyond the fruit stall stood another from which rose an intoxicating scent, complex, strange. It was laid out meticulously with rows of copper bowls, each holding a heap of a single precious commodity, spices from the east: cinnamon and pepper, frankincense and mace, galbanum, nutmegs and myrrh, onycha and the precious flakes of saffron, protected from the wind by a delicate cloth of transparent silk. The stallholders were a man and woman with dark skin and eyes black as raisins of the sun, who had come from the far east, beyond the deserts of Arabia. She was veiled so that nothing of her face could be seen but the eyes, and her clothes were of turquoise silk with gold threads running through it. Her arms were loaded from wrist to elbow with heavy gold bracelets. The man, too, wore silk, but no jewellery except a heavy chain around his neck, and his eyes darted from side to side in his unmoving face—like . . . like a lizard's—as he kept a fierce watch over his precious commodities. When a customer approached and began to bargain for nutmegs, he drew out a set of delicate scales, with weights no larger than my thumbnail.

At last we grew tired of the heat and the throngs and made our way back to the Lion's Gate, after some wrong turnings and asking the way several times. It seemed that most of the people in the streets were strangers too, and as confused as we were. I was relieved to see the gate and our fathers, and to escape from the crush of the crowds. I found I couldn't breathe easily in a great city.

I leaned back against my brother's shoulder. I caught that faint scent of him, honey and cinnamon, and tried to imagine the spice-seller's stall with all the mysterious goods I had never seen.

'What is myrrh?' I asked.

'A rare and precious spice,' he said, 'used in sacrifice and for embalming the dead.'

'Yeshûa! Mariam!' It was Shim'ôn shouting to us from further up the hill. 'You are to come home at once! Father needs you in the workshop, Yeshûa.'

He came scrambling down through the edge of the olive grove, frowning when he saw us sitting at our ease beside the river.

'So this is where you have run away to, while everyone else is working! Mariam, you'll get a whipping if you don't come back this minute and milk the goats. Mother has been searching for you everywhere.'

We scrambled guiltily to our feet.

'What about the rest of the story?' I whispered. 'You haven't told me about your *bâr mitzvâh*.'

'Later.' Yeshûa winked at me. 'When we can run away again.'

But it would be two years before I heard the end of his story.

༺

I am not quite well enough to go again to the market in Massilia and I am making a misery of life for everyone on the farm. Manilius went down to deal with the captain of the ship from Judah and sold him a consignment of wine at a good profit, because the man was in too much of a hurry to argue over the price. I had intended to go with him, so that I might question the captain for more news, but the morning after my meeting with the two sailors I felt faint and dizzy, and had to let my son make the journey on his own. Ever since, I have noticed a slight shaking in my hands and if I stand up suddenly the world seems to tip crazily around me. It reminds me of how, when we were children, we would spin round and round, so that when we stopped it seemed as though the very ground leapt like a horse. I cannot imagine now why we enjoyed the sensation. I do *not* enjoy the sensation of being not quite in control of my body.

I think perhaps I have a touch of the sun. Fulvia fusses around me like an old hen.

'Do not make such a to-do, girl!' I say to her in exasperation. 'I am not a child, to be fidgeted over. You set my teeth on edge.'

'You are not a child, Mother Mariam,' she says soothingly, showing far more patience with a bad-tempered old woman than ever I would have done. 'But you are no longer young and you always try to do too much. Please, go and lie down in your room and I will bring you a cool drink.'

'I will be well enough in the vine arbour,' I say stubbornly. I try to stamp outside with my usual vigour, but my knees, like my hands, are a little shaky.

I make my way to my favourite seat, steadying myself against pillars and the corners of walls when I hope she is not looking. I want to remove myself from the sound of their voices, hers and Manilius's, wondering what to do with me, ever since my strange talk of bishops and murder and unknown uncles, and my general odd behaviour.

A week has passed since I met the sailors, one of them a follower of the Christ cult, and their ship is long gone on its return journey. Manilius is pleased with his dealings and Sergius has come to visit us—partly for a celebration meal with us, partly (I suspect) because Manilius has told him of their worries about me, so he has decided to come and see for himself. He joins me now on the terrace, sitting on the low wall with his back to the sea and his hands loosely clasped between his knees. He is a good-looking young man, so that I am surprised that no clever Massilia girl has managed to entrap him yet.

'What is this about an uncle in Palestine, Mother?' he asks. 'I thought you had no family.'

'I never said that,' I answer. 'I simply never told you about them. Ya'aqôb was my second eldest brother. They are all dead now.'

'And was he truly the bishop of Jerusalem? A leader of the Christ cult?'

I can see that he does not believe this, but wishes to humour me.

'Does that surprise you? It is true.'

He is not convinced, I can see that, but neither is he as incredulous as Manilius and Fulvia.

'But . . . *the Christ cult!* Mehercule! That could be dangerous.'

'I did not say that I was a follower.'

'No.' He looks at me thoughtfully and a little too shrewdly. 'Are you?'

'Every man's conscience is his own affair,' I say, closing my eyes, indicating that I wish to close the subject, but he pursues it.

'Did you know that it is spreading?' he says. 'All through the Empire, and the Emperor does not like it. Even here in Gallia, it is said that they are building secret places of worship, temples to their Christ-god.'

45

Not temples, I want to say. Churches. They are called *churches*. And they are not for the worship of some new hybrid monster, a Christ-god. They are places for the worship of the one true God, but God purged of vengeance and cruelty. A new dispensation.

'Your brother,' I say clearly, keeping my eyes firmly closed, 'is planning to buy a new yoke of oxen and a new plough. He wants to plough up the wheat fields and plant another vineyard. What do you think of that?'

He takes the hint, and we turn to safer subjects.

ဢ

Once, I cannot remember how old I was, or whether it was before or after Melkha's wedding, I had gone to my father's workshop to call him to the midday meal. We ate only a light meal during the day—my mother's goat's cheese, bread, a handful of olives, with dried or fresh fruit: figs or apricots or melons. If he was absorbed in his work, my father would forget to come to the house and one of us would be sent to fetch him. As I stepped in out of the sunlight, I was part-blinded by the shadows within, but then my sight adjusted and I saw Ya'aqôb at work on the pole lathe, turning a chair leg, and Yoses and Yehûdes in a far corner, using a two-handled saw. Shim'ôn came in behind me, struggling to carry a ploughshare he had been sent to fetch from the blacksmith, who lived two streets away. It was almost too heavy for him to lift. The sharp edge had already cut his knees and blood was running down his legs. I reached out to help him, but he shouldered me aside. He was unwilling to be shamed before his father and brothers.

Shim'ôn heaved the ploughshare on to the work bench between my father and Yeshûa, who ran his hand over the beautiful simple curves of the freshly forged iron.

'*Let us beat our swords into ploughshares*,' he said. There was a curious twist in his voice, which I did not understand, though I recognised the quotation.

I saw my father look at him and smile his slow, gentle smile.

'It is fine piece of work, all the finer when we have attached it to the plough.'

46

I saw that the framework of a new plough, complete except for the iron blade, lay on the bench between them. I walked over and caressed the smooth new wood of the handles. It was pale as a newborn baby's skin, creamy and sweet, with the heady scent of new wood. I put my nose close to it and sniffed, with my eyes closed. Shim'ôn laughed.

'Mariam is always smelling things. You would think she was a dog!'

I ignored him, stroking the wood. A new plough is a lovely object, before the shining new-forged iron turns cloudy and rusty, its edge dulled, and the wood of the frame becomes stained and discoloured from wind and rain and mud.

Yeshûa began to secure the blade to the framework.

'A plough is a worthy object, fine in the sight of the Lord,' said my father.

I sensed that he was picking up a subject they had already been discussing.

Yeshûa did not lift his head.

'I know it is. Truly, Father, I know that. And the work you do is fine in the sight of the Lord, blessed be his name, and blessed be the work of your hands.'

'And yet you do not think it is for you?'

Shim'ôn had wandered off to where my brothers were working at the saw-horse, and I do not think that any of them were listening, but I saw from the corner of my eye that Ya'aqôb had lifted his foot from the treadle of the lathe and held his chisel motionless in his hands before his chest. I had taken my hand from the plough when Yeshûa picked it up, and I began to fiddle with the coiled shavings which lay on the edge of the bench.

'I do not know.' My brother's voice was strained and unhappy. 'Perhaps I am being foolish. I should be content with the life I have been called to. But are not the exact words of Isaiah: *They shall beat their swords into ploughshares, and their spears into pruninghooks: nation shall not lift up sword against nation, neither shall they learn war any more.*'

He drew a long shuddering breath, like a man saved from near drowning. 'Isn't that a wonderful vision, Father? Wouldn't it be a worthy aim in a man's life, to work for such a world?'

47

He put aside his work with shaking hands, and turned to my father with appeal in his eyes.

My father laid his hand on his shoulder.

'We all know times of discontent, my son, especially when we are young and growing to manhood. You are an excellent carpenter. You could become a fine craftsman. Give yourself time to grow into the peace of the good and simple things in life. If you want to argue the finer points of Isaiah, you must turn to the *hazzan* and other learned men, not a simple carpenter like your father.'

Yeshûa nodded, and lowered his head again. I wished I could see his eyes. If I could see his eyes, I would know what he was thinking.

'Yes, Father,' he said quietly. Meekly. And yet I thought I could hear a note of despair in his voice.

Did I really understand what he was feeling, child that I was? Could I have understood? My brother was very dear to me, and I knew every tone of his voice. Perhaps sometimes we underrate the understanding of children.

The small figure of my sister Eskha appeared in the doorway.

'Mother says you are all to come at once for the midday meal,' she said importantly. 'Otherwise, she will feed it to the goats.'

Chapter Four

Two months have passed since I received word of Ya'aqôb's death, and my health has improved a little. What has not improved, I manage to conceal. I have become skilful at hiding the trembling of my hands and I have learned the trick of rising more slowly from bed or chair and steadying myself surreptitiously. I have learned also to hold my tongue, so that my son and his wife look relieved, and no doubt think my wild words of unknown uncles and murder were due to some passing fit brought on by the bad news from Judah.

Today I have even persuaded them that I am strong enough to go to the market at Massilia, although Manilius has insisted that I ride instead of walking, and that I take our house slave Antiphoulos with me, to help with the heavy lifting. As I need one donkey for riding, we make quite a little procession: myself in the lead, riding sideways on the largest donkey (an uncomfortable posture, wrenching to the back, but the only one suitable for a woman of my years) and, following me, Antiphoulos, leading two further donkeys, almost invisible under their swaying loads.

We have brought half a dozen wineskins of Manilius's new wine (he does not use expensive *amphorae* for local sales), a basket of honey pots sealed with wax, another of preserved fruits, onions knotted together in ropes, a sack of cabbages, another of peas, and two chickens roped in a basket and protesting loudly. Antiphoulos, who is, I believe, quite an educated man, looks embarrassed to be party to such a rustic parade.

Business is excellent and by early afternoon we have sold all the wine, both chickens, and most of the other goods. I notice that the slave looks restless, his eyes constantly turning away from the ships and toward the streets of the town. There is about him an air of suppressed excitement that intrigues me. He will not try to escape, I am certain of that. The risks are too great, the penalties too horrific. Besides, he has saved enough to buy his manumission before another year is out. What is it that keeps drawing his attention?

'I can manage well enough without your help for I while,' I say. 'Do you wish to look around the town? You can meet me back here when the market closes.'

His eyes light up. I am right. There is something afoot.

'Thank you, *domina*.' He presses his palms together and bows. 'It shall be as you say.'

I give a brisk nod and turn away, rearranging the last of the goods, but following him all the while out of the corner of my eye. He makes off swiftly for the road that leads north from the port. Before I lose him in the alleyways, I ask the neighbouring stallholder, a woman I have known for years, to watch my stall for me, and set off in Antiphoulos's wake.

He does not go far. Which is as well, for I might not have been able to keep up with him. Along the main street, then right and left into narrower alleyways, until he enters the crooked doorway of a small house crouching amongst other small houses. A humble fisherman's cottage, perhaps, or belonging to a small tradesman. But he did not knock at the door and wait. He merely pushed it open and slipped inside. I hesitate on the doorstep, uncertain whether to follow. My heart is beating irregularly at this foolish prank. What do I suppose that I am doing? Then I see, scratched in the whitewash of the wall, at ankle height so that you would be unlikely to notice it unless you were looking, the looped outline of the fish. Gently, I push open the door and step inside.

It takes a moment for my eyes to adjust to the dim light cast by two small oil lamps at the far end of the room, which is windowless and, despite the cooler autumn weather, stuffy with the smell of poor and unwashed bodies. There is a considerable crowd inside, all kneeling on the beaten earth floor, except for one tall man clothed in a white robe, who stands near the lamps, with his hands clasped and his head bowed. I slip into the corner nearest the door and lower myself, with some difficulty, to my knees. Antiphoulos has vanished into the crowd.

'Beloved brethren.'

It is the tall man speaking, using κοινη, the colloquial Greek of the eastern Empire, which is also widely spoken here in Massilia, especially amongst the poor. 'We are met together today in Christ Jesus's name, to give thanks and praise to the Lord God.'

He clears his throat. 'Our Father . . .'

The prayer is taken up by those around me, who kneel devoutly, with raised hands, palm to palm, and bowed heads. I do not speak, or pray, or bow my head. Instead, I look around the room. It was crudely whitewashed some time ago, the whitewash is flaking off, showing the rough timber-and-daub walls beneath. There are no chairs or benches, as there were in our village *kenîshtâ*. The lamps are standing on a small table and, hanging above it, nailed to the wall, is a rough wooden cross. It has not even the grace of a craftsman's work. It is merely two pieces of unfinished wood, tied together, where they intersect, with knotted strips of hide. The ends of the hide hang down and stir in the air set in motion by so many bodies. They look like the strips of skin hanging from the back of a man who has been flayed near to death.

The cross, the strips of skin, the muttering voices, the crowded bodies—I feel my stomach heave and the bitter taste of gall in my mouth. I half crawl to the door, claw it open, and escape. Even the air of the alleyway, choked as it is with rubbish, seems clear after the suffocating atmosphere of the room. Back in the marketplace I thank my neighbour for her kindness, close my eyes and breathe in wonderfully the salt, fishy smell of the sea.

On the journey back to the farm, I say nothing to Antiphoulos of where he has been. And nothing in his manner indicates that he saw me in the church of the Christ cult. I wonder how long he has been a believer. Once we reach home I excuse myself from the evening meal, pleading weariness and a headache, and go to my room. There, instead of retiring to bed, I sit beside the window which looks south, out to sea, and try to regain some calmness of mind. I should never have followed Antiphoulos, never entered the building, never raised my eyes to that grotesque and macabre *thing* that the Christ cult has taken as an object of worship, a graven image. I am filled suddenly with a fierce anger and sense of betrayal.

There is bright moonlight tonight. It flows in through the window, distorting the natural shapes of the objects in the room, falling upon my clenched hands on the windowsill. On my left hand, between thumb and index finger, it illuminates a small silver scar, the shape of a crescent moon.

~

Another of my earliest memories—it must have been around the time Yeshûa rescued me from the goat shed and persuaded me to make my peace with Ya'aqôb: I am standing in the doorway of my father's workshop. There is a soft swishing sound, like the sound of the wind in the leaves of the olive orchard. It is my father smoothing a table top made of cedar wood, using a damp cloth and the finest sand brought from the beaches of Phoenicia, a place I have never seen. I love the sound of the word *Phoe-ni-ci-a*, the way it whispers with promises, and I love the rhythmic sound of my father's hands on the wood. I watch the fine gold sawdust dance in a shaft of sunlight and make a kind of glow about his head. He looks up and sees me and smiles his slow, thoughtful smile, but his hands never cease their work. I take a step inside and stroke the wood with my finger. It is as silky as my own cheek, but still he smoothes it, his body rocking back and forth, back and forth, like a Pharisee at prayer.

My father was a stonemason and builder as well as a carpenter, but it was wood he loved. Always quiet and undemonstrative, he poured all his passion into the work of his hands. Soon after this he began giving me small off-cuts of wood to play with, and he let me sand them smooth, showing me how to work with the grain. By the time I was five years old I could name them all: olive wood with its close grain and greenish ripples like waves; oak, hardening with age and mighty enough for the floors of great stone public buildings in Jerusalem and Caesarea; pliant willow, for baskets and hurdles; scented cedar for clothes chests, to drive away moths, cedar from Lebanon for the Temple in Jerusalem; prized sycamore, proof against worms and—when properly cured—as hard as iron; apple wood and pear wood with their sweet smell, apt for simple village furniture;

modest beech for spoons and kitchen stirring sticks; precious ebony to make fine caskets for the rich.

When he decided I could be trusted, he let me use his tools, and although I was clumsy in so many ways, the tools seemed to fit naturally into my hands and my hands to know how to use them. I did not make furniture or door frames or ploughs, like the men of my family, but I had an aptitude for carving. At first I carved small animals, though the *hazzan* disapproved when he heard of it. I suppose he regarded them as impious, like graven images. Later, I learned the skill of making fine joints. I still remember my pride when I made my first box and the lid fitted sweetly, after much labour. I learned to inlay woods of different colours and grains to make patterns.

My mother, however, did not approve of a girl learning what was exclusively a man's trade, although I am sure neither my father nor I ever supposed I would practise it. She must have persuaded him, a man with five sons to follow him, to exclude me from the workshop. By the time I was twelve or so, I found there was no room for me in the workshop, my brothers crowding me out, my father apologetically shaking his head at me.

The injury to my hand happened one day when I was working alone in my father's workshop, before I was excluded. I do not now remember why I was alone. Probably it was very early in the morning, for I would sometimes steal in there before it became busy and swarming with all my brothers. I am working on the carving of a box lid, using a mallet and a very fine chisel to cut the pattern of grapes and a trailing vine. It is a complex shape and I want to impress my father with my skill. For the very delicate tracery I lay aside the mallet and grip the wood with my left hand, while gouging out the pattern with the chisel in my right. Suddenly the chisel slips, and instead of meeting wood, cuts deep into the flesh of my left hand.

I let out a shriek. There seems to be blood everywhere. It wells up and flows over my hand, the chisel, the box lid, the work bench. It forms pools and rivers in the carved wood. It stains the front of my tunic and puddles in the sawdust between my toes. I can hear my voice screaming and screaming as though it is separate from me, an animal in pain.

Yet I do not feel the pain at first, only horror and cold squeezing my chest and the warmth of the blood flowing over my hand. I drop the chisel and the lid on the floor and grip my left wrist with my right hand. Then my brothers Yoses and Yeshûa are there, gaping at me. Yoses recovers first, shrugging and walking away to the far side of the workshop.

'The child should not be playing with men's tools,' he says. 'Perhaps this will teach her a lesson.'

Yeshûa takes my bleeding hand in both his, covering the wound with his palm. The blood oozes up between his fingers, but I realise I have stopped screaming.

'It will be better now.'

He releases my hand and holds up his own left hand for me to see. There, on the warm brown skin, between index finger and thumb, is a small silver scar, curved like a new moon.

'See,' he says. 'We all pay the penalty for our craft.'

Why have I never noticed this scar before? I look down at my hand. The bleeding has suddenly stopped, and I can see that the chunk cut out of the flesh of my hand is in the same place as his scar. It is only then that the pain starts.

ॐ

Mariam sits beneath the vine arbour, her eyes closed and her hands loosely clasped in her lap. Although she seems to be asleep, her hands twitch convulsively from time to time. Julia sits on the ground at her feet. When her mother was not looking, she picked a large bunch of grapes and is cradling them in the lap of her tunic, with her back to the house. She thinks of offering one to her grandmother, but does not want to wake her. Instead, she eats the grapes, one by one, bursting them between her teeth and spitting the seeds as far as she can in the direction of the terrace wall.

Each time I hit the wall, I will have a lucky day. Grandmother Mariam sleeps a lot lately. She always used to be working, or going into the village, or down to Massilia. Now she sits for most of the day. None of my friends have a grandmother like Mariam. She is . . . exotic.

Julia tries out the new word, tastes it on her tongue and smiles. She loves the sound of new words. *Exotic.* Mariam's skin is a warm golden shade, even in winter, and her hair is a rich black, almost blue, like the feather of a raven if you tilt it against the sunlight. Even now that she is an old woman, her hair is black, with just two small wings of white above her ears. Julia squints up at her grandmother. Mariam's lips move silently, as if she is talking to herself, and her eyes flicker beneath her lids, surely she cannot be asleep? Julia was proud when Mariam told her that she had inherited her grandmother's unusual blue eyes. She felt singled out from her brothers, and from her father and uncle. Unlike her parents, she is not worried when Mariam is overheard speaking to someone called Yeshûa, who is not there, for Mariam told her about Yeshûa a long time ago. Yeshûa was her brother and lived in the faraway land where she was born. Julia was never told to keep this a secret, but somehow she knew she should not mention the name.

She shifts a little closer to Mariam's chair and leans her shoulder companionably against her legs. Mariam does not speak, but Julia feels her hand come down lightly to rest on her head.

She is a good child, not inclined to indulge me with condescension as a mild eccentric. She may amount to something one day. But I have learned not to invest too much hope in children. And her innocence is precious. Let her sit peacefully eating her stolen grapes and I will spare her the world of my childhood. Gaul has suffered its own bloody times, its massacres, but they are a practical people, able to accept the inevitable, adapt, make new and perhaps better lives. Intransigence may sometimes be commendable. Noble, even. But does it lead to happiness? Not amongst the Israelites. Not in my experience.

I am a walking history—Herodotus or Thucydides on legs. I know things, I remember things. When I fled here, empty-handed, I carried within myself a scroll of memory, a library of scrolls. I could tell you things that would make the hair of your head rise up like the hackles of a dog, I could make you weep for the despair of it, and rejoice for the joy. Mariam's testament. But perhaps it would all be better left unsaid. Let them invent their myths and miracles. Perhaps that is better. Perhaps I am simply too tired.

Daniel, my youngest brother, was born a few weeks after Melkha's wedding, at the beginning of what would prove to be one of the coldest winters I ever knew in the village. My mother had a long labour, which is unexpected with a tenth lying-in. Our house being one of the largest in the village, my parents had their own room, unlike some of our poorer neighbours, and it was to this room that she retired, attended by several older women, who stepped out of the room from time to time during the hours that followed, with looks of concern on their faces.

I was too young, of course, to take part in this birthing ritual, and was exiled, like my father, brothers, and small sister, to other parts of the house. It fell to me, however, to prepare the meals, which I did without much skill, while the drama of my brother's birth went on and on under the same roof. Nearly two days, it lasted. With my mother's screams splitting the air, I fled to the roof, then to the goat shed, finally to the *midbar* above the village. It was already too cold to pasture the goats out here, and I wandered alone amongst the tumbled rocks and thin winter grass, clutching a blanket I had caught up to use as a cloak. Eskha had been deposited with Judith's mother, the potter's wife, and the men of the family took themselves off to the workshop.

The sound of those screams seemed to echo in my head even out on the hillside, and I swore that if ever I gave birth, I would not scream like that, whatever it cost me. I would not be so shamed. A vow I kept when my sons were born. Not by biting on a leather strap, as some women will do, but by forcing my mind to recall a scene where the pain was unbelievably greater. Remembering, I was shamed into biting my lips to hold back my own cries of pain.

He was born at last, Daniel, at about midnight on the second day. I was taken to see him, where my mother lay, her shift and bedclothes stained with sweat and blood. Her face was grey, pinched, and she looked suddenly old. I had never thought her old before. Her cheeks were sunken and her hair straggled around her shoulders. She looked ugly. And I made a *berâkâ* of apology, for I should have pitied her, though I could not bear to look at her. Instead, I turned to look at the baby. He was small

56

and wizened, and lay flaccid in the basket where the women had laid him. He was tightly bound, with nothing but his head showing, a tuft of black hair. His eyes, heavy-lidded and swollen, were tight shut.

'Is he alive?' I asked one of the women. He was so still, he looked as though he had been wound in his shroud for burial.

She nodded. 'For the moment. But he had a hard passage into the world and he is small and weakly. He may not survive.'

'But why did it take so long, if he is small?' I was not so young that I did not understand some of the facts about birth.

She looked at me speculatively, as if weighing up how much I should be told, then she shrugged.

'He came the wrong way into the world, feet first. For a long time there was nothing but one leg showing. Your mother has had a bad time of it. You must help her all you can.'

I crept away, feeling ashamed.

My mother was ill for a long time afterwards. When it came to the ceremony of the purification, when she was to be cleansed of the defilement of childbirth, she had to be carried to the *kenîshtâ* in a chair by her two eldest sons. Then she took to her bed again. It was as though she had given up on life. I did what I could, cooking, washing, cleaning; I could not have managed without the kindness of neighbours, who baked bread for us and brought us pots of hot food. And I realised for the first time what a heavy burden my mother carried every day. I think at that time we became the closest we were ever to be. One day, I remember, she put her arms around me and held me close. She never said a word, but pressed her cheek against the top of my head, and afterwards I felt my hair damp with her tears.

Despite her weakness, my mother did her best to feed the baby, but he had little appetite, or else her milk failed, and he grew thinner and smaller before our eyes. He slept a great deal and cried little, except in the dark of night. It was not loud enough to wake my brothers, for it sounded like the thin cry of a newborn kitten, but my ears were sharp and it always woke me.

I shall never forget the first time Daniel opened his eyes wide and looked at me. I had carried him into the main room of the house to let my mother rest and was changing his dirty clouts.

One of his legs turned out at an awkward angle and he whimpered if it was touched, so I was handling him as carefully as I could. Usually his eyes were screwed shut, as if in pain, but that day, without warning, he opened them and looked straight up into mine. I had not been told, at that age, that very young babies cannot see properly, so I was not surprised that his look held intelligence and recognition. What did surprise me was the eyes themselves. They were large and wide-set, and their colour was a deep blue, almost purple, the colour of the darkest mountain gentians, much darker than my father's blue eyes. I wondered whether my eyes were the same. Yeshûa had told me my eyes were blue, but I had never seen them myself. Mirrors were unknown in my village.

After that, I felt there was a special bond between us. Without asking permission, I decided that I would try to persuade Daniel to drink some of the goat's milk, as my mother seemed unable to feed him enough to make him strong. Each day, after I had milked the goats, I would set a bowl of the fresh milk beside me, soak a clean cloth in it, and push it into Daniel's mouth for him to suck. At first, more of the milk landed on my clothes, on him, and on the floor than went down his throat, but within a few days he grasped what to do and would open his mouth eagerly for the cloth. After two or three weeks, other members of the family began to notice the change in him and I no longer hid what I was doing. My father patted my shoulder and told me I was a clever girl, my mother accepted it wearily and even started to improve a little in health. Daniel began to grow plumper, more like a normal baby and less like a changeling. Even after my mother finally left her bed and began slowly to take up her household tasks again, it came to be accepted that I would take charge of the rearing of my small brother.

By the time he learned to stand and take a few steps, it was clear that his leg would not straighten and he would always walk with a limp. I shall never know whether he would have been born damaged anyway, or whether the women who attended my mother, wanting to end her pain, had dragged on his leg and somehow twisted it for ever at the hip. Ya'aqôb, as might be expected, saw Daniel's handicap as a judgement of Yahweh for some sin committed by the family, though he was unable to say what it was. By this time Melkha had given birth to her first son, a strong healthy boy with a decided look of Adamas about him. Although he was eight months younger than Daniel, he walked at about the same time, and could soon outrun him when my sister brought him to visit us.

It was after one of these visits that I overheard my two eldest brothers arguing outside the goat shed when I was milking.

'It is a judgement,' Ya'aqôb said, I could have sworn almost with satisfaction. 'We have not kept the Law closely enough. We have failed to say the correct prayers, or we have not washed before food, or failed to fast.'

'Are you embracing the ways of the Pharisees?' Yeshûa asked, pleasantly enough.

'You condemn the Pharisees?'

'Not at all. They are good men, good in their intentions. But too strict and unbending in their ways. Surely it is more important in Yahweh's sight that we should love one another, that we should be kind to strangers and succour the poor, than that we should always use the right dish or wear the correct garment, or follow any of these new "traditions" they have invented, which are no part of the ancient Law?'

'You may believe that, Yeshûa, but I do not. I believe that each man must start with disciplining himself, make himself as pure as possible in the sight of the Lord.'

'Then I fear we must part company in our understanding of what is right.'

They moved away, and I heard no more.

Not long after this I had taken Daniel for a walk around the village. I believed that if I encouraged him to walk as much as possible, his leg would grow stronger, even if it would never grow straight. Left to himself, he would often abandon walking and resort instead to sitting on the ground and shuffling around like a baby just learning to crawl. At two and a half he was already talking well and it shamed me to see him doing this. The walks seemed to help, though they often tired him, and that day I had given way to his pleas and carried him the last few steps home.

Yeshûa was just coming out of the workshop when we crossed the courtyard. As the men often did when it was hot, he had slipped his arms out of his tunic and let it fall in folds round his belt, so that his upper body was bare. He must have been sawing, for he was sprinkled all over with sawdust, which billowed around him in a cloud. Daniel began to strain in my arms, calling for Yeshûa and reaching out to him, thrusting his heels so hard into my stomach to push away from me that it hurt.

Yeshûa laughed and lifted Daniel from my arms, and my precious baby went to him crowing with delight, turning his back on me and forgetting me at once. I was suddenly, bitterly, blackly jealous. Jealous!

୨

When my own sons were born, Manilius and then three years later Sergius, I searched for Daniel in their eyes, but could not find him. Their eyes were blue, but that cold northern blue, like their father's. They make me think of cool skies, winter skies foretelling frost, or the blue shadows on snow high in the Alpine mountains. I made a journey once with Petradix, when we were first married and before our children were born, along the coast road and then by sea as far as Cisalpine Gaul and northern Italy. He had thoughts at the time of trying his hand at some trade with Italy and Rome, but decided in the end that the venture was too risky. He was never one to take risks. From the ship that we had boarded for the short sea journey, we could look back at the mountains and see, on their towering peaks, fields of perpetual snow, which glittered white and blue, immeasurably high against the sky.

Not that my husband's eyes, or my sons', showed a cold nature. Though cautious, they are kind. When I first saw little Julia's eyes, they reminded me of Daniel, but she did not recognise me, or reach out to me, mind to mind, as he did.

It was a cruel winter, that year he was born, such as we rarely saw in the Galilee, even in the mountain villages. The harvest had not been poor, but not abundant either, and many went hungry, though we shared, neighbour with neighbour. None starved, but we were all weakened by lack. Animals which should have been over-wintered were slaughtered for food. Many fell ill, and my mother was still not fully recovered from her lying-in. We ran short of firewood and took to sharing a hearth with our neighbours around the courtyard, turn about, four families crowding into one house and cooking over one fire to eke out our fuel. We wore many layers of clothes to keep out the cold, and for the first time in my life I suffered from chapped and split lips, and red swellings on the joints of my hands and feet, that itched and ached and kept me awake at night.

✍

Julia pads softly along to Mariam's room with a tray. When the hypocaust is lit during the winter months, she likes to run about the house barefoot, feeling the warmth of the tiled floor beneath her feet. Her mother does not approve. A well-brought up Roman girl should not go shoeless, like a common peasant. Julia does not understand her mother's objections, for the family is not rich. Her mother cannot sit elegantly, posing with her spindle like an exemplary Roman matron of the Republic, while she receives her visitors in the *atrium*. Julia has been taught morally uplifting tales of the ancient Republic, but is also familiar with the social behaviour of their richer neighbours. Her own mother has little time for making or receiving visits, and is nearer to those ancient matrons than the modern ones. Some of these neighbours cultivate the pretence of simple housewifely virtues. If Fulvia spins, she spins. It is not a pose for a portrait painter.

You can feel the difference in the floor, depending how close you are to the furnace, which is maintained by one of the farm slaves during the winter, when there is little work in the fields. The heating chamber is under the modest bath-house, adjacent to a little room, which has the next hottest floor. This is where Julia's mother retreats, on the rare occasions when she has time to herself. She calls it her *cenatiuncula*. Then comes Father's *tablinium*, where he struggles over his accounts, and the *triclinium*, for formal meals. These rooms are separated from the bedrooms, the *cubicula*, by the main *atrium* with its central garden, its *impluvium* and fountain. The hypocaust runs along either side of the *atrium*, the floors growing cooler the further

61

you go. The warmth in the *cubicula* relieves the chill nights in winter, but Julia would not want to spend all day in hers, as Mariam does.

She taps softly on the door and goes in.

Mariam is sitting in the one chair, huddled over the brazier that Father has put in here for her. She does not appear to be doing anything, merely staring ahead of her with that vague look that Julia finds disconcerting. Julia sets her tray down on the bed, moves a small table close to her grandmother's chair, and lays out the dishes within easy reach. Maia, the cook and general household slave, has made a thick and warming leek soup. Julia sniffs the steamy aroma appreciatively. There is a fresh barley bap, a dish of roasted vegetables, some smoked fish, and even a small cake made with dried apples and dates.

'I've brought your dinner, Grandmother,' says Julia.

Mariam looks at her, apparently with incomprehension. She says something that Julia does not understand. She repeats it. It sounds like a question, but the words are meaningless.

Mariam searches her mind for the Latin words, but they have fled. All she can fish from her memory is the Aramaic.

'I cannot eat all this. Will you stay and share it with me?'

Julia stares at her.

'I don't understand. What are you saying, Grandmother?'

To Mariam, Julia's Latin words sound as though they ought to hold some significance for her, but they have become twisted, a plait of vowels and consonants she cannot unravel to find the meaning.

Julia and Mariam stare at each other in consternation. Then Julia leans forward and kisses her grandmother's cheek. She tiptoes to the door and closes it softly behind her. Once she has passed the door of her parents' bedroom, which is next to Mariam's, she takes to her heels and runs. She is unaware that she is crying and that Mariam can hear the slap, slap of her bare feet fading into the distance.

This winter is proving a bitter one also. I no longer go to market, and even Manilius has made only one trip into town in the last three weeks. I cannot sit outside, for the wind is piercing, blowing down from the north, and I can feel snow on the way. All my bones ache and I feel perpetually cold, even crouched over a brazier and swathed in shawls and blankets. My hands are blue and stiff. The rest of the family are chilled, but do not seem to feel it as I do. Never until this year have I felt so old. Now, when my hands shake, I do not know whether it is from the cold or from the strange uncontrollable shaking which seized me before.

For some reason, the harsh winter has made me unsociable. I retire to my room like a hibernating animal, only sometimes emerging for meals. Fulvia humours me, and sends in food on a tray. Once or twice Julia has come to keep me company, but I can see that she finds me trying, so I send her away to more cheerful parts of the house. The cold forces me to keep the shutters closed on my window, so that my room becomes more and more like a cave, and I an ill-tempered, brooding she-bear hibernating within it.

Yet I do not sleep, as I did often in the days of late autumn. I do not know whether the cold will not let my body rest, or whether the severe weather has sharpened my mind, so that images, ideas, memories race through it in a wild torrent, like the river Rhodanus after northern rains have swollen its waters and sent it, swift as a galloping horse, to fling itself on its course to the Middle Sea.

I am living on a spiral of time. I look up or down, and all time is present, here and now. Past is not divided from present, nor present from future. I am myself as a young woman, sitting in Capernaum. Or four years old, weeping in the straw of the goat shed. Or betrothed to a lover pledged to celibacy. Or hiding amidst an alien marsh, where white horses shimmer out of the mist and dissolve again.

And I am living the time before-me, the wandering of my homeless people, the dispossessed Israelites, in Egypt and in Babylon, in slavery and in the wilderness, in a world full of wonders—water from bitter rock and bushes afire and alive; staffs turned to serpents and slithering away dry-bellied across the stony ground; seas parting and joining; the voice of Yahweh from the mountain tops and the thunderous heavens, His voice rising from the flood waters with promises, always promises, of milk and honey, or threats of punishment and damnation. Why could He never leave us alone? Just leave us to get on with our lives?

And I am living the time after-me, a time when Julia and her brothers will inherit the world, children who carry my blood, and my parents' blood. And, in a way, Yeshûa's blood also. A time when Rome will spread out further and further, conquering and absorbing all peoples as she tramps across their lands, building her unnatural roads that slice across the country like a knife, so unlike the kindly roads of other nations, that follow the contours of the land, the curve of the hillside, the river valley, the high chalk ridgeway. She will hold sway over all the world, from the frozen wastelands of Ultima Thule, to the snake-infested jungles of Africa beyond the desert.

All of this is in me, eternally present, part of me, blood and bone, running in my veins and living, thundering, in my head. I hear the voices of the past and catch the whispers of the future, and sometimes it is too much, I cannot contain it all, the voices, the pictures, the memories, so that I think that my brain will explode like a poppy head, scattering its seed to the wind, my body evaporate in an instant and float, a wisp of cloud, disperse and vanish.

Chapter Five

Festivals. All through my childhood and youth, our lives were shaped by them, from the simple weekly Sabbath to the three great annual festivals of Passover, Pentecost and Tabernacles. Some marked the seasons of the agricultural year—the sowing of grain, the planting of vegetables, the shearing of sheep, the gathering in of the harvest. Others were a memorial to the history of our people. No one could celebrate Passover—*Pesah*—without remembering that the angel of death had passed over the homes of the captives of Israel in the land of Egypt and slain instead the firstborn of our captors.

The Romans, too, have their festivals. I have never participated in those which involve worship and sacrifice to the pagan gods, but many of their festivals are the innocent agricultural ones we celebrated ourselves, with their roots so deep in time that it is almost as if we all shared a common thankfulness for the bounty of the land. In any case, the Romans pay no more than lip service to their many gods. I never knew there could be a people so freely lacking in a spiritual sense. It matters nothing to them how many gods and goddesses and semi-divines crowd their pantheon. As they have conquered more and more nations, they have simply swept up and embraced their gods, their cults, and made them Roman. The wonder is, that there should be any day in their calendar that is *not* sacred to some ass-headed Egyptian deity or some Assyrian goddess with ten arms and twelve breasts. Yet amongst all this plethora of so-called gods, none seem to be treated with any true religious devotion. The appropriate sacrifices are made, usually by priests who are no more than secular officials, the appropriate prayers are gabbled, and the citizens of Rome go about their business.

Amongst my people, we would no more have defiled the Sabbath than lain down before a charging bull. We said a *berâkâ* for every action in our daily lives, not just before and after meals. We prayed when we rose in the morning and when we lay down at night; we prayed when we pulled on a tunic or unlaced our sandals; we prayed over cookpots, looms, lathes, bread ovens, potter's wheels, cheese strainers, tanning vats, grindstones, wine presses, chisels, forges. When I stabbed myself with the chisel, I had probably forgotten to say the right prayer. A man said a *berâkâ* before he made love to his wife. And afterwards. We were forever looking over our shoulders, fearful that we might be caught out. This obsession of ours was to lead to trouble for Yeshûa.

The Romans are not a haunted people, as we were. I have never known a Roman for whom prayer was a part of life, or who felt any awe at the public prayers. As I have said, I took no part in these, but most of their festivals, while pretending to some religious purpose, are cheerful secular occasions, and the best of these is the Saturnalia.

The Saturnalia is said to recall and celebrate the 'age of Saturn', a golden age in some mythical past, when all men loved one another, the sun always shone, food was abundant, and peace reigned throughout the world. I am not sure when this age is supposed to have occurred, because it does not fit into my own people's history. After that brief moment in the first Garden, and the eating of the apple, we seem to have lurched from one disaster to the next. Mythical age or not, the age of Saturn is the excuse for a huge party amongst the Romans, when neighbour makes peace with neighbour, enemies and rivals embrace, rich men bestow alms on the poor, and in every household, the slaves sit at table with their masters and are waited on by them, in a world turned upside down in blessed chaos.

Who would ever have supposed that the Romans, *the Romans*, could have invented a festival so kindly and so joyous? Perhaps it springs from a time when they were a simpler and gentler people, before vast power made them arrogant and cruel.

The Saturnalia is a winter festival, but it celebrates the end of winter, even in the midst of snow and ice, for it falls at the time of the winter solstice, when the earth turns, and day and night pause on tiptoe, on the point of balance. The night, which has encroached on day, stealing its minutes and hours, begins to beat a retreat. The sun rises a few moments earlier, sets a few moments later, and all the peoples of the world heave a sigh of relief that, this year at least, the sun will not be swallowed up in endless night.

This year the coming of the Saturnalia has roused me from my lethargy and beckoned me out from my hibernating cave. I feel, for the moment at least, reinvigorated, and plunge into preparing food for the feast with Fulvia. It is my role always to make the cakes and sweetmeats of my native land, rich in honey and spices and almonds and exotic fruits, which our Roman Gaulish neighbours find so curious, though I do not think such delicacies are unfamiliar to the Greek house slaves. That strange aberration, when my grasp of Latin deserted me, has passed, though sometimes I hesitate over a word and find myself searching for a substitute before my handicap is noticed. Julia, however, looks at me sometimes with a small frown of worry on her smooth young forehead. I can see that she is afraid I shall begin again to speak in tongues.

The festival lasts a week, during which we exchange gifts, entertain neighbours here and feast at their houses, and eat until our sides ache. There is dancing in the village square, despite the cold. Young men drink too much. Young men are sick and fall down in alleyways. Young women are seen disappearing down other alleyways with other young men. The month the Romans call September always produces a few unexpected births in the village.

The last day of the festival celebrates, in particular, Sol Invictus. I am told by one of our neighbours, an elderly man who is something of a scholar, that this is a modern accretion to the Saturnalia. The praise of the Unconquered Sun has crept in from some of the eastern and southernmost parts of the Empire, but being also associated with celebration of the turn of the year, has been cheerfully embraced by Rome.

On the feast of Sol Invictus, then, we are happy, but a little weary from all this festivity. We sit down in our own home for the last feast of the holiday. The children have kept up the practice of cross-dressing, though I am glad to say that the adults of our household do not. The boys are cavorting about in long dresses, hitched up at the waist so that they will not trip, and Petronius has made himself a curly wig out of the ends of a fleece. Julia strides about in a short tunic, with a toy sword strapped at her waist. She has contrived a sort of helmet and breastplate for herself out of old parchment begged from her father's office. They are all three in a silly, excitable mood and will probably be quarrelling before bed, not at all in the spirit of the Saturnalia.

Sergius, who has come to spend the festival with us, captures Julia and sits her on his knee. She shows him her Saturnalia present, a *sigillum*, a wooden doll, and gradually we settle to the meal. Manilius and Fulvia, playing the part of house slaves for one last time, carry in the dishes of food from the kitchen. The three field hands cluster together at the foot of the table, made jittery even at the end of the festival by this reversal of roles. Maia and Antiphoulos, however, are quite at ease.

Antiphoulos is seated next to me and we help each other to a dish of roasted lamb cooked on sticks and dressed with (to be frank) a rather too rich sauce made with too much *garum*, the Roman fish condiment. Antiphoulos is wearing a freshly laundered tunic and his hair has been newly cut. Already he looks like a free man. If you did not know, you would take him for a citizen of modest but respectable family. This will be his last Saturnalia with us. Ever since I saw where he went on our visit to Massilia, I have been curious about him.

'What will you do,' I ask, 'when you have bought your manumission?'

He lays down his food, rinses his fingers in the finger bowl, and takes a sip of wine before he answers.

'I have not entirely decided, *domina*. I may start a school in Massilia.'

I know he can read and write, for he sometimes serves as Manilius's secretary.

'You are learned, then?'

His eyes crinkle up in a smile.

'I would not say *learned*, no. But my father saw that I received a good education.'

'You are from Greece, are you not?' I find myself dropping into Greek, educated Greek, which does not appear to have deserted me.

He looks surprised and pleased, and answers me in the same language.

'I am Greek, yes. But not from the mainland. My family had large estates on the east coast of the Middle Sea. I was sent to finish my education at the university in Athens.'

'Then how do you come to be serving my son as a household slave?'

His jaw hardens and I think he will not answer, but he is a courteous man. At last he says, 'There was a dispute about land ownership with a corrupt Roman procurator. Many of us, young men, rash, not stopping to calculate the odds, rose up and attacked a small Roman garrison. It was pointless and foolhardy. Many were killed. The rest sold into slavery. It was my education that saved me from the galleys, so I have much to thank it for.'

It is a familiar story, so familiar it does not shock me.

'If you are going to become a teacher, perhaps Manilius would employ you as a tutor for the boys. They are growing too old to be taught by their mother any longer.'

'I think not.' He smiles ruefully. 'Once a slave in this house, always a slave. It will be better to make a fresh start.'

'You are probably right.' I pass him a dish of roasted goat's cheeses wrapped in sweet peppers. 'There is warfare in my own country of Judah, a rising against the Roman occupiers.'

'Yes, I have heard. Like us, I fear they are doomed to failure. The Roman army rolls on like some great boulder, crushing everything in its path.'

I do not know what prompts me to do what I do next. I dip my finger in my goblet of red wine and trace on the table between us the outline of the fish. His reaction is remarkable. He stiffens and goes white, then red. He opens his mouth as if to speak, but at that moment Manilius comes towards us bearing a vast platter on which repose three ducks, crisp and steaming. Quick as a lizard, Antiphoulos lays his palm over my drawing. When he lifts his hand, it is gone.

A few days after the Saturnalia, Manilius made a trip into Massilia with two donkeys loaded up with as many wineskins as their patient backs could bear. There were unlikely to be any foreign merchant ships in harbour at this time of the year, but he deals regularly with a wine merchant in the city who sells to the richer inhabitants and to the owners of the large villas strung along the coast. I knew also that my son was going to enquire about the oxen he hoped to purchase. He would wait until we had fresh pasture in the spring before concluding the deal, but I could see that he was becoming anxious about beginning his new venture. I have not yet given my permission. It may seem strange, but Petradix left the farm in my name. Women have status and can own land amongst the Gauls, and my husband wanted to provide for my old age. Manilius needs my agreement before he can make major changes to the farm. I think I will probably give it to him.

Towards evening, when he was already overdue, there was a sudden commotion outside the house, and then I heard my son calling for me. I threw a *palla* around my shoulders and went outside into driving sleet. The open yard between the house and the farm buildings was full of people—men, women and children.

'Ah, Mother,' Manilius said, 'I need you to interpret. Apart from one man with a little Latin, these people speak only Aramaic.'

They were refugees, it emerged in tangled explanations: two families who had fled from the bloodshed and horrors in Judah. Everyone else from their village had been slaughtered by the Roman soldiers, because one young man had belonged to a group of Zealots which had attacked Scythopolis. The village had been razed to the ground and all the people massacred as a reprisal. These two families had only escaped because they had been away, attending a wedding in another village. They had nothing, having parted with their few items of value—the women's jewellery, worn for the wedding, one man's purse of coin—to buy themselves passage on a dirty merchant ship travelling west. It had been, it seemed, a smuggler's vessel rather than a merchant's, dodging in and out of small ports without customs posts, but finally putting in to Massilia because the whole vessel was falling apart at the seams and needed the services of a shipyard. They had barely escaped being sold into slavery by the ship's captain, who was little more than a pirate.

My son had come upon them in the harbour as he was setting out for home, where they were disputing with the captain and the slave dealer.

'I could not leave them there,' he explained to me, a little shame-faced at his spontaneous generosity. 'The women barely have clothes to cover their modesty and the children are starving.'

They heard him without understanding, but their faces turned to me full of a fragile hope.

I approached the eldest of the men, bowed, and addressed him courteously in Aramaic.

'Sir, we will gladly offer you food and hospitality. You must be weary and cold after your long journey. My son Manilius, *dominus* of this villa, will show you where the men and older boys can be lodged. Let the women and children follow me.'

I turned to Manilius.

'The large storeroom at the back of the house, next to the kitchen—it's warm, and by moving some of the barrels and jars back against the walls, we can surely make room for the men. The women can share the guest room.'

'The storeroom is hardly fitting—'

'After what they have endured, it will seem like a palace.'

'And the women and children . . . we don't own enough beds.' He grinned ruefully. 'Fulvia will be angry with me.'

'Not when I have spoken to her. And I am proud of you.'

At that he blushed and looked at the ground, as any Gaulish man will do if you praise him.

'Some of them have bedrolls,' I said, indicating the thin bundles of mats and blankets a few of the refugees wore strapped to their backs. 'They will not have been accustomed to sleeping on beds, even in their own homes. We should have enough rugs and blankets, even sacks for the men. The most important thing is hot food.'

With that I led the women into the house and went to inform Fulvia that she had just acquired fifteen guests. The duty of hospitality dictated that she must feed and shelter them, and to her credit, after the first shock, Fulvia responded gallantly. The guest room held a bed large enough to accommodate one elderly woman and a pregnant wife. I was surprised that the old woman had survived the rigours of their terrible journey, but we are an enduring race. For the rest, we laid out blankets and cushions on the floor, while Maia carried up buckets of water so that they might wash. I brought salves for several wounds and lacerations. Some looked like the result of beatings. While I attended to this, Fulvia and Maia hurried off to contrive some kind of a meal from bread and broth and dried fruits. It had grown too late to think of killing a sheep to feed them, though I could see that Manilius thought it was his duty to do so.

'Tomorrow,' I say, when Manilius, Fulvia and I have gathered at last in the *cenatiuncula*, and our unexpected guests have gone to their rest. 'Tomorrow you can roast a sheep for them and provide all the trappings of a guest-meal, but tonight I do not think they could have eaten more than broth. They were too weary.'

'They are a pitiful sight,' Fulvia agrees, 'but what is to become of them, Manilius? We cannot feed so many for long.'

Manilius looks from one to the other of us, and shifts uneasily on his cushioned bench.

'As we walked up from Massilia, I managed to speak a little to the man who knows some Latin. Zakkai, his name is. They want to find agricultural work, for it's all they know. One of the older boys has a little skill in leather work. I thought we might employ the more able-bodied to work on the farm.'

'Alongside the slaves?' says Fulvia. 'And how are they to be fed?'

'I think they would be glad of any work,' I say. 'Even alongside slaves, so long as they are not enslaved themselves. And with Antiphoulos leaving soon, one or two of the women could help with the household tasks. Surely we have stores enough to feed them for a few months, until spring comes. But is there work enough on the farm? And could you pay them wages?'

'Zakkai said they would gladly work without wages, in return for shelter and food.' Manilius looks at me cautiously. 'If we began the work of ploughing up the two wheat fields, and planting vines . . . '

I have known this was coming and know, too, when to concede graciously.

'Very well. Let's enlarge the vineyard. With so many hands at work, the planting will be done swiftly. But what of your new oxen?'

We plunge into plans for the farm. I feel curiously enlivened by this unexpected addition to our household, though I know that it may not be easy to absorb seven adults and eight children into the life of the estate.

'But,' Fulvia asks, when we have risen to retire to our own belated beds, 'where are they to live?'

'We will build,' says Manilius buoyantly. I can see how excited he is at the thought of realising his dream at last. 'There's that ruin of an old cottage beyond the orchard. It can be rebuilt. That's the first thing we'll do, before the oxen come. One family can move in there. Afterwards, we'll decide where we might build another.'

'You will keep them permanently?' I ask.

'There'll be a great deal of work with the new vines. Once they make a profit, I can pay for the Israelites' labour. And perhaps I'll sell the field slaves and work only with free men. That's how things were done in the old days, Father used to say. Before Rome came.'

It's true. I wonder, as I pick up my lamp and make my way to bed, what Petradix would have thought of all this. Later, I might ask the Israelites for more news of the Land of Judah. But not yet. I am not ready yet.

&

My brother Shim'ôn reached manhood when he was thirteen and a half, and I was ten, so he was obliged to go with our parents to the Temple in Jerusalem for *Pesah* and the ceremony of *bâr mitzvâh*, when he would become a Son of the Law and be recognised as an adult man, with all its privileges and responsibilities. Yeshûa's *bâr mitzvâh* had taken place several months before I was born, when he was only twelve. I had still been too young to remember when Ya'aqôb and Yehûdes had gone to Jerusalem, but I had a faint memory of Yoses's *bâr mitzvâh*, which would have happened when he was thirteen and I was five. In an unusual spirit of generosity, he had brought back candied plums for Melkha and me from the city. I remember that I treasured them and made them last for months.

That year when I was ten, Daniel was two and fully weaned, so both my parents would take Shim'ôn to Jerusalem. Ya'aqôb was anxious to accompany them, insisting that it was his duty to attend Passover. Indeed, the Law stipulated that every adult male should attend all three of the great annual festivals every year in Jerusalem, but the Law was drawn up generations ago, when our nation was not so scattered. Even our village was nearly a hundred miles from the capital. The journey would take at least ten days, over winding tracks and burdened with inexperienced travellers. Then a week must be allowed for purification, a week for the festival, and a ten-day journey home. In all, they would be away for more than a month. It was impossible for my father and brothers to fulfil all the rigid requirements of the Law, even more impossible for men who lived or traded in Arabia or Egypt or Greece or Italy. They attended *Pesah* when they could, a few times in their lives, and took their sons when it was time for them to dedicate themselves. Even so, I had heard it said that the crowds in Jerusalem sometimes numbered many hundreds of thousands. I could not comprehend such numbers.

It was difficult for Ya'aqôb as well as my father to be spared from the work of the carpentry shop for so long, especially as Yehûdes and Yoses had been invited by Adamas to visit his home in Sepphoris and attend the lesser *Pesah* festival that would be held there. Neither of my two eldest brothers was yet married, or showed any sign of wanting to marry, but Yehûdes, who was now nineteen, and Yoses, who was a year younger, had both raised with our father the matter of taking wives. They were still young, but he was not unwilling. There were too many sons at work in one trade in a village as small as ours. It might be better if they started their own workshops in the city, though I think we were all aware that our parents were unwilling to see them go. However, he agreed that they could make the trip to Sepphoris and meet the families that Adamas thought might be interested in a marriage alliance. Nothing would be decided until my parents returned.

Shim'ôn, Ya'aqôb and my parents left for Jerusalem as part of a caravan of pilgrims travelling from further north in the Galilee and gathering more and more people as it journeyed southward. They had paid for the use of camels, provided by the camel drivers who arranged these caravans every year. Later, they would have to pay for their accommodation in the *caravanserai* outside the walls of Jerusalem, and would buy a lamb for the sacrifice. It all meant a great deal of expense, and my father, with so many sons, had to pay, over the years, a good deal of money into the hands of camel drivers and the sellers of sacrificial animals in the outer court of the Temple.

Soon afterwards, Yehûdes and Yoses set out in the early morning on foot for Sepphoris, where they would stay with Melkha and Adamas for two weeks before walking back again. They were in a state of high excitement, never having made such a journey on their own before. Left behind, waving them off as they went without a backward glance, we made a pathetic little party. The house, which usually seemed like to burst with all of us, was empty and echoing now that Yeshûa, Eskha, Daniel and I were the only inhabitants.

By evening, as we sat down to our meal and darkness began to draw in, we were feeling somewhat forlorn. I was tired from doing all the work of the house; Eskha had taken advantage of the absence of our mother to run off to play with her friends in the village, instead of helping me; and Daniel had clung to the skirt of my tunic all day, worried by all this disruption to his normal life. When Yeshûa came in from his lonely day in the workshop, Eskha was sulking because I had scolded her and Daniel was whimpering because we had been quarrelling.

'What is this?' said Yeshûa, after we had washed and said the *berâkâ* and taken our seats on the benches at the table. 'So many long faces! When Mariam has cooked us a fine meal of fresh bread and broth, with a bean and onion stew to follow.

Eskha, why is your mouth looking like a dish turned upside down?'

Eskha giggled a little at this, though she tried not to.

'I don't like it when everyone goes away,' she said. 'Will you tell us a story, Yeshûa?'

I looked at him hopefully. He was a great teller of tales, my brother. Not only could he tell the ancient stories; he invented his own.

'Eat your dinner,' he said, 'and when you have helped Mariam tidy afterwards, perhaps I'll tell you a story. What sort of story would you like?'

'Tell us about when you went to Jerusalem to be made *bâr mitzvâh*,' said Eskha.

'Would you like that, Mariam?' He caught my eye over Eskha's head.

'Yes,' I said. 'You told me a long time ago about your journey to Jerusalem, but you never finished the story. Ya'aqôb told me once that you got into trouble.'

He threw back his head and laughed.

'Yes, indeed I did. And our mother was quite right to scold me, for I gave them many hours of worry.'

After the meal was cleared away, we all sat on the floor on a pile of cushions, with just one lamp giving a dim glow, for a story is always better in a soft light. Yeshûa took Daniel on his lap and put an arm each around Eskha and me, and he began.

I told Mariam how we travelled to Jerusalem, *he said*, and how Yehûdâ and I spent the first morning exploring the city. Our fathers had made the necessary arrangements for the purification, and after our midday meal we returned to the city together with the women. It is not permitted to participate in *Pesah* if one has corpse impurity. Perhaps you don't know this, Eskha, but you can acquire it not just by touching the dead body of a loved one, but also by walking, even accidentally, over a grave, or comforting a bereaved family, or attending a funeral. There must have been hardly a person coming to the festival who had not incurred corpse impurity at some time in the course of the year.

The whole ritual, which lasts a week, involves attending prayers at the Temple, and on the third and seventh day of the purification we were sprinkled with a mixture of water and the ashes of a red heifer. This is what our parents and brothers will be doing soon. After this sprinkling, on the seventh day, we all took ritual baths to wash away the last of the impurity, and washed all our clothes. It was a strange experience, which left me feeling clean, but empty, like a glass vessel held up to the sun, ready to be filled with light.

On the fourteenth day of Nissan that year, my father and Shim'ôn of Keriyoth went early into the city to purchase a perfect, unblemished male lamb for the *Pesah* sacrifice. It was essential to go early, for with so many people in the city it might be difficult to find a suitable animal later on. One lamb would be sufficient for our two families. Others in our caravan made arrangements to share with friends or with new acquaintances met on the journey. When they returned leading the lamb, Yehûdâ and I joined them, to go to the Temple for the sacrifice. I was given the lamb to lead by a leather thong, and it came with me happily, trotting by my side as if I were taking it to its mother. I felt suddenly like a traitor.

'Isn't it cruel, Father,' I said, 'to slaughter this young thing? It seems a shame to take its life when it's so young.'

'The Lord demands a sacrifice, Yeshûa. It is the Law. Besides, it shows our gratitude to the Lord for his protection of our people.'

I had to accept his words, but as we came nearer to the Temple, my heart began to beat faster. Everywhere people were crowding forward. The noise and the heat were worse even than the day before. And the air was full of the terrified bleating of the lambs, lost and afraid without their mothers, already sensing the approach of death. As we were early, we were amongst the first to be admitted into the court of sacrifice. There were two rows of priests standing ready in their white robes as we crowded in. Two of the assistant priests, Levites clad in saffron robes, were counting us as we filed through the gateway. Then a harsh blast rang out as a priest blew upon a trumpet made of a ram's horn, and the Temple guards swung the gates shut.

'What are they doing?' I asked. I was suddenly afraid. It felt as if we were being shut into a prison. A choir of Levites began to chant a psalm. Two of the priests advanced towards us, long knives catching the sunlight.

'There are enough now for the first sacrifice,' Shim'ôn of Keriyoth said. 'The rest must wait till we have finished.'

The priest nearest to us seized the first lamb by the wool on its back, gripped the struggling animal between his knees, and with a quick, practised stroke slit its throat. As the blood spurted out, he caught it in a cup until it overflowed, then returned the lamb to the owner and handed the cup to the priest next in line. Hand to hand, the cup passed along the row of priests until it reached the end. The last priest raised the cup above his head. His lips were moving in some sort of prayer, but the noise was so great I could not hear a word. Then he poured the blood over the altar, still steaming with the life of the lamb.

I threw myself down on my knees beside our lamb and buried my face in its wool. I put my arms around it and could not stop myself sobbing. The poor thing nuzzled me, as loving as a pet dog. The air was filled with the stench of burning flesh as the entrails were thrown on the fire, and I thought I would never be able to breathe again.

My father's hand fell on my shoulder.

'Do not shame me, son.'

I stood up, rubbing the back of my hand against my face and the lamb leaned against my legs. I could not look at it.

As the slaughter—the sacrifice—went on, the remaining lambs smelt the death and began to cry piteously. The priests were dyed to the elbows in blood, their clothes soaking, the ground around our feet flooded with it. Yahweh's altar, of shining stone, scrubbed and gleaming when we arrived, was sticky, reeking, an object of horror. Where splashes of blood had begun to dry in the sun they darkened almost to black. There was a stench of murder everywhere and all the flies in Jerusalem had found their way to the sacrifice. They waded amongst the blood, their feet clinging to it. When one landed on my face, leaving its foul footprints on my skin, I gave a cry and beat it off.

I could not watch as our lamb was killed, and I trailed after the men to the side of the court, with my eyes on my reluctant feet. They hung the lamb, which had been alive and breathing moments before, on one of the hooks fixed into the wall, while they skinned it and eviscerated it. They handed the entrails and the tail to a Levite to be burned at the altar, then wrapped the carcass in the skin and led the way out of the court.

I was glad to turn my back on the butchery and looked up at the clear sky above, wondering where the lamb's life had gone. Did a lamb possess more than a physical body? Could a lamb, who had yearned for his mother, and trusted me, and been terrified by death, be nothing more than a structure of sinew and flesh and bone and blood—so much blood? Was there not some sort of *ru'ah* in a lamb, even as in a man?

High overhead, vultures were wheeling, drawn by the sight and smell of sacrifice.

Chapter Six

Of course, that was not the story he told us that day. He left out the horrors of the sacrifice and neither Eskha nor little Daniel noticed, but I realised that he was keeping something back. It would be years before I heard the true story. The image of my brother kneeling beside the lamb condemned to die will be forever associated in my mind with a lovely shaded lane, running along the western shore of the Lake of Gennesaret. It was spring time then, too. The lane was bordered with banks of wild flowers and there were young lambs in the fields, capering in their silly games, then rushing back to their mothers. It was not many weeks before *Pesah*, and I wondered how many of them would be rounded up and carted down to Jerusalem, to that courtyard stinking of blood and sacrifice to a jealous Yahweh. I knew from the way that Yeshûa caught my eye that he was thinking the same, and it was this that had prompted him to tell me more of that boyhood visit, his only one, to Jerusalem.

'Though I must go again to celebrate *Pesah* there,' he said. 'Not this year, I think. Probably next spring. That will be best.'

And although my brother and I were so close that we could often read each other's thoughts, a curtain seemed to fall between us then, between our innermost minds, though we continued to walk companionably on from Magdala to Capernaum, where we knew there would be a good, nourishing meal awaiting us at the home of Zebedee, father of two of his followers, Ya'kob and Yôhânân.

That evening when I was ten and he told his story, with the four of us sitting together on the floor, it had grown late by the time he described leaving the Temple after the sacrifice. He said the rest of the story must wait until the next night, for it was long past the time when Eskha and Daniel should be asleep.

'Will you truly tell us the rest tomorrow?' Eskha demanded, as I herded the two of them upstairs to the room the

80

three of us shared. 'Because I don't see what you did that was so naughty.'

Yeshûa laughed.

'Ah, we have not reached that part of the story yet.'

The following evening, we settled ourselves again after our meal, and Eskha began trying to guess what he had done.

'You will soon find out, Eskha,' he said. 'Now hush, or I shall not be able to tell you what happened next.'

As we walked back to the encampment, *he said*, our father gave me two branches to carry, I think because he wanted to distract my mind from the scene of the sacrifice. They were dried pomegranate sticks, strong yet quite flexible, but I had no idea of their purpose. Beside our two tents, the women had a fire lit, and various platters of food laid ready, but we did not touch them for our midday meal. They were to be part of the *Pesah* meal, which would take place at sundown. Instead, we ate a little bread and cheese and olives, and drank only water. It was a long time until the festal meal, and I was very tired, so I crawled into our tent and fell asleep.

When I woke, the sun was dropping down towards the horizon and my father was calling me to come and help.

'Now, son,' he said, 'you must see how we prepare the *Pesah* lamb for the feast.'

I turned my face away from the flayed carcass which he had laid on the ground near the fire, but he placed his hand on my arm and squeezed it gently.

'In two days you will make your *bâr mitzvâh* dedication, and then you will be a man. A man must sometimes do things that seem distasteful. This is how we prepare the lamb.'

He picked up the two pomegranate sticks. One of them he had cut shorter than the other, and he had whittled their ends to sharp points.

'We must not break a single bone of the lamb's body,' he said, 'so we run this longer stick up through the length of the body very carefully. You see?'

I nodded without speaking. Yehûdâ and Shim'ôn sat opposite us, cross-legged on the other side of the fire.

'Now I want you to take the shorter stick and push it, crossways with the first one, through the lamb's shoulders.'

I did as I was told, though my gorge rose. The flayed animal was slippery with blood, but I could still imagine under my hands his soft young wool. My mouth tasted sour with bile. When I was done, the dead lamb looked almost human, like a man nailed to a Roman cross. I passed the whole thing to my father, numb with horror, and rubbed the palms of my hands again and again in the dust, trying to scrape away the blood. There were two forked sticks driven into the ground on either side of the fire and he balanced the carcass across them. It would roast there, turned from time to time, until it was crisp and brown.

Why was I so squeamish on this occasion? All my life I had seen animals slaughtered and eaten, and although I had never taken any pleasure in it, I had seen it as a necessary and acceptable part of life. Man must eat. The animals provide food. Yet somehow there had seemed to be a bond between that young lamb and me. I wished that I did not feel that I had betrayed him. I wished that he did not look so like a tormented soul, pierced on his cross, turning over the fire.

As the sun sank below the horizon, we chanted prayers for the ending of the day and the beginning of the next, the fifteenth Nissan. The women sprinkled the roasting meat with a special mixture of *Pesah* spices which they had brought with them in a small cedar box, and Shim'ôn of Keriyoth's maidservant cooked discs of unleavened bread on the hot stones beside the fire.

There were more prayers as my father lifted the *Pesah* lamb on to a platter and carefully withdrew the crossed sticks, still without breaking any bones. Then he and Shim'ôn carved slices of the meat and piled them on to our plates, beside the unleavened bread.

I picked up a piece of the meat and put it in my mouth. It burned my tongue and the roof of my mouth, and I felt hot tears spring up in my eyes, but whether of pain or guilt, I could not tell.

That night it was hot and stuffy in the goat-hair tent, so I crawled outside with my bedroll and lay under the stars. The fifteenth day of Nissan, which had begun at sundown, is the day of holy convocation, the most sacred of the whole of *Pesah*. The noise, stench and blood of the Temple had been succeeded by an almost eerie calm and quiet. Occasionally a snort came from the camel lines. In the distance, at the other side of the *caravanserai*, someone was softly singing one of the psalms of David. Otherwise, there was utter silence. Even the great city of Jerusalem was silent, as though some magician had laid his hand upon it and banished all sound. Apart from the dying embers of the cookfires, there was no light on the ground, so that the stars in the vast heavens seemed unusually bright. I looked for the one I had decided was my own personal star, and found it almost straight above where I lay, a reddish gold star of infinite promise.

The village *hazzan* had encouraged my enthusiasm for my studies and I had once asked him whether it might be possible for me to become a priest or a Levite in the service of Yahweh. He shook his head.

'No, Yeshûa, you cannot think of such an honour. They are all descended from the priestly castes. Their office is inherited. A simple village boy like you would never be accepted. But we can all serve Yahweh if we keep our hearts pure and obey the Law.'

I was disappointed at the time, but no longer. I wanted no part in that scene of butchery I had witnessed in the most holy part of the Temple. How could Yahweh, the One God who had created mankind and all the beauty of the earth, want His altar to be drowned in steaming blood, crawling with flies? My mind was whirling with doubts and questions, which I knew could be answered neither by my father nor by the *hazzan*, who was a man of carefully acquired learning but no profound wisdom. In this troubled state of mind, I finally fell asleep.

On waking, we began a day more quiet and contemplative than the most rigorous Sabbath. Many fasted until sundown, though my mother insisted that I eat a little of last night's leftover unleavened bread and drink some water. We were forbidden to engage in any activity, and were not even allowed to walk very far, but I slipped a little way out of the encampment and found a place in the shade of a bent and ancient olive tree, where I sat for most of the day, brooding on my thoughts of the night before. At sunset I returned to our tent where, as the day of sixteenth Nissan began, the women prepared a good meal, our first since the evening before. Everyone was loud and cheerful after our day of enforced quiet and fasting. One of the other pilgrims produced a lute, the *'ûgab*, another a double pipe, the *hâlîl*, and a boy of my own age contrived a drum from an upturned pot beaten with the palms of his hands. They played quiet tunes at first, then as the beer and wine went round they started on the merry tunes played at village festivals, and we all joined in the singing, for *matsôth*, the sixteenth, is a day of rejoicing.

'Why do we make the offering of the first fruits of the harvest at *matsôth*, Father?' I asked. 'At home we won't be harvesting for at least a month.'

'Long ago our people lived in the low-lying, sheltered lands round Jericho,' he said. 'The harvest is much earlier in those parts. So the sheaf of wheat for the offering is brought in specially from there.'

'I see.' I remembered now that, as we came through Jericho, I had seen the fields of wheat already golden, but I had not thought about its significance.

That was a good day.

Everyone streamed through the streets singing. The sheaf of wheat, the *matsâh*, was offered at the Temple, and then the crowd of boys of twelve and thirteen and fourteen, who were to be dedicated as Sons of the Law that year, were gathered together in one of the outer courts of the Temple. It was there that the moneychangers sat behind their tables with their piles of coins from every land on earth. Anyone could pay for goods in the town with Greek *drachmae* or Roman *denarii*, or Syrian coins or Egyptian. But taxes and offerings to the Temple must be paid solely in Tyrian *zuzim*, so the moneychangers did a brisk business.

'And a profitable business,' I heard Shim'ôn of Keriyoth say to my father. 'All in the hands of the priestly families, and a fraudulent rate of exchange offered, which lines their pockets while fleecing the poor pilgrims.'

I wondered that such a practice should be allowed, here in the Temple, as we hurried over to the stalls selling sacrificial animals, round which the boys and their fathers crowded. We were not expected to sacrifice a lamb for the *bâr mitzvâh* ceremony; a bird was sufficient offering for a young boy. Yehûdâ chose a cock pheasant, a handsome bird with plumage that shone in the sunlight like burnished armour.

'Well?' said my father. 'Which bird will you choose?'

I saw then that a small cage on the ground beside the stall held a white dove. It sat miserably hunched, for the cage was too small for it to stand upright. It fixed on me a look of resigned despair.

'That one,' I said, pointing.

Our fathers paid for the birds and we carried them to the sacrificial altar, where we said the requisite prayers and dedicated ourselves to uphold the Law of the Chosen People. All the time I held the dove cradled against my chest, where I could feel the rapid beating of its heart. It raised its head and looked about, sensing the open air and the movement of the wind which could be felt even in this inner court.

Yehûdâ handed over his pheasant to the priest, who cut its throat swiftly, as the lambs had been slaughtered two days before, but there was less blood and less ritual. I stayed where I was. My father gave me a small push to urge me forward, but I resisted him.

I thought of the lamb as I stroked the feathers of the dove. I had never held a dove before, never realised how soft it was, how light. I screwed up my eyes and tilted back my head. How wonderful it would be to fly up there in the pure air, so far above the earth. How could I rob this creature of such power and beauty? I raised the dove to my face, kissed the top of its head, then threw it upwards as hard as I could, reciting a *berâkâ* for its safety, for its long life, and for its acceptance by Yahweh.

There was a loud clap overhead. Could such a sound have been made by the wings of so small and light a bird? The white dove circled once, then stretched its wings and soared high into the sky above the courtyard, growing smaller and smaller until it vanished from sight.

There was silence in the courtyard. Everyone was staring at me, mouths agape.

On the altar, Yehûdâ's beautiful pheasant bled and faded, its eyes as dull as the dusty pebbles beneath our feet.

'Surely Yahweh loves a living bird, flying free, better than a bloody corpse?' I said. But I said it silently, inside my head.

'You have wasted your money, my friend,' said Shim'ôn of Keriyoth to my father.

'So that was what you did!' Eskha crowed triumphantly. 'You didn't sacrifice the dove as you should have done, and our parents were angry with you.'

'Do you think that was my crime, Mariam?'

Yeshûa looked at me quizzically. There was something in his eyes that I could not quite read.

'No,' I said slowly. 'I think it was something else. And I think, even now, you're not sorry you let the dove go free.'

He smiled.

'You are right,' he said it so softly I could barely hear. 'I'm not sorry.'

He turned to Eskha.

'Now,' he said briskly, 'do you want to hear what I really did?'

'Yes, yes!'

The rest of the *Pesah* festival passed without further excitements, and at the end of the two weeks encamped outside the walls of Jerusalem, the caravan from the Galilee packed up its tents and cooking pots, its refilled waterskins and its trinkets bought at outrageous prices from the street stalls of the Holy City. They were not the only pilgrims preparing to leave. All round the city, inside and out, people and animals milled about in a confusion of dust and shouting. At last they departed, making back towards Jericho. Having started early, they made camp a few miles before Jericho, about ten miles from Jerusalem.

While the women prepared the evening meal, my father went to the tent of Shim'ôn and said to Yehûdâ, 'Where is Yeshûa?'

'I haven't seen him since dawn,' said Yehûdâ. 'I thought he was travelling with you.'

'We thought he had gone with you,' said my father, beginning for the first time to be worried.

After that, my parents and Yehûdâ's family searched the camp from end to end, but could find no sign of me. My mother was weeping by then, and my father agreed that they must return to Jerusalem in the morning. Somehow, in the confusion of the departure, I had been left behind.

'He is not yet twelve years old,' my mother whispered to my father in the tent, where they tried to sleep, but could not.

'He will come to no harm in the Holy City,' said my father, but perhaps he did not altogether believe this.

Before dawn the next day they began the long walk back to Jerusalem, carrying what they could and entrusting their other belongings to Yehûdâ's family.

The journey was a hard day's walking in the heat and the dust, against the flow of the crowds still leaving the city. And it was hard above all for my mother, who was already carrying the child that would be you, Mariam. Over and over they enquired for their son, but no one had seen him. At last, exhausted, they reached the city just as the gates were being closed at nightfall and found a room in a cheap inn.

All the next day and into the hours of darkness they searched the city, trudging up and down streets still littered with the rubbish left behind by the pilgrims. They asked in the markets and the inns, explored back alleys with fear in their hearts, in case he had been attacked and left for dead. But why should anyone attack a young boy who, by his clothes, was poor and of no account? My mother wept without ceasing. My father was grim-faced but methodical, quartering the city from the Damascus Gate to the Dung Gate, from the Joppa Gate to the Lion Gate, searching the wide streets near the Temple and the Tower of Antonia, venturing into dark and noisome lanes amongst the huddled houses of the poor. The next morning they went to the Temple, planning to say a prayer to Yahweh for the safe return of their boy.

Every day, in an arcaded court of the Temple, away from the sacred areas and the sacrifices, scholars and teachers would gather in the shade and discuss matters of morals and the interpretation of the more obscure points of the Law. Young men came regularly to sit around them on the ground, to listen to the discussions and to put questions to them. These were the regular students. But anyone might attend the group, simply to listen or to join in.

There, amongst the young men, the despairing parents found their miscreant son, grubby of hands and face, eagerly questioning the scholars about the nature of Yahweh's mercy and what He had taught His people about the taking of life.

'Our mother was so angry, she boxed my ears, there in front of everyone!' Yeshûa grinned ruefully at the memory, and rubbed the lobe of his left ear.

'How could I be so thoughtless,' she said, 'to run off and cause them so much grief? They had searched the whole of Jerusalem, not knowing where to find me.'

'I answered in all innocence, "But you should have known that you would find me in Our Father's house."

'I did not realise the impertinence of it. I was thoughtless and rude, and they had suffered dreadful agony through my selfishness.' He paused. 'I do not think our parents will let Shim'ôn out of their sight.'

'You were *wicked*!' Eskha was awestruck. Her eldest brother to run away and stay behind in Jerusalem! 'And what happened then?'

'Then our father had to pay out more money for us to join the next caravan going north. He lost a whole week's work as well, and our mother cried often into the night. She made me promise on oath not to run away again. Never to leave our village. I think she believed I wanted to join the servants of the Temple, but that was never my intention.'

'What was your intention?' I asked.

He put his arm around my shoulders and smiled down at me.

'I wanted the answers to some questions.'

'And did you find them?'

'Not yet.'

ح

On the farm in Gaul, the Saturnalia is long past, the spring is flushing the fields and trees with early green, and the new oxen have arrived. Antiphoulos handed over the fee for his manumission last week. Manilius affixed his seal to the papers, then handed him a purse of coin to help him on his way in his new life. The house already seems strange without his presence. We have only women working in the house now, and Manilius must be his own clerk or buy the services of another. Our Israelite families have worked hard to rebuild the old cottage and have all moved in there together, for they do not wish to strain Fulvia's hospitality too far. Once the new vines are planted they will set about building another cottage. They must be very crowded, but we respect their intentions.

Under Manilius's eager supervision, one field normally put down to arable has been ploughed and trenched, and the rows of vines planted. They are cut back to just a few inches above the ground so that all their early strength will be put into their roots. We cannot expect a harvest from them for two or three years. Like all farming, this is a venture based on patience and hope. I do not expect that I shall live to drink the vintage from these vines.

The vines that are to be planted in the second field have arrived and are stored in one of the outhouses, wrapped in damp sacking, for they will have to wait a day before planting. Our labourers too are given a day of rest, though I suspect they may use the time to lay out the foundations of the new cottage. All our family is off to a wedding at the next farm, where the daughter is to marry a cousin and so enlarge the estate.

While the rest of the company attend the sacrifices to Juno and Hymen, I sit quietly dozing in the *atrium* of the neighbours' house. (My eccentricities are tolerated, if not understood. They do not fork their fingers at me here, though I think they find my scruples baffling.) When the ceremony is over, the bride, blushing and pretty, leads the party out into the terraced garden. She looks happy, even if the marriage was arranged for the convenience of the parents, and the groom, only a little older than she, is clearly pleased to have secured such a lovely wife. Soon we are seated around a table as loaded with food as Melkha's bridal table, though some of the foods would have seemed strange to her. I am thankful that the family has decided to eat, Gaulish fashion, seated at a table, and not reclining on a couch, propped up with an elbow, as the Romans do. I have never been able to adapt to this ridiculous habit, which induces cramp in the legs, numbness in the arms and shoulders, and violent indigestion. If the Romans had set out to devise the most uncomfortable posture in which to eat, they could not have bettered what they invented.

The feast is rich and delightful, the company pleasant, and the terrace—like ours, with views of the sea—charming, on the first really warm spring day this year. We are, perhaps, a little staid. There is no dancing, as there would be amongst the peasants. We are a little too conscious of our dignity here. There was invariably music and dancing at weddings in the villages of the Galilee. And at betrothals, too.

My mother always said that it would be difficult to find a husband for me. She stood me before her and looked me up and down with a critical expression. I was just fourteen years old and had reached marriageable status some time earlier. Facing my mother, with that look on her face, I was conscious of my clumsy hands and feet. I had grown suddenly in the last year and could not control my body. I was forever bumping into people and knocking things over, just as I had done when I was a small child.

'Your eyes are too far apart,' she said, 'and your mouth is too big. You never comb your hair, it's a disgrace. We might be able to do something with that, I suppose. Why have you not lengthened that tunic? Half your lower leg can be seen. I have no time to do it, with so many unmarried men to care for.'

I thought this a little unfair, for I sewed and mended my father's and brothers' clothes as often as she did, but I had learned by now to hold my tongue—most of the time. My brothers were all still unmarried, though Yehûdes and Yoses were now betrothed to girls younger than I, Yehûdes to the daughter of one of the families Adamas had recommended, Yoses to Judith's younger sister. Judith herself had married a month ago.

Awaiting the rest of my mother's criticism, which I knew would continue for some time, I stood on one leg, winding the other around it. At her look, I stood up straight again.

'Your father is in despair over you,' she said. 'He cannot think of anyone who will take you on. Your looks might not matter, but you are too outspoken, too fond of your own opinion. A man does not like that in a woman.'

I had heard all these arguments since I was ten years old.

'Yeshûa likes me,' I muttered rebelliously.

'Yeshûa is a brother, not a prospective husband,' she said crisply.

Melkha had come on a visit to us, bringing her son and three daughters, together with a retinue of servants. I suppose that had prompted this latest lecture from my mother. My elder sister wore fine silks, her maid braided her hair every morning with ribbons and strings of small freshwater pearls, and she moved and spoke like the fashionable ladies of Sepphoris. Yet I felt that she was somehow uneasy. She had given Adamas four children in six years, but only one son. He was a man with no use for daughters and I thought Melkha was worried because she had not yet fallen pregnant again. Until she bore him more sons, Adamas might dress her in fine clothes, but would treat her with little respect. I suddenly realised what I had never thought of before. I had wondered why he had chosen the daughter of a village family, but of course—we were a family of many sons!

The thought gave me a sickening feeling in my stomach, and my skin crawled as it did whenever Adamas contrived to touch me. What if I should be married to a man like that? What if I should be used like a breeding jenny, an animal useful only for labour and offspring? I wrapped my arms protectively around myself, deaf to my mother's voice. We were taught that barrenness in a woman was sinful, an insult to Yahweh. A girl who did not marry and bear children as soon as she had become a woman was better dead, for she was tainted, cursed. A married woman who did not bear children could be put aside by her husband, or he could take other wives, or father children on her maidservant. But I thought I should not be able to bear such a life, to serve the appetites of a lustful man. I stood there, numb and inwardly shaking, until my mother finished at last.

I left her and went out to my usual tasks: the endless grinding of corn and baking of bread. Eskha was old enough to milk the goats now, but she would often slip away, and was nowhere to be seen this afternoon. She had learned early the advantages of being the youngest, and even the birth of Daniel had not imposed stricter discipline on her. I decided to leave the corn in the hope that Melkha might be shamed into helping, or at least set her maid to work. Instead I carried the low milking stool and the wide earthenware bowl to the pen beyond the goat shed, where the nannies were milling about, bleating in distress because their udders were full.

Milking is something I have always enjoyed. I laid my cheek against the goat's warm side and sang softly as I began to pull. The goat stopped her crying, rested her chin on my bowed back in a friendly fashion, and relaxed, letting the milk down.

'Do you always sing so sweetly to your goats, milkmaid?'

I looked up. Someone was standing between me and the sun. I pushed the hair out of my eyes and shaded them with my hand. A young man was leaning on the stone wall that enclosed the pen and smiling down at me. He was probably in his middle or late twenties, handsome and poised, with fine clothes and skin browned from much exposure to sun and wind, although he had no look of a farmer about him.

'It calms them, if I sing,' I said. 'My little sister has neglected them and they were unhappy.' I did not mind that he had heard me singing, for there was no mockery in his tone.

'And who are you?' he asked.

'My name is Mariam.'

'Mariam?' his voice rose several tones in astonishment and he leaned further over the wall to see me better. 'It cannot be little Mariam!'

There was something about his voice that I thought I could almost place.

'You are . . . ?' I asked.

'Your brother's friend, Yehûdâ. Back from my travels halfway round the world and back.'

Yehûdâ. Of course. But it was six years and more since I had seen him. Little wonder that I did not recognise him at once. Lifting my bowl of milk, I rose from my stool and the goat ran off. Another came butting at my arm, claiming my attention.

'I must not keep you from your work,' he said. 'Is Yeshûa at home?'

'Of course. In the workshop, with my father and brothers. It's good to see you again, Yehûdâ.'

'And you.' He was looking me up and down now, taking in how tall I had grown. I was suddenly ashamed of the milk stains on my tunic, my bare feet, my wind-tangled hair. I felt myself reddening.

'I am sure my parents would be glad if you would sup with us tonight.'

'I would be pleased.'

He lingered, still looking at me intensely.

'You are not married yet, Mariam?'

I felt my face flushing even more.

'No.' I did not care to say more on the subject.

He touched me lightly on the arm and turned away.

'Do you still have that pipe I made for you?' he called over his shoulder.

'Of course.'

'Perhaps you will play for me this evening.'

I did play for him that evening. And Melkha sang. She had a beautiful voice and could always be relied upon to outshine me, though I caught Yehûdâ looking at me with that same intense expression. It seemed that Melkha had seen something of Yehûdâ in Sepphoris since his return from his travels with his father's caravans. He was now learning the less exciting part of a merchant's business, managing the money and keeping accounts. He had been at his father's Sepphoris house for some weeks before he had been able to escape (this was his word) for long enough to come to the family house in the village and take up his friendship with my brother again.

He stayed in the village for a week, during which he and Yeshûa resumed their old pastimes of fishing and swimming. I saw them often talking animatedly and wondered what they were discussing. At the end of the week, Yehûdâ courteously escorted Melkha home to Sepphoris and I did not think we would see him for a long time. And I found myself wishing that he might come again.

To my surprise, he returned less than two weeks later, and on the day of his return was soon in earnest conversation with both my father and Yeshûa. I wondered whether he might be trying to persuade Yeshûa to join him in Sepphoris, for my brother had about him that old look of restlessness.

Daniel and I were sitting on the ground under the fig tree that shaded our house, sharing a pomegranate. I had halved it with the knife I wore at my belt. With a small sharp twig, I speared the juicy seeds one by one and fed them alternately to Daniel and myself. We were both very sticky and very happy. Even now he loved best to be with me, though I knew that before long he would want to run through the village playing with the other children of his age. He still limped, and I feared that he might suffer for it. Cripples were not treated kindly amongst us.

I looked up to see Yeshûa standing before me. Yehûdâ was at the far side of the courtyard, apparently studying the distant hillside. My brother squatted down on his heels and opened his mouth to speak. I popped a pomegranate seed into it.

'Every pomegranate seed, a lucky day,' I said.

He grinned.

'An old wives' tale, but a good one,' he said. 'No, wait,' as I prepared to feed him another. 'I need to speak to you.'

'What is my crime this time?' I asked.

'No crime. Good news. I think you will think it is good news.'

I cocked my head at him. I could not tell whether he was pleased or not.

My brother continued, watching me carefully.

'Yehûdâ has asked our father if he will consider a betrothal between you. He went back to Sepphoris to ask his father's permission.'

My jaw dropped.

'Yehûdâ and *me*!'

Yehûdâ was rich, handsome, well travelled. What would he want with a girl like me?

'You know he has always been fond of you. He even suggested it to me years ago, when you were just a little girl.'

I remembered suddenly a scene long since forgotten. Yehûdâ and my brother lying beside the river and discussing marriage.

'He would not force you,' said Yeshûa. 'It shall only be if you are willing.'

I was in turmoil. Just weeks ago, my mother had lamented that I was unmarriageable. And I had feared I might be given to some rough stranger merely to breed him sons. Yehûdâ I had known and liked all my life. He was my brother's closest friend. It was like a miracle, yet I had not even prayed for it. There was a sudden tightness in my chest, as though all the air was being squeezed out of my lungs. Then my heart gave a painful lurch, so that I pressed my hand against my chest, leaving a sticky patch of pomegranate juice.

'Before you answer,' Yeshûa said, 'there is something else. For the moment, Yehûdâ is proposing a betrothal only. He knows you are of age to wed, but he—well, he and I—plan to travel a little, in the Jordan valley. There would be no wedding yet. Perhaps not for some time. More than the usual one year of betrothal. Would that matter to you?'

'No,' I said. Melkha, after all, had waited more than a year and a half, and I was in no hurry. I needed time to understand the meaning of all this.

'I . . . I accept,' I said.

'Then come and tell him yourself,' said Yeshûa, springing up and pulling me to my feet, pomegranate and all. Daniel sat and stared at us, speechless.

'Look at me!' I said. 'I cannot go to him like this.'

Yeshûa took both my hands in his, so that the pomegranate fell to the ground.

'It is not the clothes or . . .' he laughed, 'the dust and juice that he will see. Yehûdâ cares more deeply than that. It is the person inside that he sees.'

He led me across the courtyard. My father was standing in the doorway of our house, with his arm around my mother, who had her fingers pressed to her lips in astonishment.

Yehûdâ looked at me in such a way, with such passion, that I knew in my heart what my brother meant. There surged through me a feeling for him that I had never realised was there, waiting to leap out and sweep me away, like a wave of the sea.

'What is your answer, Mariam?' he asked.

I held out my hand to him.

'My answer is yes, Yehûdâ.'

He kissed my fingers and I saw from his smile that he could taste the juice on them. Then he kissed me lightly on the lips. I was not sure that he should do this, but there was nothing furtive about it. We were in full sight of my parents.

'*Thy lips are like a thread of scarlet, and thy speech is comely,*' he murmured, with laughter in his eyes, and kissed me again, not so lightly this time. '*Thy temples are like a piece of pomegranate within thy locks.*'

I had to catch hold of his arm to steady myself, for the sun, it seemed, had made me suddenly giddy.

'*Thy lips drop as the honeycomb,*' I whispered, '*honey and milk are under thy tongue. I would cause thee to drink of spiced wine of the juice of my pomegranate.*'

'*My dove, my undefiled is but one. Set me as a seal upon thine heart, as a seal upon thine arm, for love is strong as death. Oh, I am sick of love.*'

'*Turn away thine eyes from me,*' I said, '*for they have overcome me.*'

Our betrothal took place the following month, in the *kenîshtâ*, in the presence of the entire village, together with Shim'ôn of Keriyoth, and Melkha's family. After the appropriate prayers and readings from the scriptures, Yehûdâ and I stood before the company, hand in hand, and made our pledge. A betrothal is not a marriage, but it is binding in the eyes of both Yahweh and the world. It cannot be broken without documents of divorce. After the ceremony, we crossed the square to the feast, which was set up where Melkha's wedding meal had been laid six years before.

She had given me one of her dresses to wear, a beautiful deep blue silk, which Yehûdâ told me was the colour of the Middle Sea where the water is deepest.

'It will reflect the colour of your eyes,' said Melkha, in an uncharacteristic burst of kindness.

My mother had washed my hair three times before she was satisfied, anointed it with precious citrus oil, then combed it until it shone. Melkha's maid dressed it for me with a string of large sea pearls from Greece, which Yehûdâ had given me as a betrothal gift. Nervously, for I had never before worn perfume, I anointed myself from a little alabaster jar Yehûdâ had sent up to my room, containing jasmine oil. It smelled of springtime freshness, far more to my liking than the heavy scents Melkha favoured. Holding myself as tall and dignified as I could, so that I should not shame Yehûdâ and make him regret his choice, I took my place at the *mistitha*. I felt curiously outside myself, as though one Mariam talked and laughed with the guests, looking suddenly beautiful and womanly, while another Mariam watched her critically from above, knowing that inside her a fearful girl was hiding, waiting to be exposed for the impostor that she was. At the same time I felt gloriously, impossibly, released. Not to be married to some disgusting stranger! Not to be left a barren outcast! Not even to be required to fulfil the obligations of marriage for months yet! I wanted to throw wide my arms and embrace the world. Surely, to be a betrothed girl is the most enviable of all states, when the promised bridegroom is as fine a man as Yehûdâ. Throughout the meal, I saw Melkha looking at him and knew that she must be comparing him with Adamas, who had grown more greasy and offensive with time.

Shim'ôn of Keriyoth had brought a troop of professional musicians and dancers from Sepphoris, who entertained us while we ate. One man played the *kinnôr* with a plectrum, another plucked and struck a *pesanterîn* resting on a stool in front of him, while a third clashed a pair of *meshiltayim* made of brass. Most of the women were dancers, but one beat the rhythm on a *tôp* and another blew the double *hâlîl*. The dancers wore little—nothing but floating dresses of transparent silk, so that every line and movement of their sinuous bodies could be seen. As the evening wore on and the musicians drank more wine, their music became wilder, so that it seemed to make the very blood in my body throb to the rhythm. At last some of the young men ran out into the middle of the square to dance in honour of my betrothal. Yehûdâ beckoned to Yeshûa, who laughed and jumped up from the table. The young men stood in a line, linked their arms around each others' waists, and began to dance, their feet flickering in and out as they moved first to the left and then to the right, stamping and laughing and shouting. At the end of the line, my betrothed and my brother began to spin them around, faster and faster, in a great wheel, like a rope spun round in the air. Then suddenly Daniel dashed out to join the dance. I jumped to my feet, afraid that he would be crushed by the whirling mass of men as he limped into their path, but Yeshûa, who was now on the outside of the wheel, reached out with his free arm as he spun past and caught Daniel up into the air. Daniel flew past me like a bird, his eyes fierce with excitement.

I remember very little about the next few days. My life had changed so abruptly that I felt unfamiliar in my own body. Though I went about my usual daily chores, I moved in a cloud of citrus and jasmine scent which lingered on my hair and skin, compounding the strangeness.

What I do remember was the way the atmosphere in the house changed from the joyful—and perhaps relieved—preparations for my betrothal to a series of explosive arguments between Yeshûa and our parents. After he had run off during that long-ago visit to Jerusalem, he had come back home, lowered his head in obedience to his parents, and contained himself in patience, though I now know how much it had cost him. He would not leave without their permission, but he begged now to be released from his promise. The arguments continued for three days. In the end, I think our father would have given him leave, though he would miss his eldest son's skilled assistance in the workshop, because he felt that Yeshûa would never settle to his place in the family and in the village until he had satisfied his longing to travel and see the world. But our other brothers grew angry, shouting that he would be shirking his duties.

'A promise made is a promise to be kept,' said Ya'aqôb bitterly. 'You dishonour our parents.'

'At twelve years old, I promised never to run away,' said Yeshûa. 'I am a man now, and I am not running away. I am asking permission of our parents to travel for a while with Yehûdâ around Gennesaret and down the Jordan Valley. I am *not*,' he repeated, clenching his teeth, 'running away.'

'And who is to do your work while you're gone?' asked Yoses. 'If I should choose to idle away many months, amusing myself, will you step into my place, and do my work?'

'If you wish.'

The arguments went round and round in this profitless manner, but the most difficult demand for Yeshûa came from our mother.

'I beg you, I beg you, my son!' she wailed. 'Do not go! Terrible things will happen to you—I feel it in my heart!'

Then she scooped up ashes from the hearth and smeared them in her hair and over her face. And tore her tunic, like one lamenting the death of a loved one.

Yeshûa could not hide his distress. He put his arms around her and tried to calm her, but she was beyond calming, pushing him away and crying out repeatedly that leaving the village would lead to his death. In the face of her lamentations, our brothers abandoned their arguments and shambled off in embarrassment. I remained, sitting, as I so often did, withdrawn in my corner, waiting to see what would happen next. I ached for Yeshûa. I wished so much that he and Yehûdâ would remain in the village, but I knew how he longed to break free. If only I were not a girl, I would have been as fervent as he to escape.

After a time my mother grew calmer and drank a beaker of water my father fetched for her. She sat kneading her hands together, squeezing her fingers until the knuckles turned white. Yeshûa knelt on the ground at her feet, his head leaning against her knee, his face pressed against the fabric of her tunic.

At last, long after the night shadows had gathered around us, while the three of them sat in the small circle of light cast by the oil lamp, she gave a shuddering sigh and slumped forward, one hand on Yeshûa's thick curls, the other covering her face.

'If you believe it will break your heart not to leave us, then you must go, son, but my heart will never be at rest until you return.'

My brother knelt before them, and asked their blessing. They had forgotten me. I slipped away and climbed the stairs to my room.

The next morning, Yeshûa and Yehûdâ set off on their journey. They each carried a knapsack with a little food and a change of clothes, and I longed to go with them, for I had still never been beyond the village, not even as far as Sepphoris. This journey with Yehûdâ would be the first time my brother had followed his own wishes in all those long years. I was not sure then—and I am not sure even now—whether they had a definite plan in mind, or whether this was to be no more than a holiday, but it was to prove the starting point for all that followed, inexorably, from their setting forth that morning.

I accompanied them down through the olive orchard, where the scene of our many lessons prompted Yeshûa to say, 'Don't forget your studies while I am away.'

'I will not forget,' I promised, 'but I don't expect to have much opportunity.'

He patted my shoulder absently, and I knew that his mind was already on the journey ahead. I noticed that Yehûdâ was wearing the bracelet I had made him as a betrothal gift, plaited from a lock of his hair and mine, threaded with tiny gold beads I had bought two years before from one of the Bedouin traders. They had cost me ten of my goat's cheeses, and my mother said I had been cheated, but I was pleased now to see them glinting there on his wrist. His hair was fairer than mine, with a touch of chestnut in it, so that it looked almost red against my black tresses. He saw that I had noticed the bracelet, there on his arm.

'It shall not leave my wrist while I live,' he said, and kissed it lightly.

We came at last to the river bank, where we were to part. I found myself unable to speak, for fear that I should weep. They embraced me, first Yeshûa with a tender kiss to my forehead, and a murmured blessing. Then Yehûdâ took me in his arms and kissed me fiercely, so that I began to shake with a desire I had never known before. He released me reluctantly, as though he might abandon their journey.

'You must go,' I said, breathlessly, hardly trusting my voice.

'Else we will never leave,' said Yehûdâ.

They turned away and began to follow the river downstream. Somewhere far away, I had heard, it flowed into the river Jordan. At a bend in the river which would take them out of sight, they stopped and looked back, and raised their hands in farewell. Then they were gone.

Chapter Seven

I would not see either of them again for nearly nine months. It was winter by then, a heavy sky promising sleet or snow hanging over the tops of the hills. I had wrapped a heavy cloak around myself, and a mantle over my head, before going outside to chivvy the animals into the shed. This was built against one of the outside walls of the house, which would provide them with a little warmth. If the winter proved as cold as it promised to be, we would bring them in to one of the ground-floor rooms of the house, next to the storerooms which lay along one side, separated from the main room by a row of squat pillars. For the moment, though, they would fare well enough here. I pulled down more straw for their bedding and filled the goats' trough with a measure of mashed grain and hay mixed with water. We had begun keeping a few leggy mountain sheep as well, so that we now had wool of our own, instead of having to barter for it. I pushed and prodded the sheep into their own section of the shed, fenced off with hurdles, and filled their trough. If the sheep were left with the goats, then the goats, being bold and wily, would eat all the food.

When I came out of the shed, sheltering the flame of my small oil lamp against the wind, it was beginning to snow. I saw a figure crossing the communal courtyard from the direction of the village square, bundled up as I was against the cold. I lifted my lamp higher and as he came into the circle of light I saw that it was Yehûdâ.

'Mariam!' he said, hugging me, lamp and all.

'Careful!' It was good to see him, but he was in danger of setting us both alight.

'Are you alone?' I looked beyond him, but there was no sign of Yeshûa.

'Alone, yes, but no harm has befallen your brother. Can we go inside, out of this weather? Then I will tell you everything.'

Inside the house, all the family was keeping as close to the fire as possible. A new sister-in-law had joined us. Yehûdes had married and brought his wife Hannah to live in our house, for with Yeshûa gone his labour was needed in the carpentry shop. Hannah was helping my mother to prepare the evening meal, stirring a big pot of stew hanging over the fire, while Yoses, Shim'ôn and Yehûdes sat round a board game and Daniel was absorbed in some private play with a set of little animals I had carved for him. He had not been well since the cold weather had begun, and we had kept him indoors.

Yehûdâ greeted my parents and reassured them with his first breath of Yeshûa's safety, for he had seen the look of fear on my mother's face. An account of their travels had to wait, however, until all had eaten, the dishes were cleared away, and the prayer of thanksgiving recited.

'I wanted Yeshûa to return with me,' Yehûdâ said, as we sat roasting nuts over the fire after our meal, 'but he was determined to go down into Judaea, to Qumrân. We have been travelling north and south along the Jordan valley for several months. For a while we stayed in Capernaum, where we made good friends, and even crossed the Lake of Gennesaret and visited some of the towns of the Decapolis.'

We looked at him in wonder at this, for the Decapolis— those sophisticated cities far to the east, beyond Gennesaret— seemed as exotic to our village minds as Egypt or Macedonia.

'Just south of Gennesaret we encountered a group of the people known as Essenes. You have heard of them?'

Ya'aqôb nodded. 'An ascetic sect. They dwell without wives in the desert and study the scriptures. But they have some strange beliefs, and live outside the Law.'

'Well, I know little of their philosophy, but they do not live entirely outside society. They are dedicated to helping the poor and the sick. They have great skill in healing. It's said that they can restore sight to the blind.'

'None but the Lord can do that,' said Ya'aqôb.

'Perhaps,' said my father quietly, 'good men working in the name of the Lord, may do His bidding here on earth.'

Ya'aqôb opened his mouth to argue, but my mother gave him a look to say, *Let our guest continue*, and he closed it again.

'Yeshûa took a great interest in what they did,' Yehûdâ said, 'and spent many hours in conversation with them. This was when we were on our way to the Decapolis, and by the time we had returned they were gone. It seems the largest part of their brotherhood lives near Qumrân, but there are small groups scattered here and there throughout Judah. And from the main group, healers travel out to help the sick, then return to their community. They work mostly in the villages, amongst the poor country people.'

'It seems a very worthy life,' said my father.

'Yes,' said Yehûdâ, but I thought he hesitated a little.

'In Qumrân they live celibate lives,' he said, 'with much prayer and fasting. They support themselves, growing their own food, weaving their own cloth. But they are also devoted to learning. It seems they have a vast library of scrolls and spend much of their time in studying, in discussing and writing works of devotion, and in copying their sacred texts.'

I could see at once where this was tending. Study, discussion of belief, a library, works of kindness amongst the poor. This was a world my brother had been yearning for all his life.

'He has gone to join them,' I whispered. Tears began to steal down my cheeks. My mother had gone white with horror.

Yehûdâ reached across and took my hand.

'He wanted me to go with him, but such a life—living on the edge of the desert, brooding over sacred texts—that is not for me. For those who wish to join the order, there is a year of probation, while they are instructed in the way of life and tested on their commitment, heart and soul. After that, two years as a novice. If, at the end of the three years, the master of the order is satisfied, they are admitted.'

'We will never see him again,' I said in despair.

'No, do not give up hope, Mariam. I made him promise me that, at the end of the first year of probation, he would meet me on the banks of the Jordan, ten miles northeast of Qumrân. He will tell me then whether he has decided to stay in the community, and I can bring word back to you. It was a month

ago that we parted, so I will meet him again in eleven months.'
He gave my hand a squeeze. 'Not so long.'

He looked round at all of us.

'Like you, I hope that he will come home.'

There was something else that he did not tell us that
evening. I was not to learn of it for several years, and at a time
and place far from that winter day sitting beside the fire in the
only home I had then known. Their final exchange Yehûdâ kept
from me.

'I will make you this promise,' said Yeshûa, 'to do what I
am loathe to do. I will meet you in twelve months' time, because
you are my dearest and oldest friend.'

'I thank you for that,' said Yehûdâ.

'Perhaps you will not, someday, when I ask you to make
me a promise in return, to do something you are loathe to do.'

'You would never ask me to do something that is wrong.'

'Our ideas of what is wrong and what is right may be
shaped by time,' said Yeshûa, then he embraced his friend, and
they parted.

Long before I was told of this exchange of promises, I
would hear from my brother how he had spent that year of his
life, so far away from us, between the barren desert and the salt
Sea of Sodom.

෧

Desert nights were bitterly cold, colder even than winter in the
high hills of the Galilee. Somehow, Yeshûa had not expected
this. The word 'desert' had always conveyed to him barren heat,
a dry land of lizards and thorn bushes, stones cracking under a
merciless sun. All this was true, but only by day. At night it was
as if the chill wind off some faraway, snow-covered mountain
had laid a blight on the desert. At home in the Galilee, the kindly
earth soaked up the warmth of the daytime sun, like a wool
blanket wrapped round a bakestone. After a hot day, if you thrust
your hand into the upturned earth of the vegetable plot, where
your spade had lifted the soil, the held warmth could be felt. So
cruel and hostile was the land of the desert, however, that it
stored no comforting warmth. As soon as the sun dropped below

the western hills, the desert gave back not warmth, but a chill breath, like the cold flesh of a dead man.

Here, where the Community had their settlement, there was a small area of fertile ground which was cultivated for modest crops, but the nearness of the desert brought the chill down at night, so that he lay awake shivering under the one thin blanket that was allowed. It made sunrise all the more welcome, so that Yeshûa did not find it surprising that all the Community rose before dawn and gathered on the sloping ground facing the hills of Moab. In the pre-dawn light the figures of his new companions moved softly on bare feet to their allotted places like some ghostly company, their white robes dulled to grey, the Master and the priests in front, then the Levites, followed by the full members, then the novices, and Yeshûa with the other neophytes. Behind them clustered the lay members, the Sons of Israel, who would never take full vows, and were permitted to marry, but who had chosen this segregated life on the edge of the desert in preference to their villages and towns.

As the sun began to creep up the sky, still hidden from their sight by the hills on the eastern side of the Sea of Sodom, the grey robes, like the grey sky, flushed gradually to pink. They raised their arms to the heavens and, as the first curve of the sun slid golden above the mauve and purple hills of Moab, they began to sing.

Thou hast spread the heavens for Thy glory
> *and hast appointed all their hosts*
> *according to Thy will;*
The mighty winds according to their laws
> *before they became angels of holiness*
> *and eternal spirits in their dominions;*
The heavenly lights to their mysteries,
> *the stars to their paths,*
> *the clouds to their tasks,*
> *the thunderbolts and lightnings to their duty,*
And the perfect treasuries of snow and hail
> *to their purposes*
> *and to their mysteries.*

Yeshûa had never before heard such singing as he had heard in the weeks since he had joined the Community. There was singing sometimes in the village *kenîshtâ* after the reading from the scriptures, led by a rather ragged choir under the direction of the *hazzan*, but anyone who felt moved might join in—a musical sense and a good ear were not required. And most people in the village sang at their work, songs he had heard all his life: songs for sowing and for reaping, lullabies for babies and laments over the dead, songs to help drive the plough through stony ground, to encourage the goats' cheese to separate from the whey, to keep the hands working at the endless, repetitive tasks of weaving or hauling water or threshing corn. In the Temple at Jerusalem, all those years ago, the Levites had sung hymns as the priests cut the throats of the lambs and poured the blood over Yahweh's altar, but they could scarcely be heard over the screams of the dying beasts and the noise from the crowd awaiting admittance.

This music was quite different—both blissful and powerful—two hundred or more confident voices singing joyfully a hymn to the Lord God:

Thou hast brought Thy servant deliverance
>*in the midst of lions destined for the guilty,*
and of lionesses which crush the bones of the mighty
>*and drink the blood of the brave.*
Thou hast caused me to dwell with the many fishers
>*who spread a net upon the face of the waters,*
>*and with the hunters of the children of iniquity;*
Thou hast established me there for justice.
Thou hast confirmed the counsel of truth in my heart
>*and the waters of the Covenant for those who seek it.*
Thou hast closed up the mouth of the young lions
>*whose teeth are like a sword,*
>*and whose great teeth are like a pointed spear,*
>*like the venom of dragons.*

After the dawn hymn, the company dispersed quietly to their morning tasks, which were allocated by the Master in accordance with their status in the Community. But no, he must remember that the Master preferred the title *Mebaqqer*, Guardian.

107

Yeshûa had spoken only once to the *Mebaqqer*, on the day he arrived, when he was examined on his suitability to enter as a probationer. There would be other examinations later. The Community, he had learned, set great store by testing each member's faith and worthiness. Every year, at the renewal of the Covenant, each would be examined on his current state of faith and the performance of his duties and sacred practices over the previous year, and as a result would move up or down the strict hierarchy, which governed everything, from official positions to admittance at the table for the ritual meal of purity.

The *Mebaqqer* was a man of great height, gaunt from years of ascetic living and much fasting, his skin the colour of caramel from long sojourn in the desert. He had looked down his fine aquiline nose at Yeshûa standing humbly, and increasingly hopelessly, in front of him.

'Not *Maskil*,' he said. 'No one's Master. We are all brethren here. I am the *Mebaqqer*, the Guardian of the Community. Any man of the Community may become the *Mebaqqer*, given time, faith, and ability. You may become the *Mebaqqer* yourself.'

Regarding this Galilean peasant from the height of his aristocratic lineage, he did not sound as though he believed it.

'In the meantime, you will join the other new probationers in carrying dung from the latrines to spread on the fields.'

That, Yeshûa thought with some amusement, puts me very firmly in my place. Not a student of doctrine. Not even a scribe and copyist. A spreader of dung. Well, all labour is good, if it is done in the true spirit of dedication to the Lord.

Outdoor work was exhausting under the relentless sun, heat far worse than anything he had known in the Galilee. There were no trees to provide shade, except for half a dozen aged palms, dying from the ground upwards. Whenever a faint breath of wind awoke—generally only at sunset, and that rarely—the brown sword leaves rattled together like a dead man's fingers. In the past there had been more palms, but they had been cut down a hundred years ago and more to provide pillars for the buildings.

The surrounding barren countryside was inhabited by scorpions and serpents, a few gaunt hyenas, hawks circling, lizards. Above and behind the settlement, the towering cliffs shut in the deep valley, so that (if you were not careful) it could begin to feel like being buried alive in a rocky grave. Apart from the small painful fields cultivated by the Community, the only vegetation that Yeshûa could see, when he raised his eyes from his labours, was an insidious red crawling plant that marked some rocks like bloodstains and the dry white flowers of an everlasting ghost plant, whose petals, transparent and fragile as dead leaves, reminded him of the abandoned carapaces of beetles.

The buildings themselves were plain but sturdily built of stone, some dressed, some unshaped, with floors of rammed pebbles and plastered walls within. Half a century before, an earthquake had caused a great deal of damage. Cracks could still be seen in some walls and a few of the buildings were no longer considered safe to use. The tower at the northwest corner of the main building had been roughly reinforced with a pile of boulders. Fallen masonry from the damaged buildings had been heaped up outside and left when repairs were carried out. Seen from some angles, the settlement gave an impressive appearance, but if you walked round the corner of a building or approached from a different direction, you could see the makeshift repairs.

It soon became clear that not only was Yeshûa unlikely ever to become the *Mebaqqer*. He was unlikely even to become a priest or Levite of the order, for they were all descended from the ancient priestly families, just as their counterparts in Jerusalem were.

He spent two months spreading dung, digging, hoeing, labouring in the fields, work he had been accustomed to since boyhood. Then—someone having discovered that he wrote a fair hand—he was moved to the copy-room of the library, painstakingly copying the sacred documents of the Community on to fresh parchment. The calendars were somewhat tedious (and curiously different from the calendars of the Temple), but he rejoiced in the hymns of thanksgiving, some as lovely as the Psalms of King David. When he was allocated the commentaries on sacred texts, he was reprimanding for spending too long reading them and gazing into the air, when he should have been applying his quill to the parchment. He was required to confess before the whole Community to the sin of inattention and slackness in his task, and as a penance, was put on half rations for ten days. This was a more serious punishment than it sounded, for meals were always meagre.

A very small spark of rebellion kindled in his heart, for he did not feel he had been inattentive. He had been pondering the searching commentary on Habbakuk before copying it. Again and again the commentary on the prophet spoke of the enemy called the *Kittim*. Habbakuk had lived long ago, so it seemed these people, the *Kittim*, belonged to the past. Yet in every way the *Kittim* resembled the Romans—their disciplined armies, their mockery of the kings and priests of the peoples they attacked, their thirst for empire, their grinding conquests, their cruel taxation. 'They put many to the sword,' said the anonymous commentator, 'young men, adults, old men, women and children, and have no pity for the fruit of the womb.' Was Habbakuk (or his commentator) speaking of the prophet's own times, or of the present day? When he lay awake at night, his belly groaning with hunger, he could not drive these thoughts from his mind.

Every day, winter and summer, as midday approached and again in the evening, everyone laid aside his work. They walked down from the buildings of the compound or in from the fields, gathering during the dry seasons at the seven ritual baths cut out of the rock, and discarded their white robes. Naked—in winter shivering in the bitter air and even more bitter water—they plunged in for a ritual washing away of sins. During the early spring, when the melt water filled the dry river bed, they bathed in the living stream. In those brief weeks, when the fresh water seemed so much purer than the faintly stagnant water of the baths, Yeshûa had to resist the temptation to strike out and swim across the river, as if he were a boy again with Yehûdâ in the river at home, but that was not considered seemly. This was a holy ritual, in which the whole body and head must be immersed, to purify oneself before taking food. Some of the probationers, when they first arrived, were afraid of this ritual, never before having stepped into a river.

When Yeshûa had been at Qumrân some three months, two new probationers joined the Community, boys of about twenty, from a village somewhere west of Jerusalem. They had never seen a river before. Their village did not even have a stream, obtaining its water from a single well and from stone cisterns which had to be filled carefully in winter, then jealously guarded in summer. The first time they were led down to bathe in the river, they baulked like nervous horses. The bigger boy stumbled forward at last, plunged in awkwardly, dipped his head in and out, then made for the shore as quickly as he could. The other, a slender boy called Nathan, waded out slowly until he was waist deep in the water, then froze, seemingly unable to go forward or back. Yeshûa, nearby, sank deep into the water, enjoying the sensation of the fast-moving current on his skin. He opened his eyes underwater and watched as minute bubbles, caught in the hairs of his arms, broke free and swam to the surface. His skin was fizzing like newly fermented wine.

He rose slowly to the surface, finding his footing amongst the slippery rocks and flinging his wet hair out of his eyes. The river was running rapidly, swollen with spring melt water flowing down from distant mountains. The boy Nathan took another hesitant step forward, holding his arms stretched out before him, like a blind man feeling his way, then suddenly, with a great flurry and splashing, and a high-pitched shriek of fear, he vanished into the deeper water. The other bathers glanced round, but none seemed concerned. Yeshûa saw a shape, a floundering body, borne past him on the swift current. Nathan's head appeared briefly, close enough for Yeshûa to hear him gasp, then he was gone again. Yeshûa twisted round, knifed forward into the centre of the river, and began swimming fast after him.

Where the river curved, Nathan was carried towards the further shore before the main current caught him again and flung him onwards, but it had been enough for Yeshûa to overtake him, cut diagonally in front, and grab the boy as he passed in a confusion of arms and legs. Nathan fought him, as though he thought he had been seized by some malevolent creature of the river.

'Be still!' shouted Yeshûa, and swallowed a mouthful of river. 'You're safe now. I can tow you to shore. Be *still*!'

At last Nathan calmed enough for Yeshûa to grasp him by the shoulders, keeping his face above the surface, and to drag him across the river and on to the bank. They both lay there gasping, then Nathan vomited river water and moaned, curling up like a child.

'Come,' said Yeshûa, pulling him to his feet. 'We must walk back along the bank, and hurry, or we'll be late for the meal. Food is precious and the Rule is strict.'

When they reached the bathing place, the rest of the Community were gone, though their own two robes remained, neatly laid ready. This lack of concern about their fate seemed strange, but the Rule was indeed strict. They pulled on their tunics and walked back towards the compound.

'You should not go so deep in the river,' said Yeshûa, 'if you cannot swim.'

'I owe you my life,' said Nathan.

'Make it a good one then!' said Yeshûa, and thumped him on the shoulder.

They were too late for the meal, and went hungry until the evening.

Yeshûa had been drawn to the Community by tales of their life of purity, body and soul, their learning, and their good works amongst the poor, although he did not feel within himself any capability to perform exorcism or cure illness. However, part of the first year's training was an introduction to the treatment of diseases and to the practice of hypnotism, in order to cast out evil spirits. There were medical procedures to be learned, together with the magical incantations which must accompany them, herbal remedies to be studied, along with simple bone-setting. They were also taught how to breathe mouth-to-mouth, in order to restore life-giving air to a patient who was unconscious. Practising this last procedure led to some hilarity amongst the young probationers, though they tried to conceal their mirth from their instructor, who was an elderly Levite, and severe in his rectitude.

In the eleventh month of his probation, Yeshûa was allowed to accompany three of the brotherhood, Elias, Hezekiah and Alphaeus, on one of their regular rounds of visits to the villages northwest of Qumrân. Yeshûa had shown himself an apt pupil of the medical practices and had found, to his surprise, that something in him responded to this new branch of knowledge with unexpected excitement. When they reached the first village, they were welcomed into the home of one of the elders and given a meal and a place to sleep. Next morning, Yeshûa was amazed to find the courtyard crowded with people, not merely from the village but from some miles around. By word of mouth the news had spread that the Essene brothers had come to the village. Some patients had made their own way, others had been carried or led by their families. The three brothers went amongst them, assessing their problems, turning some away, telling others to wait under the fig tree. Then they began their treatment of the sick.

At first Yeshûa merely watched, but he was soon fetching medicines, helping to straighten a limb, or marshalling impatient villagers into lines. One old man was too weak to stand, and had sunk into a corner of the wall, his head bowed and his hands dangling between his knees. Yeshûa crouched down in the dirt in front of him and took his hands. He felt the old man's fingers, lifeless as a bundle of dry twigs, stir and grow warm in his. The man raised his head and Yeshûa saw that he was blind in one eye, with a cataract covering the pupil.

'Can you help me, brother?'

'I am not a brother yet, I'm afraid. Merely a probationer. I have been in the Community less than a year.'

'But surely you have the touch? I can feel it in your hands.'

Yeshûa looked down at their joined hands and was suddenly aware of them, as if they belonged to someone else. Why should he not try? It could do no harm, for one of the brothers could always treat the man later. He cupped his hand over the damaged eye, closed his own eyes, and tried to imagine the man's blindness replaced by sight. He knew the words. Words were powerful. He murmured the incantation, and waited.

At first, nothing happened.

Then, involuntarily, he shivered.

Something seemed to be brushing his skin, like the lick of cold water from a high mountain stream at the end of winter. All over his body, the hair stirred. His heart was pounding, as if he had been climbing too fast up that mountain, and it was difficult to breathe. In the depths of his chest there was a tight knot of excitement, or fear, but his mind felt very calm, very clear. As if with the old man's eyes, he saw through his own closed lids a slender young man, with dark curls and a rough, coarse-woven tunic, crouching in the dust. He could hear nothing but the rush of his own blood, as his heart galloped faster and faster.

Then suddenly all his strength drained out of him. He collapsed forward on to his knees and his hand fell from the old man's eyes. He was shaking, so weak he could barely lift his head.

The man gave a gasp.

'I can see again! You have cured me. I knew, from the moment you touched me.'

Gently, Yeshûa lifted the man's eyelid with his trembling fingers and studied the eye careful. It was clear and bright as a child's. A sense of astonishment made him rock back on his heels.

'Let us say a *berâkâ* of thanksgiving to the Lord,' he said, 'for it is He who has restored your sight, not I.'

When the prayer was finished, Yeshûa whispered earnestly to the old man, 'Do not speak of this to anyone. I am not yet learned enough to perform cures.'

'It shall be as you say, master,' said the old man, but he seized Yeshûa's hand and kissed it, which did not go unnoticed by others waiting nearby.

That evening, as they sat down to eat, Yeshûa found the three brothers eyeing him speculatively.

'So you performed a cure,' said Elias, the oldest and most experienced in treating illness and possession by evil spirits.

Yeshûa felt uncomfortable under their gaze.

'I should not have done it. But the old man begged me, and I did very little—laid my hand on his eye and said the words. I did not use the herbs. He was an old man, weak and tired.'

'You should not have done it,' Elias agreed. 'However, we will allow you to practise, under our eye, for the remainder of this trip. You will not attempt to perform cures on your own. When we return, it will be for the *Mebaqqer* and the judges to decide whether you have sinned in taking it upon yourself to perform a cure without permission.'

As they continued their round of visits to the villages, Yeshûa was permitted to treat a few more patients. Some of the procedures were simple. He set a number of broken or sprained limbs, binding them in splints. He bathed a child who had a skin disease with a cleansing lotion. Both of these treatments required the appropriate incantations, and the brothers were satisfied with him. On their last day in the last village, just as they were turning away to attend the evening meal provided by their host, a distraught man ran into the courtyard, with a girl of five or six lying limp in his arms.

'Help me! I beg of you, brothers, help me! My child fell from a tree and she has stopped breathing.'

He held the child out before him, like a man making an offering.

Hezekiah, who was the least friendly of the brothers, and who had been watching Yeshûa's treatments closely, as though expecting mistakes, turned to him now.

'Here's a fine case for our probationer to attempt.'

Elias looked at him sharply, then said to Yeshûa, 'Do you want to try?'

Without a word, Yeshûa took the child from her father's arms and laid her carefully on the ground, kneeling down beside her. He ran his hands gently over her head, then pressed his mouth against hers and began forcing air between her lips. For a long time, nothing happened. Then he felt again the same dizzying sensations he had felt with the blind man. This time he was prepared for the strength to drain out of him. As it did, he thought he saw a slight movement of her eyes behind her lids. He tried breathing into her mouth again, and the child moaned and opened her eyes. She was confused and still barely conscious, but she was breathing.

The father fell to his knees on the other side of the child, tears streaming down his face.

'You are a magician, a healer. You kissed her, and gave her back life.'

'It is the Lord's work,' said Yeshûa, relieved but embarrassed. 'It is a cure we practice. We—'

He felt the pressure of Elias's hand on his shoulder and remembered that he must not speak of the cures to any outside the brotherhood.

'Take her home,' he said to the father, 'and let her rest. In a few days she should be well again.'

For a last time, he cupped the girl's head gently between his hands. Her eyes turned towards him, and she smiled.

'The Lord go with you, *talithâ*,' he said, stumbling weakly to his feet.

Behind him, he could hear Hezekiah muttering to Alphaeus, but could not distinguish the words. Whatever they said no longer mattered. A surge of power seemed to run through him like a mighty river, unstoppable, starting from his feet, rising up and flooding his whole body with light, running out to his tingling fingertips and filling his head with a vision of such brightness that he must close his eyes and hold his breath. His very heart and lungs felt as though they would burst.

The morning after they returned to Qumrân, Yeshûa was summoned to the presence of the *Mebaqqer*, who regarded him austerely from his great carved chair, while Yeshûa stood before him, his hands clasped behind his back and his head meekly bowed, yet still filled with that sudden elation at a power he did not understand.

'I have received differing accounts of your conduct on the recent mission to the villages. All three brothers are agreed that you showed you had learned the elementary stages of our medical practices which are taught in the first year. You carried out your duties quickly and with understanding, you made no mistakes.'

Yeshûa bowed his head in acknowledgement.

'I thank you, *Mebaqqer*.'

'That is not all. Hezekiah has reported that, unauthorised, you treated a man with cataract, and—had Elias not stopped you—you came close to revealing the secrets of our treatments to one of the ignorant Sons of Israel. What do you have to say?'

'It is true.'

Yeshûa's heart was beating fast. He had not yet learned all the details of the Community Rule, but he thought that either of these two offences might entail expulsion from the order.

'Hezekiah also says you used a strange word to address the girl who had fallen from a tree. Was this some magical incantation of your own?'

Yeshûa was puzzled. 'I called her *talithâ*.'

'The word is unknown to me.'

'It means "little lamb". It's a term of endearment for children.'

The *Mebaqqer* looked at him speculatively. 'Some uncouth Galilean word, I suppose.'

I must not grow angry, Yeshûa told himself, but all the fierce loyalty to his native land boiled up in his heart.

'On the other hand,' the *Mebaqqer* continued, 'Elias believes you may have a true gift of healing. Any brother, with patience and study, can learn our medical practices. But to some is given an additional gift, a healing touch. It is a precious talent, bestowed directly by our Heavenly Father. Our great Teacher of Righteousness, who once occupied this chair and laid down the Rules of our order, possessed the touch. Do you think you have been given this incomparable talent?'

'I do not know, *Mebaqqer*. I have never experienced it before. But when I laid my hand on the blind man's eye and when I breathed into the child, I felt, as it were, something flowing through me. It was not I who performed the cures. I was no more than a conduit.'

The *Mebaqqer* nodded, as if he were satisfied with this answer.

'You must be punished for your disobedience. Ten days on half rations and field work for the same period. As for the possibility that you may be a natural healer, we shall watch and see. These things reveal themselves. Now we will say a prayer together and then you are dismissed to the fields.'

Half rations were hard to endure, especially when on field work. For the next ten days, Yeshûa sat at a low table amongst new probationers and some of the better-regarded laymen, and tried to make his tiny ration of lentils, onion and peas, with half the usual bread, last as long as the meal the others were eating. For drink he had only water, and little of that. At the high table sat the *Mebaqqer* with the Bursar, the priests and Levites, and all those brothers deemed worth of the purity of the sanctified food and new wine, the *tohorot* and *yayin*, served there. At the start of the meal the *Mebaqqer* broke the bread and blessed it, blessed the ritual cup of wine, then passed both round the table as a symbol of the foundation of all nourishment, which they shared in ritual purity and brotherhood together. A member of the Community as lowly as Yeshûa might not touch the *tohorot* or the *yayin*, for fear he should defile them. He might not touch, with his impious and impure hands, any of their ritual pots, bowls, plates, jugs or cups. To do so would blaspheme both the meal and the Lord who provided it.

At last the ten days passed and Yeshûa was just one week from the end of his year of probation. He was deeply troubled, unsure what future he should choose. If he decided to leave the Community, would this not be failure? It had seemed to him, coming eagerly to Qumrân a year ago, that here he would find what he had hungered for as long as he could remember. A life dedicated to asceticism and purity, to careful study of the great scriptures of the past and the more recent writings of the Teacher of Righteousness, and above all to the care of the sick and the poor. Wasn't this what he had always wanted?

And yet, many things hindered his perfect acceptance of the Community's way of life. It seemed to him too isolated from the rest of suffering humanity. Of course, this was how the brethren kept themselves pure. But was this truly how Yahweh wanted him to spend his life? It felt more and more selfish and self-absorbed, the longer he stayed here. To question this was to question the underlying beliefs on which the Community was founded. The final battle was near, between the pure in heart and the followers of evil, and they were preparing themselves to form an army which would ensure the victory of righteousness. He had read the War Scroll and was both fascinated and appalled. Was violence and war the true mission of those who would follow Yahweh with a pure heart? He could not accept that. Despite all the teaching here, he could not rid his mind of the belief that all the rest of humanity, outside the Community, was *not* evil. And that even sinners might find the path to goodness and to Yahweh, if someone extended a hand of loving friendship to them.

There was little time during the regimented daylight hours of the Community for him to meditate on these things. But night after night he lay awake, sick with worry. On the night before the last day of his probation, he rose quietly from his bedroll in the dormitory amongst the other probationers and novices, caught up his blanket and slipped outside. He climbed the rising ground behind the compound, which looked eastwards. Although his feet were callused and hardened from going shoeless, he could feel the cold rising from the icy ground; that bitter breath of the desert winter, which he remembered from the previous year, set his teeth chattering, even with the blanket wrapped round his shoulders. Over the hills of Moab, the moon was rising, implacable silver. He sat down on the threshold of one of the caves that honeycombed the cliffs.

Resting his elbows on his knees, he pressed the heels of his hands to his eyes. *Oh Lord, Father in Heaven, tell me what to do!*

He thought suddenly of the Teacher of Righteousness, who had founded the Community and been martyred for his faith. Was he to direct his own steps on the path to martyrdom?

All around, the desert was silent, except, far away, the lonely howl of a hyena. Below, in the valley beyond the Community's cemetery, the salt sea, deep below all the lands of the known world, lay dead and sluggish. From its surface men netted, not living silver fish, but bitter rafts of salt and a blackened devilish harvest of bitumen. This was a terrible land. He felt a sudden dreadful longing for the sweet, rich farmlands of the Galilee, for the simple people who were peasants as he was, who spoke as he did the rough Galilean dialect that so amused the aristocratic brethren.

No sign had come from the Lord, and yet he knew what his decision must be.

The next day, after the midday meal, he sought and was granted an audience with the *Mebaqqer*. As he walked through the door and confronted the *Mebaqqer* sitting on the chair of the Teacher of Righteousness, he realised that he was expected. The man sat with his hands folded quietly in his lap and his keen eyes fixed on the probationer before him. He said nothing.

With a dry throat, clenching his hands behind him to hide their trembling, Yeshûa said, 'Today I complete my year of probation.'

The *Mebaqqer* nodded, but said nothing.

'I have learned much in the Community. I love and admire the brethren, and I honour your work.' He swallowed hard. How could he explain? 'But I think the life of Qumrân is not for me.'

'You wish to join one of our camps, amongst the Sons of Israel? That can be arranged, when you have completed your noviciate.'

Yeshûa shook his head.

'No. I think I am called to something else. I think my work must be amongst my own people, in the north, in the Galilee. Amongst,' he said, not without a touch of irony, 'the poorest peasants, the *amê hâ-'erets.*'

The *Mebaqqer* raised his eyebrows.

'I have prayed for guidance, and even now I do not know if my choice is right, but I feel there is more worth in the eyes of the Lord in saving one man from sin than in . . .' he hesitated, then went on rapidly, 'than in living at ease amongst the ritually pure.'

A slight flush had risen in the *Mebaqqer's* cheeks, and his eyes hardened.

'We do not live at ease. Your understanding is still narrow and faulty. We prepare for the final war against the followers of the Evil Priest.'

'I believe that there is work to be done,' Yeshûa said, 'amongst the common people, before that day comes.'

'You set yourself up against the teachings of the Teacher of Righteousness? Who are you, an ignorant Galilean peasant, to suppose that you possess greater wisdom than he?'

'No!' Yeshûa cried in despair. 'That is not my belief. I do not know where my path lies. I know only that it does not lie here.'

The *Mebaqqer* rose from his seat. He was more than a handspan taller than Yeshûa, and his very presence made him seem taller.

'If you are cast out of the Community, you are deemed to have fallen amongst the followers of the Evil One. You may never return.'

'I know.'

'I had great hopes of you, Yeshûa. I believe you might have become a gifted healer. Now, that is not to be.'

Yeshûa could find nothing to say to this. The *Mebaqqer* paced across the room and gazed out of the window.

'As you remain a probationer until dawn tomorrow, I will not invoke the formal rite of expulsion if you leave before then.' He spoke with his back still turned to Yeshûa. 'You will leave early, and must be beyond the compound before the Community rises for the dawn prayers. You will take nothing with you but the clothes on your back. Go now.'

For the rest of the day, Yeshûa kept to himself. For the last time he worked at copying the ancient precious manuscripts, and when he finished for the day he laid aside his quill and his favourite bronze inkwell, and looked around the library with regret. He knew he would never again have such riches of the mind laid out before him. Here were not only the Book, the Psalms of King David, all the teachings with which he was familiar from his studies since boyhood. There were other writings said to date from the times of Moses and of ancient prophets like Isaiah, together with searching commentaries on the scriptures, writings which were unknown in the *kenîshtâ* at home, scrolls kept secretly here in Qumrân in the great clay storage jars. And the teachings of the greatest leader of the Community, the Teacher of Righteousness, his prophecies about the final apocalypse, were treasured and copied with devotion by his present-day followers. All this wisdom, all these ideas and speculations, which he longed to study, to dispute, to refine and purify to discover their nuggets of truth—all these he would have to leave behind forever. Lying on his bedroll that night, he could not sleep, but watched anxiously for the first lightening of the sky outside the unshuttered window.

When it came, he said a *berâkâ* for dressing, though all he had to don was his sandals—scarcely worn since coming to Qumrân—for he had slept in his tunic. Then he slipped out of the dormitory as quietly as possible. It was still dark outside, though not as dark as it had seemed inside. As he made his way up the path into the hills, he thought he could hear the echo of his footsteps behind him. When he turned at the bend in the path for a final look at the place where he had hoped for so much and which he would never see again, he realised he was being followed. He sat down on a boulder to wait.

'Did you think to leave without telling me?' said Nathan.

'I did what the *Mebaqqer* commanded.'

'You will not return?'

'No. I have chosen a different way, and so am cast out. You should not even speak to me, or the Community Rule could demand that you be cast out also.'

'Take me with you.'

Yeshûa shook his head.

'I myself do not know yet where my future lies. First, I will go back to my village, to see my family. After that, I must pray for guidance and try to find my way.'

'I could still come with you.'

'Your place may be here. At least stay and finish your probation. Try to find your own path. Perhaps it will be with the Community. Perhaps not. Perhaps we will meet again some day.'

Reluctantly, Nathan embraced him and headed back down to the compound, where the figures of the brethren could be seen making their way to the dawn prayer. Behind them the roofs, thatched with dry reeds, were already melting and vanishing into the eternal rock. Yeshûa turned his back on them and his face to the north.

By early afternoon of that day, my brother told me, he was making his way along the bank of the Jordan and knelt to dowse his head in the water and drink deeply. He had eaten nothing since the evening meal of the previous day, and then very little, so that now he felt light-headed. He rose to his feet and walked on. Ahead of him, he could see a man lying at ease on the river bank, his eyes closed, his arms folded behind his head. He reached the figure and stopped, looking down.

'So you have come,' said Yehûdâ, without opening his eyes.

Yeshûa smiled.

'I have come.'

Yehûdâ leaped suddenly to his feet and grabbed Yeshûa in a fierce hug.

'Welcome home, my brother!'

Yeshûa laughed, his heart giving a bound of delight. He knew all at once that he had been set free.

'We are a long way from home yet. Do you perhaps . . .' hungrily, he eyed the satchel lying on the ground at Yehûdâ's feet, 'do you have any food?'

Chapter Eight

Already the heat has become severe in southern Gaul, though it is only late spring. The newly planted vines are dry and exhausted, with no sign of new growth. Every day, soon after dawn, before the sun's fierce rays strike them like a withering sword, the Jewish refugees carry water to the vines, tending each stumpy plant with tender care. The thirsty earth swallows the water in moments and the vines look as lifeless as kindling. Manilius goes about the farm in a grim, tight silence. He has gambled much on this venture and with a failure in the spring rains, all could be lost. There is still other produce to bring in some income, but with the wheat fields ploughed up it will be necessary to buy flour before winter. The bees fed well at first on the spring flowers, but now the orchard blossom has fallen and the wild flowers further up the hillside are vanishing in the heat. Fulvia always finds the heat of midsummer oppressive and this early onset has left her pale and exhausted, prone to headaches.

Julia spends much of her time in her grandmother's room, avoiding her brothers, who are boisterous when released from their lessons. Although it faces south, a balcony on the upper floor projects above Mariam's window, affording some shade, and the shutters are kept half closed. A bay tree in a pot below the window has grown as high as the balcony, casting out a network of sprigs and branches which stir in the rare breeze and trace patterns of leafy shadow across the cool tesserae in the mosaic floor of the room. Over the years, Mariam has been in the habit of scattering crumbs on her windowsill for the birds and they come still, perching expectant below the swaying branches, though she is no longer able to feed them. After Julia noticed the birds, she has begun bringing scraps for them and will sit for hours watching them gather eagerly and squabble and take fright and return again. Today she has been watching a female blackbird feeding a fledgling, importunate and just as large as the harassed parent.

As usual she has drawn up a stool beside Mariam's bed and sits holding her grandmother's hand. The hand is cool and feels lifeless, but Julia has persuaded herself that as long as she holds Mariam's hand, she will not die. Her grandmother has not spoken for days, though Fulvia and Rachel manage to feed her a little each day—thin broth and water and gruel. Rachel is the Israelite woman, wife of Zakkai, who gave birth to a baby boy a month after the refugees came to the farm. Although they share few words in common, Julia likes her, for she is kind and patient with Mariam.

The young blackbird returned when it saw the new scraps that Julia has spread out. Now it is calling impatiently for its mother to come and feed it.

'Stupid bird,' Julia says softly, not wanting to frighten it away. 'You could pick up the food for yourself. You're quite old enough.'

'Sometimes young things cling on to childhood, because they don't want to grow up.'

Julia is so astonished at the sound of Mariam's voice after so long that she starts and clutches at the hand she is holding. Mariam presses her hand in return.

'Are you better, Grandmother Mariam?'

Julia jumps up and leans over the bed. Mariam opens her eyes slowly. Her face is ravaged with illness, her cheeks hollow and her nose grown more pointed, but her eyes blaze as brightly as ever. The rasping sound of her breathing frightens Julia, but there is no mistaking that fierce, vivid look.

'Child, you know and I know that I am not going to get better. I wouldn't lie to you. But I haven't left you yet.'

Julia crouches down and lays her cheek against Mariam's, so that her grandmother will not see that she is crying, but Mariam reaches across with her other hand and strokes the child's hair.

'Don't cry, *talithâ*, death comes to us all and mine is more peaceful than many, though it is slow.'

'What does that mean?' says Julia. '*Talithâ*?' She wants to put a stop to this talk of death.

'It means little lamb. We used to call a child *talithâ* in my village. It was a term of affection. My brother Yeshûa used to call me that when I was small. Sometimes later, too, when I was quite grown. My own little lamb was Daniel.'

'You've never talked about Daniel before.'

'No.'

Mariam closes her eyes. Julia sees tears seep out of the corners, but cannot tell if Mariam is truly weeping or whether it is another sign of her age and illness.

❧

It was the winter of my seventeenth year. I knew my mother felt it was long past the time when Yehûdâ should have claimed me in marriage and I should have gone to his father's house. She now had two daughters-in-law to help her, both more skilled at domestic tasks than I, the wives of Yehûdes and Yoses, who remained working with my father. Shim'ôn was betrothed and would marry in the summer. I hung about the house, neither girl nor woman, fish nor fowl. I was an embarrassment. But Yehûdâ had departed again, to the promised meeting with my brother on the banks of the Jordan, and until he returned, nothing could be decided. For my own part, despite the awkwardness of my position, I felt there was much to be said for celibacy, as I watched Melkha and my brothers' wives sink under the burden of perpetual pregnancy.

One thought was constantly on my mind: Would Yeshûa return, or had he vowed to take up the isolated life of the Essenes? I suppose all the family were wondering the same, but we never spoke of it. I presume my brothers were not overly anxious for his return, for he was the eldest son, due to inherit the largest portion. Perhaps it was cynical of me to suspect that they had such ideas. Perhaps not. Eskha was fond of him, but too absorbed in her own small affairs to give his return much thought. I am sure my parents worried about what would become of him, but my mother and I never discussed anything beyond our daily tasks. Once, I spoke to my father about it.

'Do you think Yeshûa will come back to us, Father?' I asked bluntly, when I had managed to find him alone, working

126

late over a fine casket to be sent to a friend and fellow merchant of Adamas's in Sepphoris.

He stopped his work and passed a hand over his tired eyes. His hair and beard were quite grey now. It seemed to me that he should let my brothers undertake more of the work, but none of them had his skill.

'Like you, I hope he will come back to us,' he said, 'but from his childhood he's always reached beyond us for something greater. I fear he'll never be happy, settled as a village craftsman. Even if he does not join this sect, I think he will want to move on, move away from us.'

'But we are his family. We *love* him.' I was nearly in tears. My father put his arms around me and patted me awkwardly on the back.

'We love him and he will always love us, but his path may lie elsewhere.'

I had other worries besides Yeshûa. Every winter for the last four years, Daniel had fallen ill, an illness that lasted until spring and left him weak and exhausted. Each year it started earlier and grew a little worse. At the onset of cold weather, he began to cough. After two or three weeks the dry, hacking cough would change into something much deeper in his chest, a thick, painful coughing that went on and on, leaving him gasping. In time he would begin to spit a greenish phlegm. He still shared my room and our winter nights were a strange mixture of fear, pain and closeness. When he woke me, despite trying to smother the noise in his bedclothes, I would creep down to the fire and make him a drink of honey stirred into hot water. This would soothe him for a while, though once he lay down again, the coughing would gradually return.

'Tell me a story,' he would beg as he leaned against my shoulder and sipped his drink, trying to make it—and our shared time together—last as long as possible. I was not as skilled a storyteller as my brother, but I would try to remember the stories he used to tell me when I was small, about lost lambs or greedy misers. Daniel loved to hear again the story of how Yeshûa had released the white dove in the Temple instead of sacrificing it.

'That is what I shall do,' he said confidently, 'when I go to Jerusalem to make my *bâr mitzvâh* vows, except I shall release *all* the birds from the stall.'

'That would be stealing,' I said. 'Father had bought the white dove for Yeshûa to sacrifice, so it belonged to him. Though I suppose some people would say that it belonged to Yahweh, so Yeshûa had no right to release it.'

'That's what Ya'aqôb would say.'

'Yes, I expect he would. And perhaps he would be right.'

'Would you let the dove fly away, Mariam?'

'I am only a girl. I do not make a *bâr mitzvâh* sacrifice.'

'But would you?'

'Yes, probably. Yes, I'm sure I would, if I wasn't too afraid.'

'Why would you be afraid?'

'With all those priests and Levites watching? And the other people making sacrifices? And everyone expecting you to do what everyone else has done forever? I'm not sure I would be brave enough.'

'So Yeshûa was very brave?'

'Yes, my love, he was very brave.'

Daniel's favourite story was another that Yeshûa used to tell me, about a village where everyone turned away a dirty, smelly beggar from their doors, all but one good woman, who was poor herself. She took him in and washed his feet, and gave him the last scrap of food she possessed, and laid out a bedroll for him on the dirt floor of her tiny house. In the morning he was gone. But her storeroom was filled with great jars of olive oil and wine, sacks of wheat and barley, baskets of fruit and pots of honey. Outside in her small yard was a herd of sheep and goats and even a milch cow!

'And I know why!' Daniel always broke in excitedly, bouncing up and down. 'He wasn't a beggar at all—he was an angel!'

One night, when he lay down again to try and sleep after this story, he turned to me, yawning.

'When I am a man grown, Mariam, that's what I am going to do. I shall travel about, washing all the beggars' feet, and one day I'll find the angel.'

It was past the winter solstice when they came, two weary figures trudging up the slope from the village to our courtyard. All the neighbours' dogs set up a great barking. Our own herd dog, who was new since Yeshûa left, ran at them frantically, then sat down suddenly and stared at my brother in puzzlement, as though he had called out a command, though not a word had been spoken. Both men were dusty and tattered, and Yeshûa looked older and thinner than I remembered. There was great excitement at the sight of them, the families from the other houses that shared our courtyard streamed out to greet the travellers. Soon everyone was crowding into the main room of our house, bringing food and wine, till we made a regular feast of it. There was no chance that evening to speak to either of them alone. Yehûdâ spent the night with us, but slept late, so it was my brother I finally managed to take aside from the others.

'You decided not to stay with the sectaries, then?' I did not try to conceal the relief in my voice.

We had left the courtyard and were climbing the lower hillside towards the *midbar*, where the grazing grounds were covered with a light fall of snow. He stopped and sat down on a rock, looking back over the village.

'The Community. No. It was not right for me. They keep themselves too isolated. I need to be out in the world, to live and work somehow amongst the poor. But to tell you the truth, Mariam, I don't see my way clearly even now. Though I did learn much among the brethren. And I discovered something new and strange about myself.'

He stopped.

'What?' I said. 'What did you discover?'

'It was perhaps because I was working with three skilled brothers. Probably on my own I'm nothing. It seemed that I healed a man of blindness in one eye. And a child—a little girl— she was like one dead, not breathing, and I breathed into her and she woke.'

I stared at him and shivered with apprehension. My *brother*, calling a child back from the dead?

'It's no miracle,' he said hastily, seeing my expression. 'The brethren have perfected the treatment for many ills, including this. I *think* it was not a miracle. But . . . it was what happened to me. At the time I felt . . . it was as though some power had entered into me from beyond myself. As though Yahweh himself acted through me. I have not felt it since.'

'While you were away,' I said slowly, 'and Yehûdâ spoke to us of the cures these people perform, Father said that a good man may perform a cure in the Lord's name.'

'I think it may be so. Certainly I myself am nothing, a peasant from Galilee.'

I looked at him in sudden hope.

'Daniel!' I said. 'Perhaps you could help Daniel! He is so ill every winter, and he grows so thin and weak. He barely recovers by the end of summer, when it all starts over again.'

I could see at once that he was reluctant.

'It would be a presumption,' he said. 'Who am I to attempt such a thing? I am nothing, Mariam. Before, I was in the company of the healing brethren. It was surely their presence that effected the cures. I was nothing but an assistant. I don't have the learning.'

I would not listen to his protestations, which I refused to believe.

'You cannot deny help to your own small brother, Yeshûa.'

I pleaded and argued until he said at last, wearily, 'I will not do anything without our parents' consent.'

That, I was sure, was as good as a promise. But I was mistaken. Yeshûa explained to our parents what had happened when he travelled amongst the sick villagers with the three Essenes, and how he had cured the blind man and the little girl. He did not tell them, however, about the power he had felt running through him. I thought they looked shocked rather than pleased at what he said.

'Mariam wants me to try to cure Daniel,' he concluded, 'but I will not do so without your agreement.'

I scrambled to my feet, my heart beating in my throat with hope.

'He was too ill to leave his bed this morning,' I said, leading the way to the stairs without even looking to see if they were following.

At the door of our room, I turned round. Yeshûa was close behind me, but our parents had paused at the top of the stairs and were murmuring together. My mother was shaking her head. I opened the door and went in. Daniel was propped up, half sitting, for he was more comfortable that way. As he caught sight of me he started to speak, but before he could utter more than 'Mariam', his whole body was wracked with a terrible spasm of coughing. When he took his hands away from his mouth, there was blood on them. Yeshûa knelt beside the bedroll, but did not touch him. Instead, he poured a beaker of water from the earthenware jar and passed it to Daniel.

Our parents had followed us in and my father stopped by Daniel's feet and stood looking down at his youngest child with immense pity. To my surprise, my mother stepped between Daniel and Yeshûa, and seemed to be shielding Daniel with her body. Her face was full of fear.

'Your mother will not allow it,' Father said.

'By why!' I cried. 'You can see how ill he is. If Yeshûa can help . . .'

'I will have no magic, no meddling with devils in this house,' my mother said.

And I saw suddenly that she was afraid, not for Daniel, but for *Yeshûa*. Or was she afraid *of* Yeshûa? Everyone knows that serious illness is caused by evil spirits entering the body. And they contrive this because a sin has been committed. In the case of a young child like Daniel, it is probably a sin committed by one of his family. I had feared for some time that I was the one responsible, and had prayed that his illness be transferred to me, but my prayers had evoked no response. The curing of illness, in part, depends on the casting out of the evil spirit. My mother, in her fear, would not allow Yeshûa to wrestle with the evil spirit.

I argued, but I knew from the outset that it was in vain. When my mother was this determined, however unreasonable the cause, nothing could move her. And Yeshûa had given his word that he would not make the attempt without our parents' consent. The three of them went at last, leaving me weeping and holding my little brother in my arms. I am not sure that he understood why we had been arguing. He was hot, with angry red patches like burns on his face, and the painful rasp of his breathing hurt me as if it were my own lungs fighting for air.

A few days later, Yeshûa and Yehûdâ told us of their plans. I think they had not wanted to spoil their homecoming by announcing that they were to leave almost immediately. Yehûdâ would go to Sepphoris and spend a few weeks with his parents, then they would leave together and travel down the Jordan Valley again to Beth 'Abarâ.

'But why?' Yoses asked, as we sat around the family table, after Yehûdâ's last meal before he left for Sepphoris. 'What is there at Beth 'Abarâ?'

'Not at Beth 'Abarâ itself,' said Yeshûa. 'But not far from there.'

He turned to our mother.

'We have a cousin there. Or at least, his mother Elizabeth was your cousin.'

'Yôhânân?' she said. 'He's about your age. A little older.'

'He's gaining great fame as a preacher. Many flock to him.'

'Is he another who preaches the end of the world?' asked Yoses. 'There have been a great many of them lately. We had one in the village last summer. The boys threw stones at him and drove him out.'

'He was a madman,' said Ya'aqôb, 'not a true prophet. He babbled of fire and brimstone, and the world being destroyed like Sodom and Gomorrah.'

'And the boys threw stones at him?' said Yeshûa. 'Even if he was a madman, surely . . .'

'Daniel did not,' I said bitterly. 'Daniel would have washed his feet, like the beggar in your story, hoping to uncover an angel.'

'Would he indeed?' said Yeshûa thoughtfully.

'Not this one,' said my mother with certainty. 'He was no angel. He stole two of our chickens.'

'You don't know that he did it,' I said, as much for the sake of argument as anything. He probably *had* stolen them.

'This cousin Yôhânân of ours,' said Ya'aqôb, bringing us back to the point. 'Why do you want to see him?'

'It is rather that I want to hear him,' said Yeshûa. 'I want to know what message he preaches. I did not find what I wanted at Qumrân. Perhaps I shall find it at Beth 'Abarâ.'

I saw very little of Yeshûa during the three weeks he stayed with us. He spent long hours in the workshop with Father, trying, I think, to make some amends for his long absence and his forthcoming departure. At the same time, I was occupied in nursing Daniel, who grew visibly weaker by the day. He continued to cough blood, and was no longer able to rise from his bed.

The night before they were to leave, Yehûdâ arrived from Sepphoris and the conversation I had been dreading took place. My mother challenged him about his intentions for our marriage, while I, embarrassed and ashamed, lurked in a corner of the room. Since his return, I had realised with sudden intensity how much I wanted the marriage to take place. We had been betrothed for two years, but most of that time he had been away and my feelings had not been provoked by his presence. Now, every time I saw him I became dizzy with desire. I tried to pass by him close enough to touch him, as if by accident. When he took my hand or brushed my cheek with his fingertips, I thought a raging fire had been lit in my belly. But I was humiliated when my mother spoke of it, as if it were a business arrangement on which he had defaulted. I felt besmirched.

'And when will the wedding take place?' my mother asked bluntly, while I longed for a thunderstorm to break or the roof of the house to fall in on my head.

Yehûdâ looked across the room at me and I knew that he saw my shame. He held out his hand to me.

'Perhaps Mariam and I might discuss this,' he said gently. He wrapped my cloak around me and led me, mute and unprotesting, out of the house, beyond the wall of the courtyard and through the orchard until we were well out of sight of the house. The snow on the ground was several inches deep, and I shivered, until he put his arms round me and held me close. I knew that my mother had wanted any discussion to take place in her presence, but Yehûdâ had grown into a forceful and determined man, who could assert himself firmly, yet without offence.

He turned me to face him, his hands resting lightly on my shoulders underneath both our cloaks.

'And what is your wish, Mariam? Are you anxious for this marriage to be soon?'

For answer I reached up and drew his face down to me and kissed him shamelessly. His mouth drove so hard into mine that my lower lip was bloodied, but whether his teeth had bitten into it, or mine, I did not know and did not care.

After a time I drew back breathless, gasping for air, and he laughed and brushed back my hair, which as usual had fallen over my face.

'Your answer is yes, then?'

I straightened my tunic and looked away down the hill towards the olive orchard. It was easier for me to think clearly if I was not looking at him.

'I know that my brother needs you,' I said. 'For a long time Yeshûa has been searching for something. He did not find it in Qumrân. Perhaps, as he says, he will find it in Beth 'Abarâ. I want our marriage. I want you. There is no secret between us there.'

I paused to dab at my bleeding lip with my finger. Yehûdâ took the edge of his sleeve and tenderly wiped the blood from my mouth. It made a violent crimson stain on the fresh white cloth.

'I *want* you, but Yeshûa *needs* you. I think we must wait. In any case, did you not say that you were to go to Jerusalem on business for your father, after you have visited our cousin Yôhânân in Beth 'Abarâ?'

'Yes. I will probably stay in Jerusalem about two months. I will leave Yeshûa in company with Yôhânân, then go back to Beth 'Abarâ to meet him. When we return home after that, shall we make the arrangements for the marriage?'

I smiled at him.

'By then you will know the country along the Jordan as well as our village streets. How I wish I could go with you! Take me with you!'

'You would not want to come now, with Daniel so ill.'

'No.'

'But later, perhaps, we might travel together. It can been hard, you know, and dangerous, and uncomfortable.'

'I should not mind!'

'You have not answered my question.' He looked at me quizzically. 'I think perhaps you are not sure in your own mind. Perhaps you do not really want marriage.'

'I do not want to lose my freedom,' I whispered, ashamed of my boldness, but thinking of the women of my family and the lives they led. Yet I clung to him, my heart pounding in my throat.

'I would not want to take it from you,' he said and kissed me. 'When Yeshûa and I return from Beth 'Abarâ, we will decide what is best to do.'

'Will you tell my mother?'

'I will tell your mother. Your mother does not frighten me!'

My long betrothal had become the subject of speculation in the village, but my mother must have said something to put a stop to it, some hint about what would happen when Yehûdâ returned, for now all I had to endure was the usual ribald teasing any young girl is subjected to when her marriage is forthcoming. In any case, I hardly left Daniel's bedside, except to fetch water from the well or to cook food which I hoped would tempt him, but never did.

About a month after Yehûdâ and Yeshûa left, Daniel became incoherent. The evil spirit which had been wrestling for possession of him was winning the battle and all my care and all the prayers in the *kenîshtâ* were powerless. He thrashed helplessly on his bedroll, throwing aside his blankets, alternately burning up and shaking with cold. He gabbled strange words, or else the spirit spoke through him, and when his eyes opened, they did not recognise me.

Then one night about midnight, he grew calm and lay in my arms quietly, though his breath still had that terrible laboured sound. He opened his eyes and looked at me, once again like the little boy I had loved so dearly for more than eight years.

'Mariam?' he said.

'Yes, my pet?'

He did not speak again.

✎

'Mama,' Julia says, running into her mother's *cubiculum*, where Fulvia has retreated, stricken with another of her headaches. 'Mama, please come quickly. I think Grandmother Mariam is worse.'

Fulvia slips her feet into her sandals and hurries after her daughter, to the room which has been Mariam's for the last ten years. Mariam is lying face up, drawing great shuddering breaths. She used to be such a commanding woman, Fulvia thinks. Almost as tall as her sons, with a back as straight as a cypress tree. Now she is so shrunken, she scarcely makes a mound under the light linen sheet. The room is surprisingly cool and pleasant, and Fulvia notices that someone, Julia probably, has picked a bunch of wild flowers and placed them in a vase beside the bed. It is one of Fulvia's best, a precious black and red vase from ancient Greece which she brought with her as part of her dowry, and which depicts Atalanta stooping to gather up the Golden Apples of the Sun. She moves the vase a little further to one side, so that Mariam will not throw out an arm and knock it to the floor, but she does not take it away.

'Run and tell your father to come,' she tells Julia. 'It may be nothing. No more than the heat troubling her.'

Mariam moans faintly, but does not wake.

✎

The constant coming and going of Yeshûa and Yehûdâ did not go unnoticed amongst our neighbours, who sometimes brought us news, for it seemed that my brother was beginning to arouse general curiosity. The fame of our cousin had also spread, even to remote Galilee. People were flocking to him from all parts of the Land of Judah, to listen to his preaching and to undergo baptism, a kind of ritual cleansing said to be even more potent than the rituals undergone before *Pesah* in Jerusalem. Yôhânân's

136

preaching was grim and frightening, or so it seemed to me when I heard of it. Like the madman who had wandered into our village, he warned that the world was coming to an end, that the Lord Yahweh would stand in judgement, condemning all sinners to everlasting punishment. He demanded *metanoia*, followed by baptism, total immersion in the Jordan, from which the repentant sinner would emerge transformed into blessedness.

'*Metanoia* is not merely repentance,' Ya'aqôb explained, his eyes shining with excitement. 'It is a Greek word, meaning a complete change of heart and life. How I wish I could go to Beth 'Abarâ and join his followers!'

I heard, but did not listen. Since Daniel's death, it seemed to me that everyone was far away, and their voices sounded muffled, as if a wall of water separated us. We had buried Daniel before the sunset following his death, in the family cemetery cave, around the shoulder of the hill from the *midbar*. From the slope outside, one could look down past the olive orchards towards the path Yeshûa had taken when he left us. I wished that we could leave the mouth of the cave open, so that Daniel might be surrounded by the warm embrace of the sun and the play of the wind, but the proper customs must be observed. My father and brothers rolled back the stone and I had to leave him there, cold and lonely in the darkness.

Shim'ôn of Keriyoth came from Sepphoris soon afterwards, to pay a visit of comfort to my parents. He brought news, sent from Yehûdâ in Jerusalem by a messenger, one of the men who worked for Shim'ôn as a small-time trader within Judaea.

'There is a strange story going round about your eldest son,' he said. 'Yehûdâ was present when he received baptism from his cousin Yôhânân. There was much confusion, crowds slipping and sliding on the banks of the river, some crying out hysterically, a thunderstorm brewing and approaching fast.'

He paused to drink a little wine, and my father refilled his beaker. I had retreated to a shadowy corner, where I had paid little attention to the conversation until Yeshûa and Yehûdâ were mentioned.

'It seems,' he went on, 'that because of the storm, some people were pushing to the front, wanting to receive baptism and then retreat to safety before the storm struck, for there were tall trees nearby, which might draw down the lightning. Others thought the growling thunder and the intermittent lightning, which were coming nearer and nearer, were signs of the presence of Yahweh at the ceremony and had worked themselves into a state of ecstasy. This preacher Yôhânân provokes such scenes, and the authorities do not like it.'

'But what of Yeshûa?' my mother asked.

'Yôhânân made the others wait on the bank while he took Yeshûa alone into the middle of the river. He said something about being unworthy to perform the ritual—Yehûdâ could not hear the words clearly because of the noise and confusion—then as Yeshûa rose from the river there was a mighty roar. I am sure it was the thunder, but Yehûdâ is not so certain. Some claimed it was a *bath kol*, a heavenly voice speaking, though there was a dispute about the words. "This is my son, whom I choose," or "This is my son, in whom I am well pleased". No one can say for sure. And there was talk of a white dove hovering above Yeshûa's head, though others thought a shaft of sunlight broke through the storm clouds and illuminated him as he stood in the river, the water streaming from his hair.'

He grinned suddenly at my father.

'That white dove! I think the story must have been spread about that prank he played with the dove at the *bâr mitzvâh* sacrifice. I wouldn't be surprised if it was Yehûdâ who mentioned it. He would have remembered that ritual they shared when they were boys.'

My parents looked troubled, especially my mother.

'All this attention being paid to Yeshûa,' said my father, 'it could mean danger, could it not?'

Shim'ôn was suddenly serious.

'I have had word from several sources that Herod Antipas is keeping a watch on the preacher Yôhânân, for fear he is going to bring trouble to the country. There have been so many uprisings, in our fathers' and grandfathers' times. Already Yôhânân's followers are claiming that he will lead a revolution to free Judah from the Roman occupiers, though to do him justice, I don't think that the Baptiser himself has said so. He is more concerned with matters of the soul than with this world.'

'We have an unfortunate reputation here in the Galilee,' said my father. 'Too many of these revolutions against our oppressors have been led from here. If Yeshûa, Galilean that he is, comes to be associated with such a man as Yôhânân, he could be seen as a dangerous rebel, by both the Romans and their Israelite lackeys, however innocent he may be.'

Dull though I was still in my grief, I took note of my father's words, for I had never before heard him speak of the state of our country, of the occupiers and the constant undertow of rebellion.

'I think your son is safe for the moment,' said Shim'ôn. 'Yehûdâ sends word that, after the baptism, Yeshûa decided to go south, to the Judaean desert.'

'He has not returned to Qumrân?' the words burst from my mouth and Shim'ôn looked round, surprised. I think he had not noticed me sitting there.

'No, he has not gone back to the Essenes. He's gone into the desert alone, to fast for forty days, like the prophets of old. Yehûdâ tried to dissuade him, but he would not listen. He said that ever since the baptism Yeshûa has been acting strangely. But not in any way that should worry you,' he added hastily, seeing my mother's look of alarm. 'He has been very quiet, saying little, sitting apart and meditating.'

Eskha, who had been at her spinning, but doing very little, laid down her distaff and spindle and came forward to Shim'ôn's chair.

'What do you mean?' she asked, crouching down beside him. 'I don't understand, fasting in the desert? How will he live? There's nothing there but wild animals and rocks.'

Shim'ôn, who had always been fond of her, patted her cheek.

'He will eat and drink nothing between sunrise and sundown, and in the hours of darkness will eat only what he can forage.'

'But I thought there wasn't anything in the desert.'

'There are lizards and snakes, and a few predators, like desert dogs and fowl, that feed on them. The prophets of old were said to live on locusts and wild honey.'

Eskha made a face. Some people regard locusts as a delicacy, but like Eskha I am revolted by them. They will cling to your skin or your hair and nothing will frighten them off. They regard you with their blank, mindless eyes that somehow imply a deep cunning. I think if I ever saw a devil, it would have the eyes of a locust.

As I lay sleepless that night, my mind was filled with thoughts not only of the brother I had lost to the hand of death, but of the other brother I loved, alone in the terrible waste of barren rock and dust that was the desert. There were some roots, Shim'ôn had said, which Yeshûa could dig up, which held a little precious moisture, but I could not imagine anything growing in that fearful place. And would Yeshûa know what was safe to eat, and what was poisonous?

When I had said my farewells before retiring, I raised again the subject of my brother's withdrawal into the desert.

'I do not understand,' I said to Shim'ôn, 'why Yeshûa has gone into the desert.'

'He told Yehûdâ that it was a part of his *metanoia*. He wanted to do penance and purge himself of his sins before starting afresh, reborn into a new life.'

The next morning I accompanied Eskha and two of her friends as they herded their flocks of sheep and goats out of the village and up to the pastures, which were growing succulent with the new spring grass. Now there were more women to undertake the household tasks, I was sometimes able to slip away like this, but I knew I must return before the midday meal. Leaving the girls, I continued climbing further up the hill, beyond the pockets of *midbar*, until I reached the rocky upper slopes which were too steep to support grass. There were a few stunted mountain trees, and it was here that wolves and jackals had their lairs, but I had no fear of them in the spring daylight. I used a stout staff to help me over the rougher ground and knew it would serve to threaten any unwelcome wild creature.

At last, with my breath short and my legs aching from the unaccustomed climb, I found a hollow in the rock where I could sit and look out over the village and the fall of the land to the east. I could even see, to right and left, two of the neighbouring villages, neither of which I had ever visited. In the privacy that I could never find at home, I allowed myself for the first time to give way to my grief for Daniel.

After a long time, weak and drained from weeping, I sat up and hunched over my knees, trying to drag my thoughts away from the sense of loss and desolation. I could not understand why Yahweh had visited such pain and illness and death on an innocent child. Daniel had never committed a sin which could have called down such a terrible punishment. Of course he had indulged in childish naughtiness, but never anything which could have been deemed a sin. Therefore, the sin must have been committed by the person who felt his loss the most. In other words, Daniel's death must be laid at my door.

My brother Yeshûa had gone into the desert to fast and purge himself of sin. I could not follow him into the desert, but why should I not fast? Would Yahweh accept the intention, even if my offering of penance was less painful and self-denying than my brother's? My fast would not restore Daniel to life, but perhaps if I tried to atone for my sins, it might prevent other punishments being inflicted on those I loved. I was not sure for what particular sin of mine Yahweh had exacted vengeance, but I knew I was sinful, through and through. I was guilty of laziness, ingratitude, rebelliousness, thoughtlessness—oh, the list could go on and on! I was lax in my prayers, inattentive during the readings in the *kenîshtâ*. I had never devoted my life to the service of Yahweh. I was selfishness made manifest. Tears of humiliation and self-pity crawled down my cheeks, already stiff with the salt tears I had shed for Daniel. I wrapped my arms around myself and buried my head in my knees.

The sun was growing hot and I could feel it burning the back of my neck where my hair had fallen forward, leaving the skin exposed. Sweat began to trickle down my backbone, and I welcomed the discomfort, as though it could somehow atone for my wilfulness. I was not sure how I could carry out my plan to fast. It must be done somehow in secret, for if I announced my intention, I knew that my family would frustrate me.

The heat of the sun was drawing up a faint mist from the dew-soaked early ground, so that, when I raised my head and looked about me, everything shimmered and blurred in front of my eyes. I remembered that time many years ago, lower down on this same hillside, when I had lost the kid. My brother Yeshûa had appeared suddenly before me, although I had never heard his step.

'Oh, Yeshûa, Yeshûa,' I whispered, 'you saved the kid, which was slaughtered for meat before the end of that year. Why could you not have saved your own brother? You breathed life into someone else's child. Could you not have laid your hands on my darling boy?'

The heat haze wavered and flickered before me, blotting out the hills and the valleys, the villages of whitewashed houses, the flocks, the green growing fields and the blossoming orchards. Instead, I saw before me a land that was grey and brown from horizon to horizon. Even the air was filled with dry dust. Here and there, far apart amongst the rocky outcrops that rose from the barren soil, stood a thorn bush, its jagged leafless branches clutching the air like the bony fingers of a skeleton. Nothing moved. The heat was so intense it rose from the land in waves that were visible, rippling the dust-laden air. There was no water, no life, no growing thing but those vicious thorns. Then I saw the man. He wore a tunic that had once been white but was torn and stained so that it almost blended with the earth. His face was hollowed and gaunt with hunger, his eyes looked out from cavernous sockets. They looked straight at me, and I knew Yeshûa my brother. The eyes looked through me and beyond me with a terrible intensity, as if what he saw was both marvellous and fearful.

Was this my brother?

My brother, whom I loved?

He was strange, wild. A creature of nightmare.

Could this be Yeshûa, the carpenter's son?

I was terrified, the back of my hand pressed against my mouth to hold back my cries. What was happening to my brother? What was happening to me?

Then the mist swirled again and he was gone. I was alone on the hillside. Far below me I heard, as clearly as if they were beside me, the crying of the lambs and the kids seeking their mothers.

Chapter Nine

It was not as difficult as I had supposed, to fast, in a desperate attempt to redeem myself from sin. Because so many people were now living in the house, the tables were crowded and busy at mealtimes—my parents, my brothers with their wives and children, my little sister and two unmarried brothers. In the weeks before Shim'ôn's marriage, Melkha, Adamas and their seven children joined us, so that I was able to move from table to table without anyone noticing whether or not I was eating. When circumstances made it necessary for me to sit down to a meal, I became skilled at slipping food from my plate or my mouth to the dogs, who always lurked below the table in the hope of fallen scraps. The less I ate, the more exalted I felt. My deceptions became a kind of victory, a secret triumph over my family.

Despite all my contrivances, it was not possible to fast totally, but after a while I discovered a way to rid myself of any food I had been forced to eat. I found that if I opened my mouth and prodded the back of my throat with the tip of rooster's tail feather, I could force myself to vomit. It became my practice to do this after every meal, however little I had eaten. I would slip away beyond the orchard, or down to the river, or up the hill—somewhere different each time, to avoid notice—and vomit the contents of my stomach into the grass. The taste in my mouth was bitter as aloes, but I rejoiced in it, as part of my penance.

Before long, I began to notice changes in my body itself. I grew very thin, and wore a tunic with long sleeves, even after the weather grew hot, to hide my bony arms. My breasts, which were not large, but round and firm, became shrunken, my figure childlike. When I bathed, I ran my hands over my hollowed stomach and prominent ribs with a kind of exultant pleasure. By my own will, I was transforming my physical being—I myself and no one else. In a life where I ruled nothing, I could at last rule my bodily presence. After some weeks, I found that I no longer had the monthly cycles of womanhood. Had my mother not been so occupied with the wedding preparations, she might have noticed that I had stopped washing out my bloody clouts. I felt as though I had reversed time itself, as though I could recapture the past, a past where I was a child and Yeshûa had not left us and Daniel still lived.

In those days I moved as one in a smothering dream. Sometimes the world seemed to spin around me, and I would have to catch hold of a door frame or a wall to stop myself from falling. All day long, there was a rushing in my ears, like a waterfall, that veiled the sound of voices, so that my mother would scold and shout to make me attend to my tasks. At night I lay awake, conscious of my body, which seemed to shrink and change under the very touch of my hands, and the joints of my arms and legs throbbed with pain. I welcomed the pain and rejoiced in it. It was at night, too, that the voices mostly came, echoing in my head, a strange babbling of words that individually made sense, but together tumbled over and over without meaning. Vicious, howling voices, the voices of demons. I knew that they were fighting to stay within me and torment me.

Both by night and by day I saw visions. It is said that the prophets of old had visions. Were they like mine? Sometimes I saw Yeshûa again, wandering alone and desolate in the desert of Judaea, and I would cry out to him, but he never heard me. Sometimes he was not alone. Some monstrous shape hovered fearsomely over him, or he wrestled with it, pitifully weak against its violent presence. There were other visions also. Crowds of people, shouting joyfully or menacingly, I could not tell which—their mouths were open, but no sound came out. And once I saw a garden, beautiful with flowers and lush growth under the shade of huge and ancient olive trees, yet it seemed a terrible place, full of menace, and I knew I must run for my life.

I know now that in my folly I came close to death. Someone in all that crowded house might have noticed, at last, how I was slowly killing myself—not hastening towards a lost childhood but towards a premature death. But they were all busy and happy, and I was always the awkward one—skulking in corners, as Ya'aqôb called it. Perhaps they thought that I was hurt and jealous that Shim'ôn's marriage was being prepared with such joy while my own betrothal lasted for years. In the end, it was none of them that put a stop to my dangerous game.

Less than three weeks before Shim'ôn's marriage was to take place, I was sitting on the ground outside our house, with my back propped against the wall and my eyes half shut. I was supposed to be carding wool, but I was too weak to pick up the wool-cards and the raw wool from the ground beside me. My hands lay idly in my lap. I do not know how long I had been sitting there when all the dogs set up their barking. I watched dully as a shambling figure staggered into the courtyard. Another beggar, I thought. They always know, through some mysterious message carried on the wind, when there is to be a wedding in a village and there will be food and kindness for the needy. His tunic had been torn at the shoulder and clumsily caught together with rough thread like a cobbler's twine; one sandal flapped loose from all but one of its thongs; his hair and beard were matted and filthy, and he walked with a limp. He stopped in front of me.

'Mariam?' he said.

I pushed myself to my feet by sliding my back up the wall, and peered at him. It could not be . . .

'Yeshûa?'

We stared at each other, horrified. I could not believe what I saw before me. I can only guess what he saw. He reached out and took my hands. I saw that one nail was torn past the quick, the others were rimmed with dirt. On his left hand, the old scar from the chisel stood out against skin burnt dark brown from the sun. We fell into each other's arms.

'But what has happened to you, Mariam?' he said at last. 'Have you been ill? You look as though you've been in a Roman prison and starved half to death.'

'I have been fasting,' I said. 'In penance at Daniel's death.'

I felt a sudden spurt of anger and despair.

'You would not heal him, and he died.'

A look of agony came over his face.

'He died? Oh, Mariam.' His eyes filled with tears.

'Perhaps I should have tried,' he stammered uncertainly. 'I could not tell if I should. How can I know, I who am nothing, a simple *bar nasha*, hardly more than one of the *amê hâ-'erets*?'

I shook my head. I had no answer for him.

'But what has happened to you, Yeshûa? Why do you come home like a filthy beggar?'

He smiled ruefully, and almost looked like himself again.

'Because that is what I am.'

'But how? We heard you had been baptised by our cousin Yôhânân, and then had gone into the desert to fast.' I broke off suddenly.

Should I tell him?

'I saw you,' I whispered. 'I saw you in the desert, so desolate and thin, and sometimes there was something—a monster? I don't know. An evil spirit?'

'You saw me?' He looked at me intently.

'Yes. Since I have been fasting. And once before. And I heard voices.'

He gripped my shoulders.

'The voice of Yahweh!'

'No.' I shuddered. 'No. I am sure it wasn't the voice of Yahweh. A strange babbling. I think perhaps it was the voice of the Evil One.'

'I wonder . . .'

'Yeshûa, *please*, tell me what has happened to you!'

'I returned to Yôhânân after my time in the desert,' he said. 'It seemed to me that I should join his followers and preach the coming of the final judgement. These last months, we have travelled much, throughout the Land of Judah. We even went amongst the Samaritans, though they were mostly hostile and drove us away. Then came word that Herod Antipas had put aside his wife and entered into adultery with his niece Herodias, who is also his brother's wife. He now lives with her openly, in defiance of the Law and all morality. Have you heard of this?'

I shook my head. There may have been talk of it in the village, but I had been heeding nothing but my own inner voices for weeks.

'Yôhânân preached against the tetrarch's sin, denounced him publicly as an adulterer, and Antipas sent soldiers to arrest him. There was fighting. I was hurt, a little, but Yôhânân called out to us, as they dragged him away, that we should disperse and carry his teaching to all parts of Judah. I have come home to the Galilee to begin my mission.'

He passed a hand over his face, and I saw that he was exhausted.

'Come,' I said, and took his arm, though I do not know which of us was able to support the other. 'Come and wash and eat.'

There was shouting and excitement as we came into the house. The whole family crowded round, kissing him, clapping him on the back, everyone talking at once. But I would let no one else wash his feet. I knelt before him with a bowl of warm water and a clean soft towel. As I gently sponged away the dirt from his scratched and blistered feet, I wondered whether I, too, might uncover an angel.

The rejoicing at Yeshûa's return did not last a day. By evening our brothers began to complain that during his long absences they had to do his share of the work in the fields and the workshop, and our mother was silent but tight-lipped. Our father, who was beginning to look frail with age, sat on the doorstep with his head in his hands, and said nothing. He had told me he thought Yeshûa would look for a life elsewhere, but I do not think he welcomed it. Yeshûa was gaunt, covered with suppurating sores, his skin grey and sagging, but his eyes were filled with a remote elation. Usually his calming presence was like balm to me, but now he was feverish, distracted, excited, fearful. It was the beginning of what our family saw as Yeshûa's strange behaviour, even to madness, and the beginning of the rift between them.

The next morning I took him aside, for I needed the answer to an urgent question. I knew why I had fasted: to purge myself of the sin that had brought about Daniel's death. But Yeshûa was a good man. I could not conceive that he had ever sinned. Why then, did he fast?

'Why did you do this thing? Starve, alone in the desert?'

'I wanted to draw closer to my Father.'

I looked at him, puzzled, then glanced across at the open door of our father's workshop. I was a little afraid.

'Your father is here, Yeshûa.'

He shook his head with a sad smile and touched my cheek.

'No, Mariam. My Father is in heaven.'

I stared at him, frowning. The One God, Yahweh, who dwells in heaven, is the Father of the whole nation of Israel. Of course I knew that. We are taught this from our earliest age, almost before we can even comprehend the words, and certainly before we can understand the idea. But my brother spoke the words now, the words 'my Father', so strangely, as if he possessed some secret and personal knowledge of God, as if he somehow *claimed* God as belonging to him alone, that I was shocked and angry, as if he had uttered a blasphemy.

'What do you mean? *Your* Father?' I almost shouted it. I was shaking, but whether with anger or fear, I am not sure. '*Your* Father, in heaven! *Our* father is here, among us. He is in his workshop, where he works all the hours of daylight, whether his eldest son is here to help him or not.'

I spat the words at him, and he flinched, but held his tongue. He had gone very white.

'Have you gone mad?' I cried.

No sooner were the words spoken than I clapped my hands over my mouth as if I could trap them there. I remembered the vision I had seen of him and realised that whatever had befallen him in the desert might well have driven him mad.

He took my hand.

'Some day, perhaps I can explain to you, when I can explain it to myself. Don't be angry with me, Mariam. I am groping in the dark, like a man blundering about a cave.'

He seem so sad that I was instantly contrite.

'I'm sorry,' I said, kissing him lightly on the cheek. 'We are both confused and lost at the moment. Perhaps we both need to find our way.'

Yeshûa held me at arms' length and studied my face keenly.

'You have changed while I have been away.'

I lowered my eyes, for they were filled with tears.

'I have lost Daniel,' I whispered.

Without my brother's care, I might have died even then as a result of my cruel abuse of my body. He saw at once how it was with me, and ordered me sternly to cease. I resolved to give up my fasting, my vomiting, but he would not allow me to eat normally.

'You must be careful, Mariam, or your body will be overwhelmed. Only liquids at first: broth and milk and water, perhaps a little yoghurt from sheep's milk. Believe me, I know how cautiously one must emerge from long fasting.'

He oversaw what I ate, and though the others must have been puzzled, everyone was too occupied to pay much attention. For several days I suffered violent stomach cramps and sickness while my poor body tried to accept that it was being fed again, but as the days passed I grew stronger. My headaches ceased and I was able once again to grind corn and cook and weave and milk the goats without needing to stop every few minutes to rest. Yeshûa shaved off his tangled beard, had his hair cut. He bathed and donned fresh clothes, and began to look more like the brother I had known. The gash in his leg which had made him limp began to heal.

'A sword thrust from one of Antipas's soldiers,' he explained to our father. 'I think they had been ordered to arrest none but Yôhânân, but they enjoyed giving the rest of us a beating, unarmed and helpless as we were.'

A few days before Shim'ôn's wedding was to take place, Yehûdâ arrived, bringing gifts from his family. I could tell from the way he looked at me that he was shocked at my emaciated appearance, but we had no opportunity for private conversation. He had been sent on by his father, after his stay in Jerusalem, to transact further business in Idumea and then Moab, before returning to Sepphoris shortly before Yeshûa reached us. The intention was that, as soon as the festivities for Shim'ôn's marriage were over, the planning would begin at last for our wedding.

The following day was the Sabbath and our family and visitors made a large party, walking to the *kenîshtâ*. It was a lovely early summer's day. My brother and my betrothed walked beside me through the village to the square, until we parted to take our places on the men's side and the women's side. The *kenîshtâ* was full, all the village there, the people who formed my world, whom I had known since infancy. The air smelled fresh and clean from the infusion of mint sprinkled on the floor. It was like a thousand other Sabbaths, yet it was to change our lives.

At first, the service went as usual. We stood and chanted the psalms for the day, then sat on the benches while the senior elder of the *kenîshtâ*, wearing his prayer shawl, recited the Commandments and the *Shema*: 'Listen then, Israel; there is no Lord but the Lord our God, and thou shalt love the Lord thy God with the love of thy whole heart, and thy whole soul, and thy whole strength . . .'

Afterwards, one of the elders of the village chanted the six *berakôth*, or benedictions, to each of which we responded in chorus with '*Âmên*. And then he began the final prayer: 'Blessed art Thou, O Lord . . .'

The main part of the service was always followed by the reading of one of the *pârashôt*, the selections from the scriptures. One of the congregation would volunteer or be invited to read it in Hebrew, and then interpret it in Aramaic. The *shammâsh* went forward and lifted the heavy scrolls from the lovely carved ancient '*arôn* in which they were kept. He looked around the room, and many heads turned towards Yeshûa. It was considered a courtesy to invited a visitor to read. My brother had been absent so long that clearly many in the village felt it his due to be asked to read and interpret. He nodded, rose, and went forward into the centre of the room. The *shammâsh* handed him a scroll, and he began to read in his beautiful speaking voice. I think perhaps I had never heard him speak in public before. I had heard him read scripture often enough, all through my childhood, when we sat together on the dusty ground between the coiling roots of the olive trees. This was somehow different. The well-known phrases were new made, they vibrated with sudden intense meaning as my brother read them. I saw heads go up all round the *kenîshtâ*, the silence of those listening became more concentrated. I saw that he had become something more than he had been before he went away, more urgently present. A shaft of sunlight falling through a high window lit up the soft curls of his short-cut hair and sculpted the fine bones of his face. Like Daniel, he had thick dark eyelashes, which looked as though they had been sketched against his cheek by an artist's brush. His eyes were lowered to the scroll, though I knew he could have recited the passage by heart.

The Spirit of the Lord is upon me, because the Lord hath anointed me to preach good tidings unto the meek; he hath sent me to bind up the broken-hearted, to proclaim liberty to the captives . . . to proclaim the acceptable year of the Lord, and the day of vengeance of our God . . .

Was it pure chance that this particular passage from Isaiah was the reading for that Sabbath? Did Yahweh ordain it so? My brother read the familiar words as though they were fresh, and personal to him.

Yeshûa finished the reading, rolled up the scroll and handed it to the *shammâsh* to be restored carefully to the *'arôn*. People shifted a little in their seats, sat back, and turned expectantly towards Yeshûa, awaiting his interpretation of the passage in Aramaic. And that was when the pattern of the day was shattered.

My brother said not another word but returned to his seat in silence.

On both sides of the room, men and women looked at each other in puzzlement. There were a few faint muttered words. I felt a blush rising from my neck to flood my face with shame. Why was my brother sitting down without a word? Surely he knew he was expected to say something, however brief, about the significance of the text, or its application to our lives. I could see that Ya'aqôb, who was sitting next to him, was angry. He poked Yeshûa in the ribs with his elbow. He would think that Yeshûa had humiliated the family by this extraordinary behaviour.

My brother said nothing, studying his clasped hands. The minutes stretched out in acute embarrassment. There were louder mutters from the men's side, while my mother twisted her hands together and Eskha and Hannah tried to suppress nervous giggles. The longer the silence stretched out, the faster my heart began to beat. From being embarrassed, I began to be angry. How long was he going to keep us all sitting here, his family writhing in discomfort, while that buzz of annoyance in the room became threatening?

At last my brother looked up.

'These words need no interpretation,' he said. His voice was quiet, but authoritative. 'Today is this very scripture fulfilled in your ears. I have come to show the way. To urge the wicked among you to repentance. To care for the sick and needy.'

People looked at one another in astonishment and growing anger. I could see that they thought him rude or arrogant. What kind of interpretation was this? The scripture was *fulfilled*? Through *him*? I did not understand him myself. Then a voice, louder than the others, shouted out:

'Is this not Yeshûa, the *carpenter's* son? The brother of Ya'aqôb and Yehûdes and Yoses and Shim'ôn? And are not his sisters here with us, sitting over there?' I saw an accusing finger pointing towards me and tried to shrink down behind the woman in front.

At that, my brother jumped to his feet and, stretching out his arms, looked all around at the congregation, and cried out:

'You will surely say unto me this proverb: Physician, heal thyself . . . Truly, I say unto you: *No prophet receives honour in his own country!* At the time of the great famine in Judah, Elijah was not told to save an Israelite widow. No! He was sent to save a widow in Sidon. A widow amongst the *gôyîm.*'

Puzzled, we looked at one another. What had this to do with the reading?

My brother drew a deep breath.

'Elisha the prophet did not cure any of the lepers in Israel. No! The man he cured was Naaman the Syrian. Another one of the *gôyîm.*'

Yeshûa looked around at the gaping mouths, the scowling brows. Some men were starting to their feet. He thumped his fists against his temples in frustration, but this only seemed to make them angrier.

He was shaking all over now, whether with fear or anger or some other passion, I could not tell. He began to push his way out of the *kenîshtâ,* but people crowded after him and I lost sight of him. I stood up and tried to fight my way through the angry villagers. These were our neighbours, but they elbowed me aside and ran after him shouting.

'He dares to compare himself to Elijah and Elisha!' cried the potter, Judith's father.

I didn't think that was what he had said, but I was confused myself. Once again he was behaving strangely, almost like a madman, talking incoherently. Perhaps that time starving in the desert really had turned his brain. I knew how fasting could bring on visions and hallucinations. How it changed your body and haunted your mind with delusions.

'He scorns us!' said someone.

'Aye, that fellow Yeshûa? He's nothing but the carpenter's son, but he scorns us because we won't listen to him and his arrogant words.' That sounded like the blacksmith. 'Come to fulfil a prophecy! Him! Thinks he's better than we are, does he?'

'Blasphemy!' Many of them were shouting it now.

I was running, dodging round the edge of the crowd. We were nearly at the far end of the village, beyond which the ground fell away abruptly into a deep gorge.

'Let's make an end to his pride and his blasphemy,' someone shouted. 'Throw him into the gorge! Let him break his head on the rocks and spout his dying words to the vultures. Let's see what they make of this fine prophet!'

These were the young men of the village in the lead now, boys he had gone to school with, in the same *beth ha-sefer*, with the same *hazzan*. They were his friends.

What had happened? Yeshûa's words had been strange and incomprehensible, but why were our neighbours, our *friends*, suddenly so lethally angry?

I saw that Ya'aqôb and Yehûdâ had managed to reach the front of the crowd and were blocking the way into a narrow alleyway, down which my brother must have run. For a moment everything seemed to slow down and quiver, like a set of scales when a feather or a finger-tip may cause it to dip one way or the other. Then the wild fury of the chase abated, the look of the hunter faded from the eyes of the villagers. The older men were urging the younger ones back. The crowd shifted, broke apart and drifted away, though there was still a hum of angry voices and I saw that they looked even at me with something like hatred in their eyes.

For several minutes I hid myself in the mouth of the alleyway, then, when I was sure everyone was gone, I ran home by back ways. There, everything was in an uproar. Adamas was declaring loudly that Yeshûa had brought shame on us all, that he was a madman and should be locked away. Most of the women were weeping. My father had retreated to his workshop and closed the door. The dogs, sensing the disturbance, were barking furiously. Nowhere could I see Yeshûa.

Yehûdâ caught sight of me and drew me away, out of the house and behind the goat shed.

'Where is he?' I cried. 'They would have killed him back there! What does he mean, saying that he is a prophet, unrecognised in his own country?' I was gasping with fear and running, for I was still weak.

'Take a deep breath, my love,' said Yehûdâ, 'and listen to me, for there is not much time.'

I obeyed and sank down on to the low wall. Yehûdâ knelt on the dusty ground in front of me in his best Sabbath clothes and took both my hands in his.

'Yeshûa has gone to Capernaum. We have friends there, and they will take him in. He feels himself called to continue Yôhânân's ministry. He will preach, for the moment, in the villages of Galilee.'

'But . . .' I said. He put his finger against my lips, but I shook my head. I could not be silent, for this was urgent. 'Yeshûa does not believe in the fiery message of Yôhânân, of that I'm sure. He believes in brotherly love and kindness, not punishment and damnation.'

'I know. I know. He will carry his own message. And he wants to practise the healing arts he began to learn at Qumrân, to go amongst the sick and the poor and the outcasts, healing and comforting them, body and heart and mind.'

'But why must he go to Capernaum?'

'You saw what happened here.'

I nodded. That sudden outrush of anger had been terrifying. The village had turned on him the way a herd of animals will turn on one that is strange or sick, driving it away or even killing it. It was as if, by his words, he had transformed himself into a creature alien to them. I had never before realised the power of the spoken word to arouse such emotion.

'What will you do?' I asked, though I think I already knew.

'I will go with him to Capernaum, just to ensure that he is safe. I will hope to catch up with him before too many hours. Afterwards I will come back to you, and we shall be wed.'

'Take me with you,' I said, as I had said once before.

He shook his head.

'It may not be safe, not if any of those young ruffians pick up his trail and follow him. And it would be unseemly for you. You would forever be tainted, looked upon as a woman of loose morals. You cannot travel alone with me.'

'If only we were already wed!'

'We shall be soon. Now, will you put a little food in a bag for me? Enough for your brother as well? Then I will slip away before anyone can stop me.'

'Of course.' I stood up, then as remembrance struck me, I pressed my fingers to my lips. In all the confusion and fear, I had forgotten. 'But, Yehûdâ, it is the Sabbath! You may not travel more than two thousand cubits.'

'I know. But do the scriptures not say that, to save a life, we may break the rules of the Sabbath? According to the Law, it is permitted even to save the life of an ox or an ass, if it has fallen into a pit on the Sabbath.'

'Is it permitted? Are you sure?'

'It is,' he said firmly. 'Or at least Yeshûa has told me so. Now go, say nothing to anyone about where we have gone, and meet me at the top of the olive orchard.'

It seemed I was always saying good-bye. I did as Yehûdâ asked, but I filled two bags with food and hid one beneath an old apple tree before carrying the other down to Yehûdâ. He had gathered up his belongings from the house and donned stout boots in place of his sandals. In his hand he had a fallen branch that he had picked up in the orchard, to use as a staff. The bag of food he stowed amongst his other possessions in a knapsack of goat-hide slung over his shoulder. I touched the bracelet I had given him as a betrothal gift, but did not speak.

'It shall not leave my wrist while I live,' he said. Then he kissed me and was gone, taking long strides down the hill, leaping over the roots of the olive trees. After a moment I turned and ran back to the village. At home I slipped into my room, which I was forced to share, until the wedding, with Eskha and Melkha's five daughters. I unrolled my bed and placed on it almost everything I owned, which was little enough. A few clothes, my reed pipe and the pearls Yehûdâ had given me, the set of animals I had carved for Daniel, and a lamb whose uneven legs meant that it always fell over. Daniel had made it for me not long before his last illness and had been impatient that it would not stand.

'Never mind,' I said. 'Look at his face. This is the most intelligent lamb I have ever seen.'

'Truly, Mariam?'

'Truly.'

There was also a small box of cedar wood, beautifully inlaid with the star of David in precious ivory, which Yeshûa had made for me as a betrothal gift. He had given it to me quietly, after the betrothal with all its noisy rejoicing. I found that I could fit both the lamb and the pearls inside it. Finally I added to the bundle my sandals, lacing on instead the boots I normally wore only in winter, for I had taken note of Yehûdâ's. It would be hard walking to Capernaum, and there might be snakes. I rolled up the bed with everything inside and tied it together with an old belt cord.

So far I had been lucky. None of the girls had come into the room, prying into what I was doing. I looked out of the small window, which faced the back of the house, over the yard where we milked the sheep and goats. There was no one about except the wife from the next house. When she turned away, I leaned out of the window as far as I could and dropped my bed roll into the yard. She heard something and looked round, but then went back into her house.

My heart was beating like a naughty child's as I crept downstairs again. My mother saw me and called out.

'Mariam? Fetch me a new jar of honey from the storeroom. And then you must put these loaves into the bread oven.'

I ran to obey. I must hurry. I did not know the way to Gennesaret and Capernaum, only that I should follow the river downhill to the valley, which was called the Valley of the Doves. After that, I could probably ask the way, but I did not want to be alone after dark. If I could follow Yehûdâ quickly enough, I might overtake him before then. I did not want to catch up with him too quickly, or he might bring me back. It was already past time for the midday meal, but everything was in confusion today. It seemed even my mother had forgotten it was the Sabbath and was preparing food. Why had Ya'aqôb not chastised her?

All this ran through my head as I fetched the honey, then carried the three loaves on the baking stone out to the oven in the courtyard. To my relief, someone had already lit it. I raked out the hot ashes and slid the baking stone into the domed clay interior, then wedged the stone door in place. I found Melkha's eldest daughter, a sensible girl nearly eight, and told her she must watch the bread.

'You will be able to smell when it is done. Move the stone. The bread should be golden and firm. The bread sounds hollow if you tap it with your fingernail.'

I started to run round to the back of the house, but called over my shoulder.

'Be careful. It will be hot. Use a cloth.'

She was squatting in front of the oven and nodded earnestly.

'I know.'

My bedroll was there in the dust. I picked it up, climbed over the wall and ran to the orchard where I had left my bag of food. Drawing a deep breath, I said a quick *berâkâ* for my journey. I was following my brother and my betrothed wherever they were going, and I did not look back.

My world had always been limited by the stretch of river below the olive orchard, where the boys used to swim and where we carried the clothes and household linen to wash. A well-trodden path led along the river beyond the washing-place, but I had

158

never ventured along it. I knew it was supposed to lead eventually down to the Valley of the Doves, but I did not know whether there might be other paths leading off it, serving other villages. I thought that if I kept close to the river I could not go wrong, for I knew that our river eventually flowed into the Jordan. Apart from that, my ideas about the geography were vague. I did not know whether I should turn left or right where the river met the Jordan. Were Gennesaret and Capernaum to the north or the south? Would I be able to see the lake? Would there be any village where I might dare to ask the way?

As the path turned the corner that now hid from sight everything I had ever known, I was suddenly very afraid. A girl, travelling alone, through uninhabited country—I was easy prey for anyone, and not just wild animals. I had nothing to defend myself with except the small eating knife I wore in a sheath at my belt. Since the Roman occupation and the imposition of their tribute tax on top of the traditional Temple taxes, many small farmers and villagers had lost their lands and homes, and wandered the countryside, surviving by banditry. I began to run. It mattered less now that Yehûdâ might be angry with me, might take me back to the village. I did not want to be alone. And already the sun behind me was lower in the sky.

I could not keep up the pace for long. In many places the ground was rough and I had to watch my feet. If I fell and twisted an ankle here, no one would know where to find me. I had come to fairly dense woods, where branches sometimes met overhead and roots heaved up the ground beneath the path. I adopted a sort of jogtrot in the places where I could see my way, slowing to a walk or a scramble where the going was difficult. Each time this seemed to last longer, so that I ached with impatience. I had no way of knowing how far ahead of me Yehûdâ might be.

At last I reached clearer ground. A kind of promontory of land thrust out where the woods ended, providing a place to look out over the steep fall of land below. Beyond the woods, the lower slopes had been terraced, where the remains of an old vineyard still grew. It was no longer tended, for the vines which had once corded the ground in neat rows now embraced each other in wild disarray. The blossom was over and bunches of tiny grapes could be seen between the thick growth of leaves. A prudent farmer would have cut back some of the foliage to allow more sun to reach the grapes, and would have thinned the smallest grapes from each bunch so that the remainder would grow fat and juicy. I wondered whether this was one of the farms which had been lost to the tax-collectors. If so, no new owner had taken possession, or if he had he was a careless husbandman.

Past the vineyard a smaller path led off the main one, snaking uphill again to the left, and probably led to another village. The main path continued downhill, and there in the distance I could see a man walking away, with a fast but easy stride. I knew it must be Yehûdâ. I jumped down to the path again and began to run. The slope was steep, but I flew down that hill like one of the Greek athletes of old.

The sun had dropped below the western hills behind me and it was growing dark as I reached the level ground which must be the beginning of the Valley of the Doves. Yehûdâ was only a few cubits in front of me and at last must have heard the sound of my heavy boots on the dry soil of the path. He stopped and looked round. My breath was coming in painful gasps, so that I could not call out to him, and at the last moment my luck failed me. I tripped over something—a root, a large stone—hidden in the diminishing light, and sprawled in the dust at his feet, grazing my knees and the palms of my hands.

It was at that moment, spitting dirt from my mouth, that I realised what I had done.

On all fours, my hands bleeding from the sharp stones, my tunic filthy, I saw myself suddenly for what I was. I could never go back to the village. I was forever marked as a woman cast out, befouled. In running after my brother and my lover, I had exiled myself from parents and family, from all decent society. It was as if a chasm had opened at my feet and I stood swaying dizzily on the rim.

Yehûdâ crouched down in front of me and lifted my hands tenderly from the ground. At his touch a shock ran through me, and my heart leapt in my breast, squeezing the air from my lungs. Our eyes met in a look of such perfect recognition that the world spun away from me. My body was disintegrating, falling apart into its four elements—earth and air, fire and water—and I flowed towards him on a burning river. I wanted nothing but to mingle my very essence with him, body and soul, spirit and substance.

I heard him draw a long, gasping breath, and his fingers tightened on my wrists. I strained towards him, as if I were drowning and only he could pull me to safety. Then a shudder ran through us both, as if in that moment we were indeed one flesh, and we both drew back.

'No,' I said.

He shook his head. 'No.' Then gently, as if I were some fragile creature—a newborn babe, a vessel of blown glass—he raised me to my feet. And all my body was suddenly cold, but for my face, which burned and burned, as if I had leaned too close to a raging fire, and seared my very skin.

In a few minutes he had me sitting under a carob tree at the side of the path and was dabbing the dust and grit out of my grazes with a cloth soaked in water from his water skin.

'Can I drink some of that?' I asked humbly. 'I forgot to bring water.'

He passed me the water with a smile, as if nothing had happened, and I gulped it down like a tired donkey.

'I can see you aren't an experienced traveller,' he said. 'First requisite: water. It is good that you weren't travelling in the worst of the heat, or you would never have been able to come this far. When did you leave?'

'About an hour after you, I suppose. I could have drunk from the river, but I didn't want to stop. Are you angry with me?'

'Well, there would be little point in that, my love.'

'I am afraid I am dishonoured already,' I said.

'None need know of it, if we do not tell them. We cannot overtake your brother tonight, but we must try to do so tomorrow. Then we can all arrive at Capernaum together.'

'But tonight?'

'Tonight we will make a small camp away from the road and then you will sleep while I keep watch. You will be safe with me, Mariam.'

'I know,' I said, touching his hand lightly. 'I have always known I could trust you, ever since I was a small child.'

I could trust him. But could I trust myself?

We found a grove of carob trees a little way off to the right of the path, which would provide concealment and shelter for the night. Yehûdâ refilled his water skin from the river and we made a simple evening meal of dates and cheese. I was hungry, now that I had begun to eat again, for I had had nothing since early morning, when I had eaten a piece of flatbread dipped in olive oil. We did not light a fire, for fear of attracting attention, but the night was warm. Although I would have liked to sit up with Yehûdâ, I spread out my bedroll obediently, and lay down to sleep, while he sat a little distance away, leaning against one of the trees. The carob plantation, like the vineyard I had seen further up the hill, was neglected. Once, I have been told, the Galilee was one of the most fertile farming lands in the world, but the heel of the Roman has crushed us.

To my surprise, I fell asleep almost at once and slept deeply until the morning sun, slanting down through the branches of the carob, fell on my face and woke me. I found then that I was stiff from my long trek down the hills, and there were painful blisters on my feet. Yehûdâ had already laid out food for us, but I went first to a place by the river where I could not be seen, and washed my whole body and my hair. After that I felt better, the stiffness a little eased, though the blisters were still painful.

'Do you think we will overtake Yeshûa before he reaches Capernaum?' I asked, as we ate our frugal meal.

He shook his head.

'Probably not. He fled from the village in such haste and passion, I expect he walked all night. We are used to walking great distances, he and I.'

'I have delayed you,' I said remorsefully. 'If I had not come, you would be with him now, and you feared for his safety.'

'I have kept watch all night. There's been no sign of pursuit.'

'They're nothing but dogs!' I said scornfully. 'In a pack they will attack, but they have not the courage or the craft to pursue him beyond the village.'

He laughed. 'You are very fierce this morning!'

'I despise them,' I said. 'They were his friends and they turned on him, for no reason.'

'Oh, I think they felt they had reason enough. It is a shock, when someone you have known since boyhood announces that he is a prophet come amongst you.'

I looked at him thoughtfully as I cleared away the remains of our meal and rolled up my bed.

'And was it a shock to you?'

'Yes. But I have known him better than most, and I have watched the path he has been following. He has always been set apart from us, even those of us who love him dearly.'

'Yes,' I said. 'Yes, that is true.'

We had not far to go that morning before we reached a dusty road much wider than the path we had been following. It ran north and south. Nearby our river, the river I had always known, tumbled over a wide stretch of pebbled rapids into a broader river fringed with willows.

'Is that the Jordan?' I asked, in awe. A name from our nation's past, a name almost mythical in its resonance.

Yehûdâ nodded. To him, I suppose, it was merely a familiar landmark. He turned to the left. So Gennesaret lay to the north. I hobbled after him, for my boots were becoming more and more painful.

'Why don't you put on your sandals?' he said. 'The walking will be easier here. Most of the way there is grass at the side of the road. You can walk on that.'

I sat down and removed the boots from my throbbing feet. The air on them felt wonderful. I tied my boots together and hung them round my neck.

'I think I will go barefoot for a while.'

He raised his eyebrows at me.

'Do not worry!' I laughed. 'I will put on my sandals before we reach Capernaum. I'll not shame you.'

It was a longer walk than I had expected. We followed the Jordan north for a mile or two before we had our first sight of the lake. I caught my breath in wonder. The great sheet of water glowed beneath the cloudless sky, blue as my mother's favourite mantle, but iridescent, like some exotic jewel, the whole surface shimmering and dancing with silver ripples. I had never imagined anything like this. It was so alive, like some lovely creature breathing joyously that summer morning.

'Oh!' I cried. 'Oh, I never realised . . .'

Yehûdâ smiled down at me indulgently. I must have seemed like a child confronted with some unexpected delight, which was quite how I felt. I forgot the pain in my feet and ran forward to get a better sight.

'Gennesaret,' I said, 'it means "valley of the flowers", doesn't it?'

'Yes. You'll soon see why. Flowers of every kind grow in abundance all round its shores. And it's rich in fish. Many of the people around here make their living from the fishing. It will be fish for our evening meal tonight.'

I did not answer that. We had fish from Gennesaret sometimes in the village, brought in by traders and dried until it was the texture of leather, or else salted so heavily that, however much you washed it before cooking, it made your mouth pucker. And the smell! Like corpses of animals rotting in the sun.

There was still a long walk ahead of us, but after the rocky hillside and the dark woods of yesterday, it was almost like a holiday. The air was full of the scent of oleander and jasmine. As well as the usual cereal crops and vineyards and olive orchards, and the sky-blue fields of flax, I saw smaller plots planted with precious crops like lavender, which would be harvested for their intense oils and sent to Jerusalem, or even to foreign lands.

'Further south,' said Yehûdâ, 'near Jericho, there are farms growing and processing nothing but balsam. It's so valuable that they are surrounded by high walls and guarded by armed men with dogs that would take your arm off if you ventured too near.'

I shook my head. So much that was new and astonishing!

After a while, Yehûdâ took a side road which led up away from the lake.

'I want to skirt round Tiberias,' he said. 'There are people there who would know me, merchants who trade with my father. It would be best if we were not seen.'

Looking down where he pointed, I could see the new city, raw and white against the surrounding greenery. There was a harbour, and quays with large boats tied up.

'They trade with the eastern shore,' Yehûdâ said, 'and the cities of the Decapolis.'

I could not believe that a within one day's hard walking I should be almost in touch with these magical places, which had always seemed like names conjured out of the air by a storyteller.

About midday, we came to a small town called Magdala, where I donned my sandals, and kept them on. Yehûdâ bought us a meal at an inn beside the lake. I, of course, had no money, not even a *pruta* to my name, nor had I ever eaten a meal that was not cooked in my own home or by a neighbour. I eyed it suspiciously at first, but to my relief there was no fish, just a dish of beans cooked with herbs, some flatbread and cheese, and then some rather stale honey cakes (even I could have made better). To sit under a vine arbour overlooking the Lake of Gennesaret, however, and to be waited upon by maidservants, made me feel like a great lady, were it not for my tunic, still stained from yesterday's fall, and my clumsy bundle of belongings.

After we had eaten, both of us hungrily, I sat back and looked at him across the crumbs.

'What do you think Yeshûa is planning to do?'

Yehûdâ spread his hands and shook his head.

'I truly do not know, Mariam. He fled to Capernaum because it is near and we made friends there when we visited it before on our travels. But I cannot think he means to settle there. Since the arrest of your cousin, the Baptiser, I think he's felt it his duty to carry on the mission.'

'But we agreed before that Yeshûa's ideas are different.'

'Yes,' he said. 'And your brother is a strong man, of deep convictions. I think perhaps he has not yet quite found his voice.'

'You mean, he doesn't know how to put into words what he believes?'

'Well, look at that fiasco in the *kenîshtâ* yesterday! Scraps of quotations from the scriptures. Silence. Incoherent shouting at people! No wonder they were angry. When people are afraid and confused, of course they will become angry. Especially if they feel threatened from within. Not like a threat from a Roman soldier. One of your own, coming to lecture at you, warning you that you are evil and must repent.'

Had it really been only yesterday?

'But what will you do?' I asked.

'Find out what he plans to do first, if he has any plans. Perhaps persuade him to come to my father's house in Sepphoris. Try to protect him from himself!'

He reached across the table and took my hand.

'We can be married in Capernaum, my love. Or from my father's house. It will not be the wedding your father would have given you, but wherever it is, our love will be as great.'

I lowered my eyes and lifted his hand to my lips and kissed it.

It was a relief to rest for a while, but Yehûdâ said that it was five or six miles more before we would reach Capernaum, so after our meal we set off again. After the rest, the walking seemed hard at first, but the land was quite flat around the edge of the lake, and the scent of the flowers would have made it pleasant, had I not been so tired.

'There,' Yehûdâ said, pointing to a cluster of houses ahead, lying along a curve of the shore. 'That is Capernaum.'

I loved Capernaum from the first, and I spent there some of the happiest days of my life. That afternoon, though, drawing towards evening, I thought mainly of being able to stop walking, to sit down, and perhaps even take off my sandals again. We walked on towards the little town (for it seemed to be not much larger than a village), following the strip of grass that separated the houses from the shore. They were mostly modest houses, smaller than my own home, belonging, Yehûdâ said, to the fishermen who worked on the lake. Boats of all sizes were drawn up on the beach, and a few more were being rowed in from the lake. There were nets draped over bushes to dry, and we passed a couple of men wearing nothing but loincloths who were mending a torn net with fresh twine.

And there, sitting cross-legged on the sand, talking to a group of fishermen, was Yeshûa.

Chapter Ten

Manilius and Julia crouch side by side between the rows of vines. The sun on their backs is scorching, and the soil is arid and dusty, but they ignore the discomfort. Julia is pointing to a tiny green nodule on one of the bare stumpy twigs that look like so much firewood pushed into the ground.

'See, Father. This one is alive. There's a leaf coming.'

Manilius peers more closely, his nose almost touching the plant. It needed a child's sharp eyes to make out this first sign of life, the first hint that the gods, after all, may not have deserted him. Julia crawls along the row on hands and knees, and stops a dozen feet further along.

'Here's another one!'

Abandoning all sense of dignity, Manilius crawls after her. The child is right! After that they count another twenty vines showing their first swelling buds, after weeks of worry and despair. Manilius jumps to his feet.

'They have taken! They are growing!'

He picks Julia up and throws her into the air. They are both shrieking with triumph, so that the Israelite farm hands come running.

'Another top dressing of manure,' Manilius says, 'and water it well in. Then come up to the house to celebrate. We'll broach an amphora of my best vintage, two years old, and drink to the future.'

Zakkai and the others exchange looks of relief and exultation. The success of the new vines means as much to them as to Manilius, for all their labour in the master's vineyard declares their stake in their new homeland.

Even in my room I hear them. Today is one of my better days. I am awake and sitting propped up with cushions in my bed, but aware for once of the sounds coming from the farm and of the sunlight flowing through the slats of the half-open shutters to make a geometric pattern on the floor, netted in the entwining shadows of the bay tree.

'I have brought your midday meal, *domina*,' says Rachel, coming in softly on bare feet with a tray of food. Speaking Aramaic, she is fluent and eager to talk. 'I thought you might be able to eat something more solid today. I have made lentils the way we used to do at home, with onions and cumin and coriander.'

'It smells good.'

I smile at her.

'I think my appetite has come back, a little, at least.'

Rachel straightens the cushions and lifts the tray onto my lap. Besides the dish of lentils there is a cup of chicken broth and some fresh raised bread, still warm and fragrant from the oven.

'What are they shouting about, on the farm?'

'The vines are coming into leaf. It was Julia who noticed first.'

'Oh, that's good! My son has been so worried.'

I can see that Rachel wonders how I could know this, having been lost in a dream world for days, sleeping or unconscious, but mothers have a way of reading their children's minds.

'The master would like to know whether you will take a glass of the vintage wine he has opened to celebrate? He has been very kind—he's sharing with all of us.'

'And that's only right, for you have nursed the young vines like infants. Tell Manilius yes, I will take a glass of wine.'

When Rachel returns, I have finished the broth and am eating the lentils.

'These are good, just how my mother used to make them. I'm afraid I usually overcook them.'

Rachel blushes with pleasure and sets the delicate glass of ruby wine on the tray. I lift it to the light, turning it in my hand.

'We never had glass to drink from, when I lived in the Galilee. We drank from pottery beakers. Though I remember some very fine pottery in Capernaum.'

'You know Capernaum?' Rachel asks eagerly. 'Our village was not far from there, a little to the west.'

169

'Not on the Lake of Gennesaret, then?'

'No, but only an hour's walk away. We often went there. When I was a very small child we once went to the *kenîshtâ* in Capernaum, to hear Yeshûa ben Yosef preach, him they say was the Messiah and was killed by the high priest and the Romans. He did wonderful things! I saw him lift up a lame man, and he could walk again, and he touched the eyes of a blind old woman and she could see! He was wonderful! I think it was wicked that they killed him.'

'Yes, he was wonderful. And it was wicked.'

'Did you see him too, *domina*? I did not realise.'

Rachel's eyes are glowing, her hands clasped to her heart.

'Are you,' I ask gently, 'a follower of the Christ cult?'

At once the woman's face clouds over and she lowers her eyes.

'Zakkai thinks it is too dangerous.' She looks up again suddenly and her eyes are bright with excitement. 'But I believe he did come to save us. I *saw* him!'

I point to my clothes chest.

'Will you bring me something? In the chest there, towards the bottom, on the right. A cedarwood box, a little larger than a man's hand.'

'Is this it?' Rachel carries the box over to the bed. 'Oh, it's so beautiful! The star of David inlaid in ivory.'

She runs her finger over the inlay, then turns suddenly white and trembling.

'Are you unwell?' I ask.

The woman shakes her head as she places the box on the bed.

'No. I felt for a moment . . . I do not know. Strange. Will that be all, *domina*?'

'Yes, thank you, Rachel.'

As the door closes softly, I take the box between my hands and caress it.

§

Yeshûa looked startled—and angry—when he saw Yehûdâ and me walking towards him along the beach at Capernaum.

'So you have followed me,' he said, squinting up at us against the setting sun. 'I did not ask you to come with me, Yehûdâ. I'm not sure that this path is for you.' He turned towards me, frowning. 'And you, Mariam? Have you travelled all this way, alone with Yehûdâ? Does our mother know you are here?'

'No,' I said, sitting down next to him, relieved to rest my feet. 'No. She does not. Nor any of the family. Though by this time, I expect they will have guessed. You must not blame Yehûdâ for my actions. He left on his own to follow you and to protect you against attack. You should be grateful to him. I ran after him without his knowledge or consent. After what happened . . . I could not stay in the village.'

'You were alone with Yehûdâ all night?'

'I was. But surely you know that your oldest and dearest friend is a man of honour!' I could feel the colour flushing my cheeks. 'I come to you, my brother, as safely as if I had travelled under your own protection.'

He looked from one to the other of us, then nodded slowly.

'Perhaps this was meant. Not men only, but women also.'

'Mariam,' said Yehûdâ, cheerfully ignoring him, 'these are the friends we made before, when we came to Capernaum. Ya'kob and Yôhânân, brothers, and sons of Zebedee.'

He looked around.

'Where are the other brothers, Shim'ôn and Andreas?'

Yeshûa pointed to one of the larger boats, which was drawing near the shore.

'How was the fishing?' Yehûdâ called to them.

'Poor!' shouted one of the men in the boat, a stolid-looking man, a little older than my brother. 'Never a fish in sight. We have fished all night and all day and caught nothing. They must all have fled away to the eastern shore.'

'And I promised Mariam a meal of the finest Gennesaret fish tonight,' said Yehûdâ, giving me a sly glance. He must have noticed my earlier look of distaste at the mention of fish.

Yeshûa stood up and pointed to a spot a little way offshore and to the right.

'Put your net down there, Shim'ôn, and it will come up full.' He turned to the brothers called Ya'kob and Yôhânân.

'Launch your boat and help him, for there will be too much for one boat alone.'

Shim'ôn let out a bellow of laughter, which rang across the water.

'You're become a fisherman now, are you, Yeshûa? And know the ways of the fish better than we?'

My brother merely smiled.

'Oh, let's humour the lad from the mountain village,' said Shim'ôn, and the brothers turned their boat to row out to the place where Yeshûa had pointed. The other two fishermen sauntered down to their boat, in no great hurry.

We watched as Shim'ôn and Andreas threw out a huge net that came to rest in a circle, with its edge buoyed up by floats. Suddenly the water within the circle began to churn like boiling milk. The two men in the boat struggled to hold the net steady, then Shim'ôn dived off the gunwale into the lake. He was, I could see, stark naked.

'What is he doing?' I asked.

'That kind of net is called a *mehatten*,' Yeshûa said. 'The bottom is held down with weights. Shim'ôn will dive to the bottom of the net, then draw it together and tie it off, so it forms a bag.'

Shim'ôn's head appeared above the water again and he flung himself into the boat. Both brothers began waving frantically to the other boat to come to their assistance. We could see, even from the shore, the vast waterfall of fish they tipped first into one boat and then into the other. All four men were hip-deep in thrashing silver fish. Some flopped over the side and swam away.

'The boats are sinking,' Yehûdâ said quietly, giving my brother a strange look.

'Better light a fire,' said Yeshûa, 'and find some sticks to sharpen. I think Mariam will have her fish after all.'

The two boats made it safely to shore, though the water was lapping over the gunwales. Seeing me sitting there, Shim'ôn had hastily knotted on a loincloth, but none of the men wore tunics and I tried to avoid looking directly at them. Other fishermen came hurrying along the beach, calling out to their wives and children in the houses along the foreshore. Soon it seemed as though all of Capernaum was on the beach, the women gutting the fish and packing them with coarse salt into barrels as quickly as the men unloaded them. Everywhere there were shining heaps of fish and the air was suddenly filled with gulls swooping down to seize the fish guts.

'Is it always like this?' I whispered to Yehûdâ.

He shook his head.

'Never.'

Shim'ôn's wife had gutted a pile of the finest fish, which she laid on a straw mat and smeared with oil, in which I could see flecks of herbs. Shim'ôn speared them on sharp sticks and thrust these at an angle deep into the ground beside one of the fires. For fires had sprung up all along the beach. Girls were bringing out stacks of unleavened bread and the fishermen, once they had unloaded the boats and spread out Shim'ôn's net to dry, carried great jars of wine and *shechar* down from the houses to the beach. As I sat beside my brother on the ground, sipping the rough wine, I thought that the smell from the cooking fish was not unpleasant. In fact, my stomach groaned a little in anticipation.

The fish were quickly cooked and I was handed a wooden platter holding a whole fish. I looked at Yeshûa enquiringly. He chopped the head off with his knife and threw it over his shoulder into the bushes, where two dogs began quarrelling over it.

'Just pull the flesh off the bones with your fingers,' he said. 'Take care not to burn yourself.'

Tentatively, I put a small chunk in my mouth. It melted away on my tongue. It was dill that Shim'ôn's wife had mixed with the oil, just a fragment, which blended with the delicate taste of the fish. Yehûdâ grinned at me across the bones of his first fish. Already he was reaching for another.

'Manna!' I said. 'I am converted!'

My brother shook his head at me, and laughed aloud.

That first night in Capernaum, Yehûdâ lodged with Shim'ôn, while Yeshûa and I went home with the brothers Yôhânân and Ya'kob. Their father Zebedee was also a fisherman and their mother, Salome, was a plump kindly woman who exclaimed over the state of my feet, which she washed tenderly and salved. I was given a small attic room to myself, where I laid out my bedroll and after the briefest *berâkâ*, fell soundly asleep. The long walk and the festive meal on the beach had exhausted me.

The next day, after I had helped Salome with her household tasks, I set out to explore the town. It was larger than I had thought at first, stretching back some distance from the lake, with a bustling market, such as I had never seen before, at the gateway in the northern wall. Country people had come in from the villages round about to sell their produce at stalls they set up there—planks laid across trestles, with a canopy above to protect them and their goods from the sun. A caravan of about twenty camels, with their drivers under the direction of a merchant in the bright clothes of the Bedouin, had taken up a position at one side of the market, while he bartered goods with the townspeople. Then the camels heaved themselves to their feet and began to plod away along the road leading north.

'Where are they going?' I asked the woman at the nearest stall.

'Damascus, probably. They come through all the time, between Damascus and the Middle Sea. Will you have some of my new peaches? Picked fresh this morning!'

I shook my head.

'I'm afraid I have no money. Not even a *pruta*. I came to Capernaum only yesterday. I expect I will have to find work.'

It had not occurred to me until that moment. Yehûdâ had some money, but Yeshûa was probably as penniless as I. How were we live?'

The woman smiled.

'Here. Have this one. A gift to welcome you.'

I thanked her and walked on, the peach's furry skin warm in my cupped hand. The soil here must be much richer than the land round my own village, for the houses had gardens abundantly filled with fruit trees and every tiny square or crossroads was shaded by a flourishing fig or pomegranate. There were several springs, where the water was piped through a stone conduit or carved lion's head, falling into a basin below, so that the women could fill their jars from the water spout, instead of needing to haul it up from beneath the ground with a bucket on a rope, as we did in our village. At these natural meeting places, and in shady corners, there were stone benches where the townspeople sat and gossiped, as if there was no work to be done, even in the middle of the day! In one small square I saw that there was a stone table with the board for the game of kings carved into it, and two men of working age sat there playing. Outside several of the houses stood large pottery jars overflowing with exotic flowers of a variety I did not recognise.

I wandered back at last to the shore and found a spot where I could sit on a rock out of the sun and watch the fishermen at work, while I slowly ate my peach, which was sweet and juicy and larger than a man's fist. After last night's astonishing catch, most of the men were not fishing, but were mending their nets, using wooden netting needles rather like the shuttles we used for weaving. Two men had turned their boat upside down and were caulking the seams. Just one man was fishing, not from a boat but standing thigh deep at the edge of the lake. He wound the net round his arm, then flung it out with a beautiful sweeping gesture, so that it fell in a smooth arc into the lake. It looked so effortless, yet I was sure many years' skill lay behind it. He drew the net in again. There were a few fish wriggling inside. The small ones he tossed back into the lake, the larger ones he dropped into a basket floating in the water beside him and secured by a cord around his waist.

After a time he waded ashore and I recognised the man Shim'ôn who had teased my brother the evening before. He tipped his fish into a small stone cistern in front of his house, laid his net carefully spread out to dry in the sun, and walked over to where I was sitting. I was not quite accustomed to seeing these men wearing nothing but their loincloths, and I averted my eyes.

'Well, sister of Yeshûa, what do you think of our town?'

'It's very lovely,' I said. 'And people seem well and prosperous.'

He shrugged. 'Sometimes. We are not always so fortunate in our fishing as we were last night.'

I could sense the question behind the words. He seemed a blunt, simple man, but even so he hesitated to ask me directly about that odd event.

'I expect you would have found the fish yourselves, if you had happened to cast your net there,' I said.

He shook his head.

'We had gone back and forth, all along the shore, both far out and close in. Not a fish.'

He was staring out at the lake, his hands on his hips. I saw that the casting of those heavy nets, and hauling them in when they were full of fish, had given him strongly muscled arms, like a labourer.

'Do you know what he calls me?' he asked suddenly.

I shook my head.

'*Kêphas*. The Rock.' He gave a bark of laughter. 'Thinks my head is as heavy and dull as a rock, likely.'

With that, he went off home.

By the time the next Sabbath came, the three of us were quite settled in Capernaum, Yeshûa and I at the home of Salome and Zebedee, and Yehûdâ still with Shim'ôn 'The Rock'. I had raised with my brother the question of finding employment, but all he had done was to smile sweetly and say, 'The Lord will provide.'

I bit my tongue to stop myself pointing out that it was Salome and Zebedee who were providing, not the Lord, and instead did what I could to help Salome. She seemed to hold my brother in a sort of awe since the episode of the boats sinking under the weight of fish. Me, she treated like a daughter, and when I asked if she would show me how to make the delicious sweetmeats and cakes she served after every meal, she set about teaching me. Yeshûa had been invited to preach at the *kenîshtâ* on the Sabbath, so we made our way there with Zebedee's family, meeting up with Yehûdâ, Shim'ôn and Andreas on the way.

'Shim'ôn's mother-in-law is very ill,' Yehûdâ said to me. 'They're worried about her. Shim'ôn's wife has stayed at home to care for her.'

For myself, I was worried about what might happen in the *kenîshtâ*. Were we about to be driven out of town again, if Yeshûa said something that the townspeople took amiss? I hardly heard the first part of the service, sitting with my hands clenched between my knees, dreading the moment when my brother stood.

At first all was well. He did not offer a learned and detailed commentary on the scriptural passage he had read, as the elders of the *kenîshtâ* do. He did not quote cryptic passages from the Book, as he had done at home in our village. Instead, he began to talk as if he were sitting under the awning on some family's terrace, cracking nuts and drinking *shechar*.

'My friends,' he said, reaching out his arms to us, 'I have come to tell you of a new world that is soon to come, a kingdom of righteousness.'

His eyes were alight, his smile as warm and embracing as the gesture of his arms.

'Think of it! A kingdom of righteousness! What does that mean?'

He seemed to invite us to answer, but we looked at each other, tongue-tied. It was impolite to interrupt the speaker in the *kenîshtâ*.

'Or let us think of it like this—What is *wrong* with the world now? Men are poor and cannot provide for their families. Women are bowed down with labour from dawn to dusk. Children wander the streets in rags, their bellies swollen with hunger, their diseased eyes the nesting places for flies. Is this right? Is this what the Lord God wants for his children?'

There were a few soft murmurs, and one or two people shook their heads.

'We have rich men who feed the leavings of their feasts to their goats, while the poor lie, starving, at their gates. Our wild and hilly places are filled with outlaws, many of them men who were once as honest as you or I, but have been stripped of every possession by drought and famine and taxation. They live like wild animals, preying on their fellow men. Do you not know, yourselves, of some who have been driven from their homes, even here in the pleasant town of Capernaum? And it is even worse amongst the small farmers.'

My brother seemed to light up with his passion, and he filled the whole room with that light. He burned with a sudden powerful energy, as if it had been clamped down all the years of his confinement in the village and at last had burst forth into bloom, like a desert suddenly blessed with rain. I could feel a tension in the room, as if everyone there was holding his breath. In fact, I was holding my own breath, and let it out cautiously. Everyone there knew about these terrible things of which he spoke.

'You may say: What is this to do with *me*? I am a simple person. I have little enough myself. It is for the great men, the Sadducees who control the Sanhedrin, the priests and Levites, the tetrarch Antipas, the Roman occupiers, even the Emperor away in Rome, to change the world. What can an ordinary man like me, going about his daily work, do to change things? This is the way of the world. This is how it has always been, and that's how it's always going to be!'

More people were nodding now, grinning ruefully at each other, shrugging their shoulders. Of course that was how it was always going to be.

'No!' My brother slammed his fist down so hard on the reading stand that the scroll leapt and rolled sideways. It was only stopped from being defiled by contact with the floor through the swift dive of the *shammâsh*, who caught it as it fell.

Everyone jumped. There were gasps of surprise, and perhaps even of fear.

'A new kingdom of righteousness *will* come,' Yeshûa said, 'but only through *our own actions*, each and every one of us. We must all look into our hearts and cleanse them of sin. We must feed the hungry and shelter the widow and orphan. We must heal the sick and treat our neighbours with kindness.' He smiled around at everyone, suddenly gentle again.

'It is not necessary to be a rich man to give unto others.'

I was reminded suddenly of Daniel, crying out joyously, 'He wasn't a beggar, he was an angel!!'

I caught the eye of the woman who had given me the peach and smiled. She smiled back, and I began to relax. Everyone was listening attentively, nodding in agreement. Their faces were bright with interest and hope. They seemed to approve of what he said. I thought: *It helps that here they think of him as the man who helped the fishermen to a wonderful catch, however it was done. They do not see him as a nobody, the carpenter's son, setting himself up to lord it over them.*

I had relaxed too soon. There was a movement, a disturbance, amongst the men sitting near the door. A man stood up, wild-haired and wild-eyed. He shouted out, 'Let us alone!' His voice rose to a shriek as he clambered over the benches in front, thrusting people aside, and ran out into the centre of the room. He was shaking and sweating, great damp patches on his tunic.

'What have we to do with you, Yeshûa ben Yosef? Have you come here to destroy us?'

My brother stayed quite calm. He strode forward until he was close to the man, laying his hands gently on the man's shoulders and confronting him face to face. The strangest thing was that for a long time he said nothing at all. He merely fixed the man, who was surely possessed by *mazzíkím*, with a terrible intense gaze. After he had compelled the man to look into his eyes and not turn away, he called out, 'Hold thy peace and come out of him!'

The man fell writhing to the floor, then lay there, limp. I thought at first he was dead, but then I could hear his gasping breath, until suddenly he was quiet. Yeshûa reached down and helped him to his feet. The man stumbled and looked confused, but he was quiet and biddable as a good child. He went meekly back to his seat and sat down.

The rest of the congregation could contain itself no longer. A roar of noise filled the *kenîshtâ* and for a moment I thought they were going to attack Yeshûa, as our own villagers had done. Then I realised that their faces were elated, not angry. People left their seats and crowded round him, some simply reaching out to touch him.

Salome turned a shining face towards me.

'That man has been afflicted for years. No one has ever before been able to bring him peace. Your brother must be truly beloved of the Lord.'

I followed her out of the *kenîshtâ*, where I saw Shim'ôn talking urgently to my brother, holding him by the arm. Yeshûa was standing with lowered head, almost like a man ashamed. Then he nodded and followed Shim'ôn in the direction of the shore.

'Mariam.' It was Yehûdâ, his face excited. 'Come with me. I think we may see something remarkable.'

When we reached Shim'ôn's house on the foreshore, a crowd was already gathering around it, but they made way for us, whispering, 'It's his sister and his friend.'

We followed Shim'ôn's brother Andreas upstairs and stopped outside an open bedroom door. Inside I could see a woman lying very still in the bed.

'It's the mother-in-law,' Yehûdâ whispered. 'This morning the fever was so high, they thought she could not live.'

I saw my brother step up to the bed. He leaned forward and took the woman's hands in his. He seemed to say something, but I was too far away to hear. He passed his hand gently over her face. Then he and Shim'ôn helped the woman to her feet. For a moment she looked about her uncertainly, then she patted her hair into place, and put her hands palm to palm, to greet my brother formally. As she walked steadily towards us, looking as healthy as any woman I have ever seen, a gasp went up from our little group beside the door, which parted to let her pass.

'Andreas,' she said, 'tell the maidservant to lay out the Sabbath meal for our guests. We will eat at once.'

Could this woman have truly been as ill as her family seemed to believe? I did not know what to think, for I saw no sign of illness about her.

We ate a peaceful cold meal with Shim'ôn's family, as was fitting for the midday of a Sabbath, and afterwards sat talking quietly under the vine arbour at the back of the house, looking out over the lake, which was also bathed in calm, for no boats would put out on the Sabbath. Shim'ôn's mother-in-law presided over the meal as though she had never experienced any illness, and no one spoke of it, though while we spent what was to be our last tranquil afternoon I noticed one or other of the guests stealing covert glances at Yeshûa.

In my own mind I was confused. Three times in the space of less than a week I had seen my brother do something strange. I had caught the word 'miracle' as we left the *kenîshtâ*, but could that be true? Yeshûa himself had told me of the cures he had studied while he was at Qumrân. I knew that these had including the calming of madmen and the casting out of the *mazzíkím* that possessed them. Were these miracles? I had heard of holy men who had had God-given powers, like Honi the Circle-Drawer and other miracle-workers, who had lived not long ago, in our grandparents' time, not back in the misty past of Abraham and Moses. And the glut of fish? Well, perhaps it was just as I had said to Shim'ôn the other day—the fish were there all along, and the fishermen could have found them, had they looked in the right place.

As dusk fell and the Sabbath came to an end, our party began to stir and break up. The fishermen talked of preparing their boats to go out on the lake for a night's fishing. Sometimes they would set a flaming torch in the bows of the boat to attract the fish, and they were discussing whether tonight would be a good night for spear-fishing by torchlight. Shim'ôn's mother-in-law was anxious to set about the household tasks that had been neglected while she was ill, but would not do so while we guests were present. It was then that we heard a growing noise of voices approaching the front of the house. When we walked round to see what was afoot, we were met by a press of people, crowding into the narrow street in front of the row of fishermen's houses. Some carried torches, which distorted their faces into grotesque bumps and hollows. I saw that some had rashes, others were lame, many had the unmistakable signs of blinding eye diseases. Some had made their way here on foot, others had leaned on the shoulders of their friends, some were even carried on litters.

'There are people here who are not from the town,' Shim'ôn whispered to Yeshûa. 'How can they have heard so quickly?'

Somehow, even on a Sabbath, when no man is permitted to travel far, word of what had happened in the *kenîshtâ* had reached the nearby villages. Perhaps the healing of Shim'ôn's mother-in-law, though in a private house, had also become known. I saw my brother recoil as the crowds pressed forward, almost crushing him against the front of the house.

'Heal me, master, I beg of you!'

'Please, lord, my child is lame!'

'Master, let me see your face, cure my blindness!'

Hands were reaching out towards him, groping, fumbling, tugging at his clothes.

Under the light of the torches, Yeshûa was as white as newly bleached linen. I realised that, like me, he was afraid. Partly I was proud that so many came to honour him. Then the crowd surged forward again and their excitement and hope flowed out towards me like a great wave, but I began to panic. There was such desperate urgency in their cries, they looked as though they might rip him apart, limb by limb, if he did not feed the hunger of their need.

I was terrified.

'Mariam!' Yehûdâ caught me by the arm. 'I'll take you away from here, back to Zebedee's house.'

I shook my head.

'You must stay with him. He will need you.'

'Are you sure? Will you be safe? Promise me that you will go straight back there.'

'I will go round by the beach. And Yehûdâ . . .'

'Yes?'

I did not know what it was I needed so urgently to say. All I could manage was: 'Look after him.'

It was late by the time they returned, Yeshûa and Yehûdâ and the four fishermen. Salome, Zebedee and I had waited for them, sitting silently around a table in the light of a single oil lamp. Even here we could hear the sounds of the crowds from along the street. Sometimes exultant cries reached us, sometimes what sounded like groans of despair. At last the six of them came in, all looking dazed, like the survivors of a terrible storm or an earthquake, Salome and I served them wine and a supper which had been keeping hot by the fire. No one spoke much until they had finished, then Yeshûa looked round at the fishermen and Yehûdâ.

'Will you join me in this work?'

'Lord,' said Shim'ôn, 'we cannot lay on hands and heal the people.'

I noticed that he no longer called my brother 'the lad from the mountain village'.

'I shall teach you to be a fisher of men,' said Yeshûa. 'In my name, I think you may heal them also, but much more important than that is to bring them the word. We must prepare Israel for the coming of the new kingdom. That is my mission. I am sent unto the lost sheep of Israel, above all to rescue sinners and persuade them to repent, before the final judgement.'

I shivered. There was a new note of conviction in his voice, and authority in his manner, that I had not seen before. It made the hairs on my arms rise.

'I will ask you to follow me throughout the Galilee, for it is here I must make a start. You must leave behind your homes, your wives and children, and live celibate and pure.'

At that, I saw Yehûdâ's eyes turn towards me, but I avoided them. This was not a matter to be discussed before others.

Shim'ôn alone spoke.

'If, when I have prayed and sought for guidance from the Lord, and when I have taken counsel with my family, then I will decide whether I will come with you,' he said simply. 'For now, I cannot say.'

'You do not refuse outright?'

'No. I do not refuse.'

Yeshûa looked relieved. I think I saw now why he called Shim'ôn 'Kêphas'. There was something rocklike and solid about the man, like the foundations of a well-built house. If he consented, the rest would follow.

The other fishermen nodded. I think none of them could have refused him, after the events of that extraordinary day. But to convince them to give up everything and follow him on some mission whose extent and purpose seemed unclear, that would demand all the powers of persuasion my brother could muster.

Later, when everyone else had gone home or retired to bed, I found Yeshûa still sitting by the embers of the dying cookfire. He was pale as death and shaking. Kneeling beside him, I put my arms around him and tried to still the shaking with the warmth of my own body.

'Oh, Yeshûa, what is it? Are you ill? All those sick people . . .'

He buried his face in my shoulder, so that his voice was muffled.

'I could not cure them all, Mariam. I could not cure them! And their cries of desolation, all hope gone, I cannot get them out of my head.'

'Hush,' I said, rocking him as he used to rock me when I was a child. 'Think of all those you *did* cure, how you have changed their lives forever. Had you not come here, they would have gone to bed tonight, as they have done every other night, blind, or lame, or bleeding, with corrupt flesh.'

'And besides,' he said, as though he had not heard me, 'my mission is to preach the new way, the true way to God, through love. Not to go about like a jobbing doctor, treating men's bodies and ignoring their souls.'

I held him away from me at arm's length.

'Do you not think,' I said, 'that if their bodies are healed and their pain taken away, they may more readily listen to the words you address to their souls?'

He smiled, for the first time that evening, and took my face between his hands.

'Little sister, my *talithâ*, sometimes I think you are wiser than all the sages of old.'

Then he kissed me on the forehead and got up.

'We must retire, for tomorrow, I fear, is like to be as bad as today, or worse.'

As we parted outside our rooms, he spoke softly, so as not to wake the others.

'Yehûdâ shall not come with me, for it is time your marriage took place.'

I shook my head.

'Of course Yehûdâ will come with you, and he will remain celibate as long as you ask him to. But you shall not leave me behind. Wherever you go, there also I go.' After that, he spoke no further of my marriage.

Chapter Eleven

It was as Yeshûa had predicted. For days the crowds of sick and maimed appeared outside the door, until the street was so crowded that it became necessary for them to gather in a field beyond the town. With the help of his followers, however, some order was introduced into these gatherings, and Yeshûa would first talk to them, before he began his laying on of hands. Mostly, he would tell stories, like those he used to tell us when we were children. Stories about shepherds and their care for their flocks, about husbandmen and their tillage and sowing and reaping, about stewards tending their lords' vineyards and wine presses. Always he spoke in simple terms, about the things he knew, and they knew, from daily life, then he would explain his deeper meaning, about love and kindness and compassion—the way to come closer to Yahweh.

I began to understand what he was doing. If he had preached as most men do—as I think our cousin Yôhânân did, and as Yeshûa had tried to do in our own village—speaking of nothing but moral issues, in vague and abstract terms, the people would soon have forgotten his words or, worse, would have turned on him and driven him out. But those everyday stories— and he was such a storyteller!—would lodge in their hearts.

I would sit on the outskirts of the crowd, listening to the stories and his explanations, gradually understanding more clearly what this changed world would be like, if he could bring it about. If only he could bring it about! I was excited by what he was proposing, for he made me feel that we were on the brink of a revolution, but a revolution such as the world had never known before. I was fizzing with happiness like new-brewed *shechar*, and caught myself sometimes smiling foolishly to myself. I would slip away before the healing began, because I saw how it distressed him, though I am sure no one else suspected, for he was always so patient and gentle with them. Also I'm ashamed to admit that the sight of all those diseased and maimed and devil-possessed people appalled and sickened me. And I began to

185

resent the time he spent with these strangers, so that Yehûdâ and I hardly saw him. I am not proud of these selfish feelings.

Soon after we came to Capernaum, Yeshûa, Yehûdâ and I were sitting one evening at the edge of the lake. It had been a hot day, overwhelmed with crowds of frantic people, and both men looked tired. I filled three beakers from a jug of pomegranate juice Salome had given me.

'Ah, I'm grateful for that,' said Yehûdâ as he took a long drink. 'There seems no end to these hordes of the poor and the sick.'

'Do you remember,' said my brother, 'many years ago? We talked then of the poor, in their despair and hunger.'

'I remember.'

'There are so many. More than I ever dreamed.' Yeshûa flung out his arms, taking in the whole sweep of land and water before us. 'How came there to be so many?'

'Blame the Romans,' said Yehûdâ.

My brother shook his head.

'It's easy to blame the Romans. We don't have enough to eat. *Blame the Romans*. The flock is destroyed by disease. *Blame the Romans*. The harvest fails. *Blame the Romans*. Old men become beggars on the streets of Jerusalem. *Blame the Romans*. Young men are driven to outlawry. *Blame the Romans*. The children die. *Blame the Romans*.'

'Exactly what I'm saying. An enemy occupying Judah. All these extra taxes . . .'

'No! It's much more complex than that. It's easy to blame the Romans, because that gives us an excuse for ourselves. Before the Roman occupation, had we no poor? Had they any more hope and comfort then? I think not.'

'But . . .'

'It's not just the Romans, Yehûdâ. The presence of the Romans merely masks the truth. The whole of mankind is cruel, selfish, warlike. Somehow it has to change.'

'You said the same all those years ago.'

'And you said that a village boy from the Galilee could not change the world.'

Yehûdâ smiled at him with affection.

'Perhaps I was wrong.'

We sat quietly, sipping the sweet juice as an evening breeze began to rise from the lake.

'But,' said Yehûdâ, 'there may be danger, Yeshûa.'

'Danger?'

'You keep telling these sick people that their sins will be forgiven.'

'The sick can only recover fully if their sins *are* forgiven.' My brother sounded impatient. 'There can be no other road to a final cure. I'm aware of the danger.'

'What danger?' I asked. 'I don't understand.'

'Only the priestly caste can forgive sins,' Yehûdâ explained. 'The power belongs properly to them.'

'And not,' said Yeshûa wryly, 'to a mere peasant from the Galilee. But I don't say that *I* forgive their sins. Just that they *will be* forgiven. I am no more than a channel for the works of the Almighty. I'm not trying to usurp the role of the priests.'

'Perhaps,' said Yehûdâ. 'But your nice distinctions will not be understood by many. I think you should be more careful.'

Yeshûa shook his head. 'I cannot otherwise offer them healing.'

He could sometimes be very stubborn, my brother. When he seized hold of a notion, he would clamp his jaws on it like a terrier.

'In any case,' he said, 'though they clamour for me to be their physician, my true mission is to bring them word of the new dispensation.'

'You were saying the other day,' I ventured, 'that one of the reasons you left Qumrân was that they were mistaken about the coming of the new kingdom.'

'Yes. They believe that the new kingdom will come about through a mighty battle between the Righteous and the servants of the Evil One—a terrible battle, full of weapons and bloodshed, mutilation and death. And only those who belong to the Community are Righteous. All the rest of mankind is enrolled in the ranks of the Evil One, willy-nilly. This is *not true*. I *know* it. All men are capable of goodness, worthy to be forgiven by Our Lord. The kingdom will come through love. For if we love not only our neighbours but also our enemies, how can the sons of men perish through warfare?'

Yehûdâ sighed and rubbed his tired eyes.

'I believe in your vision, Yeshûa. A vision of a better, kinder world. And I am more than glad to help you in your mission to bring it about. It will be beautiful and wonderful if we can change the world. But you must face the difficulties with honesty and accept the obstacles that lie in your path. I fear that not everyone will listen. You may not like to face the truth, but some men *enjoy* warfare and rejoice in blood-letting. If you can win them over, that will indeed be a miracle.'

I remembered these words a few days later, when a friend of Zebedee's had come to dine with us, an old man who now lived in Magdala, the village Yehûdâ and I had passed through on our way to Capernaum. Yeshûa and his followers had not yet returned from another session of healing the sick outside the town wall, and we were sitting under the arbour waiting for them. The grapes, I noticed, were nearly ready to pick, for the weeks of late summer had already flown past.

'Yes, they are saying he will be a new leader come amongst us,' said the visitor, whose name was Mihael. 'It will be like the days of our youth, Zebedee, though this leader is a man whose arm is strengthened by the Almighty One. Our enemies will perish by the sword as never before, and Israel will rejoice in her freedom.'

I suppose he must have seen the question in my eyes. All through my childhood I had heard tales of the many times that leaders had arisen in the Galilee, to battle against our occupiers, even before the Romans. The Romans saw them as violent insurrectionists and crucified them if they could catch them. We saw them as heroes, we were famous for them in the Galilee. But I had not known that Zebedee had been a revolutionary.

Mihael rolled back his right sleeve and held out his forearm to me.

'See that, sister of Yeshûa? That was a Roman sword thrust that nearly took my arm off!'

Diagonally across the arm, which was somewhat shrunken with age, a wide white scar ran from elbow to wrist.

'It must have been a fearful blow,' I said.

'Aye, it was that. I was lucky to live, and luckier still not to lose my arm. Zebedee here bound up my arm and dragged me off the battlefield, before they could come round and dispatch those of us who were not quite dead.'

Zebedee made an embarrassed, dismissive gesture.

'You were one of the Zealots?' I asked.

'Aye, both of us. Led by Yehûdâ the Galilean, as they called him, though he was born in Gamala. He was proud to be called a Galilean. And of course it was here in the Galilee that he mostly fought. And his father Ezechias before him, who was murdered by Herod. He was never a violent robber and outlaw, though the Romans and our great men—those traitors who sit at their tables—would have you think so. We too had our faith, our beliefs. But this brother of yours, he is surely come to lead us into the great and final battle, in which we shall drive the enemy into the sea.'

He gave a bitter laugh.

'Do you know what the Romans call the Middle Sea? *Mare Nostrum! Our* Sea! How like the Romans. Well, under Yeshûa ben Yosef the Galilean we shall hand them over to *Their* Sea. Let them inhabit their empire in its depths, and roll amongst the crabs and corals on the sea bed!'

He was excited now, his eyes gleaming.

'Old as I am, and my arm weakened for fighting, I'll follow Yeshûa the Galilean in the fight to liberate the nation of Israel!'

Zebedee laid his hand on Mihael's arm to quieten him, and turned the talk to other things, but I sat there wondering how many others thought as he did, and believed that my brother had ambitions to be a military leader. How little they understood him. Perhaps as his words were disseminated, things would change. But Mihael's remarks frightened me. The sooner we spread Yeshûa's message of peace more widely, the safer we all would be.

For Yeshûa was forming a clearer plan on how best to carry out his mission. As the days and weeks had passed, the first men to befriend him in Capernaum, the four fishermen, had somehow come to accept that they would travel with him when he left the town.

I was there when Shim'ôn gave my brother his answer.

'You have asked that I should give up everything, Master,' said Shim'ôn, 'in order to follow you. I have thought about this long, and with some misgiving. I have prayed for guidance. My wife weeps at the thought of my leaving, and at the uncertainty that lies ahead, but she does not forget that you saved her mother's life. She is grateful, and will accept my decision.'

'And what is your decision, my Rock?'

'I will follow, wherever you lead us.'

After Shim'ôn had made public his decision, the others soon followed.

'And what do you plan to do?' I asked my brother, as we sat over the remains of supper in Zebedee's house soon afterwards.

'We'll travel about the Galilee, mostly to the villages. I understand my own kind best. I will teach, and heal if it's demanded of me.'

'And the rest of us?'

'You will stay with me, and Yehûdâ also. But the others I'll send out in twos and threes into the surrounding countryside, to carry the message further.'

Yôhânân leaned forward eagerly.

'It would be better if my brother and I stayed with you, Lord. We are strong men of our arms. We can protect you from danger.' He shot a glance from beneath lowered lids at Yehûdâ, who had dined with us that night. 'Better than others, who are less able.'

Yehûdâ gave him an appraising look, but did not rise to the challenge. Salome snorted.

'Sons of your father!' she said. 'Your heads have been turned since you were boys by your father's stories of the Zealot uprising. Yeshûa's mission is a mission of peace. No swords and arrows are called for.'

'That's yet to be seen,' said Yôhânân sulkily.

I never knew quite what to make of this man. One minute spitting fire and brimstone, the next wandering off in a dream. A man of quarrelsome and violent nature, but weak in character. He was jealous of Shim'ôn's pre-eminent position amongst the fishermen, and jealous of Yehûdâ's position as Yeshûa's dearest friend. His unpredictable nature worried me.

Yeshûa went calmly on, as if he had not heard Yôhânân's interruption.

'Every week or so we will gather together again and move on. In that way we can cover the whole of the Galilee between us.'

He now had about a dozen committed followers, who were prepared to travel with him, as well as the many who had responded to his message but would not be accompanying us. There were also some with riches enough to give us a little money, to help us pay our way. Mostly, we hoped to find someone with whom we could lodge in the villages, but now that we were so many, we must provide for ourselves much of the time.

'Yehûdâ is the only one amongst with any understanding of money,' my brother said. 'We will hand over all funds to him, and he will be charged with purchasing supplies.'

One of our rich patrons was Yoanna, wife of Chuza, steward to the tetrarch Herod Antipas himself, who ruled in the Galilee almost like a client king to the Roman Emperor. I could not believe the news about Yoanna when Yehûdâ told me, but he swore it was true.

'A woman from the court?' I said. 'But how has she heard of my brother?'

'His fame is spreading. And that is good; yes, in many ways that is good. Though if there is too much talk of him at court, that may not be so good.'

'Particularly any of this talk about Yeshûa being a war leader. Some think he plans to lead a revolution to drive out the Romans.'

'You've heard that too? They don't understand him, and their folly could be dangerous for him. But this woman Yoanna does not wish merely to be a patron. She is going to join us, to become one of the followers. So you will not be the only woman.'

'Salome will come with us too,' I said. 'I think she feels that even a prophet and his followers will need meals cooked for them, and clothes washed and mended. Our calling also, to serve the Lord!'

And I knew that Salome would come because she wanted to keep those unruly sons of hers, Yôhânân and Ya'kob, in order.

It was about this time that I first noticed that the fishermen (not only Yôhânân), and the others like them in the group that had formed around Yeshûa, were not altogether at ease with Yehûdâ. He was different, I suppose. A rich man's son, educated and widely travelled. His knowledge of the world was much greater than theirs, though he never boasted of it, and even tried to conceal it. Besides, his speech was less provincial. He did not speak in the rough Galilean dialect that made the aristocratic Judaeans laugh and call us peasants. The others had taken to calling him 'Yehûdâ of Keriyoth', as though deliberately to set him apart. I am not quite sure what they thought of me. As Yeshûa's sister, I was honoured; as Yehûdâ's betrothed I was kept at a distance. And of course, as a woman, I was never part of that circle that closed round my brother, excluding me.

Our departure from Capernaum was postponed more than once, because of the crowds which continued to gather, and I saw that my brother was becoming exhausted as well as impatient to carry his message further. Then one morning I came downstairs at dawn to light the fire and bake flatbread for the morning meal, and he was gone.

No one knew where he might be.

'Surely he would not leave without us?' I said to Yehûdâ, when we had searched the town. 'After all the plans we have made?'

He shook his head. He was as baffled as I.

Later, when Yehûdâ and Tôma, one of the new followers, had gone to send the waiting people home, saying that their master would not preach that day, I went out of the town by the Damascus Gate and walked a little distance along the shore of the lake where it began to curve eastwards. And there I found him. He was lying asleep under the shade of some bushes, but when I knelt down beside him as quietly as I could, he sat up yawning.

'Everyone was worried,' I said.

'I needed to be alone,' he said. 'I have no opportunity to listen quietly for the voice of Yahweh, that I may know what he wants of me.'

'And have you heard him?'

'I came out early and watched the sun rise over the lake. We used to do that at Qumrân. It was the best part of the day. Their dawn hymns of praise to the Lord are very beautiful. I sang one alone here, as the sun rose in glory, and the waters of the lake shone like burnished gold.'

'It was good, then?'

'It was good. And I know what I must do. I am going to walk amongst the nearby villages for a few days quite alone, speaking to a few people, quietly helping any sick I find. That is a better way, a truer mission than these great masses of people crowding together. I feel trapped. And, I think, so do they.'

'Will you let me come with you?'

'No. You must go back and reassure the rest. Tell them that I'll return in a week or a little more, then we will all go forth.'

I did as I was told. I think this did not please the 'disciples', as they were beginning to call themselves—a Greek notion, 'students'. That was what they felt themselves to be, learning from the teachings of my brother. They thought I should have brought him back, or else told them where to find him, though that I could not do, as I did not know myself.

And a little over a week later he was back. Tired and subdued. For a short time he sat with Yehûdâ and me, before the others discovered he had returned and joined us.

'Well,' said Yehûdâ, 'did you persuade more to believe in your message?'

'A few. But I think I did something foolish.'

We both looked at him in concern.

'I healed a leper.'

'Surely that was good,' I said.

'No. He was nearly recovered already and desperate for the final purification. I took pity on him, and said, "Be thou clean". The man rejoiced, but I should not have done it. Only the chief priest is permitted to perform the final purification in a case of leprosy. I told him to say nothing to anyone, and to go at once to Jerusalem to the chief priest for the purification ritual, but if word spreads . . .'

'Yes,' said Yehûdâ. 'There will be trouble. You must be more careful, Yeshûa.'

He sighed. 'Well, our preparations are complete. We should set off within the next few days. But I have had a request from Jairus, one of the elders of the town. His twelve-year old daughter is on the point of death, and he has been here every day, begging for your help.'

I saw how tired my brother looked, but I knew he would never refuse to help a child. Not after the death of Daniel. Ever since Daniel's death, I knew he was haunted by the thought that he might have saved the life of his small brother. It was as if Daniel in his short life had made something clear to Yeshûa, illuminated some essential truth which was the foundation of his teaching. For the rest of his life, all children were precious to him.

By the time we came out of the door, a crowd had already gathered, and we set off across the town jostled and squeezed together through the streets. Suddenly Yeshûa stopped.

'Who touched me?' he said.

We looked at each other in astonishment. Some even laughed aloud. Dozens must have touched him in all that crowd. Then a woman fell at his feet, weeping. Her clothes were blood-stained and her face milk white.

'It was I, Lord. I brushed the fringe of your mantle with my fingers. I have bled without ceasing these many months, and I knew that your touch would heal me.'

'Daughter,' my brother said, 'your own faith has healed you. Go in peace.'

As we went on our way, I whispered to him, 'How did you know that she had touched you? How did you *know?*'

'I felt the power flow out of me,' he said simply. 'When Yahweh acts through me, I am nothing more than . . .' he looked across the street and pointed, 'nothing more than that conduit pipe in the fountain there.'

At the house of Jairus, we were told that we had come too late, the child was already dead. From an upstairs room we could hear the mother and the other women wailing in lamentation. Climbing up to the child's room, Yeshûa sent away all the mourners and went in with none but the parents and three of the disciples, Ya'kob, Shim'ôn and Yôhânân. I stood with the other disciples in the doorway and saw the look of agony on my brother's face. I knew he was thinking that, if he had not gone out into the countryside, he might have been in time to save the child. Had he misjudged, and failed again? And I saw the exact moment when his face lit up.

'The child is not dead,' he said, 'she is deep asleep.'

He took her hand and said, *'Talithâ, cûmi!'*

The girl opened her eyes and began to breathe. Yeshûa laid her hand down gently on the bedclothes and stroked her hair.

'Give her a little food now, some broth and milk, and she will sleep naturally afterwards. But I beg of you, speak of this to no one.'

I do not know if the parents broke their word, or some of the mourners who had been sent away, or if perhaps one of his own followers spoke of it, but by sunset everyone in Capernaum was whispering that Yeshûa ben Yosef had brought the daughter of Jairus back from the dead.

My brother promised to preach one more time in the *kenîshtâ* before we set out on our travels. By then the rich woman Yoanna had joined us, and another younger woman called Susanna, so with Salome and me there would be four women in the group travelling round the Galilee. As I came to know Yoanna, I found that despite her aristocratic upbringing she was a resourceful and doughty member of the group, never afraid to speak her mind. At first she suffered terribly from the blisters on her feet—not being accustomed to walking any distance, and certainly not on the rough surfaces of country drove roads and goat tracks. But she bore it with great patience and only the women knew what she endured in silence.

Susanna was one of Salome's lost lambs, the young childless widow of a fisherman, drowned during a storm on

Gennesaret, which had also robbed her of her father and brother. For many weeks she never spoke except in answer to a question, and kept her head veiled and her eyes turned down.

As well as travelling about the Galilee, we might also, Yeshûa said, take a boat across Gennesaret and visit the Decapolis. We were instructed to take very little with us, no more that a small bundle of belongings. A few, like me, wrapped these in a bedroll. Others vowed to live more hardily and carried no bedroll, nor even a staff to help them over the rough places. Yehûdâ insisted, however, that everyone should take a water skin.

'You and I know what can happen on a long journey on foot, without water,' he said to my brother. 'I do not forget that, when we met north of Qumrân, you were as shrivelled and dry as a fallen leaf. They must carry water.'

'The hot weather is nearly over,' Yeshûa said mildly, but Yehûdâ insisted and carried his point.

The *kenîshtâ* was so full that day that every seat was taken, people sat on the floor, and the doors were left standing open so that those gathered outside could also hear. Yeshûa spoke for a long time about the brotherhood of man, and answered questions, and entered into discussions with many of his listeners, who were eager to engage in cheerful debate. This was when he was happiest, talking informally amongst friends and setting forth his vision of a new kind of world, in which life on this earth became a kind of reflection of what the righteous might expect in the company of the Lord of the Heavens.

We began to hear a disturbance outside, but that was nothing unusual. I suppose we all thought at first that it was another hysteric, possessed by evil spirits, or some of the people arguing amongst themselves. Then one of the stallholders I recognised from the market pushed his way through the crowd that had now gathered casually around Yeshûa, who was arguing and laughing with them.

'Master,' he said, 'your mother and your brothers are outside and desire to speak with you.'

I saw then that my brother Ya'aqôb was elbowing his way through the packed doorway, with my mother beside him.

'He has run mad!' my mother cried out. 'My son Yeshûa is possessed. We have come to take him home.'

A gasp came from the crowd, and some began muttering angrily.

'Yeshûa!' Ya'aqôb shouted over the heads of the crowd, for he could force his way no further in. 'Yeshûa, your mother orders you to come home to your family, as is fitting.'

Yeshûa met his eyes from across the room and shook his head. He swept his arm out, indicating the whole of that crowded room.

'Behold my mother and my brothers!' he said with a laugh. 'They are here. For those who do the will of my Father in Heaven, they are my brothers and sisters and mother.'

Then he turned away. I saw my mother begin to sob. She drew her mantle over her face to conceal it. *Oh, that was cruel!* I thought. I pushed my way through the crowds and out into the street beyond. They were walking away, my mother and all my other brothers: Ya'aqôb, Yehûdes, Yoses and Shim'ôn. I saw that my father had no part in this. I ran after them and laid my hand on my mother's arm.

'Please, wait, Mother! He has not turned his back on you.'

She shook off my hand angrily. Her mantle had fallen back and she drew it forward, covering all her face but her eyes, which looked away, beyond me.

'Wait, Wait!' I stumbled after them, pleading. 'He speaks in symbols and stories, it's the way he teaches. What he meant was that *all* men and women are one family, one brotherhood.'

Ya'aqôb grabbed me by the shoulders and thrust me away.

'It does not depend simply on ties of blood.' I was sobbing, trying to find the words to explain. 'Of course he loves his family still. He loves you, Mother. But if we live in true faith with Yahweh, we all become part of the family of the righteous.'

She would not meet my eyes.

Ya'aqôb turned on me, his face twisted, his fists clenched as if he would strike me.

'I do not know you, woman. Who are you to speak to my mother thus? Some filthy whore, living openly with your paramour, with your brother as your pimp.'

I stumbled back, appalled at his vicious words, and could not speak.

My mother let her mantle fall from her face, which was blotched with weeping. The eyes she turned on me were cold and hostile.

'Go to your other family,' she said. 'You are no child of mine. You are an outcast and shameless. Do not touch me with your defiled hand.'

Then they turned their backs on me and walked away.

'Mother!' I pleaded. 'Ya'aqôb! Wait! You don't understand!'

They neither looked round nor slowed their pace.

Behind me, the crowds at the *kenîshtâ* were laughing and debating as if nothing had happened to disturb them. I turned away and fled down a narrow lane to the lake, then along the shore to a copse of fig trees, where I hid amongst the undergrowth, as I used to hide in the straw of the goat shed as a child. I lay with my face pressed to the dusty earth, and dry sobs shook me as if they would tear me, bone from bone, muscle from flesh. *I am lost!* I thought. *What have I done? What will become of me?*

Chapter Twelve

The room is quiet except for my own breathing, which is irregular, sometimes so faint that it seems to stop for minutes together, and at other times a painful, rasping sound. It reminds me of the sound of my father's saw, cutting through wood all those long years ago, and far away. I listen to the breathing as though it has nothing to do with me, but belongs to some creature in pain, for the pain seems also removed from me. As if I were floating in the air above the bed, I look down compassionately on the emaciated shape below and wonder whether I will actually be aware when the spirit separates from the earthly body. Perhaps they have already separated. But no. There is that breathing.

Although I rarely sit up and find talking difficult, for it interrupts that terrible laboured breathing, yet I have become acutely aware of other things. Instead of dwelling in a hazy, half-perceived world, I have found my senses sharpened. I can hear the minute scratchings of the mice in the walls of the house. I know the shadow of every leaf of the bay tree and would realise at once if someone were to pluck one from its stem. When I manage to eat a little, I can single out every ingredient in the cooking. Too much salt, and I am repulsed. And the skin of my arms, which seem to lie lifeless on the thin summer blanket, has become as sensitive as a blind man's fingertips. Every tiny motion of the air is as tangible to me as the waves of the sea.

At the moment I am concentrating on scent, and close my eyes in order to savour it more delicately. Three or four days ago—or perhaps it was longer, my sense of time, unlike my physical senses, has become blurred—three or four days ago, or a week, or two weeks, they whitewashed the kitchen. It is a long way from my bedroom, but the cheerful smell filled my nostrils for hours. Such a clean, renewing scent. It has almost faded now, just a faint undertone lingering in the air. Today there is a new scent, one even more hopeful. The scent of new-cut hay. The weather has been fine for days, so the hay is imbued with the wonderful stored fragrance of summer which it will cherish all through the bitter days of winter, holding its promise of the cycle of the seasons. I have always loved the smell of hay, with a quite ridiculous passion.

৵

Every year of my life there has been a hay-making, and they merge into one another, though they fall into a tripartite pattern. There were the years of my childhood and girlhood in the village, when I was one of the hay-makers as soon as I was big enough to wield a rake. Then there was the brief period when I followed my brother through the Galilee and Gaulantis, Phoenicia and Samaria and finally Judaea. We were not part of the labour then, but we moved amongst the hay-makers, my brother preaching and healing, and his chosen followers, the *shelîhîm*, carrying his message to hamlets and outlying farms. Salome and I and the other women would talk to the women who laboured with the men in the fields, who sometimes shared with us their cool buttermilk. And at last, the longest portion of my life, on our estate in southern Gallia, where in the early days I helped in the hay meadows, when Petradix had first begun to farm and could afford only one slave to work for him.

I remember one childhood summer with particular clarity, though it may be that the memory plays tricks and I am plaiting more than one together. Our fields lay below the village, around the lower slope of the hill, a short distance from the olive orchards. One was always put down to grass, to provide winter hay for the animals. On the others we grew wheat and barley and oats, and beans for drying. My father and brothers laboured in the fields when they were not in the workshop, and all the villagers helped each other at hay-making and harvest time. The village shared an olive-press and there were two wine-presses where the young men trod the grapes after washing in the ritual baths nearby.

The summer I remember, I must have been eight or nine, for it was not the first summer I had helped with raking the hay after the men had cut it. The women and older children would rake the hay into heaps, where it could cure in the sun. Every day or two we would come down again to turn the hay, tossing it with large wooden forks until it was dry enough to store. Then it would be tied in bundles on the backs of our donkeys—bundles almost twice as large as the donkeys themselves—and carried up to the village for storage.

I suppose I remember that summer with particular affection because for once (and it was rare) my two eldest brothers were at ease together. They were working beside each other, stripped to the waist, their arms swinging with the lovely rhythm of their sickles. I remember watching how the muscles of their backs rippled under the skin, like ripples on the river, and wondered if mine did the same as I followed along behind them, raking the hay together. I thought ruefully that probably my muscles did not show, for I was a little plump at the time, a plumpness I lost long before the time of my fasting, never to regain it. Yeshûa and Ya'aqôb were laughing together at some joke I had not heard. Usually I would have felt hurt at being excluded, but I was so happy at seeing them friendly with each other that I did not mind. I wished it could always be like this. I wished that Ya'aqôb was not always so severe, constantly finding fault with the rest of us.

Looking back now, after all these years, I realise that Ya'aqôb must have been unhappy. He yearned somehow for greatness, but must have known he did not have Yeshûa's gifts. Not merely his gift of a quick scholar's mind, but his vision of a new kingdom, his closeness to Yahweh, his sense of mission, his gift of healing. Ya'aqôb studied the Law with the dull pedantry of a man with dogged determination but no true illumination. He followed the minute rituals of the Pharisees with a kind of blind devotion, and could not understand how Yeshûa could sweep them aside in a joyous affirmation of a different kind of dispensation, in which love, compassion and brotherhood replaced the trivial rituals of washing hands and rigidly segregating dishes for different types of food. That terrible moment in Capernaum, when my mother and brothers walked away, it seemed our family would be forever rent in two. Yet afterwards, too late, after my brother's death, Ya'aqôb and my mother joined the Christ cult. By then, of course, I was far away.

When we set out from Capernaum on the first stage of our mission to the countryside, we were soon caught up amongst the *amê hâ-'erets*, the local sons of the soil. That year, hay-making was over, and most of the grain harvest too, though men and women were still working in the fields, finishing the work of the harvest and ploughing the earth for the next sowing. As chance would have it, in our early days and weeks we travelled through areas where there were large estates belonging to wealthy landlords, many of whom did not live in the country, but dwelt in fine houses in Sepphoris or Scythopolis or Antipas's new city of Tiberias. The farms were worked by labourers, many of whom had once owned land of their own, which they had lost through the grinding taxes. The Temple taxes alone were a heavy burden. But the Roman Emperor demanded tribute taxes from the tetrarch Herod Antipas and these were then exacted on his behalf from every farmer, fisherman, craftsman and trader, however poor. It was hopeless trying to evade them. A farmer might not even remove a shovelful of his own grain until the tax collector had extracted his due, for the official would press his mark into the pile of grain as soon as it was harvested. The removal of even a spoonful would cause the pile to shift and the moulded mark to collapse, so that double taxes would be imposed.

The *amê hâ-'erets* we saw labouring over the last of the harvest were being worked like slaves in their own land, like our forefathers making bricks during the captivity in Egypt. I do not know if all farm stewards were so cruel, but where we went that summer the *amê hâ-'erets* were ragged and starved and worked terrible hours, day after day. Yeshûa went amongst them, and sent out his *shelîhîm* further afield, preaching redemption through love, promising a better world in which the poor would be raised up and comforted, the rich cast into everlasting despair. Of course they listened eagerly, for such a message brought hope into their wretched lives. We shared our food with them, poor as it was, nothing but a little bread and cheese and dried figs, and they wept with gratitude.

One evening we were gathered together at the end of one such day amongst the *amê hâ-'erets*, when the labourers had returned to sleep in the hovels on their master's estate. These huts were no more than straw mats thrown over a framework of rough branches, adequate now in summer, but in winter or during the heavy rains of autumn they would provide no more shelter than a bush.

'How can the Pharisees condemn these people?' Yeshûa demanded. He tore a piece of flatbread in half as if he were wrenching a Pharisee's head from his neck.

'They call them scum and rabble and sinners, just because they don't wash before every meal or practice all these new rituals which the Pharisees have added to the ancient Law.'

He poked at the fire with a dry branch, so that it flared up and lit his face, which was filled with fury.

'How can such people be condemned if they can't wash their hands? They can count themselves lucky if the overseer allows them to pause long enough to eat a few scraps of stale bread in the midst of a day of cruel labour in the fields.'

The end of the branch had caught fire and he held it up, his eyes fixed on the burning end, which crackled and sparked in the darkness.

'Did you see that lad today?' Yehûdâ asked quietly. 'The old man working beside him was falling behind. He was bent with the stiffness of age and couldn't gather up the heads of grain as fast as the others.'

'I saw him,' I said. 'The boy worked back and forth between the two rows, so the overseer wouldn't notice and punish the old man.'

'Exactly,' said Yeshûa, resting his chin on his up-drawn knees and staring into the fire. 'There are good men and bad amongst the *amê hâ-'erets*, just as there are anywhere else in the world. But that young man showed true loving-kindness.'

'But, Master,' said Yôhânân, who would wriggle his way into the conversations of others whenever he could, 'the *amê hâ-'erets* are all very well, but should we not pursue our mission amongst the men of power? Should we not go to Jerusalem?'

Yeshûa paused a long while before answering him.

'That time will come.'

When we encountered Pharisees in our travels, and they remonstrated with Yeshûa for eating with these unclean sinners, he argued in the same way, but they still condemned him. They claimed that he was destroying the true devotion and religious practice of Israel, that he was shamed before the Lord.

As winter set in, we returned to Capernaum. We had not been there many days when a few of us received a startling invitation.

'We are invited to dine,' said Yeshûa, 'with Mattaniah and his wife at his house. Myself and four others. I will take you, sister, and also Yehûdâ, Shim'ôn and Yôhânân.'

We gaped at him.

'Mattaniah?' said Yehûdâ. 'The tax collector?'

'Even he.'

'But . . . a *tax collector*?'

I think there was hardly any class of man more hated at that time in the Land of Judah. The Romans, they were hated, yes. But the tax collectors were recruited from amongst our own people. Not only did they collaborate in the imposition of the oppressive taxes. Wherever they could, they forced more than their due out of the people, and kept the surplus for themselves. I knew nothing of the man Mattaniah, save that he was a tax collector, but I knew the reputation of his kind.

There was agitated discussion amongst the followers.

'If you think it right to go, then I will go,' said Yehûdâ slowly.

Shim'ôn was doubtful, frowning and grumbling. Yôhânân, I could see, was in a dilemma. He was always thrusting himself forward, wanting to be chosen as favourite by my brother, trying to put himself before Shim'ôn. He was flattered at being one of the chosen ones, but dismayed at the prospect of having to sully himself in the company of a sinful tax collector.

In the end, we went, those my brother had chosen, and Mattaniah seemed to me to be a man like other men I had met in Capernaum. He had a better house than the fishermen, but it displayed no sign of riches. The meal was good, but modest, his manner towards my brother eager yet humble. Perhaps, I thought, there may be such a thing as an honest tax collector, whatever men say.

When the meal was over and we prepared to leave, Yeshûa turned to Mattaniah and said simply, 'Follow me.'

Mattaniah took up his cloak, kissed farewell to his wife (who looked stunned), and followed us.

The others disciples were horrified. They felt tainted by this new disciple, who was to become one of the chosen *shelîhîm*, and they grumbled constantly to Yeshûa, until he told them sharply to hold their tongues.

'What profit is there in calling a righteous man to the Lord? I am sent to the sinners and lost sheep of Israel.'

I watched them work that out, for none of them were very quick of mind. And when they did, they were subdued and complained no more about Mattaniah.

As well as being a centre for fishing on Gennesaret, Capernaum was also a trading port. Not only did it lie on the caravan route between ports of the Middle Sea like Caesarea Maritima and the great inland city of Damascus (an important centre for the silk trade), Capernaum was also a port for goods passing back and forth across the waters of Gennesaret, thus connecting the cities of the Decapolis with the caravan route. Because of all this trade, the town was an important centre for the collection of customs dues, which had been one of Mattaniah's duties.

Although the Land of Judah was part of the Empire and under ultimate Roman control, the Galilee was ruled directly by Herod Antipas as tetrarch. This meant that, unlike Judaea, we had no garrisons of Roman troops on Galilean soil. Of course we saw them from time to time, marching across country, but in our daily lives we rarely encountered them. However, there was one task which brought Roman soldiers at certain times to Capernaum, and that was the transport of moneys collected in taxes or customs dues. Where taxes were paid in kind—grain or oil or wine—the goods were moved by ass or by ox cart to one of Antipas's palaces or some other collection point. It was too risky, however, to move the small but valuable chests of coin in this way, when there were so many outlaws and robbers at loose in the countryside. Therefore, a Roman centurion would bring a troop to escort the money at regular intervals.

One such man came to Yeshûa, and begged him to help his son, who was gravely ill. I never knew the man's name and I realise now that he was probably no more Roman than Petradix, who had also served not far away, in Syria. This man probably came from some other province of the Empire, whither he would some day return. Certainly he was one of the *gôyîm*, a pagan, a Gentile, and certainly he spoke execrable Aramaic. I have wondered why he had a son, since Roman soldiers are forbidden to marry, but many of them do form irregular liaisons. Twenty years is a long time to ask a man to remain celibate. And their women and children often follow them.

This man, this Roman centurion, bowed low before my brother, a mere Galilean peasant, and begged his help.

'I cannot ask you to come to my house, Lord,' he said, 'for it is too humble. But might you send one of your followers to see my boy?'

Yeshûa took his hand and look round at his disciples.

'See what faith this is! Go home, my friend. Your son is cured.'

I heard afterwards that at that very moment the child jumped from his bed and ran to meet his father.

෨

It is very quiet in the room. The breathing is fainter but more regular. The light is soft—it may be a little before dawn or perhaps early evening. Apart from the breathing there is a delicate watery sound, a murmur and hiss, almost beyond hearing.

'Is it raining?' she asks the empty room.

To her surprise, a voice answers.

'Yes. A good rain. Light but steady. It has been raining all day.'

'Sergius?'

'Yes, Mother?'

She forgets what she was going to ask him. She knows why he is here. He knows she is dying and has come from Massilia to be with her. She feels about the bedclothes and finds his hand.

'It will spoil the hay.'

'The hay is long gathered, Mother. It is the month of Augustus.'

'The vines. It will be good for the vines. The new vines . . . ?' Her voice trails away. It takes so much strength to speak, it is almost too much for her.

'The new vines are doing well. All but half a dozen are growing, and Manilius says he will leave even those in the ground until next year, to give them a chance.'

'Sometimes . . . Yeshûa used to say . . . For some, it takes a little longer . . . '

'Yeshûa?' His voice is puzzled. 'Who is Yeshûa, Mother?'

'Long ago. Long gone. He was your uncle.'

'I thought his name was Ya'aqôb.'

'Another uncle.'

It is so long before she speaks again that he thinks she has fallen asleep.

'We were a family of many sons,' she says at last. 'But Yeshûa was . . . different. Long dead. At your age. Crucified.'

'*Crucified!*'

The shock runs down his arm to her hand.

She cannot speak any more. Too tired.

He was so young. I am twice his age. What would he think of the world now? Of the Land of Judah destroyed by insurrection and war? Of a Christ cult that worships an instrument of torture?

'Is it raining?' she asks.

๑

There was a sinful woman. It was whispered amongst the disciples that she was a prostitute, and I saw the shiver of fascinated dread the word evoked amongst them. But I had not forgotten what Ya'aqôb had called me—*filthy whore*—and I wondered what kind of woman she might be.

We had been invited to dine at the house of a local Pharisee called Shim'ôn, a double-edged honour, for we knew that he intended to trap Yeshûa in some breach of the Law. Towards the end of the meal, the sinful woman managed somehow to slip past the doorkeeper and enter the room where we were dining. As this was a strict household, the women of the party sat somewhat apart at the back of the room, but I saw everything that happened.

The woman was very beautiful, but gaudily dressed, and at first no one moved, struck motionless by shock and disgust.

I noticed that she was carrying a little alabaster box. When it was opened, I could smell the precious scent of spikenard it contained, even at the far end of the room where we women were seated. She fell down before my brother and anointed his feet with the costly substance, weeping. She had no basin, no towel, but that did not deter her. I watched, my mouth falling open in astonishment, as she washed my brother's dusty feet with her tears, then dried them with her hair. She had lovely hair, long and glossy and interlaced with multi-coloured ribbons, very different from my own tangled mane. She kissed his feet, begging him to forgive her sins.

At that, I heard the hissed intake of breath from the Pharisee's wife, who was sitting beside me.

'That woman is a strumpet,' she whispered in my ear. 'A notorious whore.'

And she signalled to one of the servants to take the woman away.

Shim'ôn the Pharisee was also gesturing angrily at the woman, shooing her off like a street cur.

'Why do you allow this accursed woman the freedom to touch you?' he asked Yeshûa in disgust. 'A woman whose very hands are defiled?'

'*You* did not anoint me with precious balm,' Yeshûa said calmly. 'Neither you, nor your wife, nor your maidservant washed my feet when I entered this house as your guest. Yet even amongst the poor in my mountain village we would do this service for a guest. This woman has bathed my feet with her own tears and anointed me with precious oil and dried my feet with her own hair. What she did, she has done from a loving heart, and so her sins are forgiven.'

The Pharisee grew red in the face with anger and embarrassment, but what could he answer? Neither he nor his family *had* shown any of us this simple courtesy. We left soon afterwards.

The woman begged to be allowed to join my brother's followers, and despite horrified misgivings on the part of some, he welcomed her. There were some who forgot his message of universal brotherhood, fearing that such an unclean woman would defile us. Others worried at the effect she might have on the younger men. There were many whispers and sidelong glances amongst the men, and a kind of *frisson* whenever she entered a room where they were gathered. I do not think that, at first, Salome, Yoanna and Susanna were comfortable in her presence, though they came to accept her later.

Yet from that day I never saw her behave with anything other than perfect modesty and decorum. She had come from Magdala, she told us, hoping to find the *rabbi*, the teacher, because something had told her in her heart that she must serve him for the rest of her life. Her name was Maryam, though when people wanted to distinguish between our similar names, they called her 'the Magdalene', the woman from Magdala.

When I was a child, learning to read, I realised that my name meant *mâr yâm*, 'bitter sea', and I wept a sea of bitter tears over it, for I felt I was doomed to a life of pain. But Yeshûa comforted me.

'Do not cry, little sister,' he said. 'Do not be so hasty, for there are many hidden meanings in a name. Did you not realise that your name can also mean *mir yâm*? That is "beloved of God". You are blessed in your name.'

I took great comfort from this at the time, but in my declining years I am apt to think that my first interpretation was nearer the truth.

Because of this coincidence of our names, I felt drawn to the Magdalene from the first. I was fascinated too by her beauty and her strangeness. And because I welcomed her wholeheartedly, she turned to me, so that I found in her a woman friend such as I had never had before. In the hard times that were to come, our friendship remained steadfast and grew into deep affection.

Not long after she joined us, I overheard Salome's son Yôhânân talking to my brother.

'It is surely not right, Master,' he said in his unctuous voice, which always made me grind my teeth. 'Women are lesser creatures. They have not the minds and souls of men. Indeed, I've heard it said that women may have no souls. Eve was a crude being, fashioned from Adam's rib, meant for nothing more than procreation. And she disobeyed the Lord and brought about Man's fall from grace. Such creatures are vile and unworthy to be part of your great mission. I beg of you, Master, have no more to do with them. Send them away! And above all, that piece of filth, that whore, that prostitute.'

Before Yeshûa could answer, I burst in upon them, crackling with rage.

'You serpent!' I shouted. 'You would pervert my brother's message and his mission to serve your own ends! Women have minds and hearts and souls as great and as fine as men. Yeshûa has said from the beginning that he comes to all people, men, women and children, rich and poor, sick and healthy. Who are you, you vile worm, to abuse women so!'

I gasped for breath, but before he could gather his wits to reply, I rushed on.

'Maryam from Magdala is good and kind and devout. She hurts no one. She slanders no one. What she may have done in the past has hurt no one but herself, and my brother has said that her sins are forgiven. Who are you to question that? You who speak evil of people behind their backs, while you set yourself up to be a model of virtue, which you are not.'

'Mariam,' said Yeshûa. 'Peace.'

Before Yôhânân could make an answer—and before I flew at him and scratched his face—I turned on my heel and ran off. No more was said of excluding women from the mission. Indeed, from that time onwards Yeshûa called on us more often to speak, both in the private councils of his followers and in public. Yôhânân's insinuations had made him more determined than ever that women should rank with men. The Magdalene was honoured and loved along with the rest of us. But neither Yôhânân nor I forgot the encounter.

It was spring, the month of *Iyar*, with fresh grass greening the slopes above the town and the orchard trees a glory of white and pink blossom. Our hearts were high and eager, for we were on the point of setting out again on our mission to the villages and farms of the Galilee, when the news came that I suppose we had all been dreading, although we never spoke of it.

Two followers of our cousin Yôhânân the Baptiser arrived unexpectedly in Capernaum and met Yehûdâ near the gate of the town. He recognised them at once and brought them hurriedly to Zebedee's house, where Yeshûa and I had just finished our midday meal. Salome brought food and wine for the strangers before leaving us alone in the room, which opened on to the terrace fronting the lake. The two men, Benyamin and Yitzak, barely touched the food, although they were travel-stained and exhausted.

'We have come as fast as we could from Machaerus,' said the older man, Benyamin. Yitzak was barely more than a boy and looked half crazy with fear.

'You have been with my cousin?' Yeshûa asked. He sounded calm, but his face was very white and I could see a nerve jumping in his temple.

'We were not with him, no. When he was carried off by Antipas's soldiers, we followed a little behind, and in all the months since, we have stayed nearby, as near as we could. I got work as a scribe in the office of the palace treasurer. Yitzak here was taken on as a scullery boy. No one in the palace knew that we are followers of the Baptiser.'

He took a deep drink of his wine, as if to give himself courage.

'Yeshûa, your cousin is dead.'

Yeshûa said nothing, but bowed his head and pressed his clenched fists against his lips. I think we had all guessed already that this was the news they brought, but even so we were shocked at the suddenness of it.

'Executed, in the end?' said Yehûdâ tensely. 'I thought it would not come to that. There have been stories flying about that Herod Antipas was much taken with Yôhânân's ideas, that he spent many hours in discussion with him. We thought that he would be released at last.'

'That was how it seemed to us, too. The tetrarch used to summon him most evenings to his private quarters and hold long discussions. Of course, we were not privy to them, but a ruler

211

does not usually debate religion and morality with a man he plans to execute.'

'Not usually,' said Yeshûa. He seemed to have difficulty in getting the words out, as if he could not breathe.

'But why?' I said. 'Why now, after so long? Surely, if he had intended to execute our cousin, he would have done it long ago.'

'The Baptiser has always been hated bitterly by the tetrarch's mistress, Herodias,' said Benyamin, 'because of his preaching against her.'

'That was most likely why he was arrested in the first place,' said Yehûdâ. 'Preaching about *metanoia*—that was something Antipas could probably have tolerated, but condemning him publicly as an adulterer went too far.'

'Yôhânân also gave some people to believe that he would lead a military uprising against the authorities,' my brother said in a tight voice.

'Well, that was not what led to his death in the end,' said Benyamin. 'You have not heard it all.'

He glanced at Yitzak, who sat trembling in a corner. I realised that the boy had not spoken a word yet.

'Herodias was determined on Yôhânân's death,' said Benyamin, 'and used her daughter Salome as a means to accomplish it. The girl is very beautiful, like some creature from another world, and Antipas lusts after the daughter even more than the mother. But her beauty masks a heart given over entirely to the Evil One.'

Benyamin passed his hand over his face, as if to wipe away some image before his eyes. I saw that his beaker was empty and quietly refilled it, though he was staring past me and did not notice.

'The girl danced before Antipas and his guests at a banquet. Danced like a common harlot, shedding her garments one by one, till every man in the room was hot with desire. And burning up with his lust, Antipas promised her whatever she wished. She got it.'

He drew a deep breath.

212

'Yôhânân's head served up on a platter, in the midst of the banquet.'

'What!' Yehûdâ leapt to his feet. 'Dear Lord God, surely nothing so filthy!'

'That is despicable,' I cried, for I could not contain myself, though I should have held my tongue in the presence of these strangers.

My brother said nothing, but he had gone even paler and his hands were pressed to his cheeks.

Benyamin lowered his voice to a whisper. 'The boy saw it all. It has turned his mind. I am taking him home to his parents.'

Suddenly the reality of what he was telling us rushed over me. It was no longer mere words. I saw before me the man's head, pooled in blood, lolling on a gold platter, the leering tetrarch holding it high in the air, the wanton girl feverish with triumph and with a lustful delight in death.

I rushed outside and vomited into the bushes.

Chapter Thirteen

The murder of our cousin meant more than the tragedy of his death alone. We had no time to grieve, for it presaged danger for all of us. At first Yeshûa seemed so stunned by what had happened that he could not tell us what we should do. It was like those times in the past, at home in the village, when he could not find his way, did not know how to direct his path. I had thought those days were gone. Ever since we had come to Capernaum, he had been so confident, so decided. Now the old uncertainty was back, and it would be a long time before my brother saw his way clearly again.

Finally that night Yeshûa announced a change of plan. Instead of going out into the Galilee, we would go by boat to Bethsaida, on the northern shore of Lake Gennesaret but on the far side, the eastern bank of the Jordan, thus lying outside the tetrarchy and within Gaulantis, that part of the realm governed by Herod Antipas's brother Philip, who had no great love for him. Here Yeshûa would preach the message as before.

We made the short journey the next day, Yeshûa, Yehûdâ, Salome, the Magdalene and I, in the large fishing boat belonging to Shim'ôn and his brother Andreas. The rest of the disciples followed in other boats. Despite the fear brought on by the message from Machaerus, I was excited at my first journey by boat and by the prospect of seeing a new region. I sat in the bows, on a pile of fishing nets, and tried to ignore their smell. The brothers had hoisted a sail, for the wind was favourable, and I found the dip and sway of the boat thrilling. As the sail filled, the ropes supporting the mast tautened and creaked, the boat quivered and came to life, like a breathing animal. It leapt forward across the lake, towards the distant outline of houses that was Bethsaida. The water surged under the bows, curling back with foam like flowing hair, and the music of waves on wood seemed to be the very voice of the boat. The Magdalene was clinging to the gunwale, her eyes wide with fright, but I felt exultant. I have never lost that wonderful lift of the heart when a ship comes alive.

People in Bethsaida welcomed us kindly enough. Philippos, one of the *shelîhîm*, was a native of Bethsaida and quickly found lodgings for us in the town. I thought we would set off shortly to travel through Gaulantis, but Yeshûa was in a strange mood and would come to no decision. His followers too were restless. Some of the newcomers had joined us in the hope that Yeshûa was about to lead an armed rising against the occupiers and establish this new kingdom he was promising them. I suspected that some of the *shelîhîm* themselves were instigating the unrest and the demands for my brother to make a political stand. The brothers Ya'kob and Yôhânân were always violent and troublesome. I watched them with distrust.

On the third evening, as I sat beside a garden window in the house where Yeshûa and I lodged, trying to take advantage of the last of the daylight for my mending, I caught the sound of stealthy footsteps on the dry earth outside, then a voice I knew to be Yôhânân's.

'Are we all here?'

There was a murmur of assent from several voices.

His brother Ya'kob said, 'Yes, we have weapons enough. I have left them in the care of the blacksmith. Some of the swords need sharpening.'

There was a laugh, then a voice I did not know. 'Sharper the better, for slicing off Roman heads.'

'We need to go carefully.' Another stranger's voice. 'You sons of Zebedee are over-eager. You will spoil our plans by rushing the Master. He must be persuaded, and it won't be easy. From what he says, he's set against violence.'

'It's that mealy-mouthed friend of his, Yehûdâ of Keriyoth,' Ya'kob sneered. 'All he will let the Master do is lead a gentlemanly preaching campaign, when what we need is to raise up all Judah and throw off the yoke of occupation. We can do it, *he* can do it, if we can only turn his mind our way.'

'The girl is part of the problem,' said Yôhânân. 'He won't do anything to endanger her. What sort of revolution is this, with women in the party? Trailing behind, dragging us down. Maybe we should put her permanently out of the way.'

In my alarm, I let my needle slip and stabbed my finger. I thought at first that I had given a cry, but then I realised that someone outside, someone perhaps on watch, had called out a warning, and the men in the garden slipped away.

I told Yehûdâ what I had heard.

'We must warn Yeshûa,' he said grimly. 'I have seen this coming, especially since we heard the news of your cousin's death.'

My brother did not seem surprised at the news, though I had persuaded Yehûdâ not to tell him of the threat against me. Yeshûa had enough to worry him.

'Some of the followers have already been urging this,' Yeshûa said.

He paced about the room, running his fingers through his hair.

'I have warned them,' he said angrily. 'I will have nothing to do with violence. Shim'ôn is steadfast, and Tôma, and Andreas, and Mattaniah, and many of the others. These lovers of the sword—surely they will lose the appetite for it in time?'

Yehûdâ shrugged, and I said nothing.

After some days, during which the demands grew more strident, so that my brother and my betrothed would not allow me to go outside unaccompanied, Yeshûa took Yehûdâ and me aside early one evening.

'I am afraid they will try to take me by force,' he said, 'to make me king, a king to lead a military campaign against the Romans, or even against the Israelite Sanhedrin. They are blinded by folly. Such violence is contrary to the will of Yahweh. I must escape. Hot heads will cool if I am not here. I need to spend time alone out on the hillside, praying and communing with Our Father.'

'What would you have us do?' Yehûdâ asked.

'You must all go back to Capernaum and await me there.'

Then he called a small group of the faithful *shelîhîm* into the inner room, not including Yôhânân and his brother, and told them what he planned. We were to tell no one, and we must make it appear as if Yeshûa was travelling back to Capernaum with us.

'Some of us should stay,' Yehûdâ urged, 'to protect you, in case of any danger from an assassin sent by Antipas.'

'I am willing,' said Shim'ôn, 'to go into the wilderness with the Master.'

I smiled at this, though I hid my smile, for it was a generous offer. To the fishermen, anywhere more than a thousand cubits away from the lake was a 'wilderness'. Others offered themselves as well.

Yeshûa refused them all, politely at first, then with growing irritation.

He went off at once, out through the darkened garden at the back of the house, abstracted and not even saying farewell to us. Yehûdâ and I exchanged glances. We could both tell that he was deeply troubled, by fear of Antipas, or by annoyance that his planned journey through the Galilee had been prevented, or by alarm at the way the mood of his followers was turning towards an armed uprising. It was decided, since it was well into the evening, that we would wait until tomorrow and return to Capernaum in the morning.

There was no great hurry to prepare the boats next day, especially as no breath of air was stirring. The men would have to row the whole way. A milky haze lay over the lake, so that we could see only a few cubits offshore, and could not possibly make out Capernaum until we were quite near. We set off at last, not crossing directly from one town to the other, as we had done before, but following the shore round.

'It may not be a great sea,' Shim'ôn explained, 'such as I have heard of beyond the western hills, but it is just as possible to lose yourself in the fog on Gennesaret.'

Many other boats followed us, and disappointed crowds who had hoped to hear and be healed by Yeshûa in Bethsaida also began to walk round the head of the lake. We had gone some way, perhaps nearly to Capernaum—how far, it was difficult to judge in the fog—when we made out a shadowy figure keeping pace with us along the shore to the right.

'There is my brother,' I said, pointing. 'He must have changed his mind and decided to return to Capernaum at once.'

The fishermen began to row closer to the shore. In the swirling mist, the land was altogether hidden, but as it shifted, parting and closing again, we could all see Yeshûa. Shim'ôn suddenly threw down his oar and stood up, making the boat rock.

'It is a miracle!' he cried. 'He is walking upon the water!'

'Your eyes deceive you!' I said. 'The fog is confusing. He is walking along the sandy strip, just in the water's edge.'

But the man was simple and credulous, and paid me no attention. He leapt suddenly off the boat, making it plunge dangerously first to one side and then the other, calling out as he did so, 'I too will walk across the water to my lord!'

Of course, he sank like a stone.

'Help me, Master!' he began to cry out. 'I will drown!'

'I thought he was a skilled swimmer,' I said to Yehûdâ. 'I have seen him dive to the bottom of the lake, to tie off the net.'

'Aye, naked. Now he is clad in tunic and mantle, with a workman's heavy boots. They are dragging him under.'

The other fishermen jeered at first, but when they saw that Shim'ôn was struggling and in real danger, they began to row as fast as they could, closer in to shore. Before they could reach him, my brother had waded up to his waist into the lake, then swum into deeper water and grabbed him by both arms.

'Well, Shim'ôn, my Rock,' he laughed, 'today you have lived up to your name.'

We rowed the rest of the way to Capernaum with two wet and shivering men filling the boat with water and soaking the rest of us. Yet afterwards the story went around that Yeshûa had indeed walked on the water and that Shim'ôn could not do so because his faith was not great enough.

Yeshûa had not told us of his plans after we returned to Capernaum. Dressed in dry clothes he once again preached in the field outside the town and healed the sick. But the crowds were much smaller than they had been. People had come from Bethsaida, but there were not so many from Capernaum. Yeshûa was a familiar sight now. He had either cured or failed to cure their sick. They had heard his message and were waiting, perhaps a little impatiently, for the coming of his new kingdom. Even the close followers, the disciples, continued to be restive. There was no more talk, for the moment, of an armed uprising, but when would the new kingdom of bliss on earth and reward for the righteous come about? Yeshûa was tense and quiet himself, for he could not make them understand that the kingdom he spoke about would only be achieved through their own love and compassion, and through their converting the rest of the people to the same way of life. It was a *metanoia*, such as our cousin had urged, though very different in kind. There was, to tell the truth, some lack of brotherliness even amongst the *shelîhîm*, who vied with each other to stand highest in my brother's favour.

We had been perhaps two weeks in Capernaum and Yeshûa had not told us what was to happen next. He still seemed unsure of himself. The sudden flight to Bethsaida, the demands made on him there to lead an armed revolt, the sudden unpredictable decision to return to Capernaum, and his lukewarm reception in the town had left us all in confusion. Everything was suddenly disintegrating.

I was in the market one day, purchasing vegetables for Salome. As I turned away from the stall with my basket of onions, new beans and chard, my sleeve was caught by haggard-looking man who was quite unknown to me. He bore the marks of a long and rough journey, his clothes stained and worn, his hair unkempt. He was clearly fearful, for he kept glancing over his shoulder and he spoke to me in a whisper.

'They tell me . . . Are you Mariam, sister to Yeshûa ben Yosef?'

'I am.'

'I come from Machaerus. I was a follower of your cousin.'

I drew him away from the stall.

'Come with me. I will take you where you can bathe and rest and eat.'

He shook his head violently.

'No. I must not stay. I am pursued. I have a message for your brother.'

When I reached the house of Zebedee, I left my basket inside the door and went out again in search of Yeshûa. I found him on the beach, playing with a group of the fishermen's children. For the first time since we had heard the news of Yôhânân's death, he looked carefree. As he caught sight of me, he tossed the ball he had been holding into the group of children and walked towards me. When he saw the expression on my face, all the light went out of his eyes. We walked further along the shore, till we reached the rock where I had sat eating a peach so many months before.

'I have a message for you,' I said. 'From Machaerus. Herod Antipas—perhaps he is a little crazed by guilt?—has been hearing of your preaching and your cures.'

I hesitated, biting my lip. Who wants to be the bearer of bad news? And this was more than bad.

'What is it, Mariam?'

'Ever since he murdered our cousin, it seems Antipas has been acting more and more strangely. He has persuaded himself that Yôhânân did not really die. That you are our cousin reincarnated and will bring vengeance and destruction down on him.'

I gulped. The man's news was terrifying.

'Antipas is haunted, possessed by this crazy notion. And rumours of an armed uprising have also reached him. One was here not half an hour ago, a follower of our cousin. He bade me warn you that Antipas has sent out bands of soldiers to search for you and kill you.'

'That jackal!' said my brother.

He clenched his fists and looked wildly around, as if he expected to see the soldiers coming towards us.

I pressed my hand against my mouth. 'What shall we do?' I whispered. I was aghast. My brother looked confused, uncertain, then he shook himself.

'We must leave, at once.'

'Yes, but where can we go? To Bethsaida again?'

'No. If it was from there that word of an uprising was spread, his men will look there. Although it lies within Philip's domain, there's nothing to stop a small band of assassins slipping into Bethsaida.'

He sat down suddenly on the rock and put his head in his hands.

'I wish no harm to any man, Mariam. My mission is one of love.'

'People have heard you preach against the rich and powerful.'

'Even the rich and powerful can become part of the brotherhood, if they give their wealth to the poor and take up the simple life.'

'Like Mattaniah?'

'Like Mattaniah. I must think, Mariam.' He pounded his fist against his forehead. 'We will have to travel far outside Antipas's jurisdiction. The time is not yet right to go down into Judaea. We must go either to Samaria or to Phoenicia.'

I looked at him, startled. Phoenicia was a land of Gentiles, of *gôyîm*. Samaria was a strange place, where some were descendants of Assyrians and others were Israelites, many of whom had intermarried with the Assyrians. They claimed to practise Judaism, but they chose to live isolated from the rest of us and had their own religious rites, abjuring the Temple rituals, which made them almost worse than *gôyîm* in the eyes of the rest of Israel.

'Tyre, I think,' he said, getting to his feet, suddenly decisive. 'We will go to Tyre in Phoenicia. A city large enough to lose ourselves in. If we move quickly, we should be able to keep ahead of Antipas's soldiers. When did the messenger leave Machaerus?'

'He did not say, but he looked as if he had travelled hard and fast. He thinks he too is pursued.'

'We will leave tonight, after the evening meal. Only the *shelîhîm* and the most devoted of my disciples.'

'And the women,' I said firmly.

'It will be a hard journey, over the mountains.'

'I am able,' I said.

'But Yoanna or Salome?'

'Perhaps not. Susanna and the Magdalene will come, I am sure. How long will it take?'

'If all goes well, and everyone can keep up the pace, about two days, I think, or perhaps three. We must ask Yehûdâ the best way to go. He has been there before.'

'Of course!' I was relieved. I had forgotten Yehûdâ's many journeys for his father. I would feel safer with his knowledge to guide us. No doubt if Yehûdâ had not been one of us, my brother would have set off into those mountains, trusting in the Lord to show him the way, but I was glad of a more earthly guide.

There were to be only twenty of us. After eating a substantial evening meal, we filled satchels with food and carried two water skins each, for Yehûdâ said that in some places the country was dry and barren, though elsewhere there were well-watered stretches where fruit grew abundantly. Susanna and I each carried a cookpot. The plan was that we should slip away from the town a few at a time, for we did not want to attract attention. Some townsmen who were hostile to Yeshûa—and there were such, even then—might put Antipas's soldiers on our trail.

It was well past nightfall before the last of us prepared to leave—Yeshûa, Yehûdâ, the Magdalene and I. Yeshûa had insisted that the others must be safely away before he would escape. Yehûdâ would not leave him unprotected and I had demanded to stay with them. Somehow the Magdalene had attached herself to our group, and I squeezed her hand while we waited for Yehûdâ to give us the signal to leave. My heart was beating fast, but I was not truly afraid. Not then.

Yehûdâ, who was standing beside the window in the darkened room at the front of Zebedee's house, overlooking the street, finally gave us a nod and we made our way softly to the back, so we could leave by the beach. Salome kissed us with tears in her eyes. Zebedee held open the door and whispered a blessing as we passed through. It was dark as lamp-black on the shore, its far edge marked only by the faint reflected glow of starlight on the waters of the lake, for the moon had not yet risen. We held each other's hands so that we should not be parted and lost in the darkness.

The only way out of the town was through one of the gates, which were guarded at night. The rest of the group had left before the guard was mounted, but Yehûdâ had ensured that the guards on the Damascus gate were followers of Yeshûa, so that we would be allowed to pass through unchallenged. We made our way up from the beach at the northern end of the town, through the quiet streets and past sleeping houses, and had nearly reached our goal when we heard the approaching sound of marching feet. It was a sound rarely heard in the Galilee, but we knew it at once—the tramp of disciplined soldiers, Roman soldiers. The soldiers who transported the customs taxes were not in town this month. Roman soldiers could mean only one thing—the unit assigned to Antipas by the Roman governor to help maintain order, which normally remained as bodyguards around the tetrarch himself.

'They have come already!' I gasped in a hoarse whisper.

Yehûdâ pulled us into the shadows under the arcade of a butcher's shop. We could see the Damascus gate, just a few cubits away, as we pressed back against the inner wall. But between the arcade and the gate was an open area, well lit by the flaming torches mounted in sconces on either side of the gate. If we crossed it, we would be seen at once.

The Romans had stopped at the mouth of an alleyway and were peering down it, their lanterns held aloft. Yehûdâ made a move as if to lead us out of hiding, then held up his hand to stop us. The soldiers were back in the street now, nearer than before, and seemed to be arguing. My mouth was so dry that my tongue clung to the roof of my mouth and I could not swallow. I found I was squeezing the Magdalene's hand so tightly I must have been hurting her.

As we watched, one of the soldiers began beating on the door of the largest house with the butt of his spear.

'Open this door,' he shouted, in heavily accented Aramaic. 'We are searching for the miscreant Yeshûa ben Yosef. Open, or we will break the door down.'

Before those within had time to respond, one of the Romans, a heavy-built man with shoulders like a plough-ox, threw himself against the door. There was the noise of cracking wood, but the door did not give way at once. A white, frightened face appeared at an upper window. We could not hear the words exchanged, but the soldiers paused and waited until the door was opened.

'We can cross to the gate while they are inside,' I whispered, somehow loosening my tongue enough to speak.

But only four of the men entered the house. The rest remained outside, keeping a sharp watch on the street. We could hear the sound of smashing pottery and furniture overturned, and a sudden scream from inside the house. At last the soldiers emerged, one of them carrying a leather wineskin and wiping his mouth with the back of his hand. They milled about, and then turned towards a house on the far side of the street.

'The three of you must slip through the gate now,' Yehûdâ murmured, loosening the sword he had insisted on carrying. 'I will hold them off until you are away.'

'No!' The Magdalene took him by the sword arm. Her voice was low but insistent. 'The three of you must go. I know how to deal with soldiers.'

'Wait!' I said. 'It's too dangerous. You mustn't.'

But before we could stop her, she was gone, throwing back the mantel from her head so that her long luxurious hair shimmered in the light from their lanterns. She no longer looked like the woman we knew. Her very walk was different. Although she did not now wear the flamboyant clothes of a prostitute, she sauntered boldly up to the soldiers as they approached along the street, her hips swaying. Her meaning was clear. She raised her arms, letting her sleeves fall back to expose the creamy loveliness of her skin, and ran her fingers through that exotic waterfall of her hair. She did not, however, come too close to them.

We watched her in fascinated horror. The men turned away from the house they were approaching, which meant they were once again facing in our direction, but their eyes were all on the Magdalene. I was biting the back of my hand till I drew blood. She would be taken! She was throwing her life away for us! Helplessly, I stretched out my arms towards her and took a step forward, but Yehûdâ caught hold of me and pulled me back. He pushed both of us ahead of him towards the gate.

'We cannot stop her now. We must do as she said.'

The soldiers were still looking at the Magdalene. Confused, stumbling, Yeshûa and I allowed ourselves to be led through the gate on the nod of the guards. We were safely outside the wall when we stopped and looked at each other in consternation.

'We cannot leave her,' I said through my tears. 'What will become of her?'

'I will go back for her.' Yehûdâ turned towards the gate again.

'No,' said Yeshûa. 'We will wait here a little first, just under those trees. She is a resourceful woman. Brave but not foolish. Wait a little.'

We did as he said. Under the dusty trees we waited, as minutes seemed to stretch out into hours, and I bit my fingernails savagely, feeling sick and wondering if I could have done anything to prevent this.

And then at last we heard a soft murmur of voices at the gate, and a woman came through—modest in bearing, her head muffled in her mantel, but moving swiftly along the road out of the city. I leapt out from under the trees and wrapped my arms around her. She started in surprise, then she was clinging to me and we were both weeping.

'The soldiers?' said Yehûdâ.

'I'll tell you as we go,' she said, 'but we must hurry.'

As we turned aside from the road along a narrow farm path, she explained, somewhat breathlessly, what she had done.

'Easy to lead by the nose, men like that,' she said scornfully. 'A woman need do nothing but show some naked flesh, loosened hair, suggest that she is available, and they will follow.'

Even in the dim starlight, I saw that my brother blushed, but Yehûdâ chuckled softly.

'But you were not available,' he said.

'I led them down the alleyway to inn of Abel, the one-eyed man.'

'One of ours,' said Yeshûa.

'Yes. Had them sitting round a table while they thought I was preparing a room upstairs. I whispered to Abel that they were searching for you, and he promised to ply them with so much strong drink that they wouldn't be able to find their own right hands before morning. Then I slipped out the back door and ran for the gate.'

I hugged her. Her courage left me speechless.

'Abel may not have time to get them drunk,' my brother said. 'They will soon suspect that they've been tricked and will come after us. When they find we are not in the town, they'll comb the countryside round about. We must hurry.'

After that, we saved our breath for the climb.

Hard as the journey was, and edged always with the fear of pursuit, I remember it with an odd kind of joy. About midnight we had all reached the meeting place, a sheep fold a couple of miles northwest of the town but already some distance above it. I think in most of us fear had given way to excitement and exhilaration, for we were setting out upon a new adventure. Apart from Yehûdâ, none of us had ever seen the Middle Sea, or Phoenicia, or climbed these mountains that now lay ahead of us. We were fortunate in that it was a clear night with a bright moon, which had risen soon after we left the town, for otherwise it would have been difficult to find the path. Yehûdâ was leading us not by the traders' road from Capernaum to Tyre, nor by one of the regular tracks which ran from village to village, but by a barely discernible goat path through the mountains. For the first part of our journey, at least, we wanted to avoid the nearby villages, where we were known.

The darkness, the moonlight, the myriad stars overhead all added to the thrill as we set out, and I found my heart beating and a smile coming to my lips, despite the fact that we were fleeing into exile. As we climbed higher and the ground became rougher, with ruts in the track to be skirted and great boulders to be clambered over, Yehûdâ offered me his arm. I shook my head.

'If I am fit to make this journey, I am able to manage alone,' I said. 'You have your responsibilities as guide. I shall do very well by myself.'

He smiled at me and pressed my arm, then resumed his place at the front. Shim'ôn brought up the rear, ensuring that there were no stragglers. He was not a man accustomed to climbing mountains, which he regarded with distrust, but he could be relied upon to guarantee that no one was left behind. Since his foolish attempt to walk on the water he had been a little subdued, but seemed relieved that Yeshûa still trusted him.

After many hours of stiff climbing, the sky gradually lightened behind us as the sun came up, and we looked back to see how far we had travelled. Capernaum had vanished into the valley of Gennesaret and all around were the towering mountains—to right and left and straight ahead, far higher than anything we had climbed so far. Discouraged, we sank down on to boulders and earth and contemplated what lay before us.

'We can never climb that!' said Yôhânân petulantly, indicating with a sweep of his hand the massive peak that confronted us. 'Not with women amongst us.'

I glowered at him. I had climbed faster and complained less than he had, all night long, but he was the sort of man who will always make women the excuse for his own weakness.

My brother conferred briefly with Yehûdâ, whom he regarded as our leader while we were traversing the mountains, then they told us we could have a pause to rest a little and eat.

'But do not eat too much,' Yehûdâ warned. 'Small meals, taken frequently, that is best while travelling over this terrain.'

An hour or two further on and we reached a lovely river, flowing south and east towards Gennesaret. It ran through groves of wild fig trees and pomegranates, a lush bower suddenly before us, hidden away in this barren wilderness. The air was filled with the sweet scent of the fig trees, a perfume which lifts the heart, a green and purple scent, wild but beautiful. We took off our boots and sandals and waded up the river, the cool water blissful on our feet. I plucked and ate newly ripened figs and added some to my satchel of food. Yeshûa reached up and picked a pomegranate.

'Every pomegranate seed, a lucky day!' he said, handing it to me.

My legs were aching, hip to ankle, but the place was so lovely, a small Eden concealed amongst the high hills, that I could have burst into song. Later, when we had left the river and climbed higher, I no longer had the breath for it.

At last Yehûdâ called a halt. No one was talking by now, except for the occasional groan. Most had blistered feet, and our hands and knees were scraped and torn from scrambling up slopes and over rocky screes. We had been travelling for a whole night and all the next day until sunset and there was not one of us who was not exhausted.

'See there,' said Yehûdâ, pointing to a *nahal*, a small river which had sprung up from nowhere and ran alongside what he claimed was a path. 'Do you notice anything about it?'

Yeshûa walked over to stand beside him.

'It is running from east to west,' he said. 'Not west to east.'

'Exactly. We have crossed the watershed. From here the waters run down into the Middle Sea.'

Yehûdâ had chosen a spot where a few tenacious pine trees had rooted amongst the rocky outcrops, and a cave offered some shelter. Shim'ôn and Andreas gathered fallen wood and soon had a fire going, while Susanna, the Magdalene and I prepared a rough stew from any ingredients we could gather together from our fellow travellers. It was not the most elegant of meals, but it was hot, and, scooped up with pieces of flatbread from the common pot, it put some heart into us.

After we had eaten, I lay down with the other women in the cave, while the men bedded down under the trees. For a long time I tried to find a comfortable position. My body was exhausted, but my mind would not rest and skittered to and fro like a trapped rat. At last I could endure it no longer. I crawled quietly out of the cave, to avoid waking the other two, and walked over to the fire. Yehûdâ was sitting cross-legged, feeding it with dry branches. The sap in the pinewood hissed and snapped in the flames.

'Could you not sleep?' he said, making room beside him.

I shook my head and dropped down near the fire. 'You should be resting. We are all depending on you to bring us safely to Tyre.'

'The way isn't difficult to find from here, though we have some rough climbing still ahead of us. What kept you awake? Aching bones?'

'No. My mind is buzzing like a hive of angry bees.'

'Mine too.'

He reached out and took my hand. I felt that shock run through me which I sensed whenever he touched me, a touch rare now, when we had to be so circumspect. But it was dark and everyone else was asleep. I pressed his hand, but dared not look at him, for fear of what he might see of the longing in my eyes.

'I am worried about my brother,' I said, trying to keep us away from that other, dangerous, ground.

'Yes,' he said. 'This exile in Tyre is not what he wants. He has no desire to pursue his mission amongst the Phoenicians.'

'But it isn't that alone. I think he's lost his way. All this wandering about in the last weeks: Capernaum, Bethsaida. Then he says he will stay in Bethsaida while we go back to Capernaum, but suddenly there he is, walking back to Capernaum. He no longer seems to know what he wants to do. The threat from Antipas, the soldiers, the flight to Tyre . . .'

I hesitated. It felt like treachery to criticise Yeshûa, yet I whispered it. 'It is almost as if this exile has provided an excuse, saved him from making a decision.'

I looked him in the face at last. His expression, in the glow of the fire, was sombre.

'So you feel it too.'

He threw another branch on the fire, which shot a flame upwards, then fell apart in the middle and had to be raked together again. When he had done, he took both my hands in his and drew me round to face him.

'Do you think there is anything we can do? You are his sister, you know him best.'

'You are his friend,' I said. 'Sometimes I fear he still thinks of me as a child.'

'You are not that.' He cupped my face gently between his hands, and my blood began to race through my limbs.

'I mean,' I said, trying to keep my voice steady, 'that he may listen to you. But I think he must find his own way out of his confusion. All we can do is to love him and protect him, and be ready to follow him wherever he decides he must go.'

'Yes. I agree. But, Mariam . . .' he was looking deep into my soul now, his face only inches from mine, 'shall we be married in Tyre?'

My heart leapt up in sudden hope, then fell back again.

'How can we be?' I said. 'He has decreed that his followers must remain celibate. We, of all his company, must keep to the bargain.'

Once again, I had to choose between my lover and my brother. It seemed to me then that Yehûdâ was strong. Between us, we would find the strength to wait. But Yeshûa was tender, vulnerable. We had to protect him. Was I wrong?

There were tears on my eyelashes, and he bent and kissed them away.

Some faint noise from the other side of the fire caught my ear. I turned. Two eyes gleamed in the firelight. Someone was watching us. I saw that it was Yôhânân.

'I must go back to the cave,' I said, pulling myself free and scrambling to my feet.

The next morning we woke early, not merely from the sun but from our aching joints that screamed outrage at us. We filled our waterskins from the *nahal*, ate a few of yesterday's figs, and set off again. There was little talking today, but almost at once I became aware that, like the stream that crossed our path from time to time, we were climbing down the slopes most of the time, despite having to clamber uphill to negotiate some difficult places. Here the scree became somewhat dangerous, and once or twice someone slipped, until Yehûdâ warned us to go carefully. We wanted no injuries to cause us further problems.

I was following close behind him when he rounded a great out-thrust cliff and stopped. Carelessly, I trod on scree and slithered a short way, till he grabbed my arm to stop me from falling. With his free arm he pointed ahead.

'Look!' he said. 'There it is. The Middle Sea.'

At first, strange as it sounds, I could not see it. I suppose it was so vast that my mind could not comprehend it, or else some trick of vision made it appear like an inverted mirage of the sky. Then my brain or my eyes came into focus. What I saw was something so beautiful, I caught my breath.

A few times, during my childhood lessons, and if I had been especially dutiful, my brother would recite to me scraps from a Greek poet. I do not know where he had learned these, and always wished afterwards that I had asked him. Perhaps he had bought a scroll from a passing trader, or found it with the miscellaneous scrolls kept in the *beth ha-sefer* for the brighter scholars, who advanced from learning Hebrew to learning Greek. They were supposed to study the Pentateuch in its Greek translation, not secular texts, but perhaps this one had somehow found its way amongst them. I realised later that it was strange he had read those poems, written by one of the *gôyîm*, but I know he would have loved them for their stories. I remember the stories still, though few of the precise words, except for one phrase 'the wine-dark sea'.

'I cannot understand how the sea can be "wine-dark",' I said once.

Yeshûa shook his head. 'Nor can I. Perhaps a poet sees things differently from the rest of us.'

My brother came up beside us now, and I slipped my arm through his.

'Look, Yeshûa,' I said, pointing to the sea, which lay like the purple mantle of a king at the foot of the mountains, stretching out beyond sight. 'The wine-dark sea.'

Chapter Fourteen

In the farm above Massilia, the heat of late summer has become scorching. A boon to the harvest and to the ripening grapes, the hot, still, humid air fills the house with an atmosphere like the steam room in a bathhouse. Julia runs barefoot, however much her mother scolds, and hitches her tunic as high as she dares, showing her flashing legs as she runs about the house. She is the only one who runs. Her brothers, avoiding their lessons with excuses about the need for their presence in the fields, slip away to bathe, and lie as somnolent as the farm dogs under the shade of trees on the margin of the farm, swimming and dozing away the daylight hours. The Israelite farm workers endure it better than most, from long experience of blistering heat in their homeland.

Mariam, in one of her lucid periods, begs to be carried outside. Her room is like a bread oven, she complains, and she is slowly being baked alive. Manilius objects. Fulvia exclaims that the heat outside will kill her. Sergius supports his mother's request.

'Under the grape arbour,' Miriam whispers. 'There will be shade and a breeze. I cannot breathe in here.'

In the end, they give in to her demands. She has so little time left, they can all see that. Let her have her wish, however absurd. Manilius lifts her tenderly into a chair and two of the Israelite men carry it out to the terrace and place it according to her precise directions. It is exactly as she has predicted. This one spot catches what little cool air breathes up from the sea. The thick leaves of the vine cast a glorious shade and stir in a breeze which can be found nowhere else on the farm. Mariam settles back in her chair with a sigh of satisfaction. She has known every corner of this farm for thirty-five years. They think her grown into childish folly with age and illness, but she has not.

At last they go away, leaving her there with Sergius, who has told Rachel to bring out a tray. He pours from a cool earthenware jug, dewed with moisture, and carries a glass to Mariam.

'Fresh, unfermented juice pressed from the first grapes,' he says. He steadies the glass so she can drink.

'Good,' she says.

'Mmm.'

He sets their glasses down on the low table and sits on the ground at her feet, his arms around his knees.

'You said you were a family of many sons. How many?'

'Six, and another that died at birth. Three girls.'

'Ya'aqôb and Yeshûa, you said.'

'And Yehûdes, Yoses, Shim'ôn and Daniel. The girls were Melkha, Eskha and me.'

'And they all stayed behind in Palestine?'

'The Land of Judah. Yes.'

'But not you?'

'No.'

He turns his face and looks up at her. He does not want to tire her, but he is intrigued to discover all this large family he never knew he had, and the short time left to them makes it urgent. Julia told him recently that she knew something of these people.

'And why,' he asks delicately, 'did you leave?'

For a long time, she does not answer. Then she closes her eyes and says faintly:

'Because I was in danger. I was bidden to leave. That is enough now, Sergius. I need to rest.'

༄

We stayed in Tyre nearly half a year, lodging with the small Jewish community settled there, mostly minor merchants and traders, many of whom were known to Yehûdâ. The rest of our party was at first grateful to Yehûdâ for guiding us safely over the mountains and finding homes for us, but as the weeks passed, they began to look sideways again at him, and to call him 'Yehûdâ of Keriyoth' in that way which implied that he was not one of the true company.

Four of us lodged with a friend of Yehûdâ's father—my brother and I, the Magdalene and Yehûdâ. Our escape from the soldiers in Capernaum had brought us closer together, though I think, looking back, that this confirmation of Yehûdâ's special place in my brother's affection did him harm amongst the others. Shim'ôn and his brother Andreas lodged across the street and sometimes dined with us. I had come to have a great respect for Shim'ôn. I liked his quiet sturdiness, his honesty and reliability. I could see that in time he might become a leader of men. But even he was a little reserved with Yehûdâ. From several of the others there was jealousy, even at times open hostility.

Zebedee's two sons stayed at a house several streets away, where they could not be kept under a watchful eye by Yehûdâ and my brother. I wished more than once that their mother had been able to come with us, for she might have been able to check their bursts of unruliness and wild talk. I was sure they were again plotting to force Yeshûa into a position where he would have to lead an armed revolt. If he could not be persuaded to it, they might trigger an uprising themselves, and then proclaim him as their leader.

'The Sons of Thunder,' Yeshûa called them one day, teasing, and the name stuck, but I did not think he could tease them out of their eagerness for a violent confrontation with the men of power.

Much of the time he ignored their talk of an armed uprising, though I suspected that it troubled him. During our months in the city, he kept to himself, staying mostly withindoors. Partly, this was because he was anxious that word of his whereabouts should not reach Antipas or the Romans. But also he had told us that he did not want to preach to the Phoenicians, that his mission was to the Israelites. So when the brothers Yôhânân and Ya'kob arrived one afternoon at our house, leading a group of twenty or so Phoenician men, I was shocked. Ya'kob marched in at the door without knocking and confronted the four of us where we sat, talking quietly to our host.

'Behold, Master,' said Yôhânân gleefully. 'We have brought these good people to see you. They are eager to hear your message.'

The faces were eager, certainly. But to me they seemed like the faces of a crowd come to gape at a showman's prodigies—a dwarf or a two-headed sheep. They whispered and snickered behind their hands, and one man strode up to my brother and tugged at his hair, as if he thought he was an apparition or a freak.

We all jumped to our feet and Yehûdâ stood in front of Yeshûa to shield him from the crowd.

'Get them out of here!' Yehûdâ said grimly to Yôhânân. 'You know what he has said.'

Yôhânân smiled at him and folded his arms across his chest. He would do nothing to help, I could see. At that moment Shim'ôn and Andreas hurried in. From across the street they had seen the crowd arrive and had come to protect Yeshûa. Between them the brothers and Yehûdâ ushered the Phoenicians politely out of the door, then closed and bolted it.

Yeshûa stood up and confronted Yôhânân and Ya'kob. He was white and shaking, so I thought at first he was afraid, but then I saw that he was furiously angry.

'You devil's spawn!' he shouted, and for a moment he sounded like my brother Ya'aqôb. 'You dare to defy me! I will not pursue my mission amongst the *gôyîm*. These are my instructions. Why do you disobey me?'

He hardly seemed like my gentle, loving brother, but I realised that his worry and his uncertainty had been seething inside him like a boiling pot on the fire that suddenly bursts its lid.

Yôhânân was shaking now, shaking with fear, but he assumed that fawning, unctuous tone of voice that I so mistrusted.

'But, Master,' he said, 'you must act. You hide away in this house and do nothing, when we are here, ready to follow you, to rise up against the occupiers. Even Phoenicians can bear arms. All that is needed is a leader. And you, lord, are that leader. Take up your sword, and we will follow. We will crown you king of the Jews.'

'No!' Yeshûa shouted. His face was flushed red now. 'I will not take part in any violence.' Then he turned on his heel and left the room.

That was the last time Yôhânân tried any tricks in Tyre, but it would not be the last time my brother became angry during the confused and restless months of that year.

235

Living in the same house as Yehûdâ all that time was both a joy and a torment. He did not ask me again if I would like to be married in Tyre, but I saw it in his eyes every morning when we sat down to break our fast together and every evening when we bade each other goodnight, and went our separate ways. Alone of us, Yehûdâ was not idle in Tyre. He went out amongst the merchant community and transacted business on behalf of his father. In this way he was able also to earn a little money, to help us pay our way for food and lodging. Of this, too, many of the *shelîhîm* were resentful. Shim'ôn was able to find a little work at first on the fishing boats, but this was not popular with the local Phoenician fishermen, so he soon desisted.

Despite living in the same house, Yehûdâ and I were rarely alone together. For a few precious moments, on a dark turn of the stair, we might put our arms around each other and cling together, but afterwards I always felt guilty and prayed for forgiveness. I wanted to confide in my brother, but I knew he would urge us to marry and leave his following. We could not do it. His need and his danger were too great. Sometimes my whole body ached, as though I was being ripped apart, and I became sharp-tongued with everyone. I think the Magdalene guessed my trouble. Although she never spoke of it, she was especially kind to me, and it was due to her that Yehûdâ and I had one of our few times alone.

She had begun to deal with a woman who reared poultry on a small farm outside the city, a little way along the coast, buying eggs from her once a week, and sometimes a chicken.

'Could you go in my place, Mariam?' she asked one day. 'I am not quite well. My head . . .'

'Of course,' I said. 'You should lie down in our room, with the shutters closed. Tell me how to find the farm and what you want me to buy.'

I enjoyed the walk, for I was glad to be out of the city. Tyre was a busy trading post and port, with ships coming and going from all parts of the Empire, and was afflicted with all the things that grow up in a city with such a port: refuse in the streets and desperate slums and brothels and mean dirty taverns and drunken sailors gathered in menacing groups. We were staying in a prosperous part of Tyre, but when that kind of infection takes hold in a city, traces of it seep into every corner. I would never have walked the streets of Tyre alone after dusk, though I always felt safe in Capernaum.

I left the farm and made my way slowly back along the coastal path with my basket of eggs. It was a fine late summer's day, cooled by the sea breeze so that the sun was not oppressive, as it would have been inland. I had learned to love the scent of the Middle Sea, a much richer brew than that of Gennesaret. There was no need to hurry back, so I sat down on a tussock of grass, with my arms around my knees, and watched the silver flames flashing on the waves and the gulls swooping for fish, shrieking and quarrelling when one made a successful catch. A little way offshore there was a sudden rolling movement. I caught my breath. There it was again, the lovely leaping crescent of a dolphin. These beautiful creatures, beloved of Arion and all the poets, have always remained a wonder to me.

So absorbed was I in watching first one dolphin, then another which joined it, that I did not hear him until he was almost upon me.

'It's a good thing,' said Yehûdâ, sitting down beside me, 'that I am not a thief come to steal your basket of eggs.'

I turned on him a smile lit with sudden happiness. The day had become brighter, the sea more glorious, the wind carrying all the perfumes of the distant Indies!

'How did you know I was here?'

'The Magdalene directed me most carefully.'

I laughed. 'What a schemer! She told me she was ill.'

'Perhaps she could not otherwise have overcome your scruples.'

I blushed and looked down. My scruples were perhaps more easily overcome than he believed.

'Oh, my beloved,' he said, taking me in his arms and laying his cheek against my hair. 'Once you said to me, *Thy lips drop as the honeycomb, honey and milk are under thy tongue. I would cause thee to drink of spiced wine of the juice of my pomegranate.* How I long to drink that juice of you.'

'And you replied, *My dove, my undefiled is but one. Set me as a seal upon thine heart, as a seal upon thine arm, for love is strong as death. Oh, I am sick of love.*'

'I have not forgotten. I *am* sick of love. When shall I be able to take you to my bed, my beloved, my wife?'

'*Turn away thine eyes from me,*' I murmured, '*for they have overcome me.*'

He groaned, and his arms tightened round me till I could hardly breathe.

'I love you,' I whispered, too soft for him to hear. 'I love you. I love you.'

We did not break from our vow, though we trembled on the verge of it. As we walked slowly back to the city—so slowly—with our arms clinging to each other's waists, he began to talk about Yeshûa and the future.

'He wants to confer with us tonight, just the two of us. I think he means to set out his plans for the future, to see what we think of them.'

'Do you think he is any clearer in his mind than he was when we left Capernaum?'

'I don't know, Mariam. I truly do not know.'

The three of us met after supper in the small back room our merchant host used as an office. My brother had about him a greater look of resolution than I had seen all this year.

'I have been thinking hard what we should do,' he said. 'This interval in Tyre, away from home, hasn't been wasted. It has given me time to consider a plan, which I could never do in the hurly-burly of the early days of our mission in the Galilee. It was all too . . . too broken. I never saw clearly what to do, from one day to the next.'

I felt suddenly hopeful. Yeshûa seemed to have thrown aside his uncertainties. He might have been the general of an army planning a campaign, though I immediately abandoned my metaphor. I glanced at Yehûdâ, where he sat next to Yeshûa on the other side of the table, and saw that he was smiling broadly with relief.

'Exactly!' he said. 'We are going to change the world, that's what you said. Well, to do that, we must know where we are going and when, what we plan to do, how we hope to achieve it.'

Yeshûa laughed aloud. I had not heard such a merry sound from him for months. Relief flooded through me, as palpable as the wine we were drinking.

'My practical merchant!' my brother said. 'You make your list of items like a shopkeeper and check them off, one by one. Where! When! What! How!'

'It's not so bad a practice,' Yehûdâ said mildly.

'See,' said Yeshûa, dipping his finger in his beaker and drawing with wine on the table. 'We are here, in Tyre. When I judge it is safe to return, we will take the road back to Capernaum. Here.' He added more wine, to make a puddle for Capernaum.

'While we are there, we will gather together more of our followers, but then we will move on. I think we have spent enough time in the Galilee.'

He murmured, as if to himself, 'I do not know how long I shall have.'

Yehûdâ looked across at me and shook his head, but I had no intention of interrupting.

'From Capernaum I think it will be best if we go into the trans-Jordanian lands, to the tetrarchy of Philip and perhaps even on to the cities of the Decapolis, beyond the eastern shore of Gennesaret.' He drew a long, looping line, which came back to Capernaum.

'Not just Bethsaida, then?' Yehûdâ ventured.

'No, no.' Yeshûa dismissed Bethsaida with a wave of his hand. 'Then, when we are ready, we will go south. To Judaea. To the city of Jericho. And to the Holy City itself. Jerusalem.' He drew a long straight line along the table towards himself and punched his finger against the edge. Jerusalem.

I did not know why, but something in his tone made me shiver. I looked at him intently. I opened my mouth to speak, but Yehûdâ was before me.

'What are your intentions in Jerusalem? There's a Roman garrison there. And I do not think the high priest and the Sanhedrin will welcome your teaching.'

'And Yôhânân and the others,' I burst out. 'They want to make trouble, and Jerusalem is the place they will try it.'

My brother looked at me steadily. 'Perhaps I will make trouble myself. Jerusalem is where all roads end. Jerusalem is the only place for a prophet to die.'

I felt a cold sickness in the pit of my stomach. My lips shaped the word 'die?', but no sound emerged.

'But the *when*,' said Yehûdâ, more calmly than I could have done. 'When do you plan to go to Jerusalem?'

'Not this year,' said Yeshûa. 'I shall not call in your debt before then, my brother.'

They exchanged a look of some complex and deep meaning that I did not understand. Soon afterwards my brother left us, saying he was tired.

It was then that Yehûdâ told me about the promise unfulfilled between them, and the debt my brother could call in.

At last, around the beginning of the month of *Tishri*, with the grape harvest underway, Yeshûa decided that it was safe for us to return to the Galilee. This time we went by the main road, which followed, wherever possible, the valleys and lower passes between the mountains, and which made for easier walking. Despite what Yeshûa had said in Tyre, we did not return to Capernaum. Towards the end of our journey, when we were a few miles from the town, we met a young boy sitting at the roadside, a nephew of Zebedee's.

'We had word you were coming,' he said, 'so my uncle sent me to warn you. There are troops of the tetrarch in town, searching for you. My uncle thinks they discovered you were coming and have laid a trap.'

Yôhânân! I thought. He has betrayed us, to force my brother's hand. But I could never prove it. Perhaps I did him an injustice.

Yeshûa, Yehûdâ and Shim'ôn conferred together. Should we turn back, or cross the Jordan at once?

'We will avoid Capernaum,' my brother said decisively, 'and cross the river. In Bethsaida we can send word for others to join us, before we head further east.'

He turned to the boy. 'Tell your uncle that we will stay a week in Bethsaida. And I am grateful to you for the warning.'

So we skirted the north end of Gennesaret and found ourselves again in Bethsaida, where Salome and Joanna joined us, but no others. There were no crowds to greet us, and our arrival went almost unnoticed, but a few days later Yeshûa, with a few of the *shelîhîm*, went by boat to Magdala, where Yehûdâ and I had taken a midday meal at the lakeside inn all those long months ago. The girl I had been then seemed almost a stranger to me, impulsively running after her brother and his friend, shocked by that shameful attack in our village. Now I was a confident and respected member of Yeshûa's devoted followers, where men and women were treated with equal dignity and honour. Not that our roles were so very much changed in many respects. We women cooked and mended, the men fished. When the boat left for Magdala, we stayed behind because there was a great deal of washing to do, after our journey.

As we knelt together on the shore of the lake, beating the dirt out of the clothes against the smooth stones, Maryam confided in me that she was glad we had not been in the small party which had gone to Magdala.

'I should be recognised there, and shamed,' she said. 'I barely escaped with my life before, for it had been decreed that I should be stoned to death.'

'Why . . .' I was not sure how to phrase it with delicacy, '. . . why did you take up such a life?'

She shrugged. Although she now wore sober clothes and swathed her head and shoulders in a mantle, no matter how hot the weather, she was still the most beautiful woman I had ever seen. Compared with her, my sister's Melkha's looks seemed nothing but a coarse illusion of prettiness.

'I was left an orphan at the age of twelve. No betrothal had been arranged for me, no dowry laid by, I had no skills. What could I do?'

'Had you no other relatives who could take you in?'

'None but a rich uncle in Scythopolis with six daughters, who did not want another to provide for.'

'But surely the Law says . . .'

She shrugged again.

'The Law is of no account when it contradicts a selfish man's own desires.'

She flashed me a sudden smile.

'But now I have found a family, and a sister too.'

I reached out a wet arm and hugged her.

When Yeshûa and the others returned from Magdala, they seemed subdued.

'What has happened?' I asked Yehûdâ, when Yeshûa had said he wanted nothing to eat, and had gone to his room and closed the door.

'There was a party of Pharisees there. They mocked him whenever he tried to preach, and demanded a heavenly sign that he was a true prophet. None of the people wanted to listen to him. Then on the way back to Bethsaida in the boat, the other *shelîhîm* started arguing and complaining that they had no bread. It's true we were all hungry, for no one offered us a meal in Magdala, but that was little enough to bear. We knew we should dine when we reached here. They thought Yeshûa should do as Moses did, and conjure bread out of the air.'

'And what did he do?'

'He told them that *he* was the bread of heaven, the living bread, but they were too stupid to understand him.'

'They are not educated men,' I said. 'I think sometimes Yeshûa speaks too much in symbols and riddles for them.'

'Perhaps. But surely they should understand his message by now.'

He strode away, frowning. I let him go. He was tired and hungry and cross. And perhaps he too was wondering how long we must all wait for the coming of the new kingdom.

This was the beginning of a bad time for us. Many of Yeshûa's followers in the area began to drift away. We had been gone from the Galilee for so long that they had resumed their normal lives, their work on the boats or in the fields, their family duties. There was a son here to be trained in a craft, a daughter there to be married, an aged relative to be buried. Men must eat. Families must be provided for. One cannot live forever on dreams. When

Yeshûa had first come, working his cures and promising a wonderful new life—which some understood to mean a kind of second Eden, free of sickness and want and labour—a shock of excitement and hope had run through the Galilee. But now they had seen the prophet, the teacher, the *mashiha*, flee into exile in Phoenicia. On his return, nothing had happened, no easing of their labour, no freedom from the occupiers. They had begun to doubt him.

What was worse, he had begun to doubt himself again. Gone was the confident leader who had laid out his plans to Yehûdâ and me round that table in Tyre. He was hardly seen in public. Sometimes he would break off in the midst of his prayers to look anxiously at the disciples and ask, 'Who do people say that I am?'

We all tried to comfort him and restore his courage, but he seemed to have lost his way. He even began to ask the chosen *shelîhîm* if they wanted to leave him, and he talked morbidly of his own death. He was certain now that he would be executed like our cousin, with his mission unaccomplished.

'Never,' said the fisherman Shim'ôn, who showed himself loyal and steadfast in those dark days. 'It shall not happen to you, Lord.'

At that suddenly Yeshûa turned on him furiously and shouted, 'Get thee behind me, Satan.'

We were all shocked into silence as he stormed out of the room. Shim'ôn made as if to go after him, but Yehûdâ shook his head.

'He did not mean it, Shim'ôn. He is in great distress of mind.'

The next day Yeshûa announced that we were leaving at once for Caesarea Philippi, in the far north of Philip's tetrarchy. We all thought that he intended to begin his preaching again in this new region, as he had planned. When we arrived, however, after an arduous journey, he refused to allow us to go into the city—he always hated cities. Instead we took up residence in some caves on the lower slopes of Mount Hermon. They were pleasant enough, clean and dry. We had brought some food with us and more was brought as a gift by a few curious *amê hâ-'erets*, who had heard of this healer and preacher.

As we sat around our fire on the floor of the largest cave, scooping up our meal of boiled beans and dried fish with our fingers, Yeshûa said suddenly, 'I think we must disband. I shall give up my ministry. You should all go back to your homes.'

We stared at him disbelievingly. I am sure the others must have been thinking the same as I: Why bring us all this long journey to Caesarea Philippi, merely to tell us to go home again?

Yehûdâ put down his food bowl, wiped his fingers on his tunic and laid his hand on my brother's arm.

'No,' he said firmly, 'you will not abandon your ministry. All of us here believe in you and are loyal to you. Our exile in Tyre was a setback, but when was there ever a great enterprise that did not suffer setbacks? You must continue. You have told us yourself, countless times, that Yahweh wills it so. We are going to change the world!'

We all began to support him, saying that we would not abandon Yeshûa. However long it took for him to find his way, we would stay with him.

Finally Shim'ôn said, looking at him with shining eyes, 'You have been sent to the children of Israel to guide us to the new kingdom. Lord, you are the long-promised *mashiha*, as was written in the scriptures of old.'

'No,' said Yeshûa, angrily. 'No! I am not the *mashiha*. I am but a humble prophet. But it is true, the Lord has bidden me to carry forth his word.'

He ran his hand over his face and was silent for a while.

'I am sorry, Shim'ôn. I should not have shouted at you. I will think on these things. We will not disband yet.'

Chapter Fifteen

We spent many weeks on Mount Hermon, while my brother struggled in his mind. Much of the time he sat alone, unwilling to speak to us. And he was given to sudden outbursts of anger, as if that was the only way he could relieve his agony of self-doubt. It was the beginning of winter when we arrived and soon the weather turned bitter, high on our mountainside. We had little in the way of garments or blankets to keep us warm, so that we kept a fire burning, day and night. The first task of every morning, for everyone of us, even my brother, was to climb down to the lower slopes, where the forest began, and to gather as much dry wood as possible to carry back to the cave. At first the men slept in the largest cave, where we took our meals, and the women withdrew to a smaller cave at night. Once the frosts began, however, Yoanna and Salome came to Yeshûa with a different suggestion.

'It is possible to keep the small cave warmer than this one, Lord,' said Yoanna. 'The roof is lower and the entrance so small you have to stoop. Let us make that the home for all of us.'

'It is not seemly,' he said, 'for the men and the women to sleep in the same cave.'

But they had an answer for that.

'At the back of the small cave,' Salome said, 'there is, as it were, an inner room, a hollow place in the wall, large enough for the women to withdraw to at night. That way we may sleep separately but share the warmth of one fire.'

When he had inspected the smaller cave, he agreed to this arrangement, and we moved all our belongings, our small store of food, our cooking vessels and our firewood in there. At night, I slept back to back with the Magdalene. By sleeping thus in pairs, we women gained a little warmth from each other, though I lay awake many nights, shivering with the cold and the icy draughts that crept like frosty fingers down the back of my neck.

The cold might not have seemed so penetrating if we had had more food, but the store we had brought with us had nearly run out and there were no more gifts of food from the local people, who had lost interest in us. On the morning of the first snow, Yehûdâ set off with an empty sack to walk down the mountainside and then on the few miles to Caesarea Philippi to buy supplies. He was still our treasurer, though he pointed out to Yeshûa that our funds were limited.

'I will buy cheaply,' he said, 'so do not expect a banquet when I return. We will have to survive on one meal a day.'

All of us watched out eagerly for his return. He came at last, climbing wearily up to the cave and dumping his sack on the ground.

'What have you bought?' Salome asked hopefully.

'Lentils, mostly. They will fill our bellies. And barley flour, cheaper than wheat. As we have no grindstone, I couldn't buy the raw grain.'

As he spoke, she was lifting the individual bags out of his sack.

'Three onions,' she said. 'Good.'

'You must make them last, for they were not cheap.'

'And dried beans. And a marrow bone.'

'I thought you could make soup.'

'Yes, you've done well, Yehûdâ. We can use the bone more than once for broth. And when the beans have soaked, they will swell to twice the size.'

'At least we have no lack of water, with the stream almost at our door.' He reached inside the breast of his tunic and drew out a twist of cloth, tied with twine. 'I brought this too. Salt.'

After his expedition to buy food, Yehûdâ found himself in favour again. We had hot food that night and went to bed not quite so hungry. It was as well, for that night it snowed much more heavily, blowing up into a blizzard that kept us confined for several days.

It was a strange time, those winter months in the cave. Although most of us had been together for a long while, we had not lived in such intimacy before. Sometimes this was good, when we would sing and joke together. The men would scratch a board in the earth of the cave floor and play their interminable games with pebbles as counters. The women would mend clothes or tell stories. Sometimes our close confinement meant that arguments broke out, even quarrels, which upset my brother, so that he would go outside, even if it was snowing, and roam about on the mountainside. This might be enough to shame the disciples into harmony, but not always. One favourite topic of their disputes was the question of who should stand highest in the hierarchy of the new kingdom when it came. I could see how much this distressed Yeshûa, and grew so angry with them myself that once I followed him out into the snow, lest I should say something I might regret. I caught up with Yeshûa and slipped my arm through his. For a while we walked doggedly on, our feet making deep hollows in the fallen snow, while a dark mass of fresh snow whirled round our heads.

'I have failed, Mariam,' he said despairingly. 'How can they have understood my message, if they dispute about who shall stand first?'

I squeezed his arm.

'They are mostly good men, my dear. It's this confinement that wears them down. They've always been active and they need to be up and doing.'

'You're probably right.' He shrugged and would not look at me.

'Will you take up your mission again?' I asked slowly, aware that this was treading on delicate ground.

'Perhaps,' was all he would say.

Every couple of weeks, Yehûdâ would go down again to the city to buy supplies, but our money was running very short by the time the thaw came and new streams began to run down the mountain, fed by the melting snow. Soon after this, a very curious incident occurred. Few of us witnessed it, and we did not know what to make of it. One evening as it was nearing sunset, and some of the men were dozing by the fire, Yeshûa shook three of them awake: Shim'ôn and the two sons of Zebedee, Ya'kob and Yôhânân.

He said simply, 'Come with me.'

We watched them start to climb higher up the mountain, and I wondered where he was taking them. Not to gather firewood, for that was lower down. The three fishermen were still half asleep as they staggered after him. A glorious sunset was spreading itself across the western sky, and I shaded my eyes as they disappeared into it. Yeshûa had never quite given up the habit, learned at Qumrân, of rising sometimes to watch the sunrise, but he did not usually pay much heed to sunset. We had begun making the evening meal when the three *shelîhîm* stumbled into the cave, all talking at once. They were beside themselves, with a mixture of fear, excitement and exultation.

'We have seen our lord, transfigured into pure light!' said Shim'ôn.

'Moses and Elijah,' Yôhânân gabbled. 'I have seen Moses and Elijah on Yeshûa's either hand. I thought I should be lifted up on a cloud! The Lord be praised, for the Lord God is great!' And he fell on the floor, writhing in a kind of ecstasy, dribbling at the mouth.

'We *all* saw them,' his brother said, with—I thought—a slight touch of irritation. 'They were all three bathed in light.'

'Yes,' said Shim'ôn, eager not to be left out. 'Then the hand of Yahweh laid a cloud over the sun, the light vanished, and a voice from on high said—'

Yôhânân interrupted him, lifting his head from the ground, 'This is my beloved Son: hear him.'

We looked at one another. Some seemed hurt that they had not been vouchsafed this vision. Others looked as though they thought the three had still hardly woken and were dazzled by the setting sun shining in their eyes.

'Surely you are mistaken,' said Tôma.

'Where is my brother?' I asked quietly.

'I am here.'

He stood in the doorway of the cave, his head a little stooped because of the low entrance. He did not seem to me to be transformed into some kind of supernatural being. But there was something strange about him. The evening sky was all on fire behind him, so that his dark curls seemed tipped with flame. He held himself tightly together, like a runner about to spring forward at the start of a race. His fists were clenched, his eyes bright, and his voice rang out with confidence and determination.

'We leave tomorrow,' he said, ducking into the cave. 'We go forth on our mission.'

'Our mission of peace?' said Yôhânân, with a note of interrogation in his voice.

Yeshûa spun on his heel to confront him.

'Think not that I am come to send peace on earth,' he shouted. 'I come not to send peace, but a sword.'

I flinched away from him. Surely this was not my brother speaking? Was he possessed? I felt sick with shock at his words, but one or two of the *shelîhîm*, amongst them Yôhânân and his brother, exchanged looks of satisfaction.

Although the ground was still wet with the spring thaw, the walking was fairly easy back to Capernaum, where Yeshûa hoped to gather again more of his followers before we went down into Judaea. We talked as we made our way south past the reed-fringed shores of little Lake Hula and followed the Jordan down to the north end of Gennesaret. Now that we were on the move again after the months of stagnation, the *shelîhîm* were full of eagerness.

'Now, surely, *rabbi*,' said Yôhânân, 'we are on the threshold of the new kingdom.'

As he so often did, he had pushed his way forward to walk in the privileged place next to my brother. Hearing the murmurs of agreement amongst the others, Yeshûa stopped and waited while they gathered around him. I could see that he was about to tell another of his stories.

'You think we are on the threshold, Yôhânân?' he said. He thought for a moment.

'Suppose a landowner gets his labourers to plant a fig tree in his vineyard. One of those wealthy absentee landowners, like those who own the estates in Galilee, where we travelled amongst the destitute *amê hâ-'erets*. After a while, he comes from his fine house in Jerusalem, to avoid the heat of midsummer in the city and spend some time in the country. After a good dinner, he goes for a stroll in the vineyard. "I'll sit in the shade of the fig tree," he thinks, "and enjoy some of the juicy fruit." So he seeks out the fruit tree and—what! Not a fig to be seen.'

He paused, and we waited expectantly.

'He looks around for his steward. "Yeshûa!" he bellows. "Where are you, you idle scum! This tree was planted three years ago, and there's not a fig to be seen. Cut it down! It's completely useless, just like you." '

Susanna giggled when he named the steward Yeshûa, but clapped her hands over her mouth. He grinned at her and went on.

'Now this fellow Yeshûa was one of the *amê hâ-'erets* himself, but had risen to be steward through hard work and a handy way with the orchard and vines. "Please, Lord," says he bravely, "I think we should leave it a while longer. One year more. I'll dig in some manure around it, and keep an eye on it. If it bears fruit then, why that's all well and good. If not, I'll cut it down and we've lost nothing by waiting." '

Yeshûa turned on his heel and walked on.

'What does he mean?' Susanna whispered to me.

'He means we must be patient. Just as it sometimes takes longer for one plant or one tree to be fruitful, so the turning of men's hearts to righteousness will sometimes take longer than we hoped.'

She was silent for a little, digesting this.

'Do you mean that the new kingdom will be a long time coming?'

'Possibly. Probably. We must be patient. But every sinner saved and turned to good is a small step on the road. Another fig tree bearing fruit.'

'You explain things more clearly than Yeshûa, Mariam.'

I made a face. I had no wish to be compared with my brother.

As luck would have it, we arrived in Capernaum on the day the special tax was to be paid, which was a contribution to the rebuilding of the Temple. It amounted to half a *shekel* for each adult male, that is: twenty-six silver *dinars* altogether for our group. There are four *dinars* to a *shekel*. We were penniless. Yehûdâ had just one silver *dinar* left in the common purse. Yeshûa was anxious not to cause trouble by refusing to pay the tax.

'Shim'ôn,' he said, 'cast a fishing-line into the Lake. When you hook a fish, it will have a coin in its mouth. Give it to Yehûdâ, and with the *dinar* he has in his purse, he can pay the tax.'

Shim'ôn looked startled, but fetched his fishing gear from his house. Yehûdâ raised his eyebrows and shrugged, but sat down beside Shim'ôn to wait. *I'll humour him*, his expression said.

Leaving Shim'ôn to his fishing, the rest of us dispersed amongst the various houses of the town, we women going with Salome to Zebedee's house. I did not know what to make of Yeshûa's instruction. Perhaps he meant simply that Shim'ôn should fish until he had earned enough to pay the tax. Later, we heard that the first fish caught had indeed been found to have a coin in its mouth.

This is not as odd as it sounds. These fish, found only in Gennesaret, have strange habits. The male fish swims around holding the eggs of the infant fish in his mouth till they have hatched and can survive on their own, then he spits them out. Until it is time for him to repeat this curious practice, he will pick up a pebble—or a coin—and carry that in his mouth instead. Now it is quite possible that Shim'ôn caught a fish which had picked up a coin instead of a pebble. But is it not strange that my brother should have known that *that* particular fish was carrying around a coin? And that the coin would be a χρυσοῦς στατήρ, worth twenty-five *drachmae* or *dinars*? Which, together with our single *dinar*, was exactly twenty-six *dinars*. Enough to pay the tax.

Yeshûa had decided that he would not follow the direct route to Jerusalem, south on the main road along the Jordan valley. If either Antipas or the Romans should be looking for him, it would be in this well-travelled area, especially during the period leading up to *Pesah*. Instead, we would start by heading west through Samaria and only cross the border east into Judaea much further down. Then he wanted to travel over to visit Jericho, as he had told us in Tyre, before we turned back at last and headed for Jerusalem. Jerusalem! I could not believe I was to see the Holy

City at last. As a girl growing up in our village, I had never expected to travel more than a few miles from home.

Jerusalem! The very sound of it sang with the names of kings and heroes. I was filled with excitement, but also with dread. Ever since our stay in Tyre, my brother had been talking of death in Jerusalem. I clung to the hope that the Holy City itself, with all its glories, would change his mind.

So the journey to Judaea took us through Samaria, the land inhabited by those who have fallen away from faith in the Law. They claim to worship Yahweh by going up to their mountain tops, and say that this is more faithful to the practice of Moses than the rituals practised in the Temple at Jerusalem. Like all pious Israelites I had been brought up to abhor the Samaritans, though my brother sometimes told stories of kind and generous acts carried out by Samaritans when Israelites had failed in their duty of loving kindness to their neighbours. Nevertheless, we made speed through Samaria, Yeshûa trying to avoid recognition, and I was glad when we crossed the border into Judaea and were once again amongst our own kind.

We had travelled long and hard that day, and as we approached the first village I think we were all simply hoping that some hospitable villager would give us food and shelter, for we were still uncertain of our reception in Judaea. Somehow, word of our coming must have flown ahead of us, spread, as they say, by the bird's wing, for there on the outskirts of the village was a crowd of women and children, the women smiling and calling out a welcome to us, the children hopping up and down and dodging about amongst the legs of the adults.

'Lord,' the women said timidly, 'bless our children, we beg you!'

Some of the *shelîhîm* tried to hustle them to one side, for we could all see how exhausted my brother was, but he remonstrated with them.

'We're in no haste.'

He sat down at once on the low wall beside the village well, and the women brought their children to him one by one. Yeshûa had always cherished children. In some ways, for all his learning and his complex ideas, he was like a child in the loving simplicity of his heart. I remembered how he had comforted my childish woes, and played with me, despite the difference in our ages.

As the women came diffidently up to him, he cradled each baby in turn, laying his hand on each small head while saying a *berâkâ*. And the babies who were crying or fretful ceased their clamour and gazed up at him with trusting eyes. The older children he took on his lap, and he talked to them. Some of them put their arms around his neck and whispered in his ear. Some were shy and said nothing, but their faces lit up when he spoke to them.

At our meal that evening, provided by one of the village elders, the talk turned to the injustices that existed between the rich and the poor. Some had lives of ease and comfort, while others laboured for small wages, suffered illness and persecution, and often died young.

'Ah,' said Yeshûa, 'but if the poor are righteous, they shall inherit the kingdom.'

'But what of a man who is born rich?' one of the guests asked. 'If he lives a good life and obeys all the Commandments, has he no hope of a place in the kingdom?'

'Riches,' said my brother, 'are a curse to him who possesses them, for they turn his mind to the trivial objects of this sinful world. Does a man need to eat from a golden bowl? No. His food will taste the same from a wooden platter, or even scooped from the cooking pot with his fingers. Does he need garments dyed with murex and embroidered with pearls? No. He is clothed as comfortably in a simple tunic of unbleached wool. If a rich man would follow me, let him give away all that he has to succour the poor, and follow me with nothing but a peasant's garb and sandals on his feet.'

I saw that the village elder and his other guests, none of whom appeared to lack a *shekel* or two, looked uncomfortable at this, and they turned the conversation to other matters. None chose to follow him. The next day Yeshûa preached his message in the village and healed the sick who were brought to him, before we went on our way again.

Once we had walked a little way from the village, some of the *shelîhîm*, perhaps troubled by his talk of children and rich men the day before, began to ask him what they should have, as a reward for giving up their ordinary lives and following him.

'We have forsaken everything,' Shim'ôn said, 'and followed you. What shall we have?'

Yeshûa stopped in the middle of the road and faced them.

'Everyone who has forsaken houses, or brethren,' he said, 'or sisters, or father, or mother, or wife, or children, or lands, for my name's sake, shall receive a hundredfold, and shall inherit everlasting life.'

He gazed along the road ahead, that led towards Jericho.

'But,' he said at last, somewhat curtly, 'many that are first shall be last, and the last shall be first.'

Then he walked on.

Amongst the *shelîhîm* I heard murmurs.

'When?'

'What does he mean? Are we the first or the last?'

Perhaps because of their grumbling, Yeshûa was in a sad mood that evening. Despite our warm welcome into Judaea, he began foretelling his death again, saying that we would go to Jerusalem, where he would be betrayed and killed. Nothing we said could shake him out of this gloom.

გ

In Gallia, the broiling sun has dropped at last below the western horizon, and the breeze has strengthened a little, bringing with it the scent of the sea. Mariam has fallen asleep in her chair and slumped sideways, her mouth slightly open.

'Mother?' Sergius leans over her, shaking her shoulder gently. 'Mother? It is time for the evening meal.'

Mariam opens her eyes slowly. They seem unfocused and look through and beyond him. Then she sighs deeply and straightens herself painfully until she is sitting upright.

'Could we not eat out here? It is so long since we sat out on the terrace, the whole family, to eat together. Do you remember how we used to eat here, on summer evenings, when you were a boy?'

Sergius knows that Fulvia is tired and hopes to go to bed as soon as the meal is finished. He also knows, what Mariam has not yet been told, that Fulvia is with child again, after nine years of waiting. And he knows that the meal, which is already laid in the *triclinium*, will have to be carried out here with great trouble. A table and benches will have to be moved, all the dishes brought. But he does remember those long, peaceful family meals on the terrace when he was young. They were times of great contentment at the end of his father's long day of labour, when he had time at last to talk quietly to his wife and sons.

'I'll see whether it can be done,' he says, 'if you are sure you are not too tired.'

Mariam gives him a wan smile.

'I do not suppose I will have the opportunity for many more family meals.'

As he turns away and starts for the house, she calls after him.

'Sergius?'

'Yes, Mother?'

'I am glad you are here.'

ᔕ

Jericho must be one of the most beautiful places on earth. Approaching it through the barren, hostile terrain of Judaea, which seems like a place no man would ever choose to inhabit, the traveller descends into the Ghor, the great chasm through which the Jordan runs and which here seems to split the very world in half. A little way to the south lies Qumrân, and beyond it the Sea of Sodom and the unspeakable desert where my brother fasted and was visited by demons and terrible visions. But Jericho lies at the heart of an oasis, a paradise of springs and lush vegetation that stretches five hours' walk in length, a little to the west of the Jordan.

The whole town was shaded by huge palm trees, taller than any I had ever seen before, which provided shade in every street and square. And shade was needed, for there is rarely any breeze here, because the town lies so deep in the earth. But so lush, so fertile! Most of the almond blossom had fallen, but still lay like pink snow in heaps upon the ground. The citrus trees bore fruit and flowers together, and the flowers had the same sweet sharp scent as the fruit. Pomegranates glowed amongst the leaves, plumper and redder than I had ever seen before.

'What is that wonderful scent?' I asked Yehûdâ in a whisper, for something about the beauty of the place made whispering natural. I knew that he had been here several times before, and would not find it as strange and wonderful as I did.

But he smiled and reached out as if to take my hand, then remembered the others. He must not touch me. His hand fell back by his side.

'It is balsam,' he said. 'Do you see the orchard there, on the right? Behind the wall? They are gathering the sap.'

I saw that men on ladders were cutting gashes in the branches of the trees with pieces of sharp flint, then holding bowls beneath, into which the trees wept dark red tears, like blood.

'It thickens,' he said, 'and turns into precious balm.'

'Why do they not use knives?'

'It's said the trees will not give up the balm to iron. It must be stone, as when our ancient forefathers made their sacrifices with a stone knife.'

'They are cutting off the smaller branches,' I said.

'Those are boiled, and the syrup mixed with olive oil.'

'That is aromatic oil?'

'Yes.'

A little further on, a boy of five or six ran up and gave me a bunch of dates, larger than any I have seen before or since. Their taste, too was different.

'They taste of honey!' I said. 'Try them.'

I shared them with Yehûdâ and Susanna and the Magdalene, who were walking with me.

On the outskirts of town, a blind beggar touched Yeshûa's robe and asked for help. My brother cupped his hands over the man's eyes, murmured a prayer, and the poor fellow began to caper with joy, crying out that he could see once more. He kissed the hem of Yeshûa's robe, then ran off ahead of us as we made our way along the road.

Word of our coming thus went ahead of us, cried out by the blind beggar, for as we reached the centre of the town we found a large crowd waiting. They greeted us with shouts of joy. Every face was smiling, and soon we were surrounded by a mass of eager people calling out for my brother to speak to them. Suddenly, it was like the early days again, when Yeshûa had first preached in Capernaum. I felt a surge of relief. This lovely town, these welcoming crowds! The long months of exile and rejection and loneliness and doubt were swept away.

Yeshûa spoke briefly to the crowd about the new kingdom of joy and hope, but only briefly, for it was near sunset and many would be heading home for their evening meal. He began some of the easier cures, telling others to return the next day, when there would be more time to treat them. While he was working, I noticed a disturbance at the edge of the square. Some people looked embarrassed. Others were hiding smiles behind their hands. They all kept looking up at a fig-sycamore, which was shaking violently. A shower of leaves cascaded down, and I saw a bare, skinny leg slip suddenly out of the branches, to be hastily drawn up again. Then I saw an anxious face peering out between the leaves.

'Who is the little fellow up the tree?' I asked a woman standing nearby, with a baby on her hip.

She giggled.

'That is Zaccheus, the tax collector. Seems he's eager to see the *rabbi* and his cures.'

My brother noticed the man and walked over to the tree.

'Zaccheus!' he called, tilting back his head and addressing the bare leg which had again slipped into view. He grabbed the bare foot, from which the sandal had fallen, and tickled it. 'Make haste and come down, for tonight I will stay in your house.'

There was a general gasp of astonishment at this, for it seemed that tax collectors were no more popular in Jericho than in Capernaum. Zaccheus slid to the ground, tugging his robe down around his scratched legs, and bowed formally.

'Master, you do me honour.'

He looked around at the poor and the sick who had gathered around my brother and shook his head in sorrow.

'I did not know there were so many needy in Jericho.'

'And what will you do for the needy, Zaccheus?' my brother asked.

'I will give them half my substance,' he said earnestly. 'And for the rest, I will repay fourfold any man who thinks I've taxed him unfairly. Come with me now, master, and you yourself will see it done.'

'Will he do it, do you suppose?' I whispered to Yehûdâ, as the man slipped his bare foot into the fallen sandal.

'Let's watch and see. Your brother can turn even a scrawny little tax collector into a benefactor of the poor. I shall enjoy this!'

We followed the little man through the streets of Jericho to a lovely quiet square shaded with palms and pomegranate trees. A vine arbour arched over the gateway to Zaccheus's house, and a small garden laid out in the Roman style lay before it. Tax collector he might be, but he was as good as his word. He opened his strong box and drawing out several bags of coin, returned to his gate. Here, with the help of Mattaniah, Philippos and Tôma, he dispensed alms to the poor who crowded round, hands outstretched, while his wife and his maidservants bustled about preparing food for our large party. Yehûdâ looked at me across the little man's head and winked.

When we sat down at last to the best meal we had eaten for many long months, the conversation round the table was cheerful, growing ever more cheerful as Zaccheus's excellent wine circulated. The table was laid with Roman glasses. I was afraid, at first, that I would bite a piece out of mine, for I had never drunk from glass before.

'Now are we come to Judaea and the neighbourhood of Jerusalem,' Yehûdâ called out, raising his glass to my brother. 'I feel at last the joyous kingdom is near at hand!'

The other shelîhîm laughed and raised their glasses in turn. There was an air of rejoicing in the room. Yet I saw that my brother, though he smiled an acknowledgement to Yehûdâ, looked thoughtful. It seemed to me that his eyes were full of sadness and despair. I felt myself go cold, despite the warmth engendered by the wine. Jerusalem. Death. Betrayal. Then Yehûdâ too caught his eye, and I saw him flinch.

Chapter Sixteen

We stayed for several days in Jericho, and our time there was like a pleasant dream from which you wake reluctantly. When you try to recapture it by seeking sleep again, the second sleep brings only nightmares. Zaccheus and several of his friends provided lodgings for us, and when we were not in attendance on my brother we wandered about the town enjoying the pleasures of the fruitful oasis, after our exhausting walk from the Galilee through hostile Samaria and the cruel countryside of Judaea.

One early morning I encountered Yehûdâ sitting down by one of Jericho's fresh springs. It lay glittering under the sun, which had not yet reached the full heat of summer (something the inhabitants of Jericho told us could be nearly unbearable at midday). I sat down beside him on the bank, careful to keep a little distance. Most of the disciples, I believe, had forgotten that we were betrothed, but nevertheless we had always to behave with great circumspection, lest they should think that we were betraying our vow to remain chaste.

'Strange to think,' he said, 'that these lovely waters flow, in just a few miles, into the Jordan, and from there into that cesspit, the Sea of Sodom, to become something stinking and corrupt, where there's no life in the waters and none on the shores round about. The waters are bitter with salt and other unnameable substances, fumes rise from it, and the islands that float on it are not of living reeds but blocks of bitumen and rings of crusted salt. If you immerse your cut hand in the water it will burn like fire.'

'I suppose Yeshûa would say that the river Jordan is like a man's life, and if he does evil he will end like the river in the poisoned water.'

'Ah, but where is your metaphor for the *good* man's life?' he said. 'Are the sweet waters of Jordan, which bring such fertility to the Galilee, and are these springs in the oasis of Jericho, a metaphor for an *evil* life? Surely not! No, you will need to do better than that.'

'I am no preacher,' I said, lying back on the grass and resting the back of my arm on my eyes to shield them. 'I cannot tell stories like my brother.'

'It was just a little way east and south of here,' he said, 'on the banks of the same sweet Jordan, that I met your brother when he came from Qumrân.'

'Why did they choose such a desolate place as the edge of the desert to set up their Community?'

'I believe they thought that to live apart from the rest of mankind, and to mortify their flesh, and to live subject to rigid rules, made them more godly.'

'Do you believe that?' I asked, lifting my arm from my eyes so that I could look at him.

'No. And this beautiful place . . . so peaceful . . . somehow it makes me remember how much I have given up, even if you and I have not withdrawn to the desert.'

I saw something then in his eyes that made me blush and hide my face again, for I too had been wishing that I might live a more normal life. I found I was longing to be free of our vow, to be free so that Yehûdâ and I could marry at last.

'Mariam,' he said softly, 'do you wish to leave Yeshûa's following, so that our marriage can take place?'

'How can we leave him? Just when he is going to Jerusalem?'

'Yes, Jerusalem.'

He sighed.

'I think we will come to the crisis in Jerusalem. I cannot think the Temple authorities will let him preach and heal in Jerusalem as he has done elsewhere. Jerusalem is too volatile. When insurrection breaks out, it's usually in Jerusalem. That's why the Roman prefect, Pontius Pilate, always comes with armed troops at the times of the great festivals. He's there to reinforce the regular Roman garrison in the city.'

I sat up abruptly.

'But I thought we were going to Jerusalem simply for *Pesah*!'

'I think Yeshûa has something else in mind. I don't like the way he keeps referring to his death, and saying that the only place for a prophet to die is in Jerusalem.'

'You think he is *deliberately seeking* his own death?' I cried. 'I thought, when he spoke of it, he meant only that it *might* happen.'

Regardless of whether we might be seen, he reached out and took my hand.

'I told you once that, when he came from Qumrân, he made me promise that if some day he asked me to do something against my will, I would do it, in return for his promise to meet me one year after he entered the Community at Qumrân.'

'I remember.'

'Well, yesterday he reminded me of that promise. He said he might soon call in my debt. I did not like the sound of that. And I think he means to do something in Jerusalem that I will be forced to agree to.'

'He would not do anything wrong.'

'What is "wrong"? If he defies the chief priest and the Sanhedrin, is that wrong? If he preaches against the Emperor, when the Roman prefect is in the city, is that wrong?'

He was silent for a moment, then said so softly that I could hardly hear, 'And if he seeks his own death as a fulfilment of the prophecies in the scriptures, is that wrong?'

'Would he?'

'I do not know.'

'It would be a sin,' I whispered. 'Surely, surely . . . it would be a sin?'

He shook himself, as if to drive away these thoughts, and we stood up, still hand in hand. I heard a rustling in the bushes behind us and then caught sight of a figure moving away along the road. It was Yôhânân. Had he overheard our conversation? Had he seen my hand in Yehûdâ's?

'I know it is wrong of me,' I said, 'but I do not like that man.'

He smiled. 'Is it because your brother often favours him?'

'And why does he?'

'I don't know. Perhaps because he manifests so much loud-voiced enthusiasm?'

'Yeshûa would not be taken in by that.'

But perhaps it was a little true. When many of the disciples had seemed doubtful, Yôhânân had always been loud in his assertions of his belief.

'I do not like the way he stirs up trouble wherever he goes,' I said carefully. 'I do not like the way he tries to force Yeshûa into armed insurrection. I do not like his hysteria and his feigned ecstasies. I do not like his contempt for women.'

I paused.

'And I do not like the way he has been spying on us for months.'

In the cool of that evening, after we had eaten, my brother asked Yehûdâ and me to walk with him in the garden. We found a place to sit on the fresh spring grass under an apple tree, and as we talked the last of the blossom drifted down upon us like perfumed rain. I could tell that something was troubling Yeshûa, and he could not bring himself to speak of it.

At last he said, 'I am minded to release you both from your vow.'

I stared at him.

'What do you mean? Our vow to follow you? We will not leave you now, of all times.'

Yeshûa looked uncomfortable. No, he was embarrassed. The colour rose in his cheeks.

'It has been hard for you both, harder than for any of us. You have been betrothed for so long, and so long denied the fulfilment of that betrothal. To be constantly in each other's company, and to be pinioned by your vow of chastity . . . I would not blame you. I *do not* blame you, if it has proved too much, if your need to express your love for each other has overcome you.'

I was suddenly enlightened, and glanced at Yehûdâ.

'Yôhânân,' I said bitterly. 'It is Yôhânân who has been spilling poison into your ear.'

'It was Yôhânân,' he admitted.

'What has he said?' Yehûdâ asked quietly. 'I'll wager he has lied. Your sister is as pure as the day she was born. I won't

262

deny that it has been hard, to sacrifice the fulfilment of our love to the mission we have all undertaken. But Mariam and I have spoken of this more than once, and we agreed that we must wait, until you are ready to release us.'

'I am ready.'

'But we are not,' I said. 'Jerusalem lies ahead, the culmination of all we have striven for. We will not leave you now.'

I touched his hand lightly.

'We love you too much.'

He took my hand in his and turned it over, as if he would read my mind in my palm.

'Yeshûa,' I said, 'why will you not look me in the face? What has Yôhânân said to you?'

He raised his eyes to mine and I saw that he was wretched.

'He said that you had had carnal knowledge of Yehûdâ.'

I felt anger rise in my breast like a burning fire, and my head grew tight with my fury.

'He lied!' I scrambled to my feet, and they followed me. 'From time to time, Yehûdâ has taken my hand. He did so this very day, when Yôhânân spied upon us from behind some bushes, sly as the serpent in Eden. And we have kissed. Yes, a few times we have kissed. But nothing more. I swear to you, Yeshûa, by Our Holy Father in Heaven, nothing more.'

I fell at his feet, sobbing.

I felt his arms around me then. He was kneeling before me.

'Hush, *talithâ*,' he said. 'I believe you. For you have never lied to me in all your life.'

He pulled me to my feet, and embraced us both.

'I am sorry,' he said, shame-faced. 'I should never have listened to him. Both of you are so dear to me, and I bear the guilt of what you have had to endure in being kept apart. I suppose it was my own guilt that made me gullible.'

'It's forgotten,' said Yehûdâ, slapping him on the shoulder, as if they were boys again. 'Come. Didn't Zaccheus say he was to broach an amphora of vintage wine for us?'

But as we walked back to the house, I heard my brother murmur to himself, 'I pray you have not made the wrong choice.'

That was our last day in Jericho before we moved on to Bethany, a village barely half an hour's walk from Jerusalem. My conversation with Yehûdâ by the spring, and my brother's offer to set us free of our vows to him, had left me in turmoil. It was clear that Yehûdâ wanted our marriage as much as I, and soon, if it were possible. But his fears for what might happen in Jerusalem made me uneasy, and I watched my brother for any sign of what he might be planning.

In Bethany some of us—Yehûdâ, Yeshûa, Shim'ôn, Yôhânân, the Magdalene and I—stayed with two sisters and a brother, who were hospitable and kind. The elder sister, Martha, cooked us prodigious meals, until my brother groaned and patted his stomach, saying that he could have lived for a week at Qumrân on what he had just eaten at one meal. The brother Lazarus brought out his best wines for us and engaged Yeshûa in enthusiastic and intelligent discussion about his teachings, so that I saw him happy and relaxed as he had not been for a long time.

'You mean that this new dispensation,' said Lazarus, 'will come about suddenly, by a kind of miracle? We will wake one morning, and all wrongs will be righted, the sick healed, the poor no longer despised by the rich?'

Yeshûa laughed, for he saw that Lazarus was teasing him.

'Ah, that it could be so! No, nothing good comes without working for it, as you very well know.'

He sipped his wine, and I could see that he was turning phrases over in his mind.

'King David was a fine harpist. Did that come about by a miracle?'

'I expect, like any common musician,' said Lazarus, 'he was taught as a child, and practised many hours.'

'My father Yosef is a wonderful craftsman. When I was apprenticed to him, I did not expect, on the first day, to make a beautiful table inlaid with ivory and ebony, fit for the Emperor, such as he could make. No, on my first day I learned to sweep out his workshop.'

'As any boy would do.'

'Your sister Martha, as we have seen, is a fine cook. But when she was a young girl, did she not sometimes burn the stew in the bottom of the pot? Or turn out raised bread that was heavy as a brick?'

'Often!' said Martha with a laugh.

'You make your point,' said Lazarus. 'Every craftsman or artist must learn his trade, but what has that to do with the new kingdom?'

'We are still apprentices,' said Yeshûa. 'Only when every son and daughter of man has become a master craftsman in the art of loving kindness will we inherit the right to the new kingdom.'

The younger sister, who was hardly more than a child, constantly sat at my brother's feet, listening to him open-mouthed and staring at him adoringly. She followed him around like an eager puppy, until her sister scolded her for not helping to look after the guests. Yeshûa chided Martha for this, but in my heart I sympathised, and did all I could to help her with all the cooking and washing for so many unexpected guests.

On the eighth day of Nisan, we joined the stream of pilgrims heading for Jerusalem, for the beginning of the rituals and festivities leading up to *Pesah*. We had reached the outskirts of the city, a place called Bethphage, where there is a customs post, when Yeshûa called a halt and we gathered round him.

'Go over to the next village,' he said to two of the disciples, 'and you'll find a young ass colt tethered, which has never been ridden. Untie him, and bring him here. If anyone challenges you, say that the Lord needs him, and he will send the colt at once, without question.'

They did as they were bid, and brought the donkey, to the surprise of many of us. It was a fine young beast, large for a donkey and unmarked as yet by hard labour and the galls rubbed by the heavy burdens these poor creatures spend their lives carrying. There was no saddle, so we made a pad out of several mantles, and Yeshûa mounted. I watched a little fearfully, for an unbroken mount can be dangerous, but the colt stood quietly, and we set off again, Yeshûa riding in front and the rest of us

265

following on foot. I could not understand his strange behaviour, for my brother had always walked everywhere. Why should he ride now? Then I remembered what Yehûdâ had said about Yeshûa wanting to fulfil prophecies. I thought I recalled something about the *mashiha* riding humbly into Jerusalem on an ass. The ass would be important. If Yeshûa had ridden in on a horse, a symbol of power, he would have been announcing that he came as a military leader.

But Yeshûa had denied over and over again that he was the *mashiha*, for whom all Israelites longed. I remembered how he had once turned on Shim'ôn, furious at being so named. Why was he doing this now? Even in our most private conversations he had said nothing of this to Yehûdâ and me. Though indeed he had grown more secretive in recent days. Was he trying deliberately to provoke the authorities? Perhaps I was mistaken. Perhaps it had nothing to do with prophecies. Even so, I entered Jerusalem in a state of fear. Everyone's attention was on Yeshûa. He was recognised at once, even here, so far from the Galilee. The crowds of pilgrims were whispering his name amongst themselves, and soon they began to call out, 'Hosannah! Blessed is he who comes in the name of the Lord! Blessed is the son of David!'

Somewhere in the crowd a voice cried, 'Hail, the King of the Jews!'

Alarmed, I twisted round and searched the faces, trying to make out who had spoken. It sounded like Yôhânân's voice, but the press of people was too great for me to be sure. The cry was taken up here and there: 'Hail, the King of the Jews!'

I looked around for Yehûdâ. He was walking with Shim'ôn, who was transfixed with joy and excitement. I could read in his face the belief that the new kingdom was on the point of birth. Yehûdâ looked tense and worried. I was glad that we were still far from the Temple, so that there were no Temple guards or officials to hear the greetings of the crowd, for I was afraid they would seize my brother, even though it was not he but the pilgrims who were calling out these words, words which were surely seditious. I knew how nervous those in power were at the time of the *Pesah* festival, when riots and other trouble broke out.

I dragged my eyes away from the crowds round my brother and turned to look at this city we were entering, the Holy City, which I had heard about all my life. I could never have imagined such a place. Everywhere there were hills and valleys, so that the buildings climbed higher and higher above us, so crowded together and precipitous that I was afraid they might topple over and crush us. I was familiar with the usual whitewashed buildings in every village and town, but their white was flat, chalky, dull. The buildings of Jerusalem shone in the morning sun, reflecting the light from their sparkling surfaces like ice on a pond. Many of them must be marble, I realised, and reached out to touch the wall of a building at the side of the road, running my palm across the surface. The stone was hard and smooth, the white streaked here and there with faint grey lines, like the veins on the back of my hand.

In Jericho I had seen one or two buildings of marble, standing out strangely amongst the humbler constructions, but here the abundance of marble reflected the sunlight back and forth from building to building, until my eyes grew tired with the dazzle of it.

The streets were so jammed with people that we made very slow progress into the centre of the city. Everyone seemed happy and in holiday mood. Men had brought their wives and children, it was a fine spring day, there was a general air of festivity. We pushed our way through a market, like the one Yeshûa had seen when he came to make his *bar mitzvah* vow. I was dizzy with the colour of it, and the scents heaped up in almost sickening profusion. There were the clean perfumes of jasmine and astringent herbs, but I could also smell putrefying meat, and underfoot I trod on overripe grapes, reeking of sour wine and mould. I kicked something with my foot and looked down to see a rotten pomegranate roll away into the ditch. Beyond it, a narrow alley led downhill. It was strewn with rubbish and lost itself amongst a mean huddle of slums.

I realised that, behind the façades of marble, away from the streets where the priests and pilgrims walked, there lurked another, grimmer, reality.

Up ahead, a man suddenly shouted out, 'Stop, thief!' A quick-fingered robber had slashed the thong securing his purse to his belt and was running down towards us. Shim'ôn thrust out a strong arm and caught the thief as he passed, twisting the knife from his hand. It flew through the air and landed in the ditch beside the pomegranate, where a young boy seized it and made off down the alleyway. Shim'ôn forced open the thief's fingers and freed the purse, which he tossed to the victim, then kneed the thief in the back and sent him scrambling away down the alley after the boy. It all happened so quickly I hardly saw the man before he was gone.

The robbed man came puffing up to Shim'ôn.

'I thank you, friend, for saving my purse, but we should have handed over the miscreant for punishment.'

Shim'ôn shrugged his burly shoulders.

'He has gained nothing by it. Be thankful you have your gold and enjoy the festival.'

When the man had gone, still grumbling, away, my brother clapped Shim'ôn on the shoulder.

'That was well and neatly done, my Rock!'

He had dismounted from the donkey now, and was on foot like the rest of us. I saw that Ya'kob, brother of Yôhânân, was holding the animal at the side of the street, and not looking very happy about it.

'Has he told you what he plans to do today?' I asked Yehûdâ, when I could come close enough to speak to him.

'I'm hoping he is merely looking about him, scouting before the battle, as it were.'

'I don't like your comparison,' I said.

'No. A poor choice of words. Look, Shim'ôn and Andreas have cleared a way through the market for us. The others are heading for that inn.'

We sat down under the awning outside the inn, like any other pilgrims, and called for fruit juice and little cakes. Perhaps, after all, the fears that Yehûdâ and I had been entertaining were just our own fevered imaginings.

I had hoped too soon. Before we had even finished taking our refreshments, a crowd had gathered round us and was begging Yeshûa to speak to them. He drained his beaker and stood up. I shifted my stool a little closer to Shim'ôn and Yehûdâ.

My brother spoke quietly, so that people had to strain forward to hear him.

'We are all come here as pilgrims to the Holy City, my brothers and sisters,' he said, 'to the heart of our nation, the holy of holies. In a few days' time, we shall celebrate the blessed festival of *Pesah*. When Our Lord spared us in the land of Egypt, he did so because we were the Chosen People. Should we be complacent that we were given such a title? What have you done . . . or you . . . or you, to deserve it? What have I done?'

He paused, looking down at his clasped hands.

'To be favoured, to be singled out by Yahweh, does not mean that we should assume we are born *better* than the rest of mankind. No, it means we have been offered the chance to *become* better, to gain favour in the eyes of the Lord, and to enter into his kingdom. But only if we strive with hearts and minds, and in every daily action, to be worthy of it. It is a gift. Treasure it.'

Some of the crowd shifted uneasily, where they were sitting on the ground. Some avoided his eye. But some looked dazzled, as if lit with unexpected hope and understanding.

He went on to speak briefly of peace and love. There was nothing in what he said that could have offended the authorities: neither the most rigid and zealous Pharisee with his fastidious rituals, nor the most powerful Sadducee aristocrat, ruling in the Sanhedrin.

However, I noticed a group of men standing to one side, who gradually moved closer to us. They looked neither shamed nor inspired. Instead their faces all wore the same expression of sly calculation. From their immaculate dress and their way of holding themselves apart from the crowd, so that not even the edge of a robe might brush against some unclean person, I knew at once that they were Pharisees. And I knew with equal certainty that they would try to trap my brother. I was suddenly sick with fear. A barbed remark from an obscure Pharisee in some remote village in the north could do him no harm. But a group of Pharisees—wealthy men, all of them, by their appearance—here in Jerusalem . . . if they could trick him into saying something which could be taken as blasphemous or seditious, they could bring down the Temple guards on him before we could escape from the city.

I half rose from my seat and tugged at his arm.

'Yeshûa!' I hissed. 'Be careful!'

He put my hand gently aside and smiled at me. I realised that he too had recognised the Pharisees.

'From whom do you claim power, Yeshûa of Galilee?' one called, hoping to catch him out in blasphemy.

But my brother was too clever for him. He answered with another question.

'Who do you say gave power to Yôhânân the Baptiser?' he asked. 'Was it from Heaven or from men?'

The group of Pharisees looked at one another in consternation. What could they say? If they said that Yôhânân's power came from the Lord, they would acknowledge him as a sanctified prophet. If they denied it, the crowd would turn on them, for since our cousin's execution the people believed in him, if anything, more devoutly.

Then another tried to manoeuvre my brother into treason.

'What do you say—should we pay taxes to Caesar?'

Yeshûa smiled at him sweetly and said, 'Show me a coin.'

The man handed him a silver *denarius* and Yeshûa held it up for all to see.

'Whose face is on the coin?' he asked.

'The Emperor Tiberius!' several people shouted.

Yeshûa flipped the coin with his thumbnail, so that it spun, flashing, up into the sky, then fell back neatly into the Pharisee's hand.

'Give unto Caesar,' he said, 'what belongs to Caesar. Give unto God, what belongs to God.'

After that, they asked no more questions, but I saw that they took note of all my brother said. They were particularly agitated when he spoke of the coming of a new kingdom, and when the crowd dispersed they made off in the direction of the Temple. For although there was much ill feeling between the Pharisees and the Sadducees (who made up most of the

270

Sanhedrin—the council ruling under the high priest), yet if both factions of powerful men felt themselves threatened by a man whom the common people hailed as king, I knew that they would unite. I had learned much in the years I had travelled with my brother. Oh, I was no longer that green girl who had run from her home, clutching a bedroll, stumbling in the wake of her brother and her betrothed, towards an unknown future. Now, I was wiser. And I was afraid.

Later in the afternoon, Yeshûa rode out of the city and we followed. When we reached Bethphage, he dismounted and sent the colt back to its owner. Together we all walked on to Bethany. Over Martha's good dinner, I could see Yeshûa had relaxed and was talking to Shim'ôn about the fine buildings of Jerusalem as if he had never spoken of his fears about what might happen there.

When the meal was over, however, and the dishes cleared away by Martha and me, he became restless. He began to pace about the room, muttering to himself. I watched him nervously, for his behaviour in recent days had become more unpredictable. Finally, he signalled to Yehûdâ with a nod to withdraw with him into the back room. After a few minutes, I followed them. Yeshûa was sitting with his elbows on his knees and his head in his hands, while Yehûdâ stood before him, leaning forward, as if he had just been urging some point. They both jumped as I closed the door behind me.

'What is the matter?' I said. 'It went well today, didn't it? There was no trouble. You out-foxed those Pharisees.'

'Just what I have been telling him!' said Yehûdâ, striding off to the far end of the room and back again. Something unspoken crackled in the air between them.

'Yeshûa?' I said.

He simply shook his head.

I knelt on the floor beside him and gently drew his hands away from his face. His eyes looked bruised and desperate.

'Yeshûa? What is it?'

'It is not enough,' he said in a choked voice.

'I don't understand.'

'A few people heard me, but did they *listen*? Did I even begin to touch their hearts? I don't think so.'

'It will take time,' Yehûdâ protested. 'You cannot expect to convert Jerusalem in a day!'

'There *is* no time. The priests and the Romans will not allow me time, they will come after me. Sooner or later, they will take me. A few people here and there—it is all taking too long. I have to do something to make them listen, to make them understand. Tomorrow we will go to the Temple and I will *make* them listen!'

He was suddenly angry. Yehûdâ and I exchanged worried looks. What was he planning to do? But he would not tell us.

As we went to rejoin the others, he threw a final remark over his shoulder.

'A man must be prepared to die for what he believes in. I will prove by my death that the message I bring is the truth.'

I tried to hold him back, to make him explain himself, but he became suddenly urgent, calling for torches, saying that the rest of our party must be sent for, together with all who wished to follow him.

When everyone was gathered in front of Lazarus's house, he began to speak, standing beneath a flaming torch whose sparks streamed like the tail of a comet behind his head, and this time it was not about love and brotherhood.

'The Temple will be cast down, its very stones ground to dust!' he cried. 'The vengeance of the Lord will fall upon Israel, and the wicked shall be condemned to everlasting punishment! Those who do not believe shall die a thousand deaths, they shall wish they had never been born! I bring you the Sword of Righteousness!'

He seemed incandescent with anger, as I had never seen him in my life before, and I was terrified. Was this my gentle brother? The man of peace? Most of the people listening, though, after some initial unease, began to catch light from his eloquence. Oh, he could work miracles with his voice, my brother! I truly believe if he had asked them, at the height of his passion, to follow him into a raging fire, they would have gone, as obedient as a flock of sheep.

The next day we returned to Jerusalem, walking back along the dusty road all the way, and this time Yeshûa walked with us, calm now, and cheerfully resolute. At first he had not wanted the women to come, but suddenly, with a shrug, he had yielded.

'Women shall be the equals of men in the new kingdom,' he said. 'It is right that they too should bear witness.'

I was more at ease, for nothing untoward had happened in Jerusalem on the previous day, apart from my brother's strange wish to ride a donkey into the city. He had dealt calmly with the Pharisees, and they had caused him no trouble. Indeed, we had not caught sight of any soldiers or priests, and had not even gone to the Temple, though I understood that we would go there today. I suppose we were all excited at the thought, for the Temple is the most sacred of places for all Israelites. At one time, when we were not so dispersed, people were able to attend the Temple for worship regularly. Now that many of us lived far away, some people never visited it at all, or no more than once or twice in a lifetime. Certainly the fishermen from Capernaum had never been there; they had been awed on the previous day by the great walls of the city and the civic buildings we had seen.

Everywhere in Jerusalem you seem to climb. I was never able to get the shape of it into my head, but it seemed to me that if you did go down one narrow, stepped street for a little way, then immediately afterwards you climbed up another twice as far. As we made our way to the Temple we seemed to climb and climb. The streets were very narrow and crowded, and they were paved with uneven cobbles, which made them more treacherous than the dirt tracks I was accustomed to. As a consequence, I was watching my feet as we climbed until I heard the Magdalene gasp beside me.

'Oh, Mariam!' she cried, grabbing my arm. 'Look!'

Before us a great complex of courtyards and buildings arose, towering tier upon tier until its innermost and highest building seemed to touch the very heavens. I could not believe that the hand of man could have built such a place. Yet it was quite new, some parts still being completed, for the holy Temple of Solomon had been destroyed long ago. The new Temple had been started in my father's youth by Herod, him they call 'the

Great'—great in wickedness, certainly, for he slew one of his own wives and several of his sons. But a great builder, also. Despite its newness, the Temple was awe-inspiring. From the outside, it looked more like a fortress than a place of worship. A place very different from the simple village *kenîshtâ* I had known.

We joined the throng of pilgrims entering through what I was told was the Court of the Gentiles, an outer court to which even *gôyîm* are admitted, long before one reaches the inner and sacred parts of the Temple. As we walked across the great open space, I sensed more than ever that the Temple was like a fortress or even a city, self-contained within the city of Jerusalem. At the far side we were face-to-face with Solomon's Portico, through which we passed into another open secular area. What had seemed like a fortress from the outside, now appeared to be a vast, crowded and stinking marketplace. It smelled of dung and blood and, I regret to say, of too many unwashed bodies, for the people who transacted their daily business here were far from ritually pure. This was the *hanûyôth*, the merchants' quarter, and there were men of every nation to be seen, many of them *gôyîm*, though they were not permitted to enter the sacred areas, on penalty of death. Roman soldiers strolled about, keeping an eye on the crowds, but also buying from the stalls which sold everything needed for sacrifice—birds and animals, oil, precious unguents, wine, incense, grain—and a myriad other goods besides. Many of the traders were not Israelites, but Syrians, Phrygians, Nubians, Egyptians, and men whose high cheekbones and slanting eyes showed that they came from far to the east. There were even stalls selling trinkets such as travellers buy, to remind them of their visits to holy places: small pieces of stone that were said to be fragments of Solomon's original Temple, jars of local honey, *tallithim* woven in the Holy City itself, and therefore all the more efficacious when worn for prayer. At the time, I believed what the stallholders claimed for their goods, but later, I doubted. If the pieces of stone had been selling for forty years at the rate I saw them selling that day, they would have been enough to build three Temples. And the weaving looked to me like poor foreign stuff.

In pride of place amongst all this noise and dirt and stench were the stalls where sacrificial animals and birds were sold, and where moneyers exchanged all types of coinage into Tyrian silver *zuzim*, the only coins considered pure enough for Temple offerings and taxes. Yeshûa, with sudden energy, strode into the midst of these.

'My house shall be called of all nations the house of *prayer*,' he shouted, quoting scripture, 'but you have made of it a den of thieves!'

With that, he seized the edge of a moneychanger's table and tipped it up. Coins of every nation bounced and rolled in all directions. After a second's stunned silence, people began scrambling about the courtyard, grabbing the rolling coins and stuffing them into their belts and purses. Scuffles broke out, and men punched each other to reach a handful of *denarii*. The moneychanger was wailing and beating his breast, calling for the soldiers. Yeshûa went calmly on, cutting the tethers of the lambs and kids, so that they ran bleating and frightened amongst people's feet, tripping them up. Some of the animals fled out of the gates, others ran in confusion towards the sacred places of the Temple. Now my brother was unlatching the cages of doves and flinging them into the air, crying, 'Go free, brother!'

The more unruly of the disciples, including the sons of Zebedee, had joined in the tumult. They ran from table to table of the moneychangers, overthrowing them gleefully and shouting, 'A den of thieves!'

'We have to get him out of here.' It was Yehûdâ, close beside me and speaking to Mattaniah, who was also looking on, appalled.

'Mariam!' Yehûdâ turned to me. 'Take the women and go straight back to Bethany. Don't stop.'

'But my brother?'

'We'll bring him. And as many of those hotheads as we can.'

In fact, at the sound of trumpets, calling the Roman soldiers together, many of our followers has realised it was time to leave. They were melting away in different directions, slipping out of this outer court of the Temple. As I shepherded the women away,

I saw Yehûdâ and Mattaniah take Yeshûa firmly by each arm and hustle him after us.

That night, everyone was shocked and subdued. Despite Yeshûa's fiery address the previous night, I do not think anyone had expected him to initiate any really physical violence. They had somehow dreamed of a mystical intervention from the Lord, not an undignified scuffle with a crowd of dirty traders.

'Why did he do it?' I demanded of Yehûdâ and Mattaniah, who were conferring together in the garden after dinner. 'Was this what he meant last night? A violent gesture, to make the world pay attention and listen to him? Will it achieve that? Or will it just get him arrested?'

'Yehûdâ thinks he *wants* them to arrest him,' said Mattaniah uncertainly.

'But *why*?' I insisted. 'What will that accomplish? It will stop him carrying out his mission.'

'None of us are privy to that,' Yehûdâ said. 'But you heard him. He feels that our mission has stalled. The new kingdom will not come without some terrible act of sacrifice.'

'He really means to sacrifice himself?'

'That's what I fear.'

I tried to question my brother myself, but he merely shook his head at me and smiled.

'I am prepared to die, Mariam.'

'We all have to die,' I said, suddenly, furiously, angry. 'What good will it do? I think you have gone mad. I don't seek my death . . . why should you? *Please*, Yeshûa.' I was sobbing now. 'Don't leave me.'

He put his arms around me and kissed my forehead, but I could feel, even in his warm living body, the strength of his resistance to me.

Chapter Seventeen

My brother's unexpected attack on the moneychangers in the *hanûyôth* confronted us with a dangerous dilemma. If we were to take part in the *Pesah* celebrations—and that was what Yeshûa said was his intention, this was why we had come to Jerusalem—then we must go through ritual purification, Yeshûa especially, after the many sick he had touched and the *mazzíkím* he had cast out. This meant joining the groups of pilgrims in the Holy City for ritual baths and sprinkling by the priests. But how could we allow my brother to come anywhere near the priests, after what had happened in the Temple? Yeshûa listened quietly to the arguments, then agreed to go back to Jerusalem in a small group, without fuss, and with his head covered to avoid recognition. He was anxious for purification, for he never denied the proper observance of Temple rituals. It was their debasement that so angered him.

During the next few days, we behaved like any other pilgrims, joining in all the rites without disturbance and returning each night to Bethany. With each day, I grew less worried. Perhaps my brother had recovered from what seemed to be a temporary insanity. We would celebrate the festival, then leave Jerusalem and continue our mission in Judaea. Two days before the fifteenth Nisan (which would be the Sabbath and also the most holy day of the festival) my brother sent Yehûdâ with the common purse into Jerusalem, with instructions to book rooms for us at an inn and to purchase food for a meal. We would celebrate with a dinner that night, after sundown, at the beginning of the fourteenth Nisan. It was permitted to take the *Pesah* meal early if desired, any time leading up to the Festival of Unleavened Bread, though most people did so after sunset on the following day, as the fifteenth Nisan began. It was not unusual and I did not question it. I did not realise that what my brother was planning should happen the following morning could not take place on a holy day.

We made our way into the city in small numbers, to avoid attracting attention. Only the heart of our group was to attend the meal: Yeshûa, the twelve *shelîhîm*, and the women. Although we normally ate together, because my brother always maintained that men and women should be treated equally, for this formal meal he had arranged that the men should sit at the main table in the larger room, while the women sat a little apart in the inner room. Even now I do not know if he did this to avoid alerting the people at the inn, or for some purpose of his own. The two rooms were separated by no more than an archway, with a curtain drawn back, so we could converse with each other, and the dishes of roast lamb with herbs, the roasted vegetables, the wine and unleavened bread could pass back and forth.

I thought we were simply to have a peaceful meal together at the start of the holy festival, but while the inn servants were laying out the dishes and bringing in flasks of wine with the fine goblets of hammered pewter that Yehûdâ had ordered, I caught sight of my brother in an unguarded moment. He was looking out of the window at the street below, where a group of musicians was passing by, playing some soft, plaintive tune. I noticed the dark shadows under his eyes, as if he had not slept. He must have felt my gaze, for he turned on me a look that was momentarily defenceless. His eyes were sorrowful, and terrified, and seemed somehow to be asking my forgiveness. I pressed the back of my hand against my mouth and started forward to go to him, but at that moment Yôhânân tugged at his sleeve. My brother veiled his look and turned aside.

Yehûdâ was watching me and seemed as nervous as a mouse waiting for a cat to pounce. When he went through the door and began giving instructions to the innkeeper, I followed him out of the room and caught up with him at the head of the stairs.

'What is it!' I asked. 'What is happening?'

Yehûdâ looked at me with eyes that seemed to have stared into the very pit of Hell itself.

'Yeshûa has ordered me to report him to the priests of the Temple.' His voice was a harsh whisper. 'I am to bring the guards to arrest him in the garden of Gethsemane.'

He drew a long shuddering breath.

'He has finally called in my debt.'

'You cannot, Yehûdâ! You cannot!'

'This is what he demands. He believes that only in this way, with his own death, can he accomplish his mission.'

The walls began to swing around me and I grabbed his arm for support.

'You must be brave, my love, for his sake,' he said. 'He has never needed your courage more than he needs it now.'

Somehow we managed to eat that meal, Yeshûa, Yehûdâ and I, though none of us ate much. *This is our last meal together*, I thought, and the words kept on ringing in my head, so that I hardly heard what the others said, cheerfully enjoying the excellent food and wine around me. I should have been sitting with the two of them, not separated here with the women, by the conventions of our ancestors. Were we not going to make the world anew, where such divisions were cast aside? It must have been very cold in the room, it seemed to me, for I could not stop shivering. I fetched my mantle from the chest where I had laid it down, and wrapped it around my head and shoulders, but still I was chilled to the bone.

I watched the back of Yehûdâ's head. He was bowed forward, resting his chin on his hand and poking at the roast lamb on his platter with the point of his knife. My brother was leaning his head towards Yôhânân, who was trying to dominate the conversation, but I could tell from the absent way he nodded that he was not listening to him. Instead, he was trying to talk to Shim'ôn. It looked as though he was giving him some sort of instructions.

I was so filled with grief and anger I thought I should choke. How could my brother do such a wicked thing? To demand that his dearest friend and my lover betray him to his death? In exchange for that simple promise Yehûdâ had asked of him all those years ago, to meet him near Qumrân? It was monstrous, unforgivable. To bring about one's own death, suicide, was a sin in the eyes of the Lord. Was that not what Yeshûa was doing? As surely as if he had taken a knife to his own throat, it was suicide. But by doing it in this way, dragging his friend down with him . . . And how could he abandoned me, his sister, who loved him more than life itself . . . why, why, why?

I prayed, then. Prayed to Yahweh to put a stop to this madness.

When the rest of our companions had satisfied their hunger, Yeshûa stood up with a large round of flatbread in his hand. He blessed it before breaking it into pieces, which he handed out.

He said—I thought I heard him say—'This is my body. Take it. Eat it in remembrance of me.'

I stared at him in bewilderment. He had his back to me, so I could not read his face. The other women were whispering together.

The Magdalene murmured to me, 'What does he mean?'

I shook my head. I was straining to hear. They seemed the words of a madman, yet he looked calm, except for a slight trembling in the hand that held the bread.

Then he took a large double-handled cup of wine, of the sort used at marriage feasts and which some call a loving-cup. This too he blessed. He drank a little and passed it on. As it went round the table, each man drinking a little, he said, 'Take this and drink. It is my blood. Do this in remembrance of me.'

He had told me of a similar ritual with bread and wine practised at the high table for the pure in Qumrân, but without these strange instructions of his. His body? His blood?

I shivered at his words and stood up, pretending to be busy with the empty plates, carrying them through to the main room, so that I could be nearer to them both.

'Remembrance,' I whispered, but no one heard me.

'I shall not drink again of the fruit of the vine until I drink it new with you in my Father's kingdom,' my brother said, very softly, as if he was making a promise to himself.

He was still standing and moved a little away from the table, drawing Yehûdâ after him.

'What you have to do, do it quickly.'

My brother laid his hand on Yehûdâ's shoulder for a moment, then went back to the table. He glanced across at the friend on whom he had laid this dreadful burden, and gave a small nod. There was compassion in his eyes.

Yehûdâ turned on him a look of such anguish, I thought I should be sick.

'Please, Yeshûa, I beg of you!' he said.

My brother shook his head. 'Go.' Then he resumed his seat.

I followed Yehûdâ down the stairs to the street door and put my arms around him to hold him back. I did not care who saw us now.

'You cannot!' I sobbed. 'Beloved, he has gone mad! We must stop him!'

He held me close and I could feel the terrible drumming of his heart.

'I cannot break my vow. He has counted on that. He has trapped me in the web of my own honour.'

He was weeping openly and could barely speak.

'I promise you this, my dearest one. I will carry out his instructions to the letter, but that will not prevent me trying to save him from his own delusions.'

He kissed me gently on the forehead and was gone.

After the *Pesah* meal was over, Yeshûa suggested that, as it was a beautiful night, warm and still, we might go for a walk. Along the slopes of the Mount of Olives, he said, to the orchard that was called the Garden of Gethsemane, named after the large olive press located there. I was thinking desperately: Could I somehow draw him aside? Persuade him to take me back to Bethany on some pretext? Pretend to be ill? He would see through my pretence at once, or send me back with one of the others. No, I must stay here and help Yehûdâ save him.

'I wish to pray out in the open,' he said, 'under my Father's heaven.'

'Where is Yehûdâ?' someone asked.

'I have sent him,' said my brother, 'to do what is needful.'

We followed him obediently, and suddenly I understood his reasons for this walk. Perhaps indeed he wished to pray there, but Gethsemane was an easy spot for the guards and soldiers to find us. And being in the open, in the dark, it would also be easy for the rest of us to escape. I think, too, that he did not want to be

281

captured indoors, like a rat in a trap, but out under the open sky, where he had passed so much of his life.

It was very peaceful in Gethsemane. No one else was about. Because it was the middle of the lunar month, the moon was full and lit our way. It reminded me of the olive orchard at home, where I had spent those happy times with Yeshûa as a child, learning to read and write. Here too there were olive trees—from the breadth of their massive trunks, hundreds of years old, standing like ancient silent warriors all around us. But whereas in the village orchard the ground between the trees was clear of other growth, being regularly trodden by the villagers tending the trees or harvesting the olives or making their way down to the river, here we walked on fragrant grasses and herbs. I could smell camomile bruised beneath our feet, and wild thyme. I brushed against a bush of rosemary and plucked a sprig. Crushed between my fingers, its resinous scent reminded me of the meal we had just eaten, and also of the lamb roasted for my betrothal feast. Shy white flowers shone ghostly amongst the roots of the trees, wood anemones, and—barely to be seen in the moonlight—the imperial purple and blues of their larger cousins, the lilies of the field, which bled into the surrounding darkness.

When we had reached a pleasant grove amongst the trees, Yeshûa urged us to rest, for he said he wished to pray alone. As he moved away to climb a little higher, I caught his arm.

'Must this be?' I whispered.

I could not keep back the tears, and my voice was hoarse and cracked.

'Yehûdâ has told you, then? It is the only way, *talithâ*.'

'I beg you, Yeshûa,' I said. 'If you have ever loved me, come away.'

I tugged at his arm.

But he shook his head. Whatever part I had played in his life, whatever role I had in the greater story, in this I could not prevail.

Then he laid his hand on my head and blessed me. Through my tears I saw his shape amongst the trees, moving softly up the hill. Most of the group were not merely resting, they were already asleep, but I sat down cross-legged, my hands in my lap and my back against a tree, determined to stay awake at whatever cost. The great old tree, with its uncompromising shape and solidity reminded me somehow of Shim'ôn, stretched out on the ground nearby, breathing heavily from all the wine and rich food. Gradually the warm scents of the place stole over me, for it was indeed a garden, wild and uncultivated as it was, and not an orchard. The darkness and evening dew, the moonlight and starlight, made the scents of leaves and bark, of crushed grasses and delicate flowers, blend in a potent perfume that would have been undetectable by daylight. It filled the air and my fearful and sorrowing soul. I was drowsy, but my hearing remained sharp, and before long I heard hurried footsteps, not of a troop of men, but of one man.

'Where is he?'

It was Yehûdâ standing before me, pale and breathless. I pointed to the path by which my brother had gone.

'I have done what he asked,' he said grimly, 'but I am still going to try to save him from himself. They will be here in a few minutes. Will you come with me?'

A sudden unforeseen hope leapt in my breast. If anyone could save my brother, it was Yehûdâ. I sprang to my feet.

Together we climbed the hill and found my brother sobbing out incoherent prayers, begging Yahweh to spare his life. He was white and trembling with fear. Yehûdâ grabbed him by the shoulders and shook him.

'We will go *now*,' he said, 'down the other side of the hill and north towards the Galilee. We can be well away from the city before daybreak.'

Suddenly, as though transformed by Yehûdâ's words, my brother became calm. He rose to his feet, gently set aside Yehûdâ's hands, and shook his head.

'This is my bitter cup,' he said, 'and I must drink it. Now listen.' He took the hand of each of us. 'You must both flee at once. Leave the Land of Judah. You, Mariam, will be in peril as the sister of Yeshûa, the Galilean trouble-maker. You must go alone, for to accompany Yehûdâ will mean danger and probable death. You are strong now, and brave. You will do this for me. And you, Yehûdâ, will be reviled and pursued by those who believe in me. You will be called forever the Betrayer of the *mashiha*. You will have the worst of it, for your suffering will be lifelong. Mine will be over before the next sundown.'

I was suddenly, coldly, terribly afraid. I threw myself to the ground and clutched handfuls of his tunic, as though somehow I could anchor him to life, but he lifted me tenderly to my feet.

'Let me do this with dignity, Mariam.'

Then he embraced us both, holding us tightly in his arms and kissing us.

'It is time,' he said, and set off briskly down to where the rest of our group were sleeping. I could see now, beyond the clearing, the wavering light of torches coming up the hill, and men's rough voices, and the clatter of armour.

The *shelîhîm* and the women woke, bewildered, seeing us coming down the hill and suddenly in the midst of them a confusion of soldiers and Temple guards, and shouting, and the flash of torchlight on weapons. They jumped to their feet. The Magdalene screamed.

Suddenly, there were men everywhere. The soldiers were heavily armed, but some of the *shelîhîm* also carried weapons. Shim'ôn Kêphas drew his sword and flew at one of the men. Yehûdâ thrust me behind him and his sword shrieked as he pulled it from its scabbard. I fumbled for the small knife I carried at my belt for cutting my meat, but I could have done no more than scratch an assailant. In the darkness and confusion, friend was as likely to strike friend as to hurt an enemy.

'Stop!' Yeshûa shouted desperately. 'Put up your blades, my brothers! No man must spill blood on my account!'

He ran forward towards the Temple guards, holding out his spread hands in a gesture of peace.

'Take me. Don't harm my friends. I am the one you seek, Yeshûa of the Galilee. These others are nothing to you. I swear I will come with you without a struggle.'

Shim'ôn stood uncertainly, his weapon still raised. I looked past Yehûdâ's sword arm as my brother called over his shoulder, 'Go, all of you! Save yourselves!'

One of the guards struck him on the side of the head with the flat of his sword, and he fell to his knees. The others began to kick him, in the guts and the back, as a crowd of boys will kick an inflated bladder around the street. A soldier in heavy boots studded with iron nails jumped on his head. Someone was screaming. I was screaming. Then the guards produced a rope and threw a noose over my brother's neck. They twisted his arms behind his back and bound them together. His legs were tied with just enough slack to allow him to stumble along like a hobbled horse.

He looked back once towards me. Blood was pouring from a split lip and one eye was beginning to swell. His eyes held some message for me—they seemed to be pleading for forgiveness.

Then they dragged him away, and a sudden silence descended on the grove.

I looked around in astonishment.

'Where are the men?' I asked.

'Run away,' said Salome bitterly, 'even my brave sons, who talk so loud.'

Run away. Every one of them. None were left but the women.

'Let us follow,' said the Magdalene, 'and find out where they take him.'

We began to descend the hill, keeping the distant group of men and torches in sight as they made their way back into the city. I was so shocked at the speed with which my brother had been wrenched from me that I followed as if in a trance, not fully knowing what I was doing, alone in the dark of night with the women. But I found that not all of the men had fled. My arm was caught, and Yehûdâ pulled me aside from the path, into the shadow of a huge olive tree.

'Yeshûa told you to leave at once,' he said.

'I must know what is happening.'

'You must do as he says.'

I did not reply. For the first and last time in my life, I would disobey my brother.

Yehûdâ perhaps took my silence for consent.

'Listen, Mariam. Here is money for you.'

He handed me a small purse and, astonished, I tucked into the neck of my tunic.

'Where did you get this?'

'Earlier today, when I came to arrange the meal, I visited a friend of my father's to borrow money. It's not much, but it will help you. You must go to Caesarea Maritima. Do you think you can find your way?'

'I suppose so. It's on the seacoast of Samaria, just to the south of the border with the Galilee.'

'Yes. There you must go to the house of Amos, ship-builder and trader, another of my father's merchant friends. He will arrange a passage for you—the money I have given you should be enough. Go west as far as you can. To Italia. Or even Gallia or Hispania. Get away from here, to where you will be safe.'

'But can we not go together? Surely we could go together?' I was horrified.

'No. You heard what Yeshûa said. He knows my future. He knows the path I must tread, for paying him my debt. He would not condemn you to that, nor will I allow it. I will be reviled forever. I am a condemned man. If you go with me, you too will be tainted, spurned, cast out.'

'I do not care!' I cried. I was losing everything in one night: my brother, my betrothed. 'I am already an outcast. I will come with you. Don't you wish it?'

At that he kissed me, crushing me so hard in his arms that I thought he would break my ribs. His kiss was as fierce as a blow, and I could feel his tears falling on my face and mingling with mine.

'*That* is how much I wish it!' he gasped. 'But this is your bitter cup and mine. Yeshûa has brought the whole house crashing down about our ears.'

He fumbled for something else, and I heard the rustle of parchment.

'Here, you will need this.'

He thrust it down the neck of my tunic, and laid his hand for a moment tenderly on my breast.

'*O thou fairest among women! Thy breasts are like to clusters of grapes.*'

I clung to him. I could not let him leave me.

'*A bundle of myrrh is my wellbeloved unto me,*' I said, '*he shall lie all night betwixt my breasts.*'

He gave a low moan, then held me away from him.

'We cannot. It is never to be. Everything is destroyed.'

'What is this you have given me?' I asked. I was breathless and shaking.

'It is a document of *gêt*. I had that drawn up also, while I was in the city.'

'You want to *divorce* me?'

'Do you think I want it?' He sounded almost angry. 'It's the only way I can set you free. You will be able to marry. To find a new life. Forget me.'

'How can I forget you? *Love is strong as death.*'

With my fingertip, I touched his bracelet, with our plaited hairs.

'You will remember your promise?' I said.

'Forever. Now go. Be safe, my beloved. Be happy.'

Then he was gone.

When not even his shadow was left in the moonlight, I whispered for the last time, 'I love you. I love you.'

Why did I not run after him? Why? I was still so young, so accustomed to respect the judgement of Yehûdâ and Yeshûa. I was terrified, exhausted, confused, numbed by all that had happened. But I know now that if I had run after Yehûdâ, as I had run after him from the village, he would not have sent me away. I do not know where he went or what became of him. And I have regretted it all the rest of my life.

Chapter Eighteen

Blinded with grief and cold with shock, I stumbled down the hill after the other women, who drew me in and comforted me, for they were my friends, my sisters. And if any of them had seen me with Yehûdâ, they did not mention it.

We followed the soldiers to the house of Ananus, father-in-law of Caiaphas the high priest.

'Why,' I wondered, 'have they brought Yeshûa here and not to Caiaphas?'

Yoanna, from her knowledge of these men and their ways gained during her previous life at court, suggested a reason.

'Ananus, of course, used to be the high priest himself, and wields enormous power still, but behind closed doors these days. That's why they call him "Ananus the Great".' Her mouth twisted ironically. 'I expect they have gone there to confer in private, to decide what charge they can bring against our master.'

'It will be the disturbance in the Temple,' said Susanna, with certainty.

'No,' said the Magdalene. She clutched her mantle beneath her chin, and her knuckles gleamed white in the moonlight, like naked bones against the dark blue cloth.

'It will be because people hailed him as a king, that first day, when he rode in on the donkey.'

'It will be,' I said, dull with despair, 'because they see the threat to their power. The people love him and Yahweh has appointed him to his great mission, to proclaim the new kingdom. The priests and the Sanhedrin will never tolerate that.'

We waited outside the house of Ananus for several hours. Then they brought Yeshûa out, still bound, and escorted him to the house of Caiaphas. His face was more bloody and bruised than before. I felt a cry of pain rising in my throat, as though I had been beaten myself, and pressed my hand over my mouth to stifle any sound. I wanted to call out to him, *I am here, Yeshûa! We haven't deserted you!* But knew we must not to draw attention to ourselves, lest we should be driven away.

Once again we waited, as more and more men arrived at the high priest's house, men of substance and dignity, members of the Sanhedrin. It was just becoming light when they were on the move yet again, this time the short distance to the palace where the Roman prefect, Pontius Pilate, resided when he was in Jerusalem.

I found myself clutching the Magdalene's hand.

'The Romans,' I whispered, through chattering teeth. The chill spring night had drained all the warmth from my blood. 'They're taking him to the Romans. The Romans have the power of execution.'

She put her arm around me.

'Don't be afraid, Mariam. He has broken no Roman law. Why should they execute him?'

But I knew, in my heart. Despite this absurd parody of justice being played out before us, staged on the streets of Jerusalem, somehow my brother was going to find his own death, and lay himself like a lamb of sacrifice under the knife.

This time, only the soldiers went inside with Yeshûa, the priests and other notables remaining outside. And I remembered suddenly—for I was very tired with lack of sleep and agony of mind—that today was the eve of *Pesah*. Celebrants must remain ritually pure, therefore no Israelite could cross the threshold of one of the *gôyîm*. We stayed some distance away, for we were afraid to go too near the Roman prefect's palace, but after a time we saw an imposing figure in a white toga come out and speak briefly to the priests. The prefect, if that was who it was, returned indoors. The priests seemed to be arguing amongst themselves, then the troop of soldiers led Yeshûa off again.

'Where are they going now?' asked Susanna in despair. 'Are they going to visit the house of every great man in Jerusalem?'

We followed behind the stumbling figure of my brother, surrounded by his guards, but they did not go far. Downhill a little way lay the other palace, which was built by the Hasmonaean kings, in the days before Rome occupied our country.

'Herod Antipas must have come to Jerusalem for *Pesah*,' I said. 'He'll be lodging there. Perhaps the Romans have decided to hand my brother over to the tetrarch of Galilee.'

I thought of how we had fled from Herod Antipas to Tyre, and stayed there in exile for six months after he had murdered our cousin. And our long winter in the cave on Mount Hermon. The tetrarch had beheaded Yôhânân the Baptiser at the whim of a lascivious girl. In his guilt and superstitious dread, he believed my brother was Yôhânân risen from the dead. I began to weep again, a dry hopeless sobbing. After all our efforts, Yeshûa had fallen into the hands of Antipas.

Yet here too, the stay was brief. My brother was being passed from hand to hand as if each of these powerful men was afraid he might burn his fingers on the prophet from the Galilee. On we trudged, uphill to the Praetorium before the Tower of Antonia, the imposing seat of the Roman garrison, where we sank down in the dust at the edge of this great public court, paved with blocks of dressed stone. I do not think we could have walked any further. I was so numb with exhaustion, the very well-spring of my tears seemed to have dried up.

Pontius Pilate was here before us and took Yeshûa inside, I suppose for further questioning, and while they were inside, a crowd began to gather. Or rather I should say that a crowd began to be herded into the public court. I could not see any of my brother's followers amongst them. The only familiar faces I saw were some of the traders who had been in the midst of the fracas in the Temple. There were men in the garb of Temple servants, and Temple guards. There were also some ragged people who went up to one of the guards who was shepherding the crowd in, and were handed something small, which might have been a coin. Soon the courtyard was quite full, and Temple guards took up positions blocking the entrances.

The Roman prefect re-emerged, followed by my brother in the grip of two soldiers. Pilate held up his hand for silence.

'I find no fault in this man,' he said.

Caiaphas and the other priests, who were standing close to him, conferred hastily, then the chief priest said something to him.

'Speak up, man,' the prefect said, regarding him with distaste, 'you must make your accusations loud enough for all to hear.'

'He has blasphemed against the Temple and the holy religion of Israel,' the priest said loudly.

'Then it is for *you* to try him and to judge him.'

I could see that each of parties was trying to force the other to make the judgement.

Caiaphas cleared his throat.

'He has also proclaimed himself king of the Jews,' he said slyly. 'That is treason against the Emperor. It calls for the death penalty, which only you can enforce.'

It was a lie! Yeshûa had never called himself 'king of the Jews', but the Roman prefect must act now, or be seen to be committing treason himself against the Emperor. For a long time Pilate locked eyes with Caiaphas. It was Rome and the military authority in combat with Caiaphas and the priestly authority. In the end, Pilate shrugged. Perhaps he did not think my brother worth a serious struggle with the priestly caste.

'So be it.'

He called for a basin of water and made an elaborate show of washing his hands.

'I wash my hands clean,' he said, 'of this innocent man's blood.'

He dried his hands on a towel and eyed my brother thoughtfully. I think perhaps he really had no taste for this. He turned again to address the crowd.

'As is the custom at your feast of Passover,' he said, 'I will release to you one man condemned to death. Shall it be this innocent man, Yeshûa the Galilean? Or shall it be the insurrectionist and murderer, Barabas?'

At once the crowd began to chant, 'Barabas! Barabas! Release Barabas! Crucify the Galilean!'

And so *that* was why these people had been packed into the courtyard, and carefully taught what they were to shout.

I saw the smug look of triumph on Caiaphas's face as the Roman swept back indoors. I bowed my head between my knees and wept.

The next hours remain a blurred nightmare. They have haunted me all my life, but I remember them only in broken fragments. I remember we toiled after the crowds on blistered feet, seeing somewhere up ahead a man, not Yeshûa, carrying a cross.

'Is he also to be crucified?' I asked, but no one answered.

I remember that the crowds parted briefly after we passed through the city gate, and I caught a glimpse of my brother. They had pinned a tawdry cloak around his shoulders and put a kind of crown on his head, woven from briar thorns, and the blood ran down his head and shoulders. The soldiers were shouting at him, mocking, calling him 'King of the Jews'. Then they stripped off the cloak and scourged him. The thongs of the scourge were threaded through sharp pieces of metal and bone, and every time the thongs lashed down, a gasping cry broke from him, and rivulets of blood ran down his back, and strips of his skin hung down like ribbons, like the strips of leather that might hold two lengths of wood together.

Somehow we must have reached the place of execution that they call Golgotha, the Place of the Skull. I remember falling to my knees from exhaustion and calling out—silently or aloud I do not know—that Yahweh should put an end to this. Was my brother not His dearly beloved, His chosen one? How could He allow this to happen? How could He *command* it to happen? I begged, grovelled, pleaded for my brother's life, from that unspeakable god who had betrayed him. I remembered how, last night, Yeshûa had asked Yehûdâ to act quickly. If that cruel deity would not spare my brother's life, I begged at least for the end to come quickly. I knew that a man on a cross can take days to die.

The place was filled with blood and dirt and flies, and the stench of defecation and rotting flesh, and the screams of the three men the soldiers were now nailing to the crosses where they lay on the ground. Then, grunting with the effort, the soldiers heaved up the crosses and dropped them into the sockets cut into the rock. The pain, as the men's weight was suddenly taken by their pierced hands and feet, must have been excruciating, unthinkable. I heard my brother scream, and I covered my ears and wailed.

After a while, some people began to drift away. Idle bystanders, Israelites, they had come to relish the spectacle of hideous suffering, but they had taken care to stay well back from the three men, to avoid impurity. The Roman soldiers were indifferent—they seemed to have no sense of the impiety of their actions, to crucify men on the eve of *Pesah*. A dark cloud had come over the sun and I suppose most of the Israelites were anxious to hurry back to the Temple to sacrifice their lambs and make ready to enjoy their feasts for the evening. Life, after all, must go on! We sat in a little huddle together, we women who had not deserted Yeshûa, and we waited. As the crowd thinned out, I saw that Shim'ôn Kêphas was standing a little way from us. I went over to him.

'So you did not run away,' I said, 'with the others.'

He shifted his feet and would not look at me.

'I did at first,' he said wretchedly. 'Then I did worse.'

'*Worse?*'

'Aye, I denied that I was his friend. People realised that I was a Galilean and asked if I was his friend. Three times I denied it, denied him, in the city there, even before cockcrow. And he foretold it, last night as we dined together. I swore I would never do such a wicked thing. Oh, Yeshûa! My beloved friend and lord! He told me that I was to be the Rock on which his church should be built. I was to take over leadership of his mission. But I am worthless. As foul as that dung-beetle, there by your foot. At the first test of my faith, I failed him. And I betrayed him as surely as that devil, Yehûdâ of Keriyoth.'

'Yehûdâ did *not* betray him,' I cried. 'My brother ordered him to fetch the soldiers to Gethsemane. He *wanted* to be taken.'

Shim'ôn shook his head. 'I don't believe you,' he said dully. 'And even if I did, Yehûdâ should not have done it.'

'It was,' I said bitterly, 'an act of love.'

I walked away from him. I knew he would spread the word of what Yehûdâ had done, even if he also admitted his own guilt. And if he did not vilify Yehûdâ, then Yôhânân would.

They will write me out of their histories, their 'testaments', for I am an outcast of History itself, because I was the betrothed of Yehûdâ, whom they call the Betrayer. And because I fled from the Land of Judah and would not join their Christ cult. It will be as if Yeshûa never had a sister Mariam. Yet I knew him better than any did.

It seemed grotesque, but there were men selling food and drink here at the place of execution. I saw the families of the two robbers who were crucified with Yeshûa buying from the food stalls. The soldiers sat around on the ground, bored and playing dice, and arguing over who should have the condemned men's clothes, for they had been stripped down to their loincloths before being nailed to the crosses. I could not think why they would want the filthy, bloodstained garments, but it seemed this was a privilege granted to the men for carrying out their loathsome task.

There was a centurion in charge, a middle-aged man, greying at the temples, patient and somehow more respectful than the common soldiers. He was such a man as Petradix would have been, when he served the Romans as a centurion. Nervously, I went up to him.

'I am the sister of Yeshûa,' I said in Latin, 'the man you have nailed to the middle cross.'

'Best go away, woman,' he said, not unkindly. 'There is nothing here for you but sorrow.'

'How long will it last?'

'Not beyond nightfall. Because of your custom of burial before sunset, and it being your Sabbath tomorrow, we have to make sure they are all dead before then.'

I swallowed hard. There was a taste like gall in my mouth.

'How . . . ?'

'Generally, we break their legs.' He said it quite calmly, as if he were talking about slaughtering a beast. 'Then they can't take their weight on the footrest, see? The body drags down and compresses the lungs, so they suffocate. It's quite quick, really.'

He must have seen the expression on my face.

'Don't worry. That middle one, the one with the sign saying "King of the Jews", I don't think he'll last that long anyway. He isn't such a sturdy bugger as the other two.'

294

'They are selling drinks over there.' I pointed to the makeshift stalls. 'Is it possible to give my brother something to drink?'

I couldn't see how, for he was raised up so high, but it was oppressively hot, despite the clouded sky, and I could see sweat running down Yeshûa's face and mingling with the blood and the flies that had come to feed on it.

'Sure enough. We can soak a sponge in wine and hoist it up on a stick,' the centurion said. 'We often do it. You buy some wine and I'll see what I can do.'

I took some of the money Yeshûa had given me and bought a jug of the wine. It was dreadful sour stuff, vinegar more than wine, but it was all I could give him. The centurion told one of the servants to lift up the wine-soaked sponge to my brother's mouth, and I saw him feebly suck on it. At that moment I remembered he had said the previous night that he would not drink again of the fruit of the vine until the coming of the new kingdom. Was *this* the coming of the kingdom? This horror? This pain? This humiliation? This bloodshed?

In my heart I cursed Yahweh.

The screams and groans of the three men had been growing fainter and more infrequent, for they were surely dying now. Then suddenly my brother writhed as though he would drag his hands and feet free of the enormous nails that pinned him to the cross.

'*Elohî, 'Elohî,*' he cried out in agony, '*lâmâ shebaqtanî?*'

That is the question I have asked all the years of my life. Why had his God forsaken him?

After that, he said no more.

I sat in the dirt, numb, waiting for someone to tell me what to do.

It was drawing towards sunset and the soldiers set about breaking the legs of the two robbers, to hasten their deaths.

'Wait,' said the centurion as they approached Yeshûa. 'I think this one is already gone.'

He reached up and drove his spear into my brother's side. Blood ran out in a thin watery trickle, but he made no sound and did not move. The centurion stood very still, looking up at him, the hand that held the spear shaking, as though something had reached him from my brother's body. He dropped the spear as if it had burned his hand, looking from his palm to my brother's dead face, his eyes dazed.

'Truly this man was the Son of God,' he gasped, partly in wonder, partly in horror.

Why did he say that? Why now? What had he felt? Was this what Yeshûa had meant? That his death itself would make men believe in his message? Too late. He himself was gone forever. Something had been ripped, living, out of my very body.

I had noticed a man in rich clothes who had come to stand at the edge of the crowd. He had servants with him, and a litter, with a shroud of fine linen laid on it. I was astonished that either of the robbers should have such a friend. This man approached the centurion as I trailed back to my group of friends, who were sitting mute with exhaustion and shock.

'You are Mariam, the sister of Yeshûa of Galilee?'

I turned around. It was the rich man, who had followed me. I nodded dully. My cheeks were stiff with the dried salt of my tears.

'My name is Yosef,' he said. 'My town is Arimathea, but I live now in Jerusalem and I am a member of the Sanhedrin.'

He must have seen the look of revulsion on my face, for he went on hastily, 'I believe in your brother's message, and I argued hard last night against those set on condemning him or handing him over to Pilate, but I could not prevail. All I can offer him is decent burial. My own burial cave is a short way from here. If you give your permission, we can take him there at once.'

I thanked him, flooded with relief, for I had not known how my little group would be able to do what was necessary. Shim'ôn Kêphas had disappeared and we were left nothing but women. Yosef's servants wrapped Yeshûa's body gently in the pure white shroud and laid him on the litter. Then our small procession made its way down from Golgotha to the burial cave, which was set in a pleasant garden of flowering trees. A pomegranate tree stood near the entrance, which brought tears to my eyes.

Every pomegranate seed, a lucky day.

We laid him on the shelf in the cave, and the servants rolled a heavy boulder across the entrance.

'It is the Sabbath in less than an hour,' said Yosef. 'We can do no more for him now.'

I nodded. 'My friends and I will come the morning after Sabbath to wash and anoint him with spices. I am grateful to you, Yosef of Arimathea.'

༄

Mariam has returned to her room, but she is restless. Where before she slept for long stretches of time, now her body will give her no peace. She writhes under the blanket and Sergius does not know what to do to ease her pain. Julia comes sometimes to sit beside her uncle and watches her grandmother with sad eyes. *A child should not have to see such suffering*, Sergius thinks, but Julia cannot bear to be barred from her grandmother's room.

One day, a stranger arrives at the villa, and Sergius is called out to speak to him. He is a prosperous-looking man, somewhat past his middle years, a Greek merchant called Georgios, from Sidon in Phoenicia. He speaks perfect Latin, and Sergius invites him to take a glass of wine on the terrace. When they are seated with their wine and dishes of olives, Sergius turns to the man.

'You say that you have been searching for Mariam, sister of Yeshûa, a woman from the Galilee.'

'I have been searching for her throughout the whole of Gallia Narbonensis for the last month,' Georgios says. 'It is an act of kindness for a very old friend who knew that, long ago, she travelled here by ship, arranged by a friend of his. He died three months ago, but before he died he asked me to seek for Mariam. At last a man in Massilia, a Greek schoolmaster, told me I might find her here.'

'Antiphoulos,' says Sergius.

'That's the name.'

'And why do you want to find this Mariam?'

'I have this for her.' Georgios reaches into a satchel of fine tooled leather that he has laid at his feet, and takes out a very small packet, which he places on the table between them. It is wrapped in supple goatskin and tied with a narrow gold cord.

'Mariam is my mother,' says Sergius. 'I thank you for so much trouble and care in bringing this to her.'

Georgios bows politely. 'May I meet her?'

'She is very ill. Dying. Perhaps you could look in from the doorway of her room.'

They come together to the door of my room, which stands open to encourage the breeze from the window. The stranger stands silent for a long time, looking at me.

'She must have been a remarkable woman, to inspire such devotion in my friend,' he says.

Sergius offers a meal and a room for the night, but the stranger refuses politely, saying that he must return to his ship and take up again the strands of his business. When he has gone, Sergius brings a package into my room. I am still awake, gazing at the ceiling.

'Who was that, the man you brought to stare at me?'

'I'm sorry. I thought you were asleep.'

'You know I hardly ever sleep these days.'

'He has been searching for you, to deliver this package.'

'A package? For me? Who has sent it?'

'He did not say. He was a Greek, from Sidon.'

I try to untie the knots, but they are too tight and I fumble with them helplessly.

'Shall I?' he says, and I hand it to him without a word.

He unties the cord and unwraps the leather. Inside is a rolled up piece of beautiful silk, of a deep blue. Sergius holds it up for me to see.

'Exactly the colour of your eyes, Mother.'

I struggle to sit up, suddenly agitated.

'What is in it?' There is a pain in my chest and I am breathless

'A . . . bracelet, I think it is. Rather old and worn. It seems to be made from plaited hair and small gold beads. And there is a scrap of parchment.'

He peers at it.

'I can't read it. It's in Hebrew.' He hands it to me.

I know the writing at once, the exact shape of the letters, though a trembling hand has written them; I knows the way the line slopes upwards at the end.

'Not Hebrew,' I whisper. 'Aramaic.'

It shall not leave my wrist while I live. And did not.

And somewhere in the room I can hear a voice sob, not with an old woman's thin weeping, but the desolation of a young girl.

ॐ

When we returned to the tomb, at dawn on the morning following the Sabbath, to wash and anoint my brother's body, we found the great stone rolled away from the entrance and the cave empty. The blood-stained shroud lay neatly folded on the shelf. In consternation we stared at each other. Who would have defiled Yeshûa's place of burial? Even the body of an executed man was treated with respect. That was why the Romans had ensured that all the men had died before sundown. They knew our customs, even if they did not observe them themselves. If the men had lingered on and died on the Sabbath, they could not have been buried until after sundown on the following day, an act of disrespect to the dead.

'Who has taken him?' Yoanna whispered.

We shook our heads, standing there helpless, with our jars of water and aromatic oils, our spices and unguents. I walked forward into the tomb, while the others lingered fearfully outside. The air inside was clean and fresh; there was no smell of corruption as there should have been, if a mangled body had lain here for two nights and a day. But there was a faint scent of something. I closed my eyes, to smell it better.

Cinnamon and honey.

A shock ran through my body, so that my eyes flew open and I looked round, expecting to see him. There was only one person whose skin always carried that scent. But my brother was not there. Surely his bloody and mutilated corpse could not have left such a scent here? It belonged to warm living flesh, not the cold corrupt flesh of the dead.

I stumbled out of the cave into the sunlight, which caught me between the eyes like a sword thrust, so that for a moment I was dazzled. Then I saw that my companions were all on their knees.

'We have seen him, Mariam!' the Magdalene cried. 'Yeshûa has risen from the dead! The new kingdom is come, and we will all join him in bliss!'

'But where is he?' I asked, confused. 'There is no one here.'

'He stood there,' said Salome, and Susanna nodded, pointing to the east. 'He stood there, blazing in glory.'

I thought: *They have been blinded by the rising sun and by grief and by hope beyond hope.*

I followed their eager steps slowly back into the city. He was dead. I had seen him. Dead. Shrouded. Laid in the tomb. How could he have returned? He was my brother, I told myself, desperately. A man, like any other man. Dead. A man. Dead. Like Daniel. How could he have risen? My own heart was dead to hope. And if he had returned, why had he not shown himself to me, his sister? Surely it must have been an illusion. But why had I smelled the scent of his skin?

Matters moved rapidly after that. The other women found Shim'ôn Kêphas and two more of the *shelîhîm*, Mattaniah and Tôma, in the city and told them what they had seen. Shim'ôn, that stolid, quiet, sensible man, believed them at once. Without evidence, without even the vision they said they had experienced. How could he give any credit to their story? It was beyond belief. I think perhaps Shim'ôn clutched at the idea, to assuage his own guilt, though Tôma shook his head doubtfully. But I did not argue with Shim'ôn and the others. I was too weary, too weary even to speak of these things. I knew that I must not delay any longer in obeying my brother's command to leave the country, though when I found that the others planned to return to the Galilee, I decided to travel north with them, for it was on my way. No one knew what had become of the rest of the *shelîhîm* who had run away, but if the group was ever to gather together again, we all believed it would be in Capernaum.

We made the journey on foot, carrying some food with us, provided by Martha in Bethany. Where there were friendly houses, we slept under a roof. The rest of the time we bedded down on the open ground. I plodded along in silence. I could not even think about the future, stripped of my brother and my lover. I knew simply that I must go to Caesarea Maritima and take ship. Beyond that, I did not care.

At last we saw the beloved sight of the waters of Gennesaret sparkling in the distance, and I broke the news that I would not be going any further with them. The Magdalene put her arms around me and pressed her cheek to mine. They all pleaded with me to stay, but I told them I must do as Yeshûa had bidden, and that they accepted. I turned my back on them determinedly, and started on my way up a path which would join the one down which Yehûdâ and I had come so long before. Once, I turned to look back, and watched their resolute figures trudging along the road to Capernaum, out of my life and into a different future.

It was the next day when I reached the olive orchard below our village. There were the great trees under which I had studied with my brother and the stretch of the river where he and Yehûdâ had swum as boys. On the outskirts of the village a group of small children was playing. They stopped and stared at me, and I must have seemed a strange sight, a tall sun-burned woman with matted hair, her clothes soiled and dusty with travel.

In the courtyard of my parents' house, I stopped and looked about me. The dogs, at least, recognised me, for they ran forward with barks of welcome, not hostility. Then my father came out of the workshop, followed by Ya'aqôb. My father's hair was quite white and his back was stooped. I knelt before him in the dust.

'*Shalôm*. Give me your blessing, Father,' I said humbly.

He laid his hand on my head at once and murmured a *berâkâ*.

Ya'aqôb could barely contain himself till it was finished.

'You dare to come back here!' he shouted. 'You outcast, you . . . you whore! Yahweh condemns your kind to stoning.'

I had not expected much of a welcome, but nothing as bad as this.

'You do me an injustice!' I shouted back. 'I have lived celibate all these years, with good people and under the protection of my brother Yeshûa.'

'Oh?' said Ya'aqôb, sneering. 'And where is Yeshûa now, woman?'

'Dead!' I said, and I began to sob.

'You speak with a viper's tongue!' he yelled. 'Your mouth is full of falsehoods!'

'He is dead!' I screamed. 'Crucified before my eyes!'

My father sank down on the step and put his head in his hands. I knelt beside him and laid my head in his lap. I was so tired.

'Where is my mother?' I mumbled into his tunic. Suddenly, I wanted my mother.

'She has gone to Capernaum,' he said, 'to join Yeshûa's following. And Ya'aqôb plans to go as well.'

'Too late,' I said. 'Too late.'

I lifted my tear-stained face and said resentfully to Ya'aqôb. 'You need not fear contamination from me for long, brother. I came only to say good-bye. Yeshûa told me to leave the Land of Judah. He feared for my safety.'

I left early the next morning, before anyone was awake, and paid only one more visit. I went out of the village to the cemetery and knelt outside our family cave.

'Good-bye, Daniel, my little lamb,' I whispered. 'Sleep well in the land of Galilee.'

I made the journey to Caesarea Maritima without incident, for I was a seasoned traveller by now, and I found Amos, the friend of Yehûdâ's father, without difficulty. Somehow Yehûdâ had got word to him that I would be coming, and within a few days he had arranged a passage for me aboard a ship bound for Gallia Narbonensis. I was indifferent to our destination, for I was leaving behind all that I knew and loved, obeying mechanically my brother's final instructions, but caring nothing where I went or what became of me. The passage used almost all the money I had, leaving me with no more than a handful of *denarii*.

The other passengers were also Israelite refugees, fleeing for some reason or another from persecution at home. I spoke little to them, spending most of my time on deck, listlessly watching as we sailed around the shore of the Middle Sea, crossing at last to the eastern coast of Italy, then down to its southern tip and up the west coast to Gallia. The ship did not come into Massilia, but another port a little further west. The captain advised me that, if I wanted work, Massilia should be my goal, and pointed out the road.

It was strange, marshy country, where wild horses ran free, splashing amongst treacherous tussocks, and unfamiliar birds would rise suddenly, almost from beneath my feet, setting my heart beating fast. Once, I had to run for my life, for a band of rough men, robbers I supposed, tried to lay hold of me. Although I was growing a little weak from lack of food, I was still fleet of foot, for the long years wandering with my brother had hardened me. I took refuge in the marsh, hip deep in the water, my feet sinking in the mud, and I blessed the sea mist which rolled in, hiding me amongst the reeds and small white horses and wading birds.

And at length I came to Massilia.

৯

Sergius sits holding his mother's hand. For a long time her rasping breath has distressed him, but she seems easier now. She opens her eyes and smiles at him.

'Would you do something for me, which you will think very foolish?'

He smiles back. 'Yours to command.'

'I want to sleep on the roof tonight, as I used to do when I was a child.'

He raises his eyebrows at her. A strange request from a dying woman, but in his own boyhood they sometimes used to sleep up there, pretending they were Israelites.

'It will cause you a great deal of trouble,' she says meekly.

'No trouble,' he says, and squeezes her hand. The night is quite warm, he will sit with her and see that she is safe.

When at last everything is arranged to my satisfaction, I will not allow him to stay. I have refused a bed, and insisted on nothing but a bedroll, a blanket, and my inlaid box.

'I want to be alone,' I say, 'to commune with the stars. Please, my dear.'

So, reluctantly, he leaves me.

'Will she be safe?' I hear Julia ask anxiously as he descends the narrow stair.

He gives her a quick kiss. 'Of course she will be safe. Mariam is an intrepid woman.'

They are gone. How much easier it is to breathe out here under the stars. I could almost imagine myself a child again, the night of Melkha's wedding, when Yeshûa came to keep me company.

I open my precious box. It is not usually this stiff, but my fingers are growing weak. I slip the bracelet on to my arm, Yehûdâ's hair and mine, twined together forever. I think of it touching his skin for all those years, and it is as if his hand is laid tenderly on my arm. I take out his pearls and twine them clumsily in my hair. A small vanity. I would have worn them at our wedding. But what would he think of me now? A foolish, dying old woman? Then I remember. He is dead. They are all dead.

There is nothing now in the box but the scrap of parchment with his writing on it, and the little carved lamb that Daniel made for me. I lie down again, clasping Yeshûa's box to my heart. Yehûdâ. Daniel. Yeshûa.

This evening, I was thinking about the early days of Yeshûa's mission. What I remember best about that time was the laughter, the freedom. New villages, new people, new landscapes. And at the same time, the companionship, men and women together, all of us happy, full of hope. I remember long days of walking, but we talked and laughed as we went, and at the end of the day, another village, a friendly family serving an evening meal, where we would go on talking eagerly far into the night.

We were young. We were going to change the world.

They have laid out grapes up here on the roof. We do this every year with some of the grapes, so that in the winter we will have dried raisins of the sun. I can smell them as I lie here. Above me, the dome of the heavens is deep blue and crusted with stars. No moon tonight, so even the smallest humblest star can be seen.

Everyone has their own star, Mariam.

I look for the pulsing blue star until I find it, and smile. My own star, forever.

It's strange. I cannot smell the drying grapes any longer. Instead, there is something else.

Cinnamon and honey.

There is the sound of breathing. Is it only my breathing, or is someone else here?

For the first time for many years, I can see Yeshûa's face clearly, every beloved line of it. There is a glow around him, like the time in the *midbar*, when he found my lost kid.

'Yeshûa?' I say, reaching out my hands.

Then there is silence on the rooftop, and no more breathing.

The Author

Ann Swinfen spent her childhood partly in England and partly on the east coast of America. She was educated at Somerville College, Oxford, where she read Classics and Mathematics and married a fellow undergraduate, the historian David Swinfen. While bringing up their five children and studying for a postgraduate MSc in Mathematics and a BA and PhD in English Literature, she had a variety of jobs, including university lecturer, translator, freelance journalist and software designer. She served for nine years on the governing council of the Open University and for five years worked as a manager and editor in the technical author division of an international computer company, but gave up her full-time job to concentrate on her writing, while continuing part-time university teaching. In 1995 she founded Dundee Book Events, a voluntary organisation promoting books and authors to the general public.

Her first three novels, *The Anniversary*, *The Travellers*, and *A Running Tide*, all with a contemporary setting but also an historical resonance, were published by Random House, with translations into Dutch and German. *The Testament of Mariam* marks something of a departure. Set in the first century, it recounts, from an unusual perspective, one of the most famous and yet ambiguous stories in human history. At the same time it explores life under a foreign occupying force, in lands still torn by conflict to this day. Her second historical novel, *Flood*, is set in the fenlands of East Anglia during the seventeenth century, where the local people fought desperately to save their land from greedy and unscrupulous speculators.

Currently she is working on a series set in late sixteenth century London, featuring a young Marrano physician who is recruited as a code-breaker and spy in Walsingham's secret service. The first book in the series is *The Secret World of Christoval Alvarez*.

She now lives in Broughty Ferry, on the northeast coast of Scotland, with her husband, formerly vice-principal of the University of Dundee, a cocker spaniel, and two Maine coon cats.

http://www.annswinfen.com

Printed in Great Britain
by Amazon